Captured My Heart

KAREN FRANCES

Cover Design by
Kari March, Kari March Designs

Proofread by
The Word Fairy

Interior Design and Formatting by
Clydeside Publishing

My dearest husband, you are my world.
For my dearest friends and my beautiful sister.
I love you all the way you are; don't ever change for anyone. Xxx

lex

"Seriously, Alex? Why are you calling me this frigging early? Don't you ever sleep?" He's not happy. I've either woken him up or disturbed something, but I'm way past the stage of caring. My thoughts are only centred around one person…

"We have a flight to catch," I answer quickly.

"That's tomorrow. You got me up out of my bed, because you're mixed up about the days!" Michael shouts over the phone. I pull the phone away from my ear.

"No, I'm not mixed up with the days. I have changed our flights, and we need to be at the airport in an hour. Murphy and I will pick you up in what, say thirty minutes?"

"For fuck's sake, Alex! I need to pack!"

"Well, hang up then. See you soon."

I hang up, relieved that after all this time, I'm finally going to meet her. She has consumed my thoughts and dreams since Phil showed me a picture of his family. His daughter is *beautiful*. I am attracted to beautiful women, but that's all. I've never had any *feelings* for one—for anyone—ever before, especially someone who I haven't actually had the pleasure of meeting. I don't allow myself the luxury of attachment. I'm too busy with business to let a woman into my life. I really don't need any distractions.

God knows what I will tell Michael about this, about why we're leaving early. He's bound to ask, and I don't have a reason he'll understand. He'll just laugh if I tell him the truth, which is that I can't wait even one more day to meet her.

Crazy.

CHAPTER 1

"*E*lizabeth Ann Stewart! What the hell is going on?"

I hear the front door closing and the footsteps coming up the hall, which means two things: first, my parents and brother, Ethan, are back from their holiday, and second, it's time to face the music about the for sale sign with the "Sold" sticker across it in the front garden of my home. From the tone of his voice, Ethan has obviously seen it.

My house was only on the market for a couple of days when it sold, and the new buyers want to be in as quickly as possible, so I am all packed up and ready to move out tomorrow, even though I have not yet found a new place.

"Hi Mum, Dad. Did you have a good time? You both look great." I greet my parents with a hug for them both as they enter my kitchen, trying not to look at Ethan. This time tomorrow it won't be my house after the removal guys empty it; it won't be my kitchen any longer, which will feel strange. This has been my home for the last few years.

I got the house while I was still at uni. Most students start off in a flat, but not me or Ethan; we started off with a three-bedroom house. Mum and Dad bought it for our twenty-first

birthday. Dad said at the time that it would be a great invest-
ment. But it's silly having this house. It's a family home. I
would much prefer a flat, maybe somewhere in the city
centre.

My parents always look great—Mum especially. Jane
Stewart, in my opinion, is the most beautiful woman on the
planet—but then again, I am biased. She's stunning and
definitely doesn't look her age, which when questioned
about it, she will happily tell you is forty-five. I hope I look
that good when I get to that age. Mum could easily pass for
ten years younger. She is positively glowing today; the
holiday has done its job. She is slim, with curves in all the
right places for her medium height. With her black hair
and suntanned skin, she has a Mediterranean look
about her.

Dad gives me a reassuring smile and whispers, "Of course
we did, honey. And everything will be fine. Don't worry
about Ethan." God, I hope he's right. I've been dreading this
confrontation since they left two weeks ago.

Ethan and I are twins. I suppose we are similar in a lot of
ways, from our dark-brown eyes to our dark-brown hair—
we get those from Dad—and the way we talk and act and
both have a great sense of humour. Although no one has seen
much of that lately. We've always been close; we never had
any secrets up until now. I have been telling myself for the
past two weeks that I've done it all for his own good and that
maybe he will try and get on with his life, although I am not
quite sure that's how *he* will see it.

"Well? I'm still waiting on an answer, Elizabeth," Ethan
says in a quieter voice as he looks round the kitchen,
presumably at all the packed boxes. He watches me with no
hint of a smile in his beautiful face, his brown eyes piercing
straight through me.

"Well hello, Ethan. Did you enjoy your holiday? Where's

my beautiful niece? Did you miss me? Because I missed you," I say sarcastically as I put my arms out for a hug.

Ethan just shakes his head at me, staring for a few seconds before answering.

"Obviously you didn't miss me too much. Looks like you've been busy. Lucy is sleeping in her car seat. Mum put her in your front room. Now am I going to get any answers off you? Why is there a for sale sign up in your garden?" Before I open my mouth to start talking, he's beat me to it. "Mum, Dad, don't think it's gone unnoticed that you're not surprised by this, so I can only presume you both knew."

I look at Mum; she looks really uneasy and upset. I know she's hated knowing what I was doing. Even when we were little, she couldn't take sides between us. We used to fight a lot when we were kids, usually just trying to get our parents' attention. Ethan would always say I started it and vice versa. I know that this time she will take Ethan's side if things don't work out, although I hope they do.

Before any of us has a chance to say anything, a soft crying starts. Lucy is awake. "Can I go get her?" I ask. Ethan sighs and nods.

I head down the hall to the front room, and as soon as she sees me, she stops crying. I lift her out of her seat and sit down on the couch, gazing at her. God, she's gotten bigger in such a short period, and she gets more like her mother every day. As I sit with her, my mind drifts back to the day she was born. Was that really only four months ago?

Ethan and Lindsay, his wife and childhood sweetheart— and also one of my closest friends—had been out for dinner. They were on their way back home when the accident happened. A car crashed into them. The passenger's side took the full impact; unfortunately, that was where Lindsay was sitting. The staff at the hospital had fought for hours, but they were fighting a losing battle.

When the doctors told Ethan that they would have to deliver the baby by an emergency C-section, he reluctantly agreed. Lindsay was still awake, but I think deep down she knew she wasn't going to make it, and she had wanted both Ethan and me there with her for the delivery. God, it was so hard for everyone in the room. All the doctors and staff knew what was going to happen and I suppose Ethan and I knew as well, but just didn't want to admit to it.

Lindsay seemed to know everything that was going on. And when the doctors delivered Lucy, there were tears running down Lindsay's face. She had wanted a girl from the minute she had found out she was pregnant. The doctors placed Lucy on Lindsay's chest. Ethan, who was sitting at Lindsay's side, held his newborn there with one shaking hand. Lindsay didn't even have the strength to hold Lucy. I was sitting on Lindsay's other side, holding her hand. She lifted her other hand and gently stroked her beautiful daughter's head. The smile on her face was a mixture of love, happiness, and sadness.

As soon as Lucy had been delivered, the lead consultant asked to speak with Ethan outside. My brother asked if I could join them. The consultant was more than happy to leave the family together as, in his words, the three of us—well, four now with Lucy—would only have a short time together. He explained in simple words about all Lindsay's injuries. He advised me to get in touch with other family members, which I had not yet managed to do with everything going on. He also explained that although the baby was very healthy and close enough to full term, when the time came, he wanted the staff to take Lucy to the special care unit for a full check-up and observation for a few days before going home. He stressed that it was only for a few days, stating that it would allow the family to make the necessary arrangements.

I made all the calls, first to Lindsay's parents and then to our own, and it didn't take long for them all to arrive at the hospital. Ethan and I were back in the room with Lindsay when everyone arrived. I thought it would be a good idea to let Lindsay's parents have some time alone with her and Lucy, so I suggested that to our parents. But when I went to leave, Lindsay asked me to stay. Ethan went with them instead.

Lindsay turned to her mother and father first, then to me, before she spoke. Her father took over the role of holding his granddaughter. "I know I can rely on everyone to help Ethan with Lucy," she said, her voice a little shaky.

"Oh, honey," her mother sobbed.

"Please, Mum, crying is not going to help. Libby, I would really like you to keep Ethan on track. You are probably the only one who can—and you won't let him take advantage of you. I don't want our daughter being passed about; I want *him* to bring her up, with a little help. Mum, I know you will try to do everything for both Ethan and Lucy but do try and let him get on with it," she told her.

Both her parents and I gave our tearful assurances that we would all help Ethan. The four of us talked until my parents came back into the room, followed by Ethan. Not long after that, Lindsay closed her eyes and drifted away, surrounded by the family that loved her and her now more than ever precious gift to my brother.

"A PENNY FOR THEM," Ethan says as he walks into the room.

"I really don't know where to start," I say with a lump in my throat.

"Mum is going to take Lucy next door into mine and get her changed to give us some time to talk." It didn't come as a surprise to anyone when Ethan and I had both been given keys to our new homes, right next door to each other, for our shared twenty-first birthday. And when Ethan and Lindsay got married, it was great having them so close. But now it just doesn't feel right. I feel as if I haven't kept up my promise to Lindsay.

I'm spending all my free time looking after Lucy. Ethan and I both need our space, and Ethan also needs to adjust to being a dad on his own. But it is going to be really strange not to be so close to him.

I can just hear Dad talking to Mum in the hall. "Don't worry, Jane. They'll work this out."

"I am sure you're right, Phil, but I am their mother. It's my job to worry," she answers him. I can hear the anxiety in her voice.

Dad sticks his head round the door and gives Ethan a stern look. "Now, you two better behave. We're only next door. And Ethan? Please at least hear your sister out," our dad says, giving me a warm, reassuring smile. He walks towards us to take Lucy. I give Lucy a kiss on her forehead, and she smiles. God, she melts your heart when she does that. Ethan leaves the room to speak with Mum.

"Dad, truthfully, how was he while you were away?"

"Libby, I won't lie to you," Dad says. "It's going to take him a long time. But he did spend more time on his own with Lucy, which was hard on your mum, because—as you know—she wants to do *everything* for both of them. Hopefully you can help him see some sense. And if he doesn't listen today, don't beat yourself up about it. Give him more time. I'm sure he'll be fine."

"I hope so, because I hate seeing him in pain. And at the moment, I feel as if I'm going to cause him more," I reply.

"Libby, if he's going to listen to anyone, it will be you," Dad says. "Just try and be patient with him. Before your mother and I go home, we need to discuss business. You can bring me up to speed on everything. Maybe after dinner? I love you, Elizabeth." He gives me a kiss.

"No bother, Dad. I love you, too," I say as Ethan returns.

"Well, Libby, it's just you and me and no distractions," he says. "Time to tell me what's going on."

"Promise me you'll hear me out without interrupting," I say. He just nods, so I suppose I'd better start. Where better to start than the beginning. "There are a number of reasons for me leaving here. For a start, I presume that Dad told you he wants me to take over running the hotel?" Ethan nods. "He says I'm ready; although, I am sure there are a select few within the hotel who will disagree with his decision."

Dad is in public relations. He is obviously very good at what he does, going by the big-time, high-profile celebrities, politicians, and businesspeople on his client list. But he also has a few other businesses, including Stewart Country Estate on the banks of Loch Lomond and a restaurant and bar in Glasgow. The hotel is not a lavish, five-star complex with hundreds of rooms but more of what I like to think of as an intimate inn with forty-five cosy bedrooms. Although we do have some of the luxuries of bigger hotels—a great fitness suite and pool, a function suite, a cosy bar, restaurant, and sitting room—our best feature is our romantic yet prime location right on the bonny banks of Loch Lomond, surrounded by acres of land.

With his publicity business doing so well, Dad's just not got the time for running the hotel day to day. He inherited the hotel when my grandfather died. It's always been in the family, and we spent a lot of time there when we were kids, always getting up to mischief. Dad is also a silent partner in a restaurant and bar in Glasgow. I believe the previous owners, PR clients of his, got into a bit of a bother, and he bailed them out.

"This house is also too big for just me," I continue, "so I'm going to stay at the hotel until I find a flat. Something a bit smaller. I want to be really hands on at the hotel to prove to Dad that I am capable of running it. I really need the challenge. I've loved the last few weeks doing the job I've worked so hard to get. It's made me remember why I worked so hard at uni; this is all I've ever wanted to do—and you know that. But, to be totally truthful, it's also because of you."

Ethan looks a little shocked, sad, and deep in thought, probably remembering Dad's words to him before he left. He sits still and doesn't say anything. I try to choose my words carefully; I really don't want to upset him. He's my brother, and I love him.

"Since Lindsay's death, I've gone between work and caring for Lucy. She's your daughter, Ethan. And please don't look at me with those sad eyes—you *know* I love you both! She's a beautiful girl. But so far, it's been either Mum or I there to witness her firsts. Her first smile. Her first time rolling over. Her first time shaking her rattle. And her own daddy wasn't there," I say.

"I know it's hard for you because you are grieving, but Lindsay's gone, and her daughter, the little girl you and she made together, is still here, and she needs you! You've hardly spent any time with Lucy since she was born. That beautiful baby girl needs her daddy. I'm just her aunt. I will always be there for her, but I am not her mum, and that's what she's going to think I am if things keep going the way they are. I made Lindsay a promise, and so far, I've not managed to keep that up. And now I need to."

"Oh, Libby." Ethan has tears rolling down his face.

"Don't—everything will work out," I tell him as I wrap my arms around him. We sit cuddled on the couch, something we've not done in a long time. The tears keep rolling, and deep down I know he hasn't cried like this since Lindsay's death. This is what he needs to help with the grieving process.

Of course, it's not long until the tears are running down my face, too. We've shared a few tears since the accident but nothing like this. Ethan's been sitting for weeks on end, just staring into space. "Ethan, please. I didn't mean to upset you. Please stop crying." I wipe the tears off his face and see a slight smile.

"Libby, I have tears because I know you're right—just like you usually are. If I'm honest with you, it's just … I'm *scared* to do this on my own," he says. "Lindsay would have been such a great mother. And yes, I miss her like crazy. There's not a day I don't think about her." He stops and sighs. "I know she would hate seeing me the way I've been lately. I had a lot of time to reflect on these last few months while I was away. Lucy, work, friends, family, but most of all the future —I thought about it all."

"Ethan, we're all here for you—Mum, Dad, me, Lindsay's family. We all want to help, but you do have to start doing some things for yourself." I pause to judge his reaction. "Maybe you could think about joining a baby group, look into returning to work, and ring Stephen to arrange a night out. He's missed you, and he doesn't know how to help. You can't go on sitting behind four walls doing nothing."

He nods. Well, it's a start.

Stephen is Ethan's closest friend. He also just happens to run the leisure complex at the hotel. I've been giving him up-to-date reports on how Ethan's doing since my brother has stopped returning his calls.

Ethan and I sit talking for ages about the holiday, what I've been up to whilst he was away, and my plans for the hotel, not to mention Ethan's plans for the future. He's thinking of going back to work on a part-time basis. He works for an advertising company, and he was promoted a few months before Lindsay's death. They've been great with him about the time off he's needed. He assures me that he will get in touch with Stephen over the next few days. It's great just sitting, catching up. This is the brother I remember.

"So, do you want a hand packing?" he asks.

"Nope, it's all done. Even my cases for the hotel are in my car," I reply. I don't know how I managed to find the time to do it with work, but it's all done.

"Well, come on. Let's go next door to my place and put Mum and Dad out of their misery … and maybe phone out for a take-away. And Libby … thanks for today. It's what I needed." He gives me a tight hug. I do love him dearly.

Mum and Dad look relieved that Ethan and I are still on speaking terms when we go in, although Dad is giving me that *I told you everything would be fine* look. We spend the evening playing with Lucy, watching TV, and just talking about nothing of any importance. It's perfect. Just reminds me of growing up, I suppose. We were lucky; we had a great childhood and fantastic parents. Don't get me wrong. We had some ups and downs, but the ups outweighed the downs. The downs we don't really talk about.

Mum stayed home to look after us and the house whilst Dad worked. Sometimes he would be away from home for days with his various clients. Dad always kept us grounded, even though it would have been so easy to slip into spoiled-little-rich-kid mode. We each knew the meaning of hard work from an early age, and we never took anything for granted growing up. And Dad always worked so hard, although when we saw his picture in the papers or on TV with clients, it didn't look like such hard work. But as we got older, we both realised just how hard Dad's job could be, especially with some of his more challenging clients.

I remember one client of Dad's from when I was about fifteen.

The client was an up-and-coming, young actor, and his agent had wanted Dad to get the kid's name out there. But the actor wasn't that keen on taking advice; he was more interested in the club scene and girls and drink—not a great combination. I adored him, which led to a whole host of problems. Actually, it was a recipe for disaster. And that's exactly what he cooked up.

The family woke up one Sunday morning to an article in the paper. The actor had been arrested the previous night for an alleged sexual assault. Dad was furious. We had the media camped out at the bottom of our driveway for weeks, waiting on any info Dad could give them. The young man never did any acting again.

"Does someone want to phone for some food? I'll go and get Lucy bathed and ready for her bed," Mum says.

"No, Mum, it's okay. I'll take care of her. We both need to get used to it," Ethan says, looking at me with a smile. He takes Lucy off of Mum and heads upstairs.

Dad looks pleased, Mum less so.

"Mum try not worry about him. Ethan and Lucy will be fine, and they'll still need you. I know that's what's bothering you. Mum, we will always need you," I say.

"Libby, I love you. Both Dad and I are really proud of the beautiful, thoughtful young woman you've become," Mum says, her eyes brimming with unshed tears.

"Oh, Mum, don't. There have been enough tears today," I say as I walk over to the couch and sit beside her so I can give her a reassuring hug.

We order dinner. By the time it arrives, Lucy has been bathed, dressed for bed, fed, and is sound asleep. I got the privilege of feeding her—well, I did miss her when they were on holiday, and who knows when I will get time again soon? She is such a hungry, wee girl.

We sit round the table eating and talking. I fill Dad in about the hotel, telling him about what's been happening and about all of this coming weekend's events, including the wedding we have on Friday and the charity event for Sunday afternoon. He tells me he's taking tomorrow off work to spend the day with Mum and that he will come by the hotel first thing Thursday morning to go through the figures. It's nearly ten o'clock when Dad turns to Mum and says, "It's time we were going home. I know Libby has an early start as well tomorrow. What time are the removal guys here?"

"Seven," I answer. "And then the estate agent comes at eight to collect the keys for the new owner. Then I'm heading straight to the hotel. I have a few things I want to take care of tomorrow. Kieran is covering for me."

"Oh, all right, Phil ... although I did think we could stay here tonight with Ethan," Mum says, sounding disappointed.

"Mum don't worry about me, I'm fine. Lucy and I are going over to visit Lindsay's parent's tomorrow I'm sure they've missed her," says Ethan.

We see our parents out to the car. It's been an emotional day, and Mum has tears running down her face as she gives Ethan her tightest cuddle.

"Mum, please don't," he says with his softest reassuring voice. After tonight I'm sure he will be. It will still take time, but he'll get there in the end. We stand in the street, Ethan with his arm draped over my shoulder, as we wave them off.

"Libby, I do hope you've managed to clear some time off over the weekend," Dad calls from the car. "Remember I have an Alexander Mathews staying at the hotel. He arrives Thursday afternoon, and I will need you to chat him up, show him about, keep him happy."

"Of course, I remember! See you Thursday morning. Enjoy your day tomorrow."

Ethan laughs, and I know he is laughing at the face I've just made as we turn away from the car. "What?" I ask.

"Nothing. Just the expression on your face."

"Well, I can think of better things to do than spend time with one of Dad's friend's sight-seeing." I shrug.

"Libby, I don't think he's a friend of Dad's. More of a business client."

I can't remember what Dad told me about the man before he went on holiday, only that he told me to pencil in some free time to spend with a client. Actually, thinking about it, Dad was very vague. Well, this should be fun and interesting. Sight-seeing. It's not normal practice that a hotel manager would have that much interaction with a guest, but then again Mr Mathews doesn't appear to be a normal guest, according to my dad.

I say good night to Ethan, telling him to phone me if he needs me, but he reassures me that both he and Lucy will be fine. I know he will be. He has a lot of family and friends who care and want to support him. We hug for a few moments before letting go of each other. I watch him turn and go back inside his home and feel sad, even though I know it won't be long until I see him again. He's coming to the charity event on Sunday, although it's not really his cup of tea. I think he's only going to keep Mum happy. She practically begged him, saying he needs to get out more. That I can agree with. I hope he'll see Stephen and that they get a chance to talk.

I stand for another few minutes just looking at what has been my home for the past couple of years. I've had a lot of fun here, and I am taking a lot of memories away with me, both good and bad. I am a great believer that you need the bad so you can better appreciate all that's good in your life. So, here's hoping the next chapter in mine is just as good.

CHAPTER 2

Wednesday 15 October; the start of the next chapter of my life. The removal guys were bang on time; very quick and efficient, so all my things will now be in storage until I find a new place. The estate agent has also been and gone. I am not as sad or upset as I thought I would be—maybe because Ethan stayed indoors, and I've not caught so much as a glimpse of him at the window, which is a good thing since he would probably only set off my tears.

No, instead I am excited and maybe a bit scared. I'm only twenty-three; my dad must really trust me to leave the day-to-day running of the hotel to me. I just hope all the staff accepts me. There have been a few problems over the past few weeks. There are a select few who, I think, still see me as the wee girl that was always running about the hotel and grounds getting up to no good. But at least most of the main team players support me, so that will be half the battle.

Today I am off duty so I can get settled into my room. I'm also meeting my friend, Kirsty, for lunch. With work and taking care of Lucy, I've not seen her in weeks. We've still spoken every day on the phone, but it's not the same as seeing each other in person, so I'm looking forward to catching up.

The drive to the hotel doesn't take as long as it usually seems to, but that's mostly because the roads are still quiet with schools still off for a break. The sun is shining, I have the radio on, and I am singing along. I have a great feeling about today. It's been ages since I felt this good. I don't feel I have to worry about Ethan so much after our talk yesterday. I suppose I'll still worry, he's my brother after all but I am glad that he's going to start trying a little harder.

The music is suddenly interrupted as my mobile rings. "Miss Stewart? Sorry to bother you. It's Sally here. I know it's your day off, but we have a bit of a problem at reception." Sally is a lovely girl, about the same age as me, with blonde hair and blue eyes. She's very pretty, but also very shy. She's only been working at the hotel for a few weeks now, but she is extremely efficient at her job. I'd like to think we could become friends.

"What's wrong?"

"We have two guests who have arrived a day early."

"Okay, but I don't see why that's a prob—"

Sally interrupts me before I finish speaking. "You don't understand, Miss Stewart," she says haltingly.

"For goodness sake, Sally, can you please just spit it out?" I say sharply. "Surely we have rooms for them. I know we weren't fully booked."

"No, we have *rooms*," says Sally. "But these guests had originally booked two suites. We don't have any suites available until tomorrow. I've offered them different rooms for tonight and said we'd happily move them tomorrow, but they're really not happy."

"Sally, I'll be there in about ten minutes. Put them in the sitting room with tea and coffee, and I'll sort it out when I get there. Try not to let it upset you. It will work out." Sally does let things get to her. "Sally, what are the guests' names?"

"It's Mr. Mathews and Mr. Smith, your father's guests," she answers.

Dad's guests. Well, that explains a lot. I wonder if it's Dad who got the days wrong. I'll phone him later if I have to; these two sound like trouble and I've not even met them yet. God, I hope I don't need to spend too much time with them. I might need to start thinking about excuses I can use to get away from them, at least today is my day off!

"Okay, I'll see you shortly."

So much for being able to get settled in today. I'm hoping that Dad's guests don't change my good mood. No, I won't *let* them change my good mood. I suppose it won't be long until I find out. I'm now on hotel grounds. I just need to park my car.

I pull the car up to the entrance, turn off the engine, and step out, sighing as I look across the loch. The colours at this time of year are stunning, with the warm tones of autumn in the trees against the different shades of green hills in the background. And then there is the calm water in the foreground. I don't think I'll ever get tired of this view, which is still breathtaking, even on a wet, miserable day.

As my eyes drift along the loch, I find myself mesmerised by the peak of Ben Lomond. It has been a few years since I, myself, climbed the peak. There is a tourist path that takes even the most inexperienced walkers up the peak on a gentle rise to the summit at 3,192 feet. At the hotel we try to encourage tourists to make the climb with an experienced walker because if the weather suddenly changes, that smiling, green hill can become treacherous with the wind and rain sweeping across the loch.

It's incredible to think that we are less than an hour away from the hustle and bustle of Glasgow city centre. I know that's why we have so many returning guests; they love this location and our stunning hotel. Who wouldn't? It's a great base to go roaming.

I turn to find Fraser, our doorman, coming down the stairs. Fraser has been at the hotel since I was in my early teens, and he hasn't changed a bit in all the years I've known him. He's always had grey hair, blue eyes, a loving smile, and a great sense of humour. He reminds me of my grandfather. When Fraser finally decides to retire, I will miss him dearly.

"Ah, Miss Stewart. You're looking lovely today, as you do every day," he says, heading to the boot of my car.

"Flattery will get you everywhere, Fraser," I say, smiling.

"Oh, Miss Stewart, I don't think Liz would be happy with that. But if I were thirty or so years younger …" he says, laughing. "Let's get your cases inside, and then I'll take care of your car."

I grab my bag and laptop from the front of car and then go to the boot and pick up a box that Fraser has placed at the side.

"I don't think so, Miss," he says, laughing at me. "Put that back down. I aim to stay in my boss's good books, so the least I can do is take her things inside. I'll get them taken up to your room."

"I'm more than capable of carrying a few boxes and cases," I say with a warm smile. "But to humour you, I'll let you help me if you insist."

"I do, Miss Stewart; I'm only doing my job. And anyway, you have a problem to sort out, so I'll sort out your things," Fraser says, removing the last of my bags and placing them on a trolley. "Poor Sally is a bit upset. I think the American gave her a really hard time. I could hear him shouting from out here."

It's news to me that Alexander Mathews is American. Dad definitely didn't mention that. I'm picturing a paunchy, boorish man in his forties or fifties, maybe with grey hair and extremely bossy. The idea of having to spend time sight-seeing with him over the next few days makes me feel sick. No wonder Ethan was laughing at me last night. I bet he was in on this; it's just the type of thing he would have a good laugh at. I suppose I would do the same to him.

"Well, Fraser, I'll just have to use some of my Libby Stewart charm then. And if that doesn't work, we can send the American off to stay with my dad, seeing as he's here to see him anyway. But I am sure we will sort out the problem. There's always a solution; it's just about finding the right one for both parties concerned. And once we have happy guests, Sally will be fine as well."

"Not too sure your charm will work on this one. He seems a right grumpy so-and-so. But good luck."

I walk up the stairs and head inside. I am still disappointed to see that the log fire in the reception is not burning away, because with our unseasonable good weather, there is not a need for it. Yet. I know it won't be long. I love walking into this building when it's on. The warmth hits you straight away, and the glow of the flames only brings home the warm and cosy feel to this reception.

Sally lifts her head from the front desk. Her expression says, *'Thank god I don't have to deal with this anymore.'* The man standing to the side of the reception desk is talking on his mobile. I can tell from his accent that this is Mr American. He's not what I expected. He doesn't look a day over thirty, and he's quite dashing in an odd sort of way—very businesslike in his dark, sharp suit and highly polished shoes.

"M-m-miss Stewart," Sally stutters.

"Good morning, Sally. How are you today?" I ask, smiling at her as I walk over to the desk.

"I was good, but I'm better now you're here."

Mr. American, in his sharp suit, stops talking into his

phone and gives me a strange look. I know what he must be thinking. I *am* a bit underdressed today in my jeans, T-shirt and trainers, with my hair pulled back off my face. Not the first impression a guest should get of a hotel manager. I must remember not to call him Mr. American when I speak to him.

He does look pissed, so maybe Fraser was right that my charm won't work this time.

I walk over to him and hold out my hand. "Good morning. Mr Mathews, I presume? I'm Libby Stewart, the hotel manager," I say, but before I know it, I find myself adding, "It's my day off." I shake his hand.

"Sorry, Miss … or is it Mrs Stewart?" Mr American says.

"Miss."

"Well, Miss Stewart. I'm Mr Smith, Mr Mathew's assistant, but please, you can call me Michael," he says with a smile.

"Oh, okay. I do hope I can sort out this problem for you. We don't like having unhappy guests. Where is Mr Mathews?" I ask. "Perhaps he'd like to join us while we sort this out?"

"I am authorised to act on his behalf, Miss Stewart. That is a large part of my job," says Michael, with a wide grin. "In any case, he's gone off for a walk down towards the water. Hopefully we can sort this out before he comes back." He smiles sincerely; he doesn't seem grumpy at all, so it must be his boss who is grumpy.

I turn to Sally, who now has a smile back on her face. She is such a lovely girl. "Have you got all the room info up on the screen?" I ask her, walking behind the desk.

"Yes, see here," she says, pointing to the screen. "I only have three double rooms available. All the loch-view suites are full today. The suites for both Mathews and Smith are due to be ready tomorrow at lunchtime. The guests in both those rooms have early-morning flights and say that they will be checking out before breakfast."

"What's wrong with this suite?" I ask, seeing that there is, in fact, one empty suite.

Before Sally has a chance to answer, Michael speaks up. "Mr Mathews insists on having a loch-view suite." Michael seems like a reasonable man, same can't be said of his boss. *Insists, indeed.*

"Oh, Miss Stewart, that's your room. I haven't booked it out on the system yet."

I lift my head to see Fraser standing at the desk.

"Miss Stewart, your car is parked," he says. "If I can just get the key for your room, we can get your things upstairs so you can move in properly."

"Hold on a moment, Fraser." Fraser looks at me, puzzled. "Michael, I can give Mr Mathews a loch-view suite and a double room for you tonight and move you first thing in the morning," I say. "If that would be acceptable, I'll arrange to have housekeeping come in early to clean the suite you'll be moving into tomorrow, so you can move in as early as possible. Do you think this would be acceptable? It's the best solution as far as I can see."

Fraser is shaking his head at me. I know he thinks I'm crazy, but I've always been told that the guests come first.

Michael takes his phone from his pocket and walks over to the entrance, so we can't hear him. After a few minutes, he comes back to the desk. "Mr Mathews accepts your proposal and thanks you," he says with a smile.

"So, Miss Stewart, where would you like your things to go?" Fraser asks.

"Sally, please give Fraser the key for any free room. A bed is just somewhere to sleep at the end of a long day. Any one of these will do.

"Room nine okay?" Sally asks.

"Perfect." I turn to Michael. "If Mr Mathews needs me for anything more, please contact Sally, and have her page me. I'll be in the hotel all day." I say out of politeness more than anything else. I'm in no hurry to meet the moody American. Tomorrow will be soon enough.

"Thank you again, Miss Stewart. Sorry to have troubled you on your day off. And I'm sure Mr Mathews will be in touch." I can hear the sarcasm in his voice.

"Please, Michael, its Libby," I say.

Michael puts his hand out to shake my hand. "It's been a pleasure meeting you, I am sure we will be seeing much more of each other."

He then heads outside, presumably to find his irascible employer. Sally is now happy again. Gone are her unhappy guests.

"Well, that was an interesting start to the day," I say with a sigh, glad that my first problem of the Americans' stay is sorted out—although from the sound of things, I can expect more. "Sally, could you let the heads of each department know that my father's American guests have arrived a day early? I don't want there to be more problems for them to complain about. Now, as it's not even ten o'clock, and already I'm feeling a bit steamed, I think I'll go have a workout in the gym. That is, as soon as we've got my stuff to my room."

I turn to face Fraser. "And Fraser, before you say anything, yes, I *will* help take my things upstairs with you. Not because I think you need help but just so you can be done quicker in case you have to see to Michael and Mr Mathews." I turn back to Sally. "My friend, Kirsty, is coming for lunch at one. I can be paged at any time today should you need me, but please, if you can avoid disturbing us at lunchtime, that would be great. I've not seen her in weeks."

"You're just like your grandfather," Fraser says as we head

up in the lift to my room. I know exactly what he means. I don't bother unpacking anything, just grab my sports bag and iPod and then head to the gym.

I pass several members of staff on my way. They all very politely say, "Good morning, Miss Stewart," and it's got me thinking about the whole Miss Stewart thing. I would much rather be called Libby. I must speak to Karl about this today; I value his opinion.

Karl is the head chef. Excellent at his job, he has given our restaurant an absolutely brilliant reputation. In the year he has worked for the hotel, restaurant turnover is up, and profits have more than doubled. Dad started him because he is still young enough that he hasn't lost of any of his drive and ambition. It's his drive that has turned the restaurant around. It's not just hotel guests dining in anymore—we are seeing more locals use the restaurant.

When I enter the changing room, I pause. I can't make up my mind whether it's a swim or a run I want. When I see some mums with kids screaming and shouting, all ready for the pool, that makes up my mind. A run it is. That way I can stick my earphones in and not hear a thing. Kids and pools are always noisy. I make my way over to the treadmill, noticing that the gym is actually rather quiet. There are only two others here; Stephen, the leisure centre manager, is speaking with a guest. She is obviously getting an introduction to the gym, as he's telling her how each piece of equipment works. He sees me and waves; I wave back and mouth, *Speak to you later*.

Earphones in, iPod on, I hit the switch. The way I feel, I could run all day. While the miles slip by under my feet, my mind drifts. Thoughts of Ethan flood my mind. Maybe I'll phone him tonight, just to make sure he's all right. I'll also let Stephen know that Ethan's promised to call. I try to think of places that I could take Mr Mathews to see. I should have asked Dad what the man might be interested in—and what he was thinking, sticking me with the grumpy American. Ethan should have got this job. I laugh at the thought.

There's a tap on my shoulder. I take one end of my earphones out and I turn around. Stephen, so I start to slow down.

"What's so funny, Libby? I heard you laughing from the other side of the gym," Stephen says. The machine comes to a stop, and all I can do is stare at Stephen. Always—even when he's working out—he looks immaculate, with his blond hair swept back behind his ears. His soft baby blues always seem to smile at me. I've known Stephen since primary school; that's how long he and Ethan have been best friends.

I take a long drink of water when the machine finally stops and step off to face him.

"Dad has a grumpy American here on business, and I have to take him sight-seeing. I was just thinking he should have given that job to Ethan to get him out and about," I say, panting.

"I like your thinking. So how is he anyway? Did he have a good holiday?"

"He seems good. We had a long talk yesterday about the house and things," I say. "He was a bit upset, but I think I finally got through to him. He says he's going to call you. And he will be here on Sunday for the charity do, so you can see how he is for yourself."

"It will be great to see him. I miss hanging out with him, and I am missing Lucy as well. She must be getting big now?"

"She is, and she's the spitting image of Lindsay, which I know must make it harder on him," I reply.

"Hello? Excuse me?"

Stephen and I both turn towards the gym door to see a man standing there. Stephen gives me a quick kiss on the cheek. "I'll catch you later, Libby," he says as he walks towards the man. He looks vaguely familiar. He must be a member. Stephen talks to him for a moment and then points over to me. The man starts walking toward me.

Please don't let this be another unhappy guest. I can't cope with two in one day. Although I'd stand a better chance, maybe, at charming this one. He's nearer my age and *very* pleasant on the eyes.

"Miss Stewart, I believe?" he says, reaching out his hand.

"Yes." I shake the man's hand. Suddenly I'm feeling nervous. There's something about his touch that is electrifying, that sends shivers all down my spine. I try to pull my hand from his grip, but it won't move, or rather, he won't let it go.

"I am your 'grumpy American,' Alexander Mathews," he says in a rather conservative tone.

Good god. I want the ground to open and swallow me whole. Why can't I keep my big mouth shut? He still has a very firm grip of my hand as he stares at me. God, why is he still holding it? And why the hell do I recognise him? He really looks so familiar that I wonder if I've met him before. Maybe if I saw him with my father, I would remember.

I can't seem to take my eyes off the fascinating man standing in front of me. I keep telling myself it's rude to stare, but I can't help it.

"Miss Stewart, are you okay? You seem a bit distracted," he asks with a smirk.

He's noticed. Distracted—good choice of word. Can I make him think that it's not him that's distracting me? Such soft brown eyes ... still looking at me. Does he know what I'm thinking? I feel drawn to him, as if something is pulling me in. My breathing is all over the place, I feel a bit light-headed, and my legs are shaky—and not just because of the running.

"Just a bit dizzy. Must be from running," I mutter. *Pull yourself together, girl.*

He lets go of my hand and places his very softly on my shoulder. With his other hand, he guides the bottle of water I'm holding up to my mouth. His eyes remain fixed on mine. His hand is warm and soft.

"Drink." It sounds more like an order than a request.

As I take a long drink of water, I close my eyes, hoping and praying I can have a bit more composure when I open them; I really don't want to fall at this man's feet. Not yet, anyway. When I open my eyes, he's smiling at me.

The man in front of me definitely doesn't look like the grumpy American I had pictured in my head. That vision has long gone. Instead I see a man who is young, maybe a few years older than I am, handsome, and a bit rough round the edges. *Don't think I've ever seen a guy look this good in a suit.* Although I think his body would look so much better without it on. I can't believe I am standing in front of a tall, lean, handsome stranger and already imagining him naked. I wonder if the body inside the suit matches the image running through my mind?

I shake myself. *You are stronger than this. Get a grip, girl. He's only a man. But such a fine specimen of a man.*

"Mr Mathews. I'm fine, thank you," I try to say as casually as I can.

"Miss Stewart, I came looking for you to thank you and apologise."

"Please. Call me Libby. I think it's I who should apologise, after what you overheard," I say. "And why would you want to thank me?" I am embarrassed. My face must be bright red, but at least I can blame that on the running, too.

He just laughs. So glad I amuse him. Perhaps he knows it's not the running that's got me all flustered. I imagine this is the effect he has on women all the time.

"Well, I've been told that you've given me your own room. After thinking it over, I would much rather stay in one of the other rooms. I really don't want to put you out. And it *is* only for one night. I'm sure I can manage without a loch view until tomorrow."

"It's not a big deal. As I assured Michael, everything will be sorted out first thing tomorrow," I say with a smile.

"No, please keep your room. I insist. I think I've caused you enough trouble today."

"Okay. I'll have reception call you in the morning as soon as the rooms are ready. It should be about breakfast time," I reply.

"You're not what I expected, Libby."

What did he expect? Obviously someone much older and maybe not even female from the looks he's been giving me. But then he's not what I was expecting either. "Ah, you were thinking—"

"Yes, you are way too young. And … your father said that the hotel manager was a man." He answers the question that was running through my head and fires a question back at me. God, he's a mind reader.

He's referring to Luke, with whom I've worked since uni learning the trade. He taught me well, and he made it clear to my dad when he was leaving that I was more than ready to fill his shoes.

"Luke left about a month ago to accept a position in London," I answer.

"I see," he says with a sigh. "So, Libby, I guess I've been left in your care. You're spending time with me over the next few weeks?" He looks smug at the thought of that. Amusement. That's what I see in his eyes.

"Weeks?" I know my father has the rooms booked out for three weeks, but I hadn't realised I was expected to do some, let's say, babysitting for the whole duration of his stay. How can I possibly spend weeks with a man who has me so completely befuddled in such a short space of time?

"Yes, Libby. I'll be staying here for two or three weeks. Didn't your father tell you?"

"Yes, but …" I snap. Good god. I must sound like a right bitch.

"I do have various meetings to attend during my stay; it is, after all, a business trip. But I think it could also become an extremely pleasurable trip, given the opportunity to spend some time getting to know Phil's beautiful daughter."

He's openly flirting, trying and obviously succeeding in making me blush. I feel like I could fall at any moment. I am standing in front of him, visibly shaking, dripping sweat in my gym gear, my soaking-wet hair clotted to my head. Could this get any more awkward? It probably could. And here I had thought when I first saw him that I could charm him. Instead it's him using his charm on me—and it's working. I wonder what it would feel like to run my hands through his sexy, brown hair whilst in a passionate embrace.

"Could we meet up later to go over your calendar? I would also love to get a tour of the hotel and grounds. I understand that you must be busy, but there are a lot of things I'd like to do while I'm here. I've never been to Scotland before."

"I am actually meeting a friend for lunch today, but I'm free tomorrow from noon on, if that's any good," I say. "I had already cleared my agenda since that's when I was expecting you."

He's no longer smiling. There's no glint in his eyes. What does he want me to do, change my plans just for him and just because he arrived a day early? No can do. It doesn't matter how good-looking he is; I won't do it. But if he had half a mind to try, I'm sure I could be persuaded.

"Very well, Miss Stewart. Good day to you." He turns on his heel and walks away.

"Why are you here a day early?" I call after him. He doesn't answer.

～

GOD, what a morning so far. I'm really not sure what to make of the handsome American I am now going to be stuck with for a few weeks. I am definitely attracted to him, so I am going to have to figure out a way to remain professional. This could be a big problem. I am suddenly curious about what business he's in and what he's doing with my father. He must be a new client.

I can't stand here all day, dreaming. Soon I'll be meeting Kirsty for lunch, so I need to head back to my room for a quick shower and change. Stephen is busy with another guest, so I just give him a wave and mouth, *See you later*.

"No you don't, Libby. Wait up!" Stephen calls after me.

"What is it? Kirsty's coming over soon. I really need to get ready."

"So, you and Alex … how do you know each other?"

"We don't. That's the first time we've met. Dad's doing some business with him, I believe. Turns out *he's* the grumpy American I was talking about."

"From the way you were both acting, I presumed you knew each other. Surely you must recognise him?"

"Yes, I think so, but I'm not sure where from. I must have met him through Dad. He's a businessman after all."

"Libby, he is *the* businessman of the moment in America. He's always in the papers and tabloid news with a different beauty on his arm every week. I'm not really sure what line of business he's in. I've not paid much attention to the articles, just the stunning women in the pictures. Libby, promise me you'll be careful with him. He has a bit of a reputation with women. You're a beautiful woman, just his type, and I don't want to see him take advantage of you," Stephen says with a concerned voice.

"Don't worry about me. You know I'm more than capable of taking care of myself," I say, although at the moment I'm not sure who I'm trying to convince. "Now I really need to get a wriggle on. Wait just a minute … beautiful, you say? I can't make up my mind whether you want a date with the boss or a pay rise," I say, laughing as I start out of the gym. We both already know the answer to that question.

"I'd take a pay cut for a date with you any day of the week," he says, trying to make it sound like a joke, but I know he means it.

I call Sally and ask her if anyone is free to give me a hand for ten minutes or so moving my things. Poor Sally. Now she doesn't know whether she's coming or going. I send Kirsty a quick text:

Libby: What time did we say for lunch? L X

Kirsty: 1 C U soon X

Good. It's just noon, so I've got plenty of time to get ready. As I stand in the shower rinsing my hair, my mind wanders to my encounter with the American and then to Stephen's warning—because that's what it was, a warning. Stephen is sweet, but he clearly still thinks of me as a little girl unable to handle myself. But we're all the same age—Stephen, Ethan, and I.

I grab two towels, wrapping one round my body and the other round my hair, which I'll do once I've put on my makeup and clothes. When I leave the bathroom, I hear *bang … bang … bang*.

Whoever is banging on my bloody room door better have a damn good reason. I look through the peephole, surely not, Mr Mathews. I can't open the door, not like this.

"Hold on," I call out. I grab my dress and quickly put it on.

"Mr Mathews! What can I?—" I say as I open the door for him.

I don't get to finish my sentence. He's pushed his way into my room. What the hell does he think he's doing?

I stand by the open door as he pushes past then turns and comes towards me, still not saying a word. I close the door—I presume he is staying. He pushes me up against the door, bouncing my head off it. Shit. He's pinning me in place with his body, one arm up against the door. He lifts my chin with his other hand and leans his face down to meet mine. I've thought about what it would feel like to kiss him since I first clapped eyes on him, and now he's here, and I'm about to find out whether I want to right now or not.

"I am used to getting what I want," he whispers. I bet he is.

His lips meet mine, but there is nothing passionate or romantic in the way he kisses me. Hunger and need come to mind. Bloody hell. My body starts to respond, but my mind is telling me not to let this happen. His grip on my chin is getting tighter, and his other hand has moved from the door and found its way to my backside; the grip is getting tighter there too. He's scaring me. I can't stand here and let this happen. I need to do something and quick.

Think, Libby. Bloody think.

Just because I find him attractive doesn't mean he can do this. He shouldn't be forcing me … and wouldn't have had to if he had only asked. Both my arms are still free. I run one hand up the front of his shirt—I can feel the well-defined muscles of his abs and his chest—and he stops kissing me to lean away and look at me with a knowing smirk, not at all surprised that I am touching him back.

But he is very surprised when I slap him right across the face and push him away.

He takes a step back, rubbing his cheek. God, I've surprised myself. I didn't think I had the nerve to do that. I hope it bloody hurt. Who the hell does he think he is? Forcing his way into my room, forcing himself on me? Was that why he volunteered to change rooms, so he'd know what room I was in? I can't let him stay in the hotel now. What is my dad going to say when I tell him I've had to throw him out for his bad behaviour? What a mess.

"Why the hell did you do that?" he shouts.

Is he serious? "Why? Because when someone kisses me, it's because I want them to. Not because they attack me like a fucking animal. I don't know any woman who enjoys a man forcing himself on her. I should call the police. Now you have exactly five seconds to get out of my room before I call security."

"You wanted that as much as I did. Don't kid yourself," he snarls, shaking his head. He looks puzzled as he leaves my room.

I'm puzzled, too. I would have said earlier that he seemed to be a bright man. If so, he's certainly stupid about human nature. What an arrogant bastard! I slam the door shut and sink to the floor, letting the tears flow down my face.

CHAPTER 3

lex

SHE CONSUMES ME.

My head is filled with jumbled pieces of my short time with her. Filled with all the possibilities that are ahead for us both. My subconscious is playing with my heart and my fucking head, and I for one don't like the raw emotion that is pulling at me.

An angel.

And I must be the fucking devil for my behaviour.

Images flicker through my head of the hurt and devastation that crossed her face. So much raw and undiluted anger toward me, something I've never witnessed from a woman in my company before. But she wasn't just any woman. No, she's the one that has caused me so many sleepless nights over the last few months. Every time I closed my eyes, there she was, a vision of sheer natural beauty. She's the type of woman that doesn't have to spend hours in hair and make-up in an attempt to look good. She's the most beautiful woman I've ever clapped eyes on, and I've ruined it before we even get started.

"What the fuck have I just done?" I slam the bedroom door behind me, and pace back and forth to the window and the bed. This view is fucking awful. I at least hope tomorrow I have a room with a half decent view of the loch, instead of this over-grown woodland that I see.

I need a fucking drink.

I need to sort myself out.

Pull my shit together, so I don't fuck up anything else or my time in Scotland will be short lived. I walk toward the table that has a fresh decanter of whisky and a glass, *a nice touch*. I wonder if these are in all the rooms or was it just brought here because of who I am? Pouring a drink, I notice my hand is shaky. What the fuck is wrong with me?

Frustration fills me. I want her so fucking desperately that I've fucked up. She's going to be a challenge that's for sure. But I want her more than I've ever wanted anything in my whole damn life. I'll just have to prove to her that I'm worthy of her time and attention.

Taking a gulp of the whisky I close my eyes, she's every-where around me. That scent, it's one I don't think I'll ever forget. I inhale deeply and it's gone. Just like her.

I don't think, I open my eyes in time to see the glass hit off the wall before. *Fuck.* I've lost the fucking plot.

Loud knocking at the bedroom door has me turning my head toward it, but I don't move. "Mathews, open the fucking door." Michael, what the hell does he want?

He continues with his banging until I give in. I open the door without looking at him and walk away, back toward the window. "What the hell are you doing?" he shouts. I want to tell him to fuck off but he's my best friend and there's already so much that must be annoying him. Like me changing our plans last minute.

"Why is there a smashed glass lying on the floor? Alex what have you done?" The tone of his voice has changed, he sounds calm but he'll be anything but calm on the inside. I can already sense his cautious approach to me, it's one that I know so well. "Alex, talk to me. Tell me what the hell is going on."

I turn around slowly and sit on the edge of the bed, Michael stays in the middle of the room, patiently waiting. "I've fucked up."

"What have you done this time?" His question makes me sound like I always fuck up, but I don't. Well, not in business.

"Libby!"

Her name rolls off my tongue and I hear the disappointment in my voice. How could I treat her like that?

I lift my head looking at him waiting to hear what he has to say, but before he can say it, I see exactly what he's thinking. His disappointment registers with me as he furrows his brows and his lips tighten. "Yeah, you don't have to say anything."

"Oh, but I think I do. What the hell have you done? Or am I better off not knowing? She's the fucking reason you changed plans, isn't she?"

"What one of those questions do you want me to answer first?"

He sighs running his hand through his hair. "Any would be a start."

"Yes, she's the reason we are here early. And I've come on to her a bit too strong, I think."

"What the hell do you mean you think? You either have or haven't, there's no fucking in between."

He walks toward the window and I can feel frustration rolling off him in waves. "If you've fucked up that bad, we may as well get the first plane back home. Our journey will have been wasted all because you couldn't keep it in your pants."

"Hold on a minute. You might be my best friend, but I'm still your boss."

"Shut up."

"Fine," I blow out the word on a long breath. Michael takes a seat in the oversized tartan chair and waits for me to tell my not-so-happy story. I start at the beginning and try to explain my crazy thoughts and feelings about the woman who I know has given up so much to take care of her brother's baby daughter. Michael sits quietly, trying to make sense of what I'm saying. I hope he has better luck than me.

"You idiot," he exclaims when I tell him about what happened in her hotel room. "If you're lucky she'll only tell her father, but you might find that she files charges against you. Come on, Alex, this isn't you. You don't do stupid stuff like this. Me on the other hand, well, let's not go there. Look, I can understand your attraction but this is…a bit creepy and that's coming from me, your best-friend."

"You're not telling me anything I don't already know. What the hell am I going to do?"

"Firstly, you need to speak to her and apologise. Grovel if you must. Although if I were her I wouldn't want to be in the same room as you alone."

"Thanks."

"You know me, I'm truthful. She's classy, not really your usual type."

"I know but…I just can't explain it. I feel as though I know her, really know her."

"Am going to be blunt, Alex you don't know her. We're here for business. She doesn't come across as the sort of woman you could just have a bit of fun with. She would want more, and could you do more?" He shakes his head almost laughing at his last question.

"What's wrong with more? At some point in both our lives we have to grow up and stop fucking about."

"Speak for yourself. I don't imagine ever tying myself down to one woman. Now sort yourself out and go and find her to apologise. I'll go and arrange to get this mess cleared up."

He's laughing to himself as he walks out the bedroom.

I don't know what I was thinking about when I left New York. Michael is right, Libby is not the type of woman that would play games, she would want commitment.

Is that something I could possibly give?

Only time will tell.

CHAPTER 4

*K*irsty: Where R U? You're late X
    Libby: On my way X

I text Kirsty as I rush down the hall. I'm twenty minutes late, but at least I look presentable. I've thrown on a different dress to the one I had put on when Alex appeared at my room and put on sandals and pinned my damp hair up. I wasn't in the mood to fuss over it. I rushed my makeup, so even though it's less obvious that I've been crying, no doubt Kirsty will notice. I swoop through the hotel corridors towards the bar, offering up a polite greeting and smile to everyone I pass.

She's sitting at the bar, obviously flirting with my staff. I can tell. She sits twiddling her fingers through her long, blond hair, as always. She's like that; she's been a flirt since the very first day I met her. Even then she was flirting with one of the uni tutors. She doesn't see me enter—too wrapped up in a conversation with the bartender.

Kirsty and I met at university. She's been more than a great friend to me these last few months when I've needed her, even if she's just been at the other end of the phone, with her words of comfort. She decided to take a year out after graduation, and I'm not sure if she has any intention of ever looking for a job. She's more than happy to live off the bank of her mum and dad. Me, on the other hand, I enjoy and need my independence. Sounds silly, I know, considering it's my dad I work for.

"Kirsty!" I call out. "I thought we were having lunch, not a night on the tiles," I say, laughing halfheartedly. She's wearing a short dress and killer heels, and she looks stunning, but more for a night out clubbing than a lunch date with a friend.

"Libby, it's great to see you." She kisses me on both cheeks. "Let's have a look at you."

I stand back, and she twirls me round.

"You can tell me what's wrong over lunch. And I mean it. I know something's wrong." She has a concerned look in her eyes as she narrows her brows. *God, she's good ... too bloody good.*

"Just one of those mornings so far. I thought we could have lunch out on the terrace," I say, changing the subject. "What do you think? Too nice to be stuck indoors."

"Sounds good to me, although your barman here is rather dreamy. Will he attend to us outside as well?" she says with a wink.

"If you can behave yourself, I might let him. Have you looked at the menu yet?" I ask.

"I already know what I want, but I'm sure he's not on the menu," she laughs. She would chew him up and spit him out. The poor lad wouldn't know what hit him.

"Kirsty, Kirsty ... whatever are we going to do with you?"

We order our food at the bar and then head outside with our drinks. It seems everyone is taking advantage of the gorgeous, unseasonable weather. Most of the tables on the terrace are occupied. There are also some families having picnics on the grass, with kids running about. Kirsty and I find a table in the sun and sit down.

"So, what you been up to the last few weeks?" I ask knowing she'll have lots of juicy gossip to tell me.

"Well, where should I start? I've been to a few social engagements with my parents—you know, the ones that can be quite boring at times and very interesting at others?" she says, giggling.

"When you say 'interesting,' I can only presume it involves the male species."

"Ah, Libby, you know me too well."

"So do tell! I want details."

"Okay. Two Saturdays ago, I met a guy called Thomas—I think that was his name anyway—and we had a great night dancing and laughing and talking. And as you know, I don't do much talking with guys," she says. "He was really good-looking and a great kisser, so we swapped numbers. I was going to call him on the following Wednesday—really, I was —but then Dad asked me to go to a business networking event that night, so I didn't get around to calling him. Anyway, there was this really cute guy called Jay at *that* event, and I've seen him a few times since. You'll love him when I introduce you. That is, if I don't start dating your barman before then."

I laugh.

Kirsty has always been the same. She drifts from one guy to the next. I don't remember her ever having been with the same man for longer than four weeks. I wish I were more like her—carefree, always happy. I'm happy, but I'm not carefree. My last boyfriend was Jeff; we split up just after Lindsay died, when he couldn't understand my need to be with Ethan and my family.

He was heartless. I ended it, but it wasn't all about Lucy. I suppose I had been looking for an excuse even before that.

He was a bit of a bore, pushy at times and not very romantic. He was quite happy to spend most nights in front of the TV, and he didn't like me going out with my friends without him. "Controlling" springs to mind, although I didn't see it at the time. And he couldn't stand Kirsty. Me, I like to go out and enjoy myself, although I'm not quite the life and soul of every party, like Kirsty.

"So, Libby, are you going to tell me why your eyes are so puffy? Don't think I hadn't noticed." Kirsty really doesn't miss anything. Do I tell her the truth? I'm a terrible liar. Before I get a chance to talk, the waiter arrives with our food.

"Miss Stewart, how are you today?" he asks.

"Very well, thank you."

"Okay, so who is having the smoked salmon?"

"Me," Kirsty says.

"That means the king prawn is for you. Can I get either of you anything else?" he asks, placing my lunch in front of me.

Kirsty shakes her head. "I'm fine, thanks."

"Some more water would be great. Thanks," I say.

"Now, where were we? Ah, you were just going to tell me why you've been crying." She gives me that look that only Kirsty can do so well—the look that says, *you ain't getting away from this conversation that easily.*

"It's … it's nothing, really. We have a troublesome hotel guest I've had to deal with this morning. And that on top of the sale of the house and everything with Ethan … I just let it get to me. But you know me; I'll be fine. I always bounce back," I say, hoping that the shortened version of the truth will do.

"You sure that's all?"

I would question me too, but I give her a nod just as the waiter comes back with a jug of water.

"I'm sorry to bother you, Miss Stewart, but Sally has

asked if you could phone her at reception. She says she knows you are busy but that it's urgent," he says, handing me the phone he has in hand.

I press one for reception, and at the same time, I mouth *sorry* to Kirsty.

"Sally, its Libby. What's wrong?"

"Libby, I am so, so sorry. I really didn't want to disturb you—I know you're having lunch—but I didn't know what else to do." Sally is upset again. Why did I even bother to ask the question? Especially when I could put money on the answer.

"It's fine. Just tell me what's wrong, and I will sort it out," I say, trying to calm her down.

"It's M. Bloody Mathews again. He's called several times looking to speak with you, and he's also been down in person. I keep telling him the same thing—that you are unavailable at the moment and that you will contact him as soon as possible. Even Kieran tried talking to him, but he insists that he will only be dealing with you during his time with us. The other man with him—is it Mr Smith?—he looked a bit embarrassed about the whole thing. Again, I feel bad having to interrupt you, especially since you've already had to change plans for this ass. Oh, excuse the language, but … well, that's not even really what I would *like* to call him. The words I have in mind are much stronger," she says. She's almost babbling, being really apologetic, but she has no reason to apologise. She's only trying to do her job.

I knew it. Mathews. "Sally, its fine. If he calls or comes by the desk again, simple tell him that I have received the message and that I have promised to see him as soon as I am available. And try not to let him bother you," I say, although I know it's not that simple. "Why don't you get someone to cover reception for you, and take your break a little early?"

Sally agrees to go for her break to give her a chance to

compose herself again. I give the phone back to the waiter and just shake my head. "Sorry, Kirsty. It's the troublesome guest I mentioned. I'll have to deal with him straight away after lunch. He's upset my staff, *again*. I wish he'd be more patient. I really wanted to spend the rest of the afternoon with you."

"Don't fret, Libby," she says. "We can have a good catch-up on Sunday."

"So, you're still coming on Sunday then?"

"Of course! Wouldn't miss it."

"Why don't you come here early, and we can get ready together. I have the hairdresser coming to do my hair, and perhaps she can do yours too. We've not done that in such a long time."

"Sure, that sounds like a plan."

We continue talking whilst eating our lunch. I don't dawdle, but neither do I rush. I am not in that much of a hurry to see Mr Mathews again. What is his problem? Although at this moment, I really don't want to know. I don't even want to think about him. I fill Kirsty in on how Ethan and Lucy are doing and let her know that he will be here on Sunday. I remind her again *not* to flirt with him; I don't think he's quite ready for that yet. We both laugh at that.

Kirsty stops talking mid-conversation. She's just sitting there staring into space over my shoulder. It must be the view; it does that to me as well. It's something about the clear water going on for miles and seeing all the way over to the rolling hills on the other side. Even with the sound of boats and Jet Skis, the loch still has a calming effect on me.

"Oh my god, I think I've died and gone to heaven," Kirsty says, her head tilted to one side, her mouth open, and her eyes sparkling.

I laugh. "I presume you've just seen the man of your dreams." As I finish saying it, I cringe. An icy shiver runs all the way down my back. I really wish I hadn't said that, as I have a feeling I already know whom she's looking at. I slowly turn. Alexander Mathews.

"Who is that?" Kirsty asks.

"*That* is my ongoing problem. Could you excuse me a minute?" I say, pushing my chair back quietly to get up from the table. I draw in a deep breath and try to mentally prepare myself for this confrontation.

"No way! How could a man like that be a problem? Look at him; he is sex on legs. He can be my problem any day," Kirsty says, all smiles. "Introduce me. I'll deal with him for you."

"I'm sure you could. But no."

I walk over to where he stands, looking tall and confident. Michael had been standing with him but has just walked away shaking his head. I'm a lot more confident about this brief meeting with him; since we're in a public place, I probably won't need to slap him again. I hope.

"Mr Mathews." I hold out my hand to shake his. I hope he realises I am not intimidated by him. Well, maybe I am just a little, but I won't admit that. He brings both his hands up to meet mine and takes my hand. The palms of his hands are warm and soft, very soft, but I already knew that from my earlier encounter.

"Miss Stewart, it seems I am going to spend my entire time here apologising to you. I'm sorry for the way I acted earlier." He's studying my face, which I am hoping gives nothing away, because I think I could crumble at any time.

"Are you? Because I don't think you are. What was it you said? Something along the lines of always getting what you want?" I snap.

"Please, I'm trying to say I'm sorry. That's not something I do very often, and so far today I've already had to do it twice," he says.

"Look, I am really not sure an apology is going to cut it. What you done … What gave you the right to think it was okay to take?"

I can feel my hand getting sweaty with his hands still wrapped round mine. His eyes are locked on mine as if he's in a trance or trying to read my mind. I go with the latter. I try to pull my hand away from his, but he keeps a tight grip.

"Miss Stewart, I'm sorry if my actions earlier upset you. That wasn't my intention." He looks sincere enough, but I for one am not buying it.

"Really? What *was* your intention?"

"Please. I've obviously misread you," he says. He looks hurt at my curtness and genuinely surprised. But really, what *was* he expecting? That I would just roll out the red carpet, so to speak, because he's so bloody important? I still don't even know who he is.

"But you have to admit there is some chemistry between us. You must have felt it earlier?"

"Seriously! That's your excuse for your behaviour?" I snap trying to pull my hand free. "Can you let go of my bloody hand before I make a scene."

"Alex …" It's Michael's voice that distracts me from the man in front of me. Alex lets go of my hand and glares at Michael, who is shaking his head at him.

"Miss Stewart, I don't know what else to say, except sorry." His eyes are pleading with me. "If it's any consolation my behaviour was totally out of character"

"That I wouldn't know about. But I will say this; you being here is obviously important to my father and yourself and for the time being I will not discuss this matter with my father, but so help me god, you step one foot out of line and I can assure you any business you have with my father will come to very abrupt end." I have confidence in my words.

"Miss Stewart, you have my assurance that I won't step

out of line, unless I am invited to." He winks at me. Seriously this man is going to be detrimental to my health.

"Apology accepted. Now if you would excuse me, I have a friend waiting." I look back at Kirsty, who has the biggest grin on her face.

"Yes. I can see that you're busy. If I could, though, Miss Stewart, I would still like a tour later today. Michael will join us." He's obviously sensed my apprehension about spending time alone with him and with good reason. "And remember we need to check both our schedules for the next week. Perhaps you and I could do that over dinner this evening?"

Dinner. Why on Earth would I want to go for dinner with a man like him? Arrogant and domineering. He reminds me of someone.

"This is my day off. You don't want much, do you?" I say, trying to sound stern but not unprofessional. I fear I just sound petulant. "I could meet you both at reception in say, an hour. We could review our schedules in my office, and then I can give you both a tour of the hotel and the grounds. As for dinner, I don't customarily dine with guests."

He looks very disappointed.

"Miss Stewart, we will be spending a lot of time with each other over the coming weeks. I think we can both agree that my extended stay means that I am not your normal hotel guest, so I can't see why dinner would be a problem."

I suppose that is true. Would it be so bad? I glance at Michael from the corner of my eye; he's standing about ten feet away from us. Has he been there the whole time listening? Does he know what happened earlier in my room, or does he think Mathews is apologising for his rudeness over the accommodations? With the expression on his face I think he knows only too well what happened.

"I'll consider it and let you know."

His eyes light up with a half-smile on his face. "That is

already more than I expected after earlier. I mean it when I say I am sorry." He lifts my hand to his lips and places a very gentle, warming kiss in the middle of my hand. "An hour then. We'll see you soon." He turns and walks away with Michael, leaving me in the middle of the terrace staring after him.

"Oh, Elizabeth? Elizabeth Stewart!" Kirsty shouts, startling me as she walks towards me.

"What?" I snap.

"You'd better start talking, lady, and he had *better* not be the reason you've been crying," Kirsty says. She sounds pissed at me.

"Let's go back to the table. I'll tell you everything this time; I promise."

We sit down, and I start at the beginning, telling her everything that has happened with Alexander Mathews and his assistant, Michael Smith—what I first thought of him, how pushy he is, how he tried to force himself on me, and how angry it made me feel.

"He likes you, and it's obvious you like him. There's chemistry between you, and don't you dare try to tell me otherwise," Kirsty says, smiling. "He's also gorgeous. But he sounds like a spoiled, rich brat. That kind of man is trouble for innocents like you, but I know how to handle them. You should tell him to push off, but you should push him my way." She chuckles.

"What do you mean, 'chemistry'?"

"Where do you want me to start? I've only seen him with you for a few minutes, and already I have a list. Maybe it will take him throwing himself at you—again, that is—because you're sure as hell not going to make a move, are you? He couldn't take his eyes off you the whole time. It's not often you see a man with such a longing, needing, wanting look in his eyes. His hands stayed touching yours the whole time, and if I am not mistaken, his hands were caressing yours. Go on, tell me I'm wrong."

"Okay, okay, yes, I'm attracted to him. Who wouldn't be attracted to him? But after how I've seen him behave, I'm not sure that's enough. I need to spend the next few weeks with him and remain professional, if only for my dad's sake, although I'm really not sure what his connection is to my dad. So, Kirsty, my question to you is: what the hell am I supposed to do?"

"Relax. He likes you and you like him. You have to spend time with him anyway, stop worrying, and just enjoy his company. And if things do end up going too far, try thinking of it as a holiday romance. Once his business with your dad is done, you probably won't even see him again. My advice, for what it's worth, is simple. Have some bloody fun, girl! You deserve it. All work no play leads to a very boring life. And all you've done lately is work." She's smirking at me.

"So, you're saying I'm boring?" I stare at her. God, am I boring? I shouldn't be boring. I do have fun when I have the time. Although she's right; time isn't something I've had a lot of lately. "You know, it's funny. Earlier today Stephen tried to warn me off him. He recognised Alex, said he's always in the papers with a different woman on his arm each week."

"No, you're not boring, honey, but it would be nice seeing you have some fun for a change," Kirsty says. "And as for Stephen, why do you think he's done that? You know how Stephen feels about you. He's never tried to hide it. If you're that worried, do some research on the Internet, and then give him a grand tour of this place. Take him down to the marina, and finish off with a tour of your room." She's laughing at me now. That is just the type of thing she would do. "Now, why are you still sitting with me when you're meeting him shortly?"

"I'm meeting him and his PA. But you're right; I should get a move on. Now, Sunday—you'll come over early?"

"You just *try* keeping me away now! I'll want all the info on what you get up to," she says.

"By then you'll have had three full days together for some fun."

"Not quite. I still have other work to do each day round here. We have a big wedding on Friday, and I need to be round for that." Bolstered by Kirsty's words, though, I have to admit that the prospect of having some fun, even if it's with Alexander Mathews, sounds rather appealing. That thought has me grinning.

When we say our good-byes, Kirsty makes me promise to relax and have fun. I plan to try and keep that promise, but at the moment I'm still apprehensive about spending time with him. I wonder if I should spend the time before our meeting looking him up on the Internet. But then maybe I'm better off not knowing.

CHAPTER 5

I'm sitting at my desk, staring at the computer screen. Do I really want to do this? I've already typed in his name, and my hand is hovering over the search button. No. I pick up my phone and call Dad. He answers on the second ring.

"Hello, honey! Is everything all right?" he asks.

"No, it's not. I thought you said Mr Mathews wasn't arriving until tomorrow. He's arrived a day early, and he's upset my staff already," I say, taking a deep breath. "Americans! They're always so bloody damn pushy, wanting their own way. What kind of business are you doing with him?"

"Okay. One thing at a time. It was definitely tomorrow he was due to arrive, but I take it you have things in hand?" Dad says.

"Yes, of course I've sorted out the initial problems when he arrived," I say with confidence. "And I have another question: why the hell am *I* stuck with him for a few weeks?"

"All right. I've not known Alex that long, but I never got the impression that he was pushy. As for the business I am doing with him, I'll fill you in tomorrow morning when I come by the hotel. Does that answer your questions?"

"I suppose so."

"Oh, Libby. I *was* planning on having Ethan spend time with him—they have similar interests—but then I thought maybe Ethan's time would be better spent with Lucy. And you're at the hotel anyway, so it makes sense." The softness of his voice pulls at my heartstrings. "Don't worry. Most of Alex's time will be taken up with meetings with me. I hope you're not too upset with me."

There's a knock on my office door.

"Hold on a minute!" I shout.

"No, Dad, everything's fine. I have to go. That will be Mr Mathews at the door now. I'm going to give him a tour and sort through my schedule. I will see you in the morning. Early. Love you."

"I love you too, honey," he says, hanging up.

"Come in!" I shout. I look at the computer. His name's still in the search box. I need to switch it off; I don't want him thinking I'm interested in him. Even if I am curious. I quickly switch it off.

Alexander Mathews enters my office. He's no longer in his business suit. Instead he's wearing a bright white T-shirt that shows off his lean arms and a hint of the fabulous torso beneath it, along with jeans that sit just on his hips. And I thought he looked good in a suit. He's also just out of the shower; his hair is still wet. *Just out of a shower*. I need to get that thought out of my head, it sends icy shivers through my body. I need to relax.

"I hope I'm not too early, Miss Stewart," he says.

"No, you're just on time. Please, could you stop with the 'Miss Stewart'? It's driving me mad. My friends just call me Libby."

"Okay then, Libby. We should start again." He smiles and

holds out his hand to me. "I'm Alex. Very pleased to meet you." He lifts my hand to his mouth and places a soft kiss in the back of it. I feel myself blush. He slowly lowers my hand. Michael is trying to hide a laugh – although not very successfully.

"Michael, have you got my calendar open?" Alex turns to Michael, who is standing in the doorway to my office with an iPad in his hand, smiling at me. He seems the calmer of the two, and he has a sense of humour—always a good thing.

I pull my calendar up on the computer screen so we can start going through each day. I also call Kieran, my duty manager, into the office. I want to run my free days past him to make sure he can cope on his own. I introduce Kieran to Alex and Michael. I know they met earlier, but I also know that the meeting didn't go very well. I catch Kieran eyeing Alex. As soon as Kieran sees me watching him, he mouths, *handsome son of a bitch, isn't he?* The four of us sit and start at the beginning.

"I'm free from noon onward tomorrow. I presume you are as well, seeing as it was tomorrow you were meant to arrive?" I say with a smirk, looking at Alex. He smiles. I wonder if he will tell me why he has arrived a day early. "If there is anything in particular you would like to do, just say."

"I'm sure we'll think of something." His soft, brown eyes are firmly fixed on mine as he speaks, and there's also a smug grin on his face.

God, we could be sorting out schedules all day if we go through each day like this. "Friday?" I ask.

"Friday morning, I will be with your father. He's showing me around the office. Then lunch … I should be back here about three."

"We have a big wedding here Friday, so I'm tied up until after the meal is served." We do weddings most weekends, and I have been here for lots of them, but this is the first one

I've been in charge of. This is a part of my job. I love knowing that we've helped a happy couple create their perfect day and seeing that everything runs smoothly.

Kieran pipes up. "You know, Libby, as soon as the ceremony is done, you should be good to go." Kieran is great. I don't know what I would do without him at times. "I have the schedule of the day's events with me, and as long as everything goes as planned, you should be able to get away about four. As long as the rain stays away," Kieran says with a laugh.

"Rain? What does rain have to do with it?" Alex asks Kieran with a puzzled look that shows frown lines across his head.

"For one, the lovely couple are getting married outside on the front lawn. And two, they plan on getting beautiful photos taken on the grounds. If it rains, the lovely Libby and I will spend the day rolling out the backup plan to accommodate them inside." Kieran flashes me his big, cheesy, white smile. I wonder if Alex has realised yet that Kieran is gay; surely he must have, with the admiring looks headed in his direction.

"So ... Saturday?" I say.

"You're free all day, honey, as long as you do an early check in the function suite on Sunday morning and let me have a lie-in—seeing as I'm working all day, and you get to play. Life is so unfair." I think Alex has just caught up. He glances between Kieran and me.

"Your father has already taken care of Saturday. I believe you are taking me to a football match. I can't come all this way and not see a Scottish football game. I understand that you Scots have a real passion for the game," Alex says. From the look on his face, I can see that he is no longer talking about the football.

"Football, seriously? I'm supposed to take you to football?"

Kieran sits laughing, clutching his belly—genuine, proper laughing. *Why bloody me? A whole day at football!* That's Ethan's thing, not mine—not anymore. I used to love going to football with my dad and Ethan on a Saturday afternoon. It was always a good way of spending time with Dad. But it's been so long since I was last there that I couldn't even name a single player now. Dad was always taking some client or another to both Rangers and Celtic games—always the neutral supporter. The amount of business my dad has done over the years at football matches, I suppose it is a great day out, if you like that sort of thing.

"Yes, and then we are going for dinner with your parents," Alex informs me. He looks pleased with himself, like the cat that's got the cream. How come no one thought to tell *me* what I was doing?

"Will you stop with the bloody laughing? I take it you knew about this?" I ask Kieran, who is still in stitches.

"Of course, I knew. I had to sort your tickets. Your face was a picture!" says Kieran, finally collecting himself. "Okay, I have hospitality booked for you at the Motherwell vs Celtic game. So no slumming it in jeans. Smart dress. Alex, I know you were happy to see *any* game, so it will be a bonus seeing the current Scottish champions. If you're interested, I think Phil can arrange a stadium tour of any of the clubs at a later date during your stay."

I turn to Alex. "This is more my brother's thing than mine, Alex. Maybe I will get Ethan to go with you instead."

"Missy, there are *four* tickets. Ethan *is* going," Kieran says smugly.

Ethan's first outing. Well, that's a bonus. And I don't have to wait until Sunday to see him. He did always love the football, Lindsay didn't share his passion. "So that's Saturday taken care of," I say resignedly. I might just strangle my father when I see him.

"Now Sunday. If I'm correct, there's some sort of a charity function here at the hotel?" says Alex. "Your dad has invited me along."

Naturally. "Yes, there is, and there will be many of his business colleagues here."

"Michael, am I right in thinking that we are tied up all day Monday, Tuesday, and Wednesday?" Alex turns to Michael, who's been sitting quietly at his side.

"Yes, and we also have to arrange a meeting in London for the following week, but we can't plan that week's meeting until we see how the first lot go."

"We can arrange some sight-seeing for Thursday and Friday then?" Alex glances at both Michael and me. Michael just nods his head.

"I'm sure we can manage without you on both those days, honey," Kieran says, looking rather happy with himself. "Fabulous! So, I'll play at being the boss." He winks at me.

I humour him. "Yes, you'll be in charge then. Do try and keep the damage to a minimum, won't you? I think that's as sorted out as I can be for the time being. And plans are always subject to change in emergencies," I say. "Now are you both ready for a tour?" They both nod, and we all stand up. "Kieran, could you let chef and the department heads know that we need to have a meeting tomorrow morning, ten o'clock? Could you also ask Karl for an updated Christmas menu? I think that's everything. If you have any problems, ring my mobile. Otherwise I'll see you in the morning," I say to Kieran as we all leave my office.

"No worries, honey. Enjoy the rest of your day." Kieran leans in to give me a kiss on the cheek and to whisper in my ear, "I would *love* a piece of him, but he only has eyes for you. Don't do anything I wouldn't do."

God that could be hard. Don't think there's anything I've not known Kieran to do.

WE WALK THROUGH THE HOTEL. Alex is at my side, and Michael walks just behind us. I fill them both in on the history of the building, an eighteenth-century baronial mansion that has been in my family for the last century. Alex asks lots of questions, which I answer to the best of my ability, but I realise that all I know is what my grandfather told me. I tell him there is a book with the whole history of the building and estate that I can have sent to his room, and he seems interested in this. My grandfather had commissioned the restoration of the main house to turn it into a hotel. Then he had the extension built about thirty years ago. My father has plans to extend the hotel again, more bedrooms, but I'm not sure his heart is in it. Alex seems interested in what I tell him. Michael doesn't say much. A man of few words.

I give them a full tour, showing them all the staff areas as well, including the very modern and well-equipped kitchen. I introduce them to Karl, who spends some time describing the various menus. When we leave the kitchen, we head to the leisure centre. This is probably the most modern part of the hotel when compared to the rest. Stephen smiles when he sees me, but when he recognises my companions, the smile leaves his face. I introduce them, but Stephen is very dry. He is always polite—even on an off day, he can hold it together —but there's tension in the air, so we don't spend much time with Stephen. I'm sure both Alex and Michael have picked up on the awkwardness.

As we leave I turn back to Stephen. "I'd like to speak with you later. I don't know what's wrong with you."

I make our last stop inside the hotel the bar, where I offer them both drinks. I love being in this part of the hotel; it has an old village pub feel to it, warm and inviting. We have a full range of malt whisky from all over the world. Michael asks for water.

"What would you recommend, Libby?"

"Do you like whisky?"

"Yes, but if I am honest, I prefer a nice, cold beer."

"If I can interrupt," the bartender says, "can I recommend the Glendronach nineteen- year-old -single-malt whisky? It has everything you would expect in a good scotch whisky; it's oaky, sweet, and woody."

"Will you join me in a glass, Libby?" Alex asks.

"I suppose I can. Could I have a dash of water in mine, please?"

"Stephen … is he your boyfriend?" Alex asks studying me.

"God, no! He's my brother's best friend. Whatever gave you *that* idea?"

"Just the way he looks at you. And earlier today he kissed you," Alex says. "He really didn't like seeing you with me, so I just presumed."

"Well, you presumed wrong. For your information, there *is* no boyfriend. I have no time for that. I'm totally focused on running this place," I say. Then, lest he think me a cold fish, I add, "Well, there was one, but the relationship had run its course. I broke it off." *Why am I explaining myself to him?*

Alex's mobile rings, and he steps to the side to answer it— far enough away that he won't appear rude and yet, oddly, not so far away that I can't still hear his side of the conversation. "No, it's not going to happen … I have business in the UK to attend to. Surely you can deal with it? Or are you that incompetent?" He pauses, waiting on the reply from whomever is on the phone. "Michael can call you shortly and go through the paperwork with you before you e-mail it to me. If it's all in order when my lawyer looks at it, I'll sign it—

then, deal done. If there are any other problems, direct them to Michael first. He can decide whether I need to know about them." Alex hangs up, returns to the bar, and takes a drink of the whisky.

"A problem?" Michael asks.

"Yes. It seems the Vegas deal is hanging in the balance. Vince is going to send over the details. Can you deal with it?"

"Of course. I'll take care of it right now." Michael doesn't wait for a response from Alex. He places his water glass on the bar. "Good day, Libby," he says, with a nod of his head.

Now I'm a bit apprehensive. There is tension running through my whole body. Do I want to continue with a tour of the grounds now that I know Michael won't be joining us? I could call an end to it just now instead of going outside. Michael felt like my safety net, and now that is gone.

"So, Libby, are we ready to head outside now?" Alex asks with a reassuring smile as he places his empty glass on the bar. I don't finish mine.

"Yes." My brief reply is all I can manage.

We head outside via the leisure centre. We pass Stephen on the way out, and he eyes me cautiously, mouthing, *'Remember what I said; be careful!'* We pass the tennis courts and the kids' play area, which is quite noisy with kids running around playing, but there is an awkward silence in the air between Alex and myself—as well as a huge amount of sexual attraction, at least on my part. We walk in silence towards the riding stables. Every now and then, I glance over to find him looking at me. When we get to the stables, we stop.

"Surely we are not going riding, with you in a dress?" Alex says with a laugh.

Maybe we could do that one evening, I think to myself. "Not today, but it's probably the best way to see the whole estate. We could ride at some point during the next few days." We stop in front of the paddocks, where two small girls are getting riding lessons while their parents watch from the side. We have six horses on the estate, stunning creatures. Ethan and I used to go horse riding most Sundays with our parents.

"Yes, I would like that," Alex says with a warm smile.

We continue walking and engage in some polite conversation. I tell him about various activities the hotel has to offer, including clay pigeon shooting, hiking, and the seaplane trips, which I highly recommend. It still feels a bit strained, but I'm hoping it will get easier. I ask a few questions about him, and I learn that Alex has an older brother named Connor who is twenty-nine and a lawyer just like both his parents. He has a sister, Sophie, who is the same age as me and is still at university studying fashion. He already seems to know all about my family; Dad has already told him a lot about Ethan and me. It turns out that Alex had been due in the UK four months ago, but he cancelled the visit when my father told him about Lindsay's death.

I ask him what line of business he's in, and he tells me that he has several casinos and a hotel in the states, which sets my mind racing. *Surely his being here has nothing to do with this place? My father wouldn't part with it.* But he says that what he's best known for is buying struggling businesses and turning them around so they are profitable and then selling them on. An investor then? But I've seen the books for this place. Why would we need an investor? I don't want to jump in with all guns blazing, but I really need to know about the business my dad is doing with him.

I HAVE to admit it's been a very pleasant few hours walking round the estate, something I've not done in a long time. I've forgotten how beautiful the whole estate is. I really should do this more often; it's so easy to take things for granted and not truly appreciate what's right on my doorstep. The company hasn't been too bad either.

Our last stop is at the water's edge. As the water splashes against the pebbles, I notice a seaplane has just landed at the jetty, and an excited couple is about to go for a tour. There's no better way to see the loch than a bird's-eye view from the sky. From up there you see the real majesty of the vast loch and surrounding highlands. From the sky the hotel glistens like a jewel against the unspoilt water's edge.

"I love this view," I say, looking over my shoulder at Alex, who's standing just behind me. "Don't think I'll ever get tired of looking at it." The water is still and has a calming effect on me.

"I have to admit that I don't think I will either, although I think my point of view is especially spectacular," he says with a smile so full of promises. He slips his left hand around my waist and places small kisses on the nape of my neck, which sends shock waves through my body.

"Libby, I'm going to turn you around and kiss you. I am warning you to give you a chance to say no. I'd rather not be slapped again." Alex slowly turns me to face him, and all I see is a wanting look in his eyes. My breathing has altered, picked up pace, and my heart is racing. I *do* want this.

"Well, what are you waiting for then?" I whisper in invitation.

That's all it takes. One hand is still on my waist. The other reaches up to my chin and tilts my face, so I am watching as his face comes closer. His soft, wet lips meet mine, and they taste so sweet. And before I know it, I'm kissing him back.

When we eventually pull ourselves apart, all I can do is sigh. He still has one arm held firmly round my waist. I notice his smile. What a beautiful smile it is.

"I hope that makes up for my mistake earlier today?"

"It certainly does. But as you recall, I already accepted your apology hours ago," I say, smiling back at him.

What time is it? It's a lot cooler now. How long have we been out walking? I glance at my watch; it's nearly seven.

"What's wrong? Do you have somewhere you need to be?" he asks.

"No, not really. But I should check in and make sure everything is okay back at the hotel. I didn't realise how long we've been away. Michael must be wondering where you are. We've been gone a few hours."

"Michael must still be working. At least he hasn't called or texted to say otherwise," Alex says checking his phone. "I probably should go and see how he's getting on. But before we head back, you haven't answered my earlier question about dinner tonight. Do you have an answer?"

"What about Michael?"

"I would much rather have dinner with you by myself," he says with a smile but also sadness in his voice. "But if you'd like, I'll ask him. Would you like to eat at the hotel, or do you want to recommend somewhere else?"

"I don't dine in the restaurant at night since I don't let any of the staff do it," I say. "So it's either the staff canteen, or we go out."

"Well, let's head back up, and we'll take it from there. Although we could just stay here. I can't remember the last time I had a few hours off work and didn't give it a moment's thought. I think the company had a lot to do with it."

I hate to admit it, but the company *was* great. I think I could get used to his company. But it isn't going to be just the two of us over the next few weeks. Michael will be there and others as well, on occasion at least. I think of Kirsty's words to me earlier in the afternoon: *Just enjoy yourself. Enjoy his company.* Maybe it won't be as bad as I first thought.

Alex leans forward and gently places a small kiss on my forehead, saying, "Come on, then." He places one hand in the small of my back as we walk back towards the hotel. Even this small gesture has sent my heart racing again; the feelings are all completely new to me. Even Jeff, the man I dated for two years, never sparked this intensity of feelings within me.

We walk the short distance back to the hotel in silence, but it isn't an awkward silence. As we pass through the doors and enter reception, Fraser smiles. Sally is still at the desk. She's looking flustered, but that isn't too unusual for her.

"Sally, what's wrong?" I ask her as she fumbles about the desk.

"I can't seem to find the financial reports Kieran gave me. I was meant to give them to all the department heads tonight for your meeting in the morning."

"Don't worry about it, Sally. We can print off copies in my office. It's fine, really."

Poor Sally. She's not had a great day. I know that the man standing at my side has caused most of her problems today. Sally looks at me and then at Alex; he just gives her a slight smile, which makes her turn quickly away.

"Sally, why don't you get off home now? I can get copies. It's been a long day for you. Go home. Relax. I'll see you tomorrow."

"Are you sure?"

"Go—before I change my mind."

"Thanks, Miss Stewart. See you in the morning, then."

Alex sniggers at my side.

"What's wrong with you?" I ask as I turn to face him.

"I get the impression you're a soft touch with your staff and—"

I don't let him finish. "Don't. Just don't. *You* caused most of that poor girl's problems today. The least I can do is let her get off home, and the least you could do tomorrow when you see Sally is apologise to her," I snap. I turn and head to my office. Soft touch, indeed. That's new, even for me. I've been called a lot of things but never a soft touch. Dad would laugh at that.

Kieran is in my office working on the computer when I go charging in. "Oh boy," he says. "I take it this afternoon didn't go so well? I thought that since you were gone so long you'd have an exciting story to tell."

"This afternoon was fine—more than fine—it's just … oh, nothing," I say, shaking my head. "Will you be long on the computer? I need to print off extra copies of the reports. Sally has misplaced the copies you gave her."

"No, I'm just about finished. But we don't need extra copies; I have them right here," he says, lifting a pile of papers from the desk and waving them at me. "I did give her them, but then I needed to check something. Poor Sal. She's had a bit of a stressful day, with one thing and another."

"Yeah, I know. I've sent her home."

"So, missy, are you going to give me details on your day?" Kieran asks with a wicked smile.

"No." I walk back out of the office.

Kieran shouts after me, "You can't leave! Get back here!" I ignore him. Kieran's mind will be going into overdrive.

Alex is still standing out in reception. He's talking on his phone. As soon as he sees me, he hangs up. "So, Libby, what time will you be ready for dinner?" he asks.

"Eh, I think I'll have to pass on dinner. Maybe another night, Alex. I have a few calls to make."

"Oh, I'm sorry to hear that. I just finished speaking with Michael, and he was looking forward to it," he says looking disappointed. I see Kieran from the corner of my eye. His eyes are dancing between me and Alex. I know he's desperate to find out what's going on; Kieran and gossip go hand in hand. Alex glances at Kieran and shrugs.

"Okay. I'll see you tomorrow?" Alex leans forward, and I know he is about to kiss me, but I lean away ever so slightly and reach my hand out to shake his hand, which isn't going down well.

"Yes, I'll see you then," I say sharply.

With that, Alex turns and walks away. I let out a sigh of relief. Kieran comes rushing towards me, grinning. I know he's going to grill me about Alex.

"Right. You and me … I think we should go have some dinner in the canteen. It will be quiet, and I have questions that I want answered—and I'm not taking no for an answer."

"Okay, okay. You know, Kieran, you and Kirsty are so alike." I laugh.

We make our way to the staff area and head to the canteen, which is empty except for a junior chef who is sorting out food in the hot plate. Most of the staff would have already had breaks before the evening service in the restaurant. Kieran walks along the hot plate looking at the food.

"Tonight's choices are as follows: chicken curry, haddock and chips, or a mushroom stroganoff. So, what'll it be, Libby?" Kieran asks.

"Kieran, I'm not really that hungry."

"Oh, Libby. You need to eat to keep your strength up. I think you're going to need it." He laughs teasing me. "What if I go and ask Karl if he'll rustle you up something else? I am sure he will if it's for you." Kieran turns and heads towards the kitchen.

"Hold it. Stop right where you are," I say. I turn towards the junior chef at the counter. "Kieran, Karl is a busy man. And anyway, all I want is a sandwich, which I am sure— what's your name?" I ask the chef.

"Thomas, Miss Stewart."

"Which I'm sure Thomas is more than capable of putting

together."

"Yes, ma'am. Any kind in particular you would like?"

"Anything at all. A round of sandwiches for two would be great. Is that okay with you?" I ask Kieran, who just nods and heads towards the coffee machine.

"Kieran, can you get me a tea? I don't want coffee."

I sit down, waiting for Kieran to join me, knowing that he wants me to give him the details of my afternoon. He can read me just as well as Kirsty can. It's no wonder that we are all friends, although sometimes it would be good if they *couldn't* read me so well. Maybe one day I will get to keep a secret.

"Right, Libby, now spill it. What happened with you and the American after you came back from your looooooong walk?" Kieran asks sitting down and waits for the gossip.

"He called me a soft touch because I let Sal go home early."

"He obviously has a lot to learn about you," Kieran says with a halfhearted laugh. "I mean, where the staff are concerned, you are always firm but fair. And I would have done the same thing. Poor Sally—she's had a rotten day from start to finish. Between your American and her rat arse of a boyfriend."

"What's the boyfriend done now?"

"He's only gone and dumped her by text this afternoon."

"If I had known about that, she could've gone home much earlier. That's such a shame." What a day she's had! I now feel *really* bad for her. She had seemed really happy with the boyfriend too and thought he was the one.

"I did offer, honey, but she refused to go home and feel sorry for herself. She's such a great girl, with a big heart."

We stop talking when we see Thomas coming from the kitchen with our sandwiches.

"These look great, Thomas! Thank you so much for

making them," I say to the young boy. He must only be about seventeen.

"You're very welcome, Miss Stewart. I hope you both enjoy," he says, heading back to the kitchen.

Kieran and I chat briefly about things that have happened in the hotel over the course of the day as we eat our sandwiches and drink tea and coffee. I can tell by the expression on Kieran's face that he is dying to know how it went with Alex today but wants me to tell him without him having to ask.

Should I just put him out of his misery? Yes.

"Okay, we kissed."

Kieran seems to choke on his coffee. He's coughing and spluttering everywhere.

"Oh. My. God."

"Are you okay? Can't have you choking to death." I lean over to pat him on the back.

"You can't just say that and leave it hanging. You have to tell me more. I want all the details, honey, and I mean *all* the details. I *knew* there was something between you, but if I'm truthful with you—as I always am—I really didn't think you'd act on it. And especially not on day one. I need answers."

His last statement is definitely a demand, so I tell him the whole story—the start, the middle, and the end. Kieran hangs on every word I say, jaw dropped, mouth open. I think for the first time in all the time I've known Kieran, I've managed to shock him, but listening to my story I've also shocked myself. It so doesn't sound like me. God, it took months of Jeff chasing me before I finally gave in and went on a date with him. And at the end of our first date, I only let him kiss me on the check.

"Well, Libby, you might not believe it, but I am almost at a loss for words. That sounds like a story from Kirsty, not my sweet and much-too-innocent Libby," Kieran says, shaking his head in mock disbelief. "Have you told Kirsty any of this yet? She'll be as speechless as me. But seriously—all this really happened today?"

"What can I say? I've surprised even myself with today's chain of events. And yes, Kirsty knows about earlier, although I know she'll be waiting by her phone for an update. I'll give her a call when I'm in my room."

"Oh, honey, I knew there was some sexual tension earlier in the office between you and that *gorgeous* man, but I have to say I did think you would be able to resist. Although I can't blame you. I wouldn't have been able to either. I'm so disappointed to have it confirmed that I'm not his type." Kieran pretends to pout. He has a wicked smile on his face that lets me know he's not *too* disappointed that Alex isn't his type.

"Kieran, don't you dare make fun of me. And anyway, Kirsty told me to have fun, so that's what I've done," I say. "Although after I refused his offer of dinner, I'm not sure how much fun I'll have for the rest of his stay here. He's a bit … unpredictable. Who knows how he'll react?"

"Libby, he wants you; that much is obvious," Kieran says, getting up from the table. He walks round to me and takes my hand to help me up. He draws me in close for what he calls a Kieran Special, a tight hug and a kiss on my forehead. As I stand tight to him, resting my chin on his chest, I find myself totally relaxed in his arms. Kieran is up there with my dad and Ethan; they are all able to take tension away from me.

"We'll see." That's all I can say.

We head out of the canteen. It's way past time for Kieran to head home, and I have a few things to take care of, such as unpacking all my stuff, then giving Ethan and Kirsty both calls before I turn in for the night. We say good-night at reception, and I tell him to make sure he's not late in the morning for our meeting.

CHAPTER 6

$\mathcal{A}$lex

ARE YOU FUCKING KIDDING ME?

I don't know how the hell I managed to fuck that up, *again*.

I'm a guy. I really don't know if I can figure her out. She's nothing like anyone I've ever met before. I smile because I'm glad she's different.

Elizabeth Stewart, an accomplished woman in her own right. Hard working, with an abundance of determination to succeed in life. She's caring and compassionate about those that she loves. But there is something so much more to her...

She intrigues me. I have a need to know more, to have more. I want her and badly. I've never felt a connection so strong and I know I'm not the only one who feels it. And that kiss, it was magical. The look in her eyes after our kiss had my heart skipping a beat.

Then, what do I do?

Fuck up by saying something stupid and no not the lyrics from a song. She's no push over, I can see that. So why did I open my big mouth. I pick up my phone from the bed and type out a message.

I have your number. It's only fair you save mine. Alex

I stare at the phone in my hand, hoping that she'll reply, needing her to reply. I need to explain myself and apologise yet again. Something I don't want to start getting used to, but here I am only a day in Scotland and I'm breaking all sorts of damn rules and aplogising to a woman. A woman who is more than capable of bringing me to my knees and I'd happily surrender to.

I stand and pace the floor a few times, then pour myself a drink. This time trying to keep all my thoughts in line and not throw the tumbler in anger. Checking my phone, there's no messages. Should I or shouldn't I. My finger hesitates over calling. Fuck it. I press the button and wait, nervously. It rings out. Maybe she doesn't want to speak to me tonight. I should just wait until tomorrow.

I've got some work I could be doing to occupy my time, but will I be able to concentrate?

I take a seat at the desk where I left my laptop and power it up, checking through my emails first. Nothing on here from Michael, so I presume he ironed out the details for the Vegas deal and got it back on track. Michael is a lot of things, but when it comes to business he's certainly the best and having him onside is worth every damn dollar I pay him. I skim through my emails and there's nothing important that needs to be dealt with, which I was hoping there would be.

I need a distraction. With a sigh I pick up the phone and hit call and wait. Still no answer. So, I type out another message.

I've called a few times. I hope you're not ignoring me.

Libby doesn't seem the type to just ignore me, I'm sure she'd tell me straight up what the problem is.

Fuck it. I need to see her, and now.

CHAPTER 7

When I get to my room, I take my phone and put it on charge, as its dead. I start unpacking my cases and hanging clothes up in the cupboard, putting other bits and pieces, namely my underwear, in the drawers. My phone starts buzzing, indicating that I have messages. I look at it; god, there's quite a few.

Ethan: Had a great day with Lucy. Going to crash and have an early night. Catch you tomorrow xx

Kirsty: Give me a call when you have time xx

Kirsty: I so hope you will call me. I want to know how it went xx

Kirsty: SO HELP ME GOD, LIBBY! CALL ME. NOW GETTING WORRIED.

I better call her. Kirsty and her capital letters. There are also a couple of texts and calls from the same number.

Alex: I have your number. It's only fair you save mine. Alex

Alex: I've called a few times. I hope you're not ignoring me

Just as I finish reading his last message, my phone beeps. There's another message from him.

Alex: I need to see you. I am on my way

I send Kirsty a quick text.

Kirsty: I will call in the morning. My battery died. Everything's OK but have loads to tell you xx

Why is Alex coming to my room? Whatever the reason, I'm sure it could have waited until the morning … unless he just wanted to see me. That thought seems crazy. I hurry round my room picking things up and trying to put them all away quickly. Although I'm not sure why—he won't be in my bedroom. Whatever has to be said can be said in the sitting room. One of the benefits of being in a suite.

When I hear a slight knock at my door, I answer, not even noticing I have several pairs of lacy underwear in my hand until Alex smiles. I must look really foolish. I smile and let him enter my sitting room. Closing the door behind him, I turn to find him standing only feet away, gazing at me. I hold his gaze for as long as I can, but it only fuels the attraction between us, fanning the flames, and I have to look away.

"Libby?" Alex starts to say.

"Give me a sec. Let me put my … er, *things* away." I turn and head to my bedroom. Alex nods.

I open a drawer of the dresser and throw the underwear in, then stand staring in the mirror. I close my eyes and take in a long, deep breath. I don't need to open my eyes to know that he's followed me into the room.

I sense him.

He's getting closer.

I can smell him. It's hard to describe—a sweet, rich, masculine scent. I've not even heard his footsteps coming across the floor. So silent, like a predator creeping up on its prey.

I can feel how close he is as he leans in. I feel his breath against the back of my ear. Then it travels ever so slowly to the nape of my neck. I know what he's doing. This is sheer torture of a pleasurable kind. He's tormenting me on purpose. *Don't think I can take much more of this. But I don't think I can move either.* My brain has shut down. I should tell him to go; that would be the right thing to do. But the parts of my body that have lain dormant for the past few months won't let me speak.

He slowly slips one hand round my waist as he trails small kisses along my neck. My head automatically tilts to one side to give him more access. His other hand starts at my neck, and with gentle strokes, he starts working his fingers down my back, then up again. I can't even bring myself to open my eyes.

I must be dreaming. I've only known this gorgeous man who is standing behind me for … how long? Not even a day. This can only be a dream.

"Libby, please. Open. Your. Eyes. And. Turn. Round," he says slowly in between the kisses that he's placing on my neck.

I don't want to do as I'm told because at this moment, I'm more than quite content where I am. And I'm also a bit afraid that he won't finish what he has started.

He stops kissing me. "Libby, please?"

I shake my head, and still my eyes refuse to open.

"I need you to look at me. What's wrong? One minute you're right here with me, nice and relaxed, and now I can feel tension in your whole body. If I've done something wrong, please just tell me."

Slowly I open my eyes. I stare at our reflections in the mirror. It's not been a dream after all. He is here with me, and the look in his eyes tells me he wants me just as much as I want him. I feel the tension leave my body only to be replaced by another feeling altogether.

A desire.

A hunger.

He must feel it too as he pulls me in tighter. That's when I know he wants me. I can feel his hard erection against me.

I try hard to give nothing away in my reflection, but all hope of that is gone. I need to get my breathing back under control before I speak.

"You can't fight this, Libby. This is going to happen," he says quietly.

After a few moments, I turn to face him. I think I am almost able to speak now. He keeps both his hands wrapped tightly round me, stroking my back. I know this is wrong on so many levels. God, I don't even know him. Earlier, I push thoughts of that to the back of my mind. Then there's the business he's doing with my dad. My dad—he *so* won't be happy about this.

"What if I don't want to fight this?" I find myself saying. I put my arms round his neck and pull him towards me.

It's been a day filled with surprises, so why do my words shock even me? But at least Alex is smiling as he tilts his head. Our lips meet, so gentle and slow. He tastes divine. He might be prepared to take this slowly, but I don't think I can. I have an overwhelming need to up the pace; I try to deepen the kiss as I run my hands through his soft, silky hair. But he slowly pulls away from me and takes a step back, although he's still holding onto me by my shoulders. My arms fall to the side of my body.

What the ...? I knew this was too good to be true. He's just playing with me.

"Libby, please don't rush this. I want to savour the moment with you. I've thought of nothing else but you since I first saw you in person in the gym this morning. And I intend to enjoy every moment of it." He runs his hands up my back and then trails his fingers along the nape of my neck, back and forth, back and forth. The sensations running through my body I can't put into words.

Instead, the words I say are a question. "What do you mean, 'in person'?"

"Well, I have to admit that I feel like I've known you for months. Through all my calls and meetings with your father, I've learned all about you ... and Ethan, of course. And I have to admit that I have been looking forward to meeting you." He's smiling at me playfully. "Now if you'll let me, that's what I want to do. I want to savour this moment with you."

Even if I wanted to say no, I can't. My emotions are over-ruling my head. Not a good sign.

"So what exactly are you waiting for? The invitation won't get any better. I've not thrown you out. You're still here."

He stands staring, eyes ablaze. If I looked hard enough, I'm sure I would see the flames. Flames of passion. That's what I'm thinking as he pulls me in tight against his body. Once again I feel his erection. He leans down, his kiss much more demanding than his last. His tongue meets mine. I can only respond with a soft moan. *I could kiss this beautiful man all day.*

The pace has definitely picked up. He's squeezing me tighter against his body. His hands seem to have a mind of their own, traveling up and down my back, caressing my neck, my shoulders, my backside. My own hands are doing a fair bit of traveling, from his soft hair to his back to his strong shoulders and then down the front of his muscular chest to the hem of his T-shirt. My hands stop there at the hem, and I take hold of it and gently pull upwards. Our lips break contact, but we never break eye contact. He nods in approval of what I am about to do. We really need to lose the T-shirt. He dips his head so I can pull it off. I take a step back to enjoy the view. *What a body.* I smile, remembering one of my earlier thoughts.

"You seem to have a wicked smile on your beautiful face. Care to enlighten me, Libby?"

I can only shake my head and grin in response; I'd like to keep that secret to myself for the time being. He steps out of his shoes, one at a time, then bends down and ever so slowly removes each of his socks. And still his eyes are on mine. I know he wants to savour the moment, but this is torture. I need him, and I need him *now*.

"Well, Miss Stewart. It seems you are wearing far too much clothing. Turn around. It's about time we got you out of that dress, don't you think?"

I nod and slowly turn around. He lays his hands on my shoulders and places a small kiss at the nape of my neck, at the same time drawing in a long, deep breath.

"Ah, Libby, you smell so sweet."

His voice and touch will be my undoing. My need is building, the pressure growing deep within me. Slowly his right hand moves from my shoulder and glides to the zip at the back of my dress. He takes the zip between his fingers and slowly pulls it down; at the same time, he trails small kisses down my now-exposed spine. My eyes are closed. I am completely lost in the moment. I sense him bending down at my back. Good lord, what is he going to do now?

His hands are on my ankles. He starts working his way up, massaging my legs, higher, higher … higher. I've never experienced sensations, emotions, like these before. Wanted. Sexy. Nervous. Jeff never made me feel this good about myself. No, thoughts of Jeff have to go. His hands are back at the hem of my dress. In slow motion he starts to lift my dress up as he stands. I am positive it would have been quicker to step out of the dress, but …

"Arms?"

I lift up my arms so he can completely remove my dress, which he tosses on the floor. I glance down at myself. I have indeed got on matching white lace underwear. I feel a bit embarrassed standing in just my underwear in front of a man I barely know.

He unhooks my bra and slides the straps off my shoulders and then lets it drop to the floor. It's not just my breathing that's out of control now as his hands slide round my waist and over my tummy and travel upwards. They stop on my breasts, gently cupping them both as he nuzzles my neck. And if I'm not mistaken, the moan I hear this time is not coming from me.

"Turn around. I want to see you."

I slowly turn. He stands gazing at me for what seems an eternity, but it can only be a few seconds. Suddenly I feel shy; I can feel the colour rush over my cheeks. I have an urgent need to cover up.

"You have nothing to be embarrassed about," he says with a warm smile. "I can feel all the tension in your body. You are an extremely beautiful young woman with an incredibly sexy body. Please, relax. We're not going to do anything you don't want to do." I know he's trying to reassure me, but I've never left myself this open and exposed to any man.

He leans down and places a quick, soft kiss on my lips. He has one arm round my neck. With one quick move, he slides the other arm beneath my legs. He's lifting me up and walking the short distance to my bed, where he places me down gently, as if I were made of glass, and he's trying not to break me. He lies down beside me, resting his chin on his left arm. With his right he pulls me closer and tighter towards him, closing the distance.

I reach out and take his chin in my hands as I make eye contact, suggesting by the smile on my face what I am about to do. But I don't get the chance; his lips are on mine first with passion and lust. Consuming me. *So much hunger*. The kiss deepens, and he pushes his tongue into my mouth, exploring. There's no soft, slow approach this time.

"Libby, you and I are going to be so good together."

He's holding himself on top of me, running a hand up and down my chest, each time pausing on my breast for a few moments. My heart is pounding. His lips leave mine but continue with a kissing assault down my neck. I tilt my neck and moan at the same time. This feels too good. He continues traveling with his lips until they reach my breast. I can feel his teeth against my nipple pulling slightly, but it's not painful. He continues licking and sucking until I can hardly take the throbbing any more. Then he switches to the other breast and repeats the same torture-pleasure.

Just when I am on the edge again, his lips move and continue with their travels down my navel. *Oh, I see where this is heading.* With only a simple raise of his eyebrows and the intensity of those beautiful eyes, he is seeking my permission to continue. I can only nod. In one quick motion, my knickers have been removed.

Bright, brown eyes look straight at me as he continues; he extends his tongue and slowly starts to lick at my swollen sex. My eyes close, but I can still feel his gaze burning through me. I've never experienced anything like this before. Just as the pressure is starting to build, he inserts one finger, then two, inside me and starts moving them slowly. But I need the pace quickened. As if on cue, the pace picks up and takes me right over the edge in what I can only describe as an earth-shattering orgasm. I cry out.

"Alex," I start to say, but he just presses a finger to my lips to stop me.

"Libby, I told you we would be good together, and it's about to get so much better."

I am unable to move. I lie on the bed, and desperately I

try to get my breathing under control, which isn't happening quickly enough for my liking. Alex lifts himself off the bed, and I can only stare, admiring the view. He makes quick work of unfastening the belt on his jeans, and in one swift motion, he drops his jeans and boxers, leaving me breathless again. Well, I did wonder earlier on today what he would look like without the clothes. The vision in my mind definitely didn't do the vision standing in front of me any justice.

Alex slowly crawls back up the bed until his face hovers in front of mine. His thick shaft is between my legs, gently teasing my swollen sex. I pull his face towards mine. So much lust in his eyes! As his mouth descends on mine, he lets out a soft groan. He's still teasing me with sliding movements.

"Alex, please," I cry.

"Libby, don't ask me to stop now, because I don't think I am capable of doing that."

"No, I need you, all of you. *Now.*"

And with one forceful thrust, he is exactly where I want him—inside me. So deep. Slow in. Slow out. Slow in. Slow out. I wrap my legs round him, telling him without words what I am needing and wanting. His mouth is all over me—my mouth, neck, even my earlobes. This is a man who has done this before.

He adapts the pace. Thrust for thrust, coming quicker. Deeper and deeper. I am building higher and higher. God, I never knew this could feel so good. I thought sex was good before, but this ... this night of passion has taken me to a whole new level. Again the pace changes. Quicker now. I match him thrust for thrust. I can see that he's close, so close, to the edge. I can read it in his face, his eyes ablaze with passion, with pleasure.

A moan escapes me. His hands grip me so tightly against him that there is no room between us. Skin on skin. Mouth on mouth. I am climbing higher and higher, so close to the edge I can feel myself falling. With each thrust now, the pressure builds until I completely and utterly shatter round him, crying out his name. I hear him whispering mine, a strangled moan, and then he collapses on top of me.

He swiftly rolls onto his side, pulling me with him so we are face to face, both of us panting. I am smiling, almost laughing out loud. Until he starts shouting, that is. "Shit! Fucking hell! Fuck!"

I look at him in alarm. He lowers his voice, at least somewhat. "We shouldn't have done that. I can't believe I let it go as far as I did." He slides off the bed and starts pacing the floor. The pain is etched all over his face.

What the hell have I done to deserve this shouting? Here I was thinking I've just had the most amazing sex ever, and I do mean *ever*, with an equally amazing guy. Obviously the feeling wasn't mutual. I think Alex could give Dr. Jekyll a run for his money with his Mr. Hyde mood swings. I don't know whether I am coming or going, but I am starting to wish *he* were going.

Straight out the fucking door.

"What the hell are you talking about?" I shout back at him, pulling the covers up round me. I feel as if I need their security.

"Fuck, Libby. Do you need me to spell it out? I didn't use anything for protection." He's shaking his head at me.

"Take a step back. One, I'm on the contraceptive injection and have never missed a shot. And two, I'm clean. So …"—I take a deep breath—"are you trying to tell me there's a problem at your end?"

"Thank fuck for that," he says calmly, walking back towards the bed. "No, no problem at my end. I've just never been in a situation where I didn't act rationally."

That was the answer I was hoping for. God knows what I

would have done if he'd said otherwise. Although I do think he needs to explain his last statement.

"Well?" I ask, waiting. "What do you mean by a 'situation where you didn't act rationally'? Seriously, after the amazing sex we just had, you're not trying to tell me you've never had sex before, are you?"

"Jesus, Libby! Of course that's not what I'm saying. It's just ... I didn't stop to think before we ... I've never been so affected by anyone."

Control freak springs to mind.

"So you're telling me that everything you do in life, including sex, is planned?"

"The only risks I take are those in business, Libby, nothing else. Until tonight."

He really needs to stop with the pacing; it's starting to drive me mad.

He sits down on the bed with a huge sigh of relief. He brushes the hair off the side of my face, which sends a small, electrifying shock through my core. Such a simple gesture has completely turned me on again. He smiles, sensing what I am thinking, and laughs.

"Baby, I am more than ready for the next round. I hope you are?" His gaze into my eyes is questioning.

I just smile and pull him closer. "I am sure it can be arranged."

CHAPTER 8

*E*verything is a bit hazy. I am hoping this isn't a dream. Although if it is, I'm in no hurry to wake up. I am lying in my bed with a gorgeous guy who has both his arms wrapped tightly round my waist, his head resting at the back of my neck. He is still asleep. I want to turn around and watch him, but I'm frightened that if I move, I will wake him.

Would that be such a bad thing? If he woke up, maybe we could continue where we left off during the wee small hours of the morning? I don't even remember falling asleep in his arms. I do remember lots and lots of pleasure. I should get up, but to be honest I am too comfy and content in his arms. I close my eyes again, but I hear a noise. It seems so distant. It's only after a moment that I realise it's my phone buzzing.

"Shit!" I say, leaning over to the cabinet to get it. Too late; it's stopped.

"What's wrong, beautiful?" the voice behind me asks.

I don't even look at my phone as I place it back on the cabinet and slowly roll over to face him. His arms are still round me. How can he look this good first thing in the morning? There must be some kind of law about it, especially when I know how bad I can look first thing.

"Good morning, yourself."

A silence hangs in the air between us as we lie face to face, not taking our eyes off each other. He gently strokes the side of my face, leans his head towards me, and places a small kiss on my forehead. He smiles. He looks so damn sexy as he gazes at me.

"Who was on the phone?"

"I don't know. I never checked."

"So, a question. How are you feeling on this fine morning?" he asks with a mischievous grin.

"I think the answer would have to be *exhausted*," I say, smiling shyly.

He laughs as if he'd known my answer would be along those lines.

"How exhausted?" he asks, pulling me tighter to him and leaning in to kiss me. And just as things are starting to get a bit more heated and interesting between us, another phone interrupts us. His. *Leave it*, I mouth as he picks it up.

Can't, he mouths back. "Mathews," he says. "Ah, good morning, Phil."

"As in my dad?" I whisper. Alex nods.

"Sure, Phil, I can meet for breakfast shortly. Just let me grab a quick shower. I'll see you then." With that, he hangs up.

"So, breakfast with my dad. You'd better not keep him waiting," I say. I plant a soft kiss on his lips. "God, what time is it anyway? I better get a move on too."

"It's going on eight," he says, getting up and out of the bed. "I'd better head to my room shower and change."

"You could always shower with me."

"Oh, Libby, I don't think that's a good idea. Do you? You

were the one who just said I shouldn't keep your father waiting. And if I get in a shower with you, it's going to take a whole lot longer than ten minutes."

He picks up the clothes that are scattered on the floor and dresses quickly as I look on. What a sight. I smile. I could watch him all day. With that thought, my phone rings, and Alex smiles as he picks it up and passes it to me.

"Your dad."

"For the love of god. What does he want with me?"

"If you answer it, Libby, you might just find out." He's smirking at me, the smart arse.

"Morning, Dad."

"Morning. Would you like to join Alex Mathews and me for breakfast?" he asks.

"Dad, I've just woken up, and I need to take a shower, do my hair, and get dressed," I say, staring at Alex.

"Libby, honey, I think you should. It might help you get back on the right footing with Alex," Dad says. "It might make things easier, having me there. You said it was very awkward yesterday." *Awkward. If only he knew the half of it. Shit!*

"Okay, Dad. Give me thirty minutes tops. And will you order an omelette for me?"

"Yes, honey. See you shortly."

"So, breakfast should be interesting, don't you think, Libby?" Alex heads to the door with a smug grin on his face. "See you soon."

He's gone. Oh. My. God. How can I sit beside Alex and my dad without my dad picking up on things between Alex and me? I can't do it. I need to call him and cancel … but then he'll think there's something wrong. Whatever I do, I won't win. What a dilemma. God, this is going to be hard. What possessed me to let things get carried away between us?

85

I have what has to be the quickest shower in my life, in and out with hair washed in under five minutes. I head to the wardrobe and start sifting through the hangers. I know what I want to wear; I'm just hoping it's here. Finally. Why is it that when you are looking for something, and in a hurry, it's always the last thing you get to?

My red shift dress; I pull it on and slide my feet into black heels. I glance at the time. Not really enough time left to do my hair but needs must. I spend a good fifteen minutes blow-drying my hair to bring it under some sort of control. The end result is better than I expected, although I do pin the front back to keep it off my face. A quick look in the mirror to make sure I am presentable: I suppose I will do.

On my way to breakfast, I call reception and leave word for Kieran to call me as soon as he's in. Hopefully if things are uncomfortable during breakfast, Kieran will be my excuse to leave. That's my plan, and I'm sticking to it.

As I enter the large room, one of the waiting staff stops me for a chat. I'm not really listening to what the girl is saying; I'm too busy scanning the room. I spot those gorgeous, brown eyes staring at me, and I flush as a slow smile spreads across Alex's face. I stand hypnotised by his gaze, ignoring the poor girl in front of me.

He's sitting by the window with my father and Michael, whose eyes are going back and forth between mine and Alex's. Shit, Michael must know. My dad looks as if he's in full conversation, then stops suddenly, looks at Alex, and follows the direction of Alex's gaze straight to me.

I walk away from the girl and mumble, "Thanks. Bye." As I get closer to the table, Dad stands to greet me, and the other two men follow suit.

"Good morning, sweetheart," Dad says. With a touch of concern, he adds, "Are you all right? You look tired. Or are you unwell?"

"I'm fine. Just a bit tired. I didn't get a great sleep … new surroundings and all that," I reply, giving him a kiss on the cheek. Michael lets out a small cough. Oh, he knows, all right. Awkward.

"Morning—Alex, Michael," I say, taking a seat next to my father and opposite Alex.

"Morning, Libby. That's such a shame that you didn't get a good sleep," Alex says, with a hint of a smile. Michael, on the other hand, seems to choke on thin air. This could get embarrassing.

"Have a drink," Alex says to Michael with a stern look.

"We've already ordered. I got you a cheese, ham, and mushroom omelette. That's okay, isn't it?" Dad asks as he pours some orange juice into a glass in front of me.

"Yes, that's fine."

The three men continue their conversation—work-related nattering about schedules and meetings. I find myself not following their words but drifting into my own daydream. One that involves Alex and a steaming-hot bubble bath. *I'm enjoying a nice, relaxing soak in the tub. I open my eyes when he enters the bathroom with a wicked grin on his face. He kneels down at the end of the bath and reaches his hands down into the water, then starts gently massaging my shoulders. I close my eyes. After a few moments, he ever so slowly starts to move his hands down the front of my neck, heading south, stopping on my breasts. He starts to massage them as well. Oh, the sheer pleasure …*

"Libby!" I hear my father's raised voice. "You were a million miles away. You've not heard a word that's been said to you."

"Sorry," I say with a shrug. I can feel myself blush as three sets of eyes stare at me. With a quick look down, I realise my breakfast is already in front of me. I lift my eyes back up, and the only one who is still staring at me is Alex. Of course he would be.

You okay? he mouths to me. I just nod and pick up my fork to start eating.

The men are still talking, and I do try to follow them this time. But something doesn't quite add up for me. Or maybe it does. After all, it did cross my mind yesterday. It suddenly hits me what business they are doing together.

"Please, for the love of god, tell me you are not selling this place to him!" I say rather loudly to my father. So that's the grand plan—sell the estate! My grandfather would be turning in his grave.

"For goodness sake, keep your voice down," Dad says sharply.

I can't believe Dad would sell this place off. It's been in the family for years. And no wonder Alex was so keen on hearing about its history.

"So, is it true? Am I right?"

"No, Libby. You're way off the mark. I'm not the slightest bit interested in buying this place. My business in the UK has nothing to do with this hotel. I'm interested in a casino group. The chain I am looking into has gone into administration. You will have probably heard about the company in the news, it's been all over the media."

"Libby, my job is to make sure we get enough PR for Alex both through his business and charitable dealings. Alex has a certain … shall we say … *celebrity* status in America, and I would like to ensure that he has the same here in the UK," Dad says in his best reassuring voice. "With that in mind, I'm giving you fair warning. I'm informing the press today of Alex's business dealings in the UK, so there will be a lot of interest in him very soon. You should expect the press to be there at the football match on Saturday and here on Sunday as well. Good PR is all about getting the right coverage at the right times."

"Good PR, bad PR it's all the same. You get the same effect from both, your name in the papers." I hiss.

I am a bit apprehensive of press coverage if I'm totally honest. Dad has always done his best to ensure that Ethan and I were kept away from that side of Dad's business, but there have been a few times when he wasn't able to keep the two parts separate, and I found myself having to deal with the not-so-nice aspects of PR. I know there are loads of people who do love the attention and seeing their names and pictures in the paper. But it's not for me.

"Libby, what's wrong?" Alex asks. I obviously look either concerned or terrified. Well, I am.

"It's just that I hate being put in the spotlight for anything," I say, turning to face my dad. "It's fine. I will do whatever is required of me—you know I will. But I don't get why your business path and family path have to cross. After everything that's happened in the past, you've tried so hard to keep parts of your life separated—and for very good reason. And with the upcoming trial of the driver who has been charged with Lindsay's death, Ethan needs me to be focused, not worrying about whatever the press decide to write about his sister again. Now if you'll excuse me, gentlemen, I have a hotel to run," I say calmly as I push my plate away and rise to my feet. I turn on my heel and walk away.

"Libby, wait!" Dad says, but I just keep going.

"Phil, don't. I'll go after her," I hear Alex say.

Alex catches up with me in the hotel corridor. He reaches out and grasps my elbow, stopping me in my tracks, which sends a shiver down my spine.

"What is it, Alex? I have work to do this morning, if you don't mind?" I say tiredly, trying to shrug him off.

"Libby, I didn't know your dad was planning this. Well, I knew he was going to get press coverage, but not that he would involve you," Alex says. "I'll tell him to stop if it upsets you so much, but I guess ... I guess it would be good to know why you're so against it. Because I would *love* to be seen with you."

"I'll tell you my reasons later on, but I have a meeting in less than an hour, and I really do need to do some work before I take off with you this afternoon," I say, more civil this time. "But you've just given me another reason why I don't want to be seen in public with you."

Alex looks puzzled and bewildered by my statement. I leave him standing in the corridor, and I can feel his stare following me. I head straight to my office, passing Sally at reception and slamming my office door shut behind me. I march over to my desk and throw myself down in my seat. I am so angry with my dad at this moment. He knows how I feel about the press.

There's a knock at my door, and Kieran enters without waiting for me to call him in.

"I've brought you a cup of tea. Looks like you could do with it," he says. "It's just past nine o'clock. Surely the morning can't be *that* bad?" He holds the cup out to me.

"You've no idea, Kieran. Why does everything have to be so damn complicated?"

"Can I to presume this involves a certain American?" I nod and let him continue. "If he's hurt you, so help me god!"

"No, no ... nothing like that. My father has just informed me that the press will be here on Sunday and at the football to get, as he phrased it, 'the right sort of press coverage for Alex'—meaning him being seen with *me*. And now Alex has said he would *love* to be seen out with me, so there's little chance he'll be especially discreet." I pause and draw in a deep breath.

"I'm not sure I see the problem, love."

"Well, I'm thinking about what Stephen said yesterday, about all those photos out there of Alex with numerous women. I don't want to be someone's handy prop—a way to further Alex's fortunes over here—and I'm brassed off at Dad for using me that way. And anyway, I have no desire to see myself in the papers in a good light or bad. That's it—rant over for this morning. I want to get on with the jobs at hand." I sip the tea gratefully.

"Are you sure, honey?" Kieran walks round the desk and puts both arms round my neck. "You know I'm a great listener, and my advice for you is always free, love."

Kieran is great, but right now I am not sure I want to go into all the gory details about my history with the press. It's out there if you know where to look, and Kieran and I have only been friends a short time. It's not something I reveal to everyone. Maybe I will in time, but not right now when I'm this upset about it.

"Yes, I'm sure. Now let's get a wriggle on. We have a lot to sort out this morning before I leave you in charge."

The rest of the morning runs smoothly. We have a meeting with all department heads to go over all the arrangements for tomorrow's wedding: food, wine, flowers, staff. My father sits in, listening quietly from the corner of the room, taking notes. I hardly look at him. I'm still too angry. I hope I can talk some sense into him. Everything is in order for the wedding; all we need is for the sun to be shining and for the bride and groom to both turn up.

We go through each department's budgets and running costs, increasing and cutting where necessary. We need more servers in the restaurant, so Kieran needs to advertise for waiting staff. We could also do with another chef, but Karl wants to hold off for a few weeks to give the chefs he currently has a chance to prove their worth. I tell him not to leave it too long to make a decision, because we have to think about Christmas.

I give credit where it's due: Karl is doing an amazing job

in the kitchen, which is inspiring other departments to do well. Everyone seems happy enough, although Kieran and I have decided that we need to spend a bit more time on the leisure centre—not because it's underperforming, as it's still meeting all targets, but because it could do with a facelift. That's a conversation to have with my dearest dad.

The meeting finishes at half past eleven, and everyone heads back to get on with his or her own job. This leaves my dad, Kieran, and me to go through some of the points that came up in the meeting. On a whole I think my father is impressed with how we're running the place, and he has even given me the go-ahead to have some plans drawn up for the leisure centre. I don't want to change everything dramatically—fresh paint throughout and a bit of an upgrade in the changing rooms might do it—but I'm willing to listen to suggestions from a designer. Kieran, probably sensing tension between my father and me, announces that he has a few errands to do round the hotel and leaves us to it. Dad and I head back to my office.

"Libby, sorry about earlier. I just didn't think."

"No, you didn't. Surely you remember how bad it was when the press wrote all that stuff about me and Tony? Dad, it was *awful*. I still remember the police questioning me on and on after he was charged with all those sexual assaults on young girls," I say. "The stories in the papers ... well, the less said about those, the better." I try to give him a smile, but I can't even manage that, thinking about the past.

Tony was a young actor. I thought he was great. Both Ethan and I looked up to Tony. He was eighteen, and we were fifteen. He was one of Dad's big clients, and he was always around. Dad considered him part of the family. Ethan and I were often invited along to the interviews if we were around, and I always jumped at the chance to go, just to hang out with him. I would stand at the side, listening in awe of everything he said.

I admit it. I was fifteen. So naturally I had a huge crush on him. Who wouldn't if they had seen him? After he kissed me at one of my father's parties, I thought I was in love. I was young and naïve, and Tony always showed a lot of interest in me when I was around. Maybe too much interest. It started off with chance remarks about my appearance or him accidentally brushing against me.

But the more famous he got, the more he changed, and not for the better. He started to make me feel very uncomfortable with his suggestions of what could happen between us. I shut myself away, and I stopped going with him to interviews and events. Dad says that Tony's fondness for drink, drugs, and the fame got him thinking he could do what he liked with whomever he wanted. When the news broke that Tony had been accused by a young girl of sexual assault, Dad shook his head sadly and said there would be more. I don't know if he knew that for sure or if he just expected that the first victim's courage would embolden the others to come forward. I do know that he never thought that *my* name would show up in the papers. It was just gossip, unfounded rumours, but the damage was out there. My dad was furious with himself for letting Tony get so close, but he had trusted him. He still blames himself. After that, Dad always kept his clients away from us. Until now. So why is Alex so different?

"Libby, sweetheart, I can assure you that there will be nothing like before, with Alex in the papers. Anyway, Alex is nothing like Tony. He has an extremely good business reputation. I would never put you in harm's way again. You have to trust me on this." He gives me a reassuring smile, but I'm not convinced. I smile back weakly as we enter my office. *What the hell have I done? Should I 'fess up to Dad about my ... romantic interest? I might be better off throwing myself into the lion's den.* We are chatting about what exposure my dad hopes to get for Alex and his companies when the phone rings.

"Miss Stewart?" It's Sally from reception. I love her voice —always so professional and courteous.

"Yes, Sally. What can I do for you?"

"I have Mr Mathews and Mr Smith at reception for you."

"Send them through. Thanks."

"Okay."

"Dad, that's Alex and Michael on their way through. I'm really not sure what to do with them today. Any suggestions?"

"What about going out on the loch?"

Just as they enter my office, my mobile rings. Kirsty. God, I forgot to call her. I'd better answer.

"Hey, you," I say to her.

"Hey, yourself. What're you doing today? I'm bored." Kirsty is always bored. She really needs to get a job.

"Well, I have Dad's clients today. We're planning on going out. Is everything all right?" I ask.

"Yeah, it's fine. Maybe we can catch up later or tomorrow?" She doesn't sound fine. There's obviously a problem. Kirsty's not usually this vague.

"Um … not sure what my plans are yet for the rest of the day or tomorrow. It would have to be tomorrow night. Can I give you a call back in a bit?"

"Yeah, sure." She hangs up on me. This has to be one of the strangest conversations I've ever had with her. I hope she's all right.

"Alex, Michael," I say, greeting them both now that I'm off the phone. Dad has been chatting away, keeping them occupied.

"Your dad has suggested going out on the loch. Is that all right with you? Maybe we could do a picnic lunch?" Alex asks me with a smile that melts my heart.

"Yes, I think that would be perfect. I'll ask the kitchen to make us up a lunch to take along and have Sally make arrangements for the three of us."

I'm pleased that at least the bloody press won't be following us around today, unless they have their own boats. I'm safe for another day.

CHAPTER 9

*T*hirty minutes later I am changed out of work clothes, and we are on board the hotel's private tour boat preparing to set off. Stephen is our official tour guide, and to everyone else he probably seems fine, but so far he's not been able to string two words together with me. I just don't know what his problem is. Oh, that's right. I do. It's a certain American that he has taken an instant dislike to without even knowing him.

The kitchen rustled up a rather elaborate picnic for the four of us. It looks and smells divine and includes a couple of bottles of wine, some water, and a selection of juices. So far it's been a day for clearing the air. Dad and I sorted things out, and now I need to do the same with Stephen. Then it will be time to deal with Alex, whom I have purposely avoided since leaving my office.

"Stephen, can I have a minute?" I ask, approaching him.

"Yeah. Sure, Libby. What's up?" He smiles at me weakly probably already knowing what I'm about to say.

"Listen. Alex is an important client for Dad. Do you think you can at least be civil? Try and stay professional?" I didn't mean for my words to come out so snappy, but it's done now.

Libby, if there had been someone else available to take you out today, I would have chosen not to be here. But as it is, I am here, and yes, I will be civil," Stephen says quietly. "I'm not paid to like him, though. I'm paid to do a job, and that's what I'll do this afternoon. There's just something about him that bothers me. I can't quite put my finger on it."

"You don't even know him," I say. I want to say, *you're just jealous!* I hold myself back, though. I suppose there could be something more to Stephen's attitude; he's always been a good judge of character.

"Neither do you, Libby."

I raise my eyebrows at him. Stephen's never been that abrupt with me before, not in all the years I've known him. Is he mad because he thinks I like Alex? Or out of some genuine concern?

"Stephen. Enough."

"It's not you, Libby. You're my friend, and I care—probably too much—but I know we'll only ever be friends, and I accept that. But I don't trust him. Let's leave it at that so we don't fall out," he says with a halfhearted smile. Stephen then turns around to face the others. "Are we all ready to go? If so, we'll set off. I can answer most questions you'll have about the loch and the surrounding area, so gents, don't be shy."

And with that, we set sail, so to speak; the boat is a speedboat, so it doesn't actually have any sails, just a fast, purring pair of inboards. I take a seat opposite Michael, who just smiles at me. He really is a man of very few words. Alex is talking to Stephen. That could be an interesting conversation. But it's not long before Alex turns, stares at me, and heads over to take the seat right beside me. I try to ignore the force that draws me towards him. I don't turn to look at him; instead I focus on the water and the truly breathtaking scenery: the Munros and the Corbett's, the plentiful islands, the bountiful wildlife and fish.

"You were right about the view; it's postcard perfect," Alex says in a low voice, leaning towards me. "I can understand the attraction of the loch. It's beautiful."

I really don't want to turn to face him, because I know if I do, everyone on this boat will be able to read me like a book. I've never been very good at hiding my emotions, and in this case my emotions are running riot. Maybe I shouldn't have taken Kirsty's advice from yesterday … and I probably shouldn't have jumped into bed with Alex. I could end up ruining things between him and my dad. Why is my life never straightforward? I close my eyes in a bid to shut him out, if only for a few minutes. I need to focus on something, anything, other than Alex.

With my eyes still closed, I hear rather than see some birds overhead, the sound of the boat swooshing quickly through the water, leaving its lacy wake behind. I hear Michael's voice and then Stephen's, giving him some info about the loch.

"Loch Lomond is about thirty-nine kilometres long and eight kilometres wide at the broadest point. At its deepest point, it is approximately one-hundred and ninety metres. The loch has a host of islands in various shapes and sizes. We will see some of these today. There are rumoured to be about thirty-eight islands, but some will tell you there could be a lot more, many of which you will only see when the water levels are at their lowest point. We will stop shortly at one island, Inchcailloch, for our picnic lunch. There you can go for a short stroll and see the remains of an old farmhouse."

"Loch Lomond and The Trossachs National Park became fully operation in 2002. There are 720 square miles here of some of the finest scenery in Scotland. Within the park there are twenty-one Munros. Munros are mountains that are over 3,000 feet. We have nineteen Corbetts, mountains that are between 2,500 and 3,000 feet, and there are two forest parks …" Stephen is talking, but I let his voice trail off.

I almost forget where I am. Then I suddenly feel him, even though he's not actually touched me. I know he has his arm resting on the boat just behind my back and that he's moved ever so much closer in the seat to me; his scent, that rich masculine smell, has gotten stronger. I open my eyes and turn to look at him, and I am greeted with his gorgeous smile.

"Have you even listened to a word Stephen has told you about the loch?" I ask him.

"Sure, I have. I can tell you all the details if you want because I know *you* haven't been listening to him," he replies with a grin. "But I'm more interested in finding out the reason you are ignoring me, so we can deal with it. You know, sort it out and move on to enjoy our day together."

"You'd think it were just the two of us spending the day together. Have you forgotten Michael and Stephen are here as well?"

"No, I've not forgotten they are both here, although I'm *wishing* it were just the two of us. That would make for a much more enjoyable day. That I can assure you of."

I feel my face redden with embarrassment. After last night, why am I surprised that I still get embarrassed so easily? All it took was a few simple words from him. I glance at Michael from the corner of my eye. He's chatting away with Stephen, taking pictures. They both seem relaxed—Stephen especially. I hope this is an indication of how the rest of the afternoon will pan out. Now if I could just do the same. *Relax*.

"What's the reason you're ignoring me?"

"I am not ignoring you. I've spoken to you several times

today, but I do have a lot on my mind, so if I've been rude, it's not been intentional and I apologise."

"I can't help thinking that I am partly to blame for whatever's on your mind. If it has to do with me, tell me, and maybe I can help fix it," he says with a typical boyish grin on his face. He looks so confident and sure of himself.

"Alex, where will I start? Last night with you? The press? My dad? At the moment my head is doing somersaults."

"Oh, Libby," he says. He runs his hand through my hair. "I have no regrets about last night, and I really hope you don't either. I really enjoyed it—and you had no complaints at the time. I told you, I don't usually do anything like that. And as for the press, I told you not to worry about that. I don't think your dad intended to upset you. And you don't have to go into the details about why you hate the press. Phil mentioned something about a previous client of his and the tabloids making up some garbage linking you with him."

Good god. Does Dad never think before he opens his mouth? Why would he tell a complete stranger about my past? That's a very good question, but not nearly as good as the question I am asking myself: *Why would I sleep with a man I had known for less than twenty-four hours?*

"So daddy dearest has been talking! You must have really made a good impression on him. That's something that doesn't get spoken about—and especially not with strangers," I snap, my voice raised. Stephen turns and gives me a questioning look. *Its fine*, I mouth to him.

"Libby, I am certainly not a stranger to your father," Alex says drily. "And I don't want to be a stranger with you. Your dad gave me brief details, but I mostly put two and two together and came up with four. If you feel like talking, I am more than willing to listen."

"I don't want to talk about it. It's in the past, and that's where I want it to stay. But I do want you to understand that

I will not be just another woman on your arm posing for the press." Alex looks puzzled. "Stephen told me that you're always in the papers, pictured with a different woman every night or week or whatever. If that's helped you get ahead in the world, then that's your concern, not mine. But I will not —and I repeat, *will not*—join the parade just to help you get noticed here in the UK. I believe my father was bloody stupid to even let the thought cross his mind."

There. I've told him. I turn away and fold my arms across my chest for some security. I feel three sets of eyes on me, but I hold my own and don't glance at any of them. Bloody men. I am outnumbered today. I'm not sure how long I sit staring into space in what can only be described as a childish huff. Not even my surroundings are lifting my mood.

It's Stephen's voice that finally distracts me. "Libby, we're here. Time for some lunch," he says, holding out his hand to me. I take it and let him help me up. "You okay? You know you can talk to me anytime."

"Stephen, I'm fine. Honestly. I was just trying to sort out the shit in my head that my dad caused earlier. It's really nothing." I hope my words sound convincing, although I've not convinced myself. "Come on. Let's go and feed our American friends. I'm hungry."

American friends. Where did that come from?

Stephen and I head over to where Michael and Alex are and begin setting out the picnic. Lunch turns out to be rather interesting, and it lifts my mood. Michael is definitely not as quiet as I thought. He can be quite talkative, and he has a great sense of humour once you get past his cool exterior. It turns out he is not just Alex's PA but also his closest friend. He seems to be a really nice guy. Although Michael did drop a few hints about Alex and me. That had Stephen questioning me with raised eyebrows and a silent glare.

Lunch is delicious, and amongst the four of us, we devour

almost everything that we brought. I feel the need to keep a clear head, so I refuse the wine that Alex offers me. Stephen refuses a drink as well for much the same reason. After eating lunch and generally just enjoying each other's company, Stephen and I take the lead, walking the short distance to the ruins of an old farmhouse. I know it is only a matter of time before Stephen brings up the subject of Alex, and the silence between us is deafening.

"Libby, I really hope you have a good reason for not listening to my warnings."

"What?"

"The tension in the air is unbearable. But seriously—I warned you about him. You are far too good for him. You're a lot more than arm candy." Stephen pauses, waiting for my reaction. Judging by the look on his face, he's not looking forward to it either.

"Stephen, you're like family to me. And I appreciate what you're saying, so I'm going to be honest with you," I say, although I wonder if I am even being honest with myself. "I'm only going to have some fun, nothing more. Yes, I'm attracted to Alex. But I'm not naïve enough to truly believe that he's seriously interested in me. So, as Kirsty so eloquently put it, I'll just have 'a bit of rumpy pumpy' and move on."

"I might have known. Bloody Kirsty—this is so her. Well, he's a fool if he isn't seriously interested in you. Look at you. You are at times an intelligent, although sometimes I have to wonder about this, educated, accomplished, funny—my list could go on." His words are so sincere. "In truth you're far too good for him, and so help me god, if he hurts you, he'll have to answer to me!"

"Stephen, I really don't want to go into this here, now," I say. He just shakes his head and watches me closely. I really need to lighten the mood again. "You know, you've been hanging about Ethan too long. You really sounded like him just then." And with that the two of us burst out laughing.

Having one brother is bad enough, but Stephen has always felt like family to me. So between him and Ethan giving my boyfriends the brotherly chat, they've managed to scare off most of the boys I've fancied. I turn around and call to Alex and Michael to hurry up.

Just then my phone rings. It's the estate agents.

"Hi, Lynn. How are you? Good, I hope?"

"Libby, I'm great … and I think you will be too when you see the apartments I've got to show you. I've already sent the details over to you for three flats, but one of them has only come into the office today, and I'd really like you to see it tonight if you could manage—before it goes on the market."

"Okay. I think I can manage tonight," I say excitedly.

"Right, then. I'll send you the address. Meet me there at six thirty tonight. See you then!"

I send Kirsty a quick text:

Libby: U free tonite to go c a flat with me? xx

Straightaway I get a reply:

Kirsty: Yes. Do you want a lodger? xx

Something is obviously wrong, so I'm glad I'll be seeing her tonight. She can tell me all about it. When Kirsty is down, it is one of two things—men or her parents. Judging from her comment, I'm guessing it's her parents this time. They can be quite controlling, and *Kirsty* and *controlled* don't go well together.

Libby: Will send u details shortly xx

I slip into a world of my own and don't even notice that I have fallen behind the pace Stephen has set. I'm thinking about how excited Lynn sounded about the flat, insisting that I see it before anyone else. It must be really good. God, I've not even got settled in the hotel. Maybe I won't like it after all. I was really hoping for a month or two at the hotel to really get into the job.

"*Elizabeth?* What bloody planet are you on? I've been calling your name," Stephen shouts as he marches back towards me. "Everything okay?"

"Yes, sure. Why wouldn't it be?"

"You had a call, and then you drifted off. I thought something was wrong." It's so like him to catch the slightest change in my moods. He's good that way.

"Sorry, Stephen. I have a viewing tonight of a flat going on the market. I was just deep in thought about that … and Kirsty," I say.

"Well, if that's all, can we start walking again? Because we need to be heading back to the boat shortly. Things to do, places to see, and all that." Stephen winks at me.

I can only smile back. Sometimes I wish I had the same feelings for Stephen that he has for me. That would make for an easier life. Stephen is actually a really great guy—hardworking, great sense of humour, and good-looking as well. He has the complete package … for the right girl … and I am sure that someday he will find her. Michael and Alex are talking just in front of me, although I can't make out what they're saying. They overtook me while I was in a daze.

Alex stops and waits for me to catch up. Michael carries on walking with Stephen. I can already sense the air shifting between us; that undeniable force is ever present, which is why I have been avoiding him. I don't know what it is about him that draws me in.

"Sorry." Alex's voice takes me by surprise.

"What are you sorry for?"

"For upsetting you again. I sense a pattern here." He chuckles.

"Really. You're going to apologise, then laugh at me? You

have some nerve." I say, smiling back. "And anyway, I'm not sure you've done anything wrong."

"I told you yesterday that I rarely apologise, but that's all I've done since I got here. You must bring out the best and worst in me." Alex gives me a smile that makes my heart skip a beat. "Did I hear right that you're going to view a flat tonight? Do you want some company? It would be interesting to see what there is on offer in this country."

"My friend Kirsty is coming with me. And why would you need a place here?" I ask, puzzled.

"I like to keep my options open. And who knows what else will come off the back of the casino deal?" he says with a smirk that shows off his dimples. That smile must bring women to their knees. Alex stands gazing at me, probably trying to judge my reaction or read my thoughts. Which I hope he won't because at this precise moment my thoughts are of only one thing. Him.

Getting lost in the beauty of Alex is not hard to do, but I'm also sure it's not the smart thing to do. I think I will need to spend most of my time with him with Kirsty's words going over and over in my mind: *Just think of it as a holiday romance, and have some fun, girl.*

"What can you tell me about the casino?"

"Well, I've had a good look at the figures, and on a whole it looks like the turnover was high, which is an advantage in any business. But I think the problem was it was poorly managed; the overheads look far too high, which led to the losses the business sustained over the last few years."

"Do you think that if you're successful, you'll be able to keep the business whole, or will you have to separate it, even close some of the outlets down? How many are there?" I ask.

"There are six. I do hope to keep them all, but there are two that I could let go of because I believe these are bringing the rest of the company down."

"What about job losses? I can only imagine that if you are going to restructure the company, job losses will be included."

"You seem to have a good business head on those shoulders. Yes, Libby, there are always bound to be some losses when you do this, but it should also save jobs in the long term."

"Yeah, I know *that*. The hotel had to do a bit of restructuring a few years back when my grandfather was still around. It was hard on him because he had known most of the staff for years. I learned a lot from him over the years of hanging about; most of it is experience you won't learn at college or university."

"You have an idea of what's involved then." He smiles. "Can I tag along tonight? I promise I'll try and behave." His last sentence leaves me intrigued.

"Oh, why not? The more the merrier. I presume Michael will be joining us?"

"Only if you're sure you don't mind. And maybe after the walk-through, we could all go for a bite to eat? You pick, and it will be my treat."

"Yeah, that sounds fine."

I stop and stare at the man who continues to walk in front of me. In the space of twenty-four hours, my emotions have been all over the place. This gorgeous man has left me completely and utterly distracted, and as much as I crave being around him, I have a feeling that these next few weeks are going to be up there as some as the hardest weeks of my life.

"All right, everyone. Time to head back to the boat," Stephen says.

"But we haven't …" My voice drifts off as I take in my surroundings.

"I've done the whole history part with Michael—at least

he was interested. You and the hotshot over there were on a completely different planet. Come on. As I said before, places to go, people to see." Stephen chuckles.

He places his arms on my shoulders and turns me slowly round so I'm facing the way we have just come. Once again Alex and Michael are walking behind us. Stephen is talking to me, but truth be told, I'm not listening to a word he's saying. I do know he will have a field day telling Ethan everything he thinks he knows. God, Ethan … what the hell will *he* make of this?

I don't need eyes in the back of my head to realise that Alex hasn't taken his eyes off me the whole walk back to the boat. Michael has been talking to him, but his only replies have been very short yes or no answers. The walk back isn't long, and before I know it, we are all back on the boat and ready to continue with our tour of the loch.

The rest of the tour is pleasant. Stephen seems much more at ease around Alex now, at least if I can judge by the conversations flowing between them and the laughter. Stephen talks steadily about the loch and the surrounding towns and villages. I join in when I'm asked a question, but I'm more than content to enjoy my surroundings. Yet I'm always aware of the deep, brown eyes focused on me, trying to gauge my mood.

"Libby," Stephen calls, distracting me from my thoughts.

"Yes."

"Libby, it might be good for the guys here to go to one of the distilleries for a full tour—see how our whisky is made, sample some of our finest, and maybe purchase a bottle or two to take home."

"Yeah, I'm sure we could fit that in over the next few weeks," I say, "along with a few other historical tours, including Charles Rennie Mackintosh's Hill House. Mackintosh was an architect, designer, and artist. Hill House is only a few miles from the hotel."

We arrive back at the hotel shortly after four. I have already called Kirsty and told her of the plans for the evening. She shrieked down the phone when I told her we were going for dinner with Alex and Michael. She thinks it's great that we're going on a double date, which makes me laugh. A double date, really. She's told me that she'll meet us at the apartment at since she's already in town.

"Well, Libby, today has been full of surprises," Stephen says to me.

"What do you mean?"

"Well, it turns out I might have been a bit hasty in my comments about Alex. He's kind of grown on me today. I didn't think I would like him, but to my surprise I do." He winks at me. *Really.* "But I still mean what I said earlier; if he hurts you in any way, there'll be trouble."

"Well, I can assure you, Stephen. He won't get the chance to hurt me."

"Okay. Time to mind my own business, I guess." I nod with a smile. "Right, well, you know where I am if you need me. I should make sure everything is okay in the gym before I head home. Good luck with the flat hunting tonight."

"I will. And thanks for today. I mean that." He smiles before walking away.

I'm left standing with Alex and Michael in reception. Suddenly I remember the original problems with their rooms; I haven't even checked yet to see if everything is okay. "Did your rooms get changed this morning as planned? Was everything satisfactory?" I ask. I shouldn't be surprised that it's Michael who answers.

"Yes, Libby, the loch view suites were ready for us after breakfast, so we both must thank you and your staff for

being so efficient … although I was fine with the room I had."
Michael glares at Alex with the barest hint of a smile.

"Sorry. I forgot to thank you earlier. What must you think
of me?" Alex says.

I answer Michael first. "It's fine. No need to thank me, it's
my job to make sure all guests are happy. And Alex, you don't
really want to know what I think of you." I smirk.

"I think I do; I'm curious now."

"Well, you asked for it, but I don't think you'll like it. I
think you're an arse." I turn and walk away from them both,
laughing. I'm not the only one laughing; Michael is in
stitches. Alex looks shell shocked.

"We need to leave here at five thirty to leave plenty of
time; traffic will be busy in the city centre. My friend Kirsty
is coming along too." I call back to the both of them as I head
towards my room. I only just close my room door when
there is a light tap. For the love of god, maybe I am not
meant to get any sort of peace here. I open the door to find
Alex standing there. He looks deep in thought.

"Can I come in, or do I need to stand in the hallway?"

I open the door wider, and he walks into my room. My
thoughts go back to the last time he was in my room. Was
that just this morning? God, I hope he's not here for a repeat
performance, because as much as that thought appeals to me,
I don't really have time for that. I close the door behind him
and turn to face him.

"Libby." His voice caresses my name. "Come here, please."

I walk towards him. He's standing at the window, looking
stunning as usual. His gaze is intense and follows every step I
take across the room. The closer I get to him, the larger I see
his delicious smile grow. Dear god, my desire for him moves
up a notch, and by the look on his face, his feelings are the
same. I want to touch him, but I know I can't let anything
happen, or I'll never get to my six-thirty appointment.

I stop right in front of him. He lifts his arms and wraps them round me tightly. *Oh, this feels so good.* I lean into his strong chest and hear his heart racing. My own heart has been racing since I opened the door to him.

"Libby, I've wanted to take you in my arms all day," he says, caressing my back. "I knew I would never have made it all through dinner tonight without at least holding you. Although now that I'm here, I'm not sure it's enough."

I lift my head and glance up at his brown eyes, still intense and burning straight through me. There's something in his look that excites me. My imagination is running riot. I could stay in his strong arms forever; he makes me feel safe.

Alex places a small, soft kiss on the top of my head and moves his hand up towards my face. Slowly he lowers his face to mine. The thrill of being this close to him has moved my desire for him up yet another level, which really isn't good. Alex draws out the moment between us. I can't stand this. I need him to kiss me—now. His gaze is so intense.

Suddenly his lips are on mine, softly, delicately—so different from his earlier fiery kisses. Actually, I don't think I've ever been kissed like this before in my life, so tenderly and with so much meaning. I don't want to think about what it could mean. He trails his tongue along my lips, but he's still so delicate with me. I want to shout at him, tell him I won't break, that I am not made of glass, and to pick up the pace, but I am also enjoying the tenderness. He pulls back and just looks at me.

"Alex," I say softly, as I look into his eyes.

"Yes."

"We do need to leave here at five thirty, and after our outing I really could do with longer than half an hour to get ready." Alex just laughs at me.

"What? It's not funny? That's all I had this morning before

meeting with my dad, and it was the same yesterday for my lunch date with Kirsty."

"Well, in both cases you looked stunning, so I don't see the problem," he says, stroking the side of my face. There is so much promise in his eyes.

"Alex, please. I don't know what's going on between us, but right now I need to be getting showered and ready." Although I know what I would much rather be doing.

"Okay, you win. I'll go and let you get ready—although I want it noted that I'm leaving, reluctantly. We'll have to wait until after dinner to finish what we've started." He leans down and places a quick, soft kiss on my lips. Then he leaves with me staring after him. I give myself a shake and head to the shower.

CHAPTER 10

*S*ally is talking with Kieran behind the reception desk as I approach. Alex and Michael are standing near the main door deep in conversation. Kieran whistles. "You are one seriously smoking-hot, sexy lady tonight," he says, running a practiced eye up and down me. "Seriously, love, you look fantastic."

"Yes, Miss Stewart, I have to agree with Kieran. You look great," says Sally. "Going somewhere nice?"

"Thanks, guys. And Sally, you really need to call me Libby," I say. "I'm going to look at apartment with Kirsty, then out for dinner."

"Well, have a good night then, Libby," Sally says.

"I take it a certain someone is going as well?" Kieran points towards Alex, who has turned to look in our direction.

"Yes, Kieran, Alex and Michael are going to dinner with us."

"Ah … a double date. Enjoy!"

I grin at Kieran, his statement mirroring Kirsty's. As I walk towards Alex and Michael, Alex stops talking and stares at me, his expression unreadable. I suddenly feel nervous, although I'm not sure why. We aren't *really* going on a date; he's tagging along on an errand of sorts … right? I pause in front of the two of them.

"Ready to go?" I ask

"Yep," Michael replies and walks out the main door.

"Libby, you are full of surprises," says Alex, leaning towards me and whispering in my ear. "You look stunning, but I know you'll look even better later when I get you out of those jeans."

"Who says you'll get me out of these jeans?" I say as I take a step past him.

He stops me, taking hold of my arm. I smile at him. "I'm so glad I paid you a visit earlier. But right now, I really wish I could just pick you up and take you to bed."

What can I say to that? I am completely lost for words. He places his hand in the small of my back, which sends shivers down my spine, as we walk outside together. He must know the effect his touch has on me. It's hard to put into words. But now I am looking forward to how my night might end. I can only imagine the look on Kieran's face behind me—it must be priceless—but I don't give in to the temptation to look back. I know I will face the Spanish Inquisition tomorrow, but I'll deal with it then. Right now, I just want to enjoy my night.

"So where are we heading?" Alex asks.

"Glasgow's West End. I'm only viewing the one flat tonight. Then we can go to dinner."

"Sounds good," Michael says. "Alex mentioned your friend Kirsty's coming as well?"

"Yes. I'm sure you'll both like her. She's great—so much good fun. She's meeting us at there," I say. "Come on. My car is parked over there." I point to the back of the car park where my red convertible is tucked between two vans.

"Nice car." Alex looks between the car and me. "It suits you."

"I like it, but maybe I should have gotten one of Dad's cars and a driver for tonight." I didn't plan this very well. This means no alcohol will be passing these lips tonight—but then again, in Alex's company, maybe that's a good thing. I need my wits about me.

The journey from Loch Lomond to Glasgow doesn't take as long as I thought it would at rush hour. Rush hour seems to last longer than an hour, which begs the question of why it's called rush hour at all, but right now I'm puzzling over more pressing questions. *Will I like the flat? Is it too soon to leave the hotel? What does Alex really think of me?* Alex is sitting in the passenger seat next to me, and Michael is in the back. The conversation is flowing amongst the three of us, and it's nice and relaxed. Alex and Michael seem to have a really close relationship. I'm learning a lot about them both, although I still get the feeling Alex is holding back.

I pull up in front of a traditional red sandstone building in what appears to be a good neighbourhood. The tree-lined street gives me a good first impression. Lynn and Kirsty are already there, waiting for us on the walkway. I introduce everyone, but from the look on Lynn's face, I take it that she already knows exactly who Alex is. *For the love of god, close your mouth, woman!* Kirsty has also noticed Lynn's reaction and she smiles. S

"So," I say to Lynn grabbing her atttention, "what can you tell me about the flat before we go in?" Yeah, that's right. I'm the reason we are all standing here, not him … or has she completely lost her mind?

"Oh. Right. Okay, so from the outside, this building looks like all the rest on the street—your typical eight flats within the one close, with two flats on each landing," Lynn says. "It's not, though. This building was redeveloped a few years ago, and it has just three apartments—two on the ground floor and one on the third. But let's not stand here talking when we could be inside. The one that's going on the market is the one on the third floor. Let's go and have a look."

I'm excited about the possibilities, and I can see by the look on Kirsty's face that she is thinking the same as me—the flat must be huge. I can't wait to see inside.

"Are you two going to keep standing out here on the pavement, or are you coming in?" I ask, already regretting the words since I can't quite hear what Alex mutters under his breath in response. Michael obviously has; he's grinning like a Cheshire cat.

We follow Lynn into the building and the close, or shared entrance, is still very traditional, with light-tiled walls and floors. As we climb up the three flights of stairs, I admire my surroundings.

We arrive at the third floor. Lynn opens the solid wooden door into the flat, and I step inside. God, the first thing that hits me is that it's so light. I glance at Kirsty, who looks like an excited kid on Christmas morning.

"Can I?" she asks me, stepping away from me. She wants to explore on her own.

"Go ahead." Kirsty doesn't have to be told twice before she heads off.

I'm still standing in the doorway admiring the view in front of me. There's a gorgeous, wooden double staircase that rises on both sides of the entry to the upper level of the flat. It's stunning. It's a very grand hallway for a flat. The floor is a light oak, the walls are cream, and there's a beautiful chandelier hanging from the ceiling. A few pieces of contemporary artwork are already hanging on the walls. It has a great mix of old and new.

"I thought you were here to view this apartment, not just

stand in the hallway." Alex's voice snaps me out of my daydream. He places his hand on my shoulder.

"Yes, of course I am."

Lynn is standing beside the staircase watching my reaction. Or is it Alex she is watching? Alex motions for me to enter first, and then together we walk towards Lynn, with Michael behind us. Kirsty is nowhere to be seen. There is a set of double glass doors to both my right and left.

"Shall we? I'll give you the tour," Lynn says.

"Yes, please."

Lynn opens the doors on the right side and starts talking. I follow her through, but to be honest, I don't hear a word she says. I am in total awe of the beautiful room I have just entered—the living room. It's a huge space, with beautiful bay windows that allow loads of natural light in. Again, the mix of new and old works well; the room has some great period features, like the high ceiling with the beautiful cornice and stunning fireplace, but it feels open, airy, and modern. It looks like the original. The room also has a real warmth to it, a homely feel to it. One room down, and already I'm in love.

Off the living room is another set of glass doors. These lead to an ultramodern eat-in kitchen. Sleek and white with plenty of units, lots of built-in gadgets, and a state-of-the-art cooker. In the dining area is a large table with eight chairs, and there is still plenty of room. I love this room; it's huge.

"*Oh. My. God.* Libby, this place is stunning. It's so … you!" Kirsty shrieks as she enters the kitchen. Both Alex and Michael laugh. Kirsty gives them a puzzled look.

"I know. I'm just trying to take in what I've seen so far."

"Libby, maybe you should go have a wander round by yourself. I'll come find you in a bit. Let you get a feel for it," Lynn says, although she is still looking past me straight to Alex.

"Do you mind if I go off by myself for a bit?" I ask Alex and Michael.

Both guys tell me to go ahead. I leave them all in the kitchen. Lynn offers to make them tea or coffee, saying the current owners won't mind. I head back through the living room and out into the hall, then walk through the opposite set of doors into a sitting room. It's similar in size to the living room but feels more formal than the living room, which felt cosy despite its size. This room has more period features, including another exquisite fireplace. I'm starting to get a bit frightened to ask Lynn the price of the place. I do have a rough idea about prices in this part of the city, but I have to admit, this one is probably way out of my league. I didn't even read the details she e-mailed over earlier.

Off the second sitting room is a much smaller hallway. Three doors open off it. One leads to a very modern WC, another to a home office that looks very practical, and the third and final door opens into a smallish but beautiful bedroom with a large window that overlooks the shared back garden. The room reminds me of the seaside, with its soft blues and whites and white-painted, wood furniture. The large en suite bathroom and the proportions of the bedroom suggest that this is a guest bedroom. So far I am very impressed.

I head back to the staircase. I'm smiling at the irony; there I was thinking my *house* was too big. This place is *huge*. I slowly head up the stairs to a wide hall with four doors. The first room is currently used as a games room, with a full-sized pool table, TV, and games console. The colours of this room are really bright compared with the rest of the house, but they work well because there is lots of natural light coming in from the bay window that overlooks the front of the property. This room also has an en suite bathroom, so it's obviously been used as a bedroom. The next two rooms I go into are identical in size. Both have en suite bathrooms and overlook the rear of the property. So far, so good.

The last room takes my breath away as soon as I step through the door. It's beautiful and light. The bay window has old, wooden shutters that can be closed. The cornice around the ceiling is exquisite. There's also another fireplace, and again it looks like an original feature. The room itself has a very romantic feel to it. I step through the door into the en suite, and … wow, what a room! Whoever said bathrooms were the smallest rooms in a house has obviously not seen this place. There is a huge, Victorian-style tub in the middle of the room. I can see myself relaxing in there after a long day at the hotel. There's a shower big enough to fit god knows how many people in it at once, and along one wall is a marble worktop fitted with an extra-large sink. I love this place.

I step back into the master bedroom and walk towards the window. I lean on the windowsill and look down on the street. I hadn't noticed when I arrived earlier, but there are some right fancy cars in the street. Maybe it's time to speak to Lynn. While I'm checking on the price, I'll ask about the neighbours and find out some more about the area.

I hear soft footsteps walking across the room. I know without looking that it's Alex. Suddenly two arms snake round my waist. His touch alone could light a fire.

"Do you make a habit of sneaking up on people?" I ask.

"I wasn't sneaking. I was looking for you."

He pulls me tighter. This feels good. Comfortable. Safe. And so right. I lean my head against the warmth of him. My heart is racing. Is he always going to have this effect on me when we are this close? He brings his hand to my face and gently brushes his fingers along my cheek and across my lips. I place a small kiss on his fingers, and he quickly turns me round in his arms until I am facing him.

"Why were you looking for me?" I ask, looking deep into his eyes. "Did you miss me?"

"Oh, Libby, you have no idea." His gaze is intense, burning with desire. That much I can tell. "What do you think of this place?"

"I love it, but …"

"There's a but? I wasn't expecting that."

"It's amazing—it really is. I didn't expect it to be this good. But it's far too big for just me," I say. "What about you? Is it very different from what you're used to?"

"You're right that it's nothing like where I live back home. It's incredible. I would love to have a place like this."

That surprises me. We're standing face to face, gazing into each other's eyes. There's passion and desire running through my veins. My eyes dart to the bed and back again; Alex shakes his head at me, as if reading the thoughts running through my mind.

"No you don't, Libby. Not here. I promise the wait until tonight will be worth it." The grin on his face is wicked and so full of promise that now I want to skip dinner and head straight back to the hotel.

I turn in his arms to face the window. He's holding me possessively now. I am so relaxed in Alex's arms. I turn my head a little to gaze up to the incredible man, who leans down and brushes a light kiss on my lips.

"What was that for?" I ask, smiling at him.

"Do I really need a reason?"

"No, I don't suppose you do."

I don't get to say another word before his lips are on mine again—this time with passion and force. I moan and lean back, kissing him with the same passion and force. When he breaks our kiss, I can only gape at him. I must look like a love-struck schoolgirl.

"Now," he says in a soft voice, "shall I tell you what I plan to do with you later at the hotel? Or keep it a surprise."

"Not too sure I am that keen on surprises, so I think you'd better tell me."

"Close your eyes then," he says. His voice is commanding. "First I'm going to get you out of those clothes. Then start by kissing every single inch of your body, and then—"

We're interrupted by someone coughing. We both turn, but Alex refuses to remove his arms from around my waist. Lynn is standing in the doorway. *Oh god, how long has she been there, and what exactly has she heard?* If looks could kill! Lynn might end up costing her boss a sale if she keeps this up.

"Sorry to interrupt," she murmurs. "I do have another client to meet soon in another part of the city."

"Sure, Lynn. Sorry if I've kept you back." I try to sound apologetic. "We'll be downstairs in a minute." She doesn't even answer me before turning on her heel and walking away.

"What was her problem?" Alex asks with a sly smile. He already knows the answer to that.

"Would you really like me to tell you? No, on second thought, don't answer that. You really don't need the ego boost."

"Come on. We better go," Alex says. He grabs my hand, and we head down the stairs and out of the apartment. I am a little amused by this show of affection.

When we finally reach the outside, the others are standing by my car chatting. Kirsty is the first to look in our direction, and I know the question she's asking without her even opening her mouth: *What the hell is going on with you two?* The smile on her face gives it away, along with the glances between my face and my hand, which is still in Alex's. Michael looks up briefly, but he returns to his conversation with Lynn. Lynn looks up as we approach.

"Libby, what do you think?" she asks, with a hint of hesitation in her voice.

"Truthfully, Lynn, I love it. I can see myself living here, but can you let me have a few days to think about it?" Lynn nods. "Tell Eric I'll call him tomorrow to get a few more details."

I hold out my hand to Lynn and shake hers firmly. She does the same with the others, leaving Alex until last. Her hand lingers on his for way too long before he finally pulls away from her and smiles at me. And then she is gone, away to her next appointment. I unlock my car.

"Libby, wait a minute," Kirsty says. "Before we head off to dinner, I think you have some explaining to do. What exactly is going on with you two?"

"What? It was your idea after all. I'm just having some fun and enjoying a beautiful man's company."

"Maybe my advice wasn't the best. I've learned a little more about who he is, and I don't want you to get hurt."

"Kirsty, there's no way I can get hurt if I just keep things simple. There's no chance of a real relationship with someone like Alex, so I'll just enjoy it and take it one day at a time." But as I finish my sentence, I doubt my own words.

"It doesn't look like things are going to be simple," she frowns.

THE RESTAURANT I've chosen is the one my dad has shares in. We arrive on time for our reservations for eight thirty. The manager, Sean, greets me by name and plants a kiss on each cheek. I introduce him to the others before he shows us to our table. As we sit down, I start to order some wine and drinks, but Alex butts in.

"I think we should have some champagne, seeing as I

think Libby has something to celebrate. Am I right?" He gestures to me.

"Yes, I think I *will* put an offer in on the flat tomorrow. But no alcohol for me; I'm driving. Please, though, you all feel free."

We order drinks, including a non-alcoholic cocktail for me. The conversation is light as we look over the menu. Alex is sitting beside me with Michael opposite him, and Kirsty is opposite me. Kieran's words come back to me; I suppose it does look like a double date. I suddenly feel a bit uptight and uneasy, as if someone is watching us. I shift in my seat and glance round the restaurant. There are a few other diners nearby, but no one's bothering to watch us. So why do I have this really bad feeling?

"Libby, what's wrong?" Alex whispers in my ear, obviously not wanting the others to hear.

"Not sure," I say, looking around again. "It's probably nothing more than an overactive imagination."

"Are you sure? We can leave if you want."

"Don't be silly. And anyway, I'm starving. We're not leaving here until we've eaten." I am teasing him.

Sean brings over our drinks and opens the champagne, much to Kirsty's delight. He takes our order. I try desperately to relax, but I still have an odd feeling that I just can't seem to shake. It's really beginning to bug me.

"So, Libby, how would you feel about a lodger?" Kirsty asks with a grim expression.

"It depends. Tell me what happened with you and your parents."

We listen to Kirsty's moans and groans about her parents, but the short version is that her dad told her to get a job or move out. I find this so amusing that I burst out laughing, and soon Alex and Michael are laughing as well. Kirsty does not look very happy at me. Her face is grim. I think I've pushed her too far. But it's not long before there is a grin on her face too, and I can tell she's trying hard not to laugh.

"Kirsty, you know your parents are right. You need to get a job," I tell her.

"I know, I know. Don't suppose there is anything open at the hotel?"

"You suppose right, honey, but if something comes up, I'll let you know," I say, although I'm not sure I could work with Kirsty. She's my friend, and I love her, but her working at the hotel could really push the boundaries of our friendship. Work is not her strong suit.

I'm much more relaxed now, and Alex must sense it. The atmosphere at our table is perfect, and the rest of our evening goes well. Starters and main courses come and go, and we empty every plate. We send our compliments to the chef. The drinks have been flowing, although I do notice that Alex is drinking more water than alcohol. Kirsty seems to be enjoying Michael's company, although she's not in full flirting mode.

Alex has been very attentive throughout our meal, topping me up with water, making sure I am okay, which I assure him I am. And then there's his touch. At every opportunity he's touched me, from slight brushes on my hands when they've been resting on the table to the gentle stroking of my back when he's had his arm on the back of my chair. He has my body tingling with desire. In fact, I'm growing so excited that I want to get out of here *now*.

I look around for Sean to get his attention, which isn't hard. Whenever we've needed him, he's been right there. I wave him over. "Sean, can I have the bill, please?" He looks at Alex before answering me.

"Libby, the bill is already taken care of," he says.

"When?" I ask as I turn to Alex, who just shrugs.

"I gave him my card earlier when you went to the ladies' room."

"Well, thank you, but you really didn't need to."

"I offered, if you recall." Alex stands up and reaches his hand out to me. I take it and pull myself out of the seat. He pulls me towards him in one swift movement until I am in his arms. I place one arm on his chest as he leans down and places a soft, lingering kiss on my lips. "Now I think it's time for dessert," he whispers in my ear as he pulls away from me. I blush. "I do have this uncanny knack of putting a smile on your face."

He's right. Just then I notice a woman who has been sitting with friends at a table in the corner. She has a phone in her hand and is taking pictures of her friends. They all look happy. That's how I feel at this moment: happy.

We all say good-night to Sean and thank him for a wonderful evening and then head outside to my car.

"Right. I'm not ready to go home," Kirsty exclaims. "I feel like a few more drinks and maybe a club. Who's up for joining me?"

"Kirsty, I need to head back. I am up early; we have a wedding tomorrow. I can drop you home."

"No!" she shouts at me. "I am so going out, with or without you."

Alex and I exchange glances, and I shake my head. There is no way I am going clubbing. Alex and Michael can keep her company if they like. If I didn't have such a big day at the hotel tomorrow, it wouldn't be such a big deal, but although I've worked at loads of weddings, this is the first since I've taken charge, and it has to go without a hitch.

"Guys, if you want to go to a club with Kirsty, go ahead. I can have the hotel send a car for you later, or you can get a cab back. But I really need to be up early. Any other night I wouldn't hesitate."

"We have early morning meeting as well," Alex tells Kirsty, who is slightly staggering beside us.

"Kirsty, honey, I'm not happy about the idea of you going to a club on your own right now. What if you come back to the hotel and we have a couple of drinks together in the bar?"

We all wait, trying to gauge her reaction. She seems to be thinking it over. I hope so. But in all fairness, she's had too much to drink; if she insists on going clubbing, I know I will go just to keep an eye on her. Michael and Alex are talking, but I can't quite hear what is being said between them.

"Libby," she says with a sigh. "Maybe you should just take me home."

I nod my head in agreement and relief. The guys look relieved as well. I hook an arm with Kirsty to give her the support she might need to make it to my car without falling. I can cope with the staggering, as long as she stays on her feet. The distance to my car is short, which is just as well. Kirsty climbs in the back and snuggles up to Michael, who looks amused. It *is* quite funny, I suppose. I start to walk round the back of the car, but Alex stops me, grabbing me by the waist. He really is making a habit of this.

"You know what you said about having an early night. There is really no chance of that happening," he says with a glint in his eye and a teasing smile. He leans towards me and places his lips on mine, where they linger for a moment. Then passion overtakes us both, and we kiss with a bit too much ferocity for a public place. I pull myself away.

"I promise there is much more to come," I say, slightly embarrassed.

"Oh, you got that right. You will most definitely be coming." Alex turns away and gets in the car, and I am left standing in shock.

CHAPTER 11

$\mathcal{W}$e have barely make it into my room before Alex is pressing his body against me and pushing me up against the wall. I gasp. His lips are quickly on mine with such hunger and passion, his tongue sliding along my bottom lip. Instinct takes over, and I wrap my arms round his neck and return his kiss with the same intensity. My fingers run up his neck and through his soft hair.

My heart is racing. Surely this speed can't be good for my health? My legs feel weak, as if I might collapse in a heap to the floor, but Alex has a firm grip on my waist, and I know he won't let that happen. I trust him not to let it happen. Can you trust someone you've just met?

"Alex, we need to …" I say, panting. "We need to close the door."

He kicks the door closed without removing his hands from me. We're still against the wall, our lips attacking each other. I taste Alex on my lips. My breathing has quickened. Between our kisses, Alex's breathing matches my own. His grip loosens on my waist, and his hands start running up and down my back, touching the bare skin between the waist of my jeans and my top. My own hands are still running through his hair, slightly pulling it. He moans.

One hand is caressing my ass, drawing me closer to him. But god, there is no space left between us. The only way we could be any closer is if we were naked, and I'm sure that's only a matter of time. He moves his hand round my ass, roughly parts my legs, and shifts us both slightly. His arousal is very evident, as his erection strains against me, seeking a means of escape. He groans. This is way too intense. I tighten my hands in his hair, and a softer moan escapes his throat. Our lips are still locked. I need him. Every last inch of him. And I don't think my body is prepared to wait. The ache is almost unbearable.

"Alex," I say, pulling away from him, though it's the last thing I want to do. But I'm moaning, and I realise that anyone passing by in the hallway could hear us. "Alex, you do remember that I have a very comfortable bed, right?" I really don't want to hear tomorrow that we've had a complaint from guests about the antics coming from this room. All the staff knows this is my room.

Alex's lips travel down my throat and round to the side of my neck. This I like. This feels softer. I moan and groan again. I rub myself against him, trying to relieve the ache that has built up, but it's not working. There's only one way that's going to happen.

He chuckles. He's loving this, teasing me. Tugging a bit harder, I pull my hands out of his hair and bring them down to his firm chest. Splaying my fingers, I push him back slightly. He frowns and then laughs. He looks so hot right now.

"Is there a problem, Libby?" He's smirking at me.

"Oh, I think you know what the problem is, and you're the one causing it. Now, you need to decide whether you're

going to be the one to fix this *problem*, as you put it, or …"
Two can play this game—if that's what he wants, to play.

He does. He smiles at me and brings one hand up to cup
my chin. He kisses my lips. Not a long, smouldering kiss but
more like a quick peck. He leans back and watches me. I'm
struggling to get my breathing back to something close to
normal.

"So, Miss Stewart, you would like to go to bed?" His eyes
shift from me to the bedroom door. "Or we could have a
drink?"

*A drink. A bloody drink. He's got me all hot and bothered, and
now he wants a drink?* I want to scream at the top of my voice,
No, I don't want a drink; I want you inside me, now! But I don't. I
smile wickedly. "I have some white wine if that's what you
really want, but I am sure the minibar in your room is better
stocked than mine."

He glares back, fire burning in his eyes, challenging me.
God, the desire running through me is intense. I am not sure
about the game he's trying to play at the moment, but my
body needs a release, not a game.

"I know exactly what you need, Libby, and I think I
started to tell you earlier tonight what I want to do with your
body." His voice is light and sexy.

He takes my hands away from his chest, places them
round his neck, and then starts backing me up through the
room. He stops at my bedroom door and lets out a sigh as he
opens it. "I do hope you can function on very little sleep
because once we make it to your bed, sleep will be the last
thing on your mind."

The grin on his face tells me a story. *Oh my god. What have
I let myself in for?*

He throws me down on the bed a little rougher than I
expect. There's a serious look in his eyes, which now give
very little away. He bends down and removes both my shoes

at the same time, tossing them across the room. Instantly I feel relief. Why hadn't I taken them off as soon as I got in? Oh yeah. I was a bit preoccupied.

He takes my right foot in his hands and gently massages it, all the time keeping his eyes fixed on mine. The feeling is so sensual. I usually hate anyone or anything touching my feet. He continues for a few moments and then leans down and places small kisses all over my foot. Once he's finished with the right foot, he does the same for the left. Would now be a good time to say I could do with a drink after all?

"I think you are wearing far too many clothes for what I plan." He crawls up onto the bed, so he's almost on top of me. He stops at my waist first and unbuckles the belt on my jeans. He loosens the button and pulls down the zip. He sits back on his heel and pulls his own T-shirt over his head and throws it on the floor. What a mighty fine sight he is before me. His chest is rising and falling quickly with every rapid heartbeat.

With a slight smile on his face as he leans towards me, and before I know it, the smile is gone again, and his face is unreadable. He takes the hem of my top and starts pulling it slowly, very slowly, up and over my head. He tosses it on the floor beside his.

I reach up and put my hands round his neck and pull him towards me, and I'm greeted with his dazzling smile. I close my eyes and draw in a deep breath. I open my eyes and smile as his lips come down to meet mine. With passion and fire burning in his eyes—or is that a reflection of my own?—he kisses me. This is going much too slow now for my liking. I needed him the moment we entered the room.

His lips move away from mine, and I let out a moan, missing the contact. But they don't leave me altogether; instead, they start a slow descent of my body, starting with my neck, kissing and sucking, which leaves my skin tingling.

He's trailing downwards towards my breasts, where he stops. He tugs gently on my nipple with his fingers. My bra? How did I not notice that he had already removed it? His teeth scrape lightly against my nipple as he takes it in his mouth. Sucking and licking. The pleasure is building within me. I need a release.

"Alex …" I'm panting.

"Yes, Libby?" The long pause is almost unbearable. His eyes question me. He still has my nipple between his teeth.

"I'm … I mean, I'm not sure I can take much more of this."

"Libby, if you want me to stop, just say so. I can end this as quickly as you like. There's a great deal of pleasure in the build-up, but I do hope there is no pain."

Alex starts stroking the side of my face. This is going to be a long night. I tense, and to be honest I am not sure why.

"Libby, baby, I just wanted to be sure that I wasn't hurting you," he says, taking a deep breath.

"Sorry, I don't know what's come over me."

He flops to the bed by my side and stares up at the ceiling. It's usually me and my big, bloody mouth. I kind of have a knack of saying the wrong thing at the wrong time, but this time it's my actions that are letting me down.

"Alex." I turn to face him. "I'm sorry. It's just … the words scared me a bit. What you were doing was extremely intense, but when I heard the word *pain*, it frightened me."

He turns to face me, and it's then I can fully appreciate the pain he is in. A tormented soul. I reach out and gently stroke the side of his face, hoping the contact will help soothe his pain. Pain that I seem to have caused. I've hurt him, and right now I don't know how to fix it. A single tear trickles down my face.

He brushes my tear away. "I don't deserve your tears. I'm sorry that I upset you."

"Alex, please, I just took it the wrong way." I pause,

waiting to see how he is. There's distance between us. This powerful, confident man is totally unreachable as he searches my expression.

I watch slowly as he comes back to me. His gaze has me hooked. His attention has refocused. He's smiling now; the pain that was there only moments ago seems to have vanished without a trace.

I run my eyes over his fine body. His muscles are well defined, sculpted. He follows my eyes as I glance at my own body. I feel the blood rush to my face, a bit embarrassed about where my thoughts are heading. We are both wearing only our jeans. His lip twists into a devilish grin as if he's reading my mind.

"Well, what are we waiting for?" I say. I am sure my face must be bright red. *What the hell am I doing?* I am never this forward.

His smile grows wider, and he falls back onto his back with a chuckle. Without even thinking and before he can change his mind, I lean over and straddle him.

"Why, Miss Stewart! You're in a very interesting position. So exactly what do you intend on doing?"

"Now, Mr Mathews, that would be telling …" I tease playfully. I have surprised myself with my boldness. *God, I am feeling brave or do I just feel alive?*

I lean down and place a quick kiss on his lips, which he tries to deepen, but I am having none of that. I sit back up in his lap quickly, and our gazes lock. Fire and passion are burning once again in his eyes, and relief sweeps through me. I run my hands down the front of his muscular chest all the way to the edge of his jeans and fumble with the buckle on his belt. When you see this in the movies, it looks so bloody easy.

I loosen the buckle and undo all the buttons on his jeans without too much trouble. I look back up into his handsome face to find his eyes wide and excited. Just as I am about to finish what I've started and remove his jeans, he sits up.

"Hey …" I start but don't get the chance to finish. In one swift movement, I find myself lying on the bed with Alex hovering above me. *What the hell?* I never saw that coming.

"An interesting thought you were having, but maybe next time. This time we both need to be naked. Now."

He climbs from the bed and I watch on as he removes his jeans and underwear quickly. He does have a point; that probably would have taken me all night.

"Admiring the view, Miss Stewart?"

"Well, it is a mighty fine view I have." I know I must be blushing again.

He kisses my lips softly.

"Well, I think it's about time you lost the jeans," he whispers, pulling away from me. He makes quick work of removing the last two items on my body. He crawls back onto the bed until he's on top of me. I giggle, although I'm not sure why. The desire is clear in his smoky, brown eyes. Hunger.

His eyes trail over my body, and it takes every ounce of energy not to squirm. "So who's enjoying the view now?" I ask. Alex shrugs.

I reach my arms up and around his neck, pulling him closer to me. I need the closeness. He brings his lips down, and they collide with mine. Fire, passion, desire, hunger— they're all there. His shaft is between my legs, teasing me. The throbbing between my legs has intensified. I moan.

"God, Libby, do you have any idea how beautiful you are? And how much I want you at this moment?" I see the desire in his expression, and I feel how much he wants me. At this moment I feel the exact same way.

He runs a hand over my breasts and straight down past

my stomach, down until he's touching me between my legs. "You're very wet. More than ready for me, I think."

I flush at his words. He is right, though; I am ready for him—and have been all night. He's gently stroking me, pushing me closer to the edge. I'm waiting for the fall, but he leaves me dangling, so close, right on the edge.

"Alex, please. No more teasing right now. I need all of you." I need to feel him inside me.

In one quick thrust, he is inside me. I let out a groan as my body wraps snugly around him. He waits a few seconds for me to adjust before moving slowly inside me.

"Is this what you were wanting?"

I don't answer. I can't answer. Surely, he knows it is.

Arching my back to meet his thrusts, allowing him to go deeper. My muscles clench around him, already anticipating what is still to come. My body's response to him is undeniable.

He knows exactly the response my body is having to his. I grip my legs around him, silently telling him what I want and need. That is all it takes. Each thrust is going in deeper. This is going to shatter me into a thousand pieces. The sensation of him inside me is perfect. We move in unison. Thrust for thrust. Heading straight to the edge. Every moan together bringing us closer to the fall.

Our rhythm is steady. I am close … so close. The look on Alex's face tells me he is just as close. Part of me wants to drag it out—I don't want to lose the closeness between us— but I know I'm being selfish.

Deeper and deeper.

Thrust for thrust.

And then we fall together. My orgasm has shattered me as I thought it would. Alex slumps on top of me.

"I have no words …"

He is still inside me, growing soft. He lifts his face to look directly at me. Smiling, he places a gentle kiss on my forehead.

I feel sleepy, drained, and content at the same time. I don't have the energy to move. Alex moves positions, I turn on my side with my back to him. He wraps his arms around me, pulling my body closer to his. I welcome the warmth between us. Silence fills the air. With a smile on my face I close my eyes, and let sleep overtake me.

$\mathcal{W}$earily, I open my eyes and glance at the clock. Six thirty. It's a big day—that is, *someone*'s big day. I try to move, but Alex's arms are still wrapped tightly round me, and our legs are tangled together. I could get used to waking up like this. Two mornings in a row. I lift his hands one at time so I can get up as gently as I can, but it's too late. He's stirring.

"Going somewhere, Miss Stewart?" His voice is playful. *God, I don't have time to play.*

He pulls his arms back round me as if that's where they belong. How I wish I could stay here all day. He trails small, soft kisses around the back of my neck. I moan.

"Alex …" My voice tails off, and I take in a deep breath. "Alex, please don't start something that I don't have time to finish. I need to be downstairs shortly to start setting up and receiving deliveries for today's wedding."

I turn my head, and I am rewarded with a passionate kiss. When we break away from each other, his hands loosen their grip as well.

"Okay, okay. If you have to go." The boyish grin lets me know he's teasing.

I head to the bathroom. *Good god, I look terrible.* I switch on the shower. It's going to take a lot more than a shower and makeup to make me look presentable today. Sleep deprived. Today of all days. But it was *so* worth it. I am standing in the shower letting the water fall over my aching body when the door creaks open. Alex is standing there in all his glory.

"May I join you?" His grin is wicked.

"Well, it would save water," I say, laughing.

He slips in the shower behind me, snaking his arms round my waist. His lips are on my wet neck, trailing kisses along my shoulders and caressing me with his arms at the same time. I feel the hardness of him behind me. *So much for a quick shower. That's not going to happen.*

"Alex—" I start to object, but I'm distracted by his touch. "Please, Alex, we can't," I say, as a moan escapes me.

"Are you saying 'no' because you've not got time or 'no' because you don't want to?" he asks. "And I will find it hard to believe you if you say you don't want to."

"Well, I think you already know the answer to that question. But you're going to make me late for work."

"You may be late, but if you're good, I might even wash your back." His voice is soft.

Thirty minutes later I emerge from the bathroom with just a towel wrapped round me. Half dressed, Alex paces the floor, talking on his phone. Anxiety etches on his face. I stop. Something doesn't seem right.

"How many papers is the story running in?" He's angry. Who is on the other end of the call? "Fuck, Phil is going to be pissed when he sees this."

I wasn't trying to eavesdrop, but hearing my dad's name catches my attention. It wasn't as though Alex left the room to take a private call. "Shit, I'd better call him. No, don't do anything until I speak with him. And … I need to talk to her." He ends the call.

"Her?"

"You."

"What's wrong?" I ask, not really sure if I want the answer. He looks angry.

"That was Michael. It seems we made the papers," Alex says. "Kieran is on his way up with a copy."

"Seriously, can my bloody Dad not leave things alone? He knows how I feel about this kind of thing. I can't believe he would go ahead and do something like this!" I am shouting, but just now I don't care who hears me. I'm doing exactly what Alex was doing moments ago, pacing the floor. He grabs my shoulders and pulls me into a tight embrace.

"Libby, this wasn't your dad's doing. He's on his way over here, though, so I suggest we both get ready before he arrives. Because if he arrives to find us looking like this, I am sure it won't go down well."

He's right. I can just picture Dad's face now.

"It will be fine. Try not to worry." His voice is soft and reassuring. There's a knock at the door. Alex opens it to a very wide-eyed Kieran. I know that expression on his face only too well; I suppose he'll want to hear all about it later, after finding me in only a towel and Alex half-dressed. Alex gives me a quick kiss on the cheek before turning to Kieran. "Make sure she's okay for me." He pulls on his T-shirt, grabs his shoes, and dashes down the hall.

"Kieran, give me a minute to get dressed, okay?" I say, leaving him in the sitting room. I fumble through drawers and my wardrobe looking for clothes. I throw on a grey work dress and grab a matching jacket in case I need it.

"Kieran, come on in. I'm decent now," I call to him.

"Right, missy. Do you have a plan of attack? Why didn't

you answer your bloody phone when I called you earlier? You know this makes for some good headlines. And the picture they got of you—I can't remember the last time I seen you looking so damn hot. Well actually I do, when you were leaving here last night." Kieran sits down on the bed, looking at me with curiosity. He picks up my phone and hands it to me. "See? Look at all the missed calls you have. And messages. You are a very popular young lady this morning."

Good god, there's a dozen missed calls from my dad, a couple from Ethan, and—of course—from Kirsty and Kieran, along with several text messages as well.

Kieran: Your dad's looking for you. He woke me xx K

Kieran: Phone me xx K

Kieran: OMG!!! HAVE YOU SEEN TODAY'S PAPERS? PHONE ME!!! XX K

Ethan: Well you've done it this time, Lib. But you look fab in the pic. Love u.

"I suppose you better give me the paper. Let's see what all the fuss is about."

Kieran moves from the bed and steps over to the dresser, where I am trying to do something with my hair. He gives me the paper and picks up the hairdryer from the floor and takes the brush from my hand.

"You read," he says. "I'll do your hair. You need to look professional today."

Oh my god. There are two pictures on the front page with a big headline:

HAS ALEX FOUND HIS VERY OWN FLOWER OF SCOTLAND?

That is so cheesy. Who comes up with these headlines? Not the most original I've seen.

The pictures are both from inside the restaurant last night. One shows Alex and me looking relaxed and comfortable with each other. His arm is draped round me or rather the chair, it's hard to tell which. The other one is of just me, and Kieran is right; I *do* look good in this one, and I know why I looked so happy. Alex had just teased me about dessert.

Has one of America's most eligible bachelors been snapped up by our very own Miss Elizabeth Stewart? "Libby" Stewart is the beautiful daughter of Phil Stewart and his wife, Jane. Phil is said to be working alongside Alexander Mathews. Does that mean Alex already has her father's seal of approval? We can only imagine there are a lot of broken hearts today with this news. We have it from a very reliable source that they have already started house-hunting in Glasgow. Both are said to be impressed with what they've seen so far but will continue looking until they find the perfect property. Our source has said they look "very much in love."

Alex has in the past been linked with various women in the States. As recently as just a few weeks ago, he was spotted arm in arm with American actress Katherine Hunter. Sources close to Miss Hunter say she is still looking forward to her trip to the UK next week for her film premiere and that she plans to catch up with Alex as well. The rumour mill stateside has been in overdrive for weeks, speculating on Alex and Katherine's relationship and saying she was 'the one.' But one look at our pictures will have you believing otherwise.

Our pictures show a young couple very much in love, enjoying a romantic night out. Other diners at the restaurant said that the couple looked very happy in each other's company and spotted them kissing and cuddling several times throughout the evening. Management at the restaurant had no comment to make on the loved-up couple, but that comes as no surprise seeing as Phil Stewart is part owner.

I stop reading. I've read enough. I can't agree with one thing that's been written. At least I know Dad isn't responsible for this story. I glance up at Kieran, who is standing behind me admiring his handiwork. I have to agree; he's made a great job of my hair. All I have to do now is put on some makeup and *hey presto!* I might just be presentable.

"Well, love, I think it makes for some damn fine reading. And breathless readers like me anxiously wonder if there's any truth to the story."

"Oh, Kieran," I say with a sigh. "There is no truth in it. I went and viewed a flat for me. Alex, Michael, and Kirsty all tagged along for something to do, and then we all went out for dinner."

"That much I know. But come on—these pictures tell a story. You look radiant! You're positively glowing," he says. I know what he is waiting to hear. "I've seen the chemistry between the two of you. Now I find you both half-dressed and looking like ... well, I know that look, honey. Tell me everything!"

"There's really nothing to tell. Now do we not have a wedding today?" I say, standing up changing the subject. I head to the bathroom to put on some foundation, face powder, and mascara. That's as good as it's going to get today.

We head downstairs. Already the hotel is busy, with staff all in early to set up. Kieran's checked and double-checked the weather forecast for today, and its full steam ahead for a romantic outdoor wedding, with the reception in our grand hall. Fussing over the details will help me keep my mind off everything else. I'll be too busy to fume about the photos.

My phone bleeps with an incoming text:

Alex: Beautiful pic in the paper. Your dad will be here soon to speak with you and pick me up.

Shit.

"Kieran, can you delegate some staff to start setting up for the ceremony and preparing the hall? The cake will be delivered shortly, along with the flower arrangements for the tables and the arrangements for outside." I pause, hearing a loud voice coming from the entrance. I don't need to turn to see who it is. Dad. "I need to speak with my father. I'll be in the office if you need me."

"No bother. Can we do breakfast at nine? If we don't, who knows when we'll have a chance to eat later?"

"Yeah, sure." I turn to greet my dad, who looks furious. I really don't need this today.

"Morning, Dad. What brings you here this fine morning?" I say without making eye contact.

"*Office. Now.*" His voice is commanding. Shite. He sounds furious with me.

I nod my head. He walks on in front of me, muttering under his breath. What he's saying, though, I don't know. I send Alex a quick text:

Libby: He's here. Not happy. My office.

Dad's pacing the floor. Well, I may as well get comfy. I could be here for some time. I walk round my desk and sit down. I wish Alex would hurry up and get here.

"Do you have any idea how I feel being the last to know what my own daughter is getting up to? My phone has been ringing off the hook since before five. Your poor mother is worried sick."

"Stop right there," I say, taking a deep breath just as Alex walks in. *Thank heavens*. He's changed into a suit, and he looks so different from when I saw him last. He looked hot then; actually, he still looks hot. I have to turn away, as I am desperately fighting the urge to go straight into his arms. My dad turns to him.

"And as for you—" he starts to say, but I cut him off.

"No, Dad, enough." My voice is raised. "First things first. Do you always believe what you read in the paper?" Dad shakes his head. "Do you *honestly* think I would move in with someone without telling you first?" He shakes his head again. "I went to look at a flat—for me. *Only* me. Alex, Mathew, and

Kirsty all came with me because, as per your request, I'm spending time with your client. We all went out to dinner. I am not really sure what the problem is, you wanted us to be seen together. Is it because you didn't orchestrate it yourself?" I snap.

He still doesn't look happy. But he can't argue: he *was* the one who asked me to spend time with Alex. He'll have to deal with the consequences.

"And the pictures?"

"Oh, Dad. Alex's arm was resting on the back of my chair, not round me. And we were all laughing at Kirsty, who was moaning that her dad told her to get a job."

Dad studies me for a moment before laughing. He knows Kirsty as well as I do. Alex looks at me and mouths, *well done*. Thank god for that. But I'm not happy telling a lie.

"What about the one of you on your own?" Dad asks.

"That must have been taken when we were leaving the restaurant, but I can't remember what we were all talking about then," I tell him.

"Do you have any idea where they got the pictures and their information?" Alex asks.

Suddenly I remember the woman taking pictures on her phone. "There was a diner with a camera phone taking pictures of her friends … I thought," I say. "And as for the flat, I will be phoning Eric at the office when it opens to make a complaint about Lynn. It could only be her who made up that story. Although what she hoped to gain from it, I'll never know."

"Okay. I suppose the whole story could work in our favour. We could end up with some extra PR out of this. I'll work on a press release straightaway." There's always an angle Dad can use, usually to his advantage. I'm not at all happy that his angle now involves me. "Now, the flat, did you like it?"

"Yeah, Dad, I loved it, although it is much bigger than the house I just sold, but I do love where it is. Why don't you come and see it with me … maybe tonight before I put an offer in?"

"Okay, I'll let your mother know. We could go for dinner."

"Sounds good," I say turning back to Alex. "Now if we're set here, I have plenty of work to get on with."

"Yes, sweetheart, of course. And we need to be heading into the city. Call me later with the plans for tonight. Love you." Dad leans in and gives me a kiss on my cheek before heading out of the office.

"Alex," I call as he follows my dad.

He walks back towards me and leans down. I tremble in anticipation of his touch. He places a soft kiss on my lips and then turns walking away without saying a word. I sink into my chair, overcome with emotions.

I AM STILL SITTING STARING into space when Kieran walks into the office a good fifteen minutes later. "Right. Come on, missy, we have work to do," he says, casually walking round the desk and taking my hands so I get up.

The rest of the morning whirls by, and before we know it, it's one o'clock. There were a few teething problems that I've had to sort out. The restaurant had forgotten to put its wine order into the supplier, so I made the call and pulled a few strings with a promise of a complimentary meal for two. Then there were the flowers—the delivery driver dropped the flowers for our wedding at another hotel, an easy mistake to sort out, although it did put us behind schedule a bit.

Kieran was right that we should have stopped for break-fast. Now it's time for a break. I go in search of him, which could be a task in itself today. Moving about the hotel is not easy today; I'm constantly getting stopped by staff asking questions—most of which relate to today's wedding but some of which are innocent queries about when I'll be making a happy announcement of my own. I set them straight and focus on the wedding. The bride and her attendants are all here and getting pampered in their room. An endless supply of food and drinks has been taken up to them.

I finally find Kieran in the hall putting the finishing touches on the room. It looks *spectacular* in a black, white, and silver theme. I think it's the first time I've seen these colours all together in this room. Striking.

"There you are."

"What do you think? Lovely, isn't it?" he asks, super-excited.

"It is, but—"

He cuts me off. "But what?"

"No, it's perfect. You've done a fantastic job," I say. "I presume you've not seen outside? Come on—let's go get something to eat and drink, and then we'll head outside."

"I knew we wouldn't eat if we missed breakfast. I told you so, didn't I?"

"Yes, you were right. Come on then. Because I *am* hungry," I say, grabbing his hand.

"How is it possible that you manage to stay so slim? I've seen the amount you can put away. Me, I *look* at food and put on weight," Kieran says with a laugh. He's being silly. His body is perfect.

"I just find time to burn off the extra calories."

"Yeah, after seeing Alex in your room this morning, I know exactly *how* you burn off those extra calories too," he says, giggling.

"Jealous?" I ask, perhaps a little smugly.

"Hell yeah! What I wouldn't do for a piece of that right now."

We head to the canteen, where the chefs have been busy, not just for the number of staff in the building today but for the restaurant and the wedding feast. Bottles of water and juice have been set out, along with fresh fruit and trays of wrapped sandwiches. On days like today, no one has time for proper breaks; it's just a case of grabbing something on the go. We each take some water and sandwiches. I promise Kieran we'll sit down for five minutes outside.

We head through the building, straight to reception, where we find Sally busy with some guests. She looks rushed off her feet. I am so glad I got someone else in to give her a hand today. I give her a wave when she looks up on my way past.

"Miss Stewart, could I have a minute? Please?" she calls after me.

I nod. Kieran and I wait until she has finished with her guests. Kieran is tapping his hand against the bottle impatiently. I mouth at him, *Stop it.*

"Libby, we have a bit of a problem," she starts to say. She has our full attention. The last time Sally had a problem, it was Alex. Why do I get the feeling he's involved again?

"Go on," I say.

"Stephen has gone with security to the main entrance of the estate. It seems we've attracted some journalists who have been ... let's say ... making it difficult for people to get in or out." She pauses before continuing. "I've also taken a lot of calls for you, asking if anyone can clarify your relationship with Mr Mathews."

I bloody knew it.

"Shit, I thought my father would have dealt with this by now." I'd better call him. "Sally, have Stephen call me as soon as he has a moment."

"Yes. What do you want me to do about the calls?" she asks.

"Tell them a press release will be issued later on today, but if anyone is insistent, call me, and I will deal with it."

"Will do," she replies before dealing with her next guest.

Kieran and I head outside. I am desperate for him to see it. Fraser is busy with more guests, all of whom look as if they are here for the wedding. We both give him a wave when he glances up. I love days like this here at the hotel. There is a real buzz in the air. Excitement.

"Oh my god! Libby bloody Stewart, you have excelled yourself this time!" Kieran shrieks. "It's stunning! You've done good, girl!"

"Do you think so?"

I think it looks great. I just hope the happy couple likes it. I've kept to their colours—black, silver, and white —and I'm really pleased with the outcome. I must admit, when I was told about the colours, I was a bit worried about how it would look outside. I needn't have worried. The focal point is the stunning silver arch by the lochside. It's entwined with white flowers and black ribbon. Everything is picture perfect. We've created a temporary aisle with grey stones trailing from the road all the way down to the arch. The white chairs on either side have silver ribbons on one side of the aisle and black ribbons on the other. The floral arrangements are exquisite: white lilies, black roses flown in especially from Turkey, and dried heather sprayed silver, all in shiny silver vases on white columns.

"Oh, Libby, it's perfect! I'm sure they will love it."

We sit down on the lawn to eat while we have the chance. God, my feet ache. Actually, I ache everywhere now that I've stopped moving, although remembering the reason for it makes me smile. Alex. *I miss him. How is this possible?* I wonder what he's doing just now.

"I can take a guess who you're thinking about. Is he tall,

dark, and handsome with an awesome accent?" Kieran teases me.

"How can you tell?"

"Libby, sweetie. You're a million miles away. I've seen the look before. Granted, not on you, but I know it well enough. You have it bad," Kieran says.

He's right. I do have it bad. Now that I've paused, I'm thinking of Alex and realising that I probably won't see him today at all, what with the wedding, then the flat, and then dinner with my parents. *Shite*. Three days ago he wasn't even in my life, and in about three weeks, he will be gone back out of my life. I was so looking forward to seeing him later too. *Ah well, I suppose I had better get used to it.*

We are just finishing our lunch when I see Stephen walking towards us. I can only guess what he thought if he saw the papers today. He looks happy enough now, though, so maybe he's not too mad.

"Well, Libby, the problem at the main entrance has been taken care of. Although you could have given us a bit of warning about the papers so we could have stepped up security for today," he says. "The guests are all worked up about having to show their wedding invitations or reservations to get past the gates today."

"Thanks, Stephen. If I'd known about the story, I would have warned you—especially with this wedding today—but it was all news to me too. I had no idea I was in a serious relationship," I said jokingly. I wink at Kieran. "I wonder if I'm getting married?"

"Yeah, I get it. So, you're okay?" Stephen waits for me to reply. He knows my history with Tony and the media and I am sure he will be just as concerned as Ethan will be. I nod. "But I know that there's *something* going on with you two. Remember—I had the pleasure of spending the day with the two of you yesterday?"

Kieran looks between Stephen and me. "Oh, what did I miss? Stephen, do tell, because a certain young lady is revealing absolutely nothing."

"Nothing. Nothing at all," I reply.

"Seriously, Libby. Talk to me," says Stephen.

"Thanks, but honestly, I'm fine. Now I'm sure we all have work to be done. After all, there is a *real* wedding here soon." I stand up.

Kieran and Stephen glance at each other, then at me. I have a rough idea what they are thinking, but I am far too busy to discuss it anymore today. It will have to wait. We only have a short time before the ceremony takes place, and I need to check on Karl and the rest of the kitchen.

We all head back inside. Stephen heads towards the leisure centre, and Kieran goes to check in with the events team. I head for the kitchen.

My phone buzzes with an incoming text from Dad:

Dad: I will be at hotel shortly. We can leave together from there.

Libby: Ok. See you soon but I am still busy x

Dad: That's fine. I have things to do in the office.

Everything in the kitchen is going according to plan. The restaurant expects to be busy tonight as well, and with a four-course meal for the wedding, the chefs all have to be at the top of their games. It helps that we have a great staff. Let's hope the team doesn't let Karl down.

At twenty minutes before three, Kieran and I head back outside. There's a sense of excitement in the air. Guests are starting to take their seats. The minister is speaking with the groom and best man, who both look very dashing in their matching MacFarlane tartan kilts. There are a few staff members outdoors to make sure everything runs smoothly; the rest should be inside ensuring that everything is perfect. The wedding photographer is taking a few shots of some kids running around. All we need now is the bride.

Jack, is the photographer we recommend to all couples who book their special day with us, makes his way over to Kieran and me. Jack's work is stunning. Even the posed pictures look so natural.

"Hi, Jack," I say as he gets close. "What a great day it is."

"Kieran, Libby. It's perfect. You couldn't wish for a better day. I always worry when it's an outdoor wedding, especially this late on in the year." He pauses, and a concerned look crosses his face. "And how are *you*, Libby?"

"I'm well, Jack." I'm puzzled by the tone of his question.

"Well, I will say, that was one hell of a picture of you in the papers today. I've been trying to get one like that of you for years."

Ah, so *that's* where he was going with the question. Well, in all fairness, everyone in the country must have seen it by now, so his curiosity shouldn't surprise me.

"Ah, there's the bride waiting just over there. I'll catch up with you both later," Jack says as he heads in her direction.

"Libby, look at her. She looks splendid!" Kieran says with a look of awe in his eyes. "Although she doesn't outshine my current company."

"Smooth … real smooth," I say, slapping his arm.

Kieran and I stand back under an old oak tree to watch the proceedings. Two bridesmaids and two beautiful little flower girls walk down the aisle, followed by the bride's father walking her down the aisle. He looks handsome in his kilt. The bride's dress is an elegant, slim, off-the-shoulder gown with a small train. The bridesmaids' dresses are black, and boy, do they look good, which really surprises me. And the little girls are adorable in their white dresses with matching black sashes around their waists.

While we're watching the procession, Kieran's phone

vibrates. Stephen tells him that there is a problem at the gym, something about the ventilation, and Kieran heads back inside to sort it out. I offer to go, but I am told to stay put.

A small crowd of other hotel guests gathers at the edge of the lawn to watch the happy couple. I smile to myself as my thoughts wander off. I find myself thinking of Ethan's wedding. So many things have happened since then to turn his world upside down. How I wish things were different for him. As I stand watching, I hear someone approach me. Arms curl round my waist. I know its Alex. He leans down and rests his head on my shoulder, and I turn slightly to look at him. God, I have missed him today. He gives me a quick kiss on the lips.

"You look tired," Alex says, watching me closely.

"If someone hadn't, how shall I put it, taken so much out of me last night, I would be fine," I answer, slightly embarrassed. "Should I assume that Dad is here now?"

"Yeah, he went straight to the office. Said he had a few calls to make. How's your day been?"

"Do you really want to know?" I say. I sigh, thinking about how busy it's been.

"I wouldn't ask if I weren't interested."

"Well, then … it's been hectic here, but seeing this beautiful wedding, it's all been worth it," I say. "My feet are killing me, though. Kieran and I only sat down for about ten minutes all day. If you want me to be honest, yes, I'm shattered. There have also been a few other things preying on my mind as well."

"What other things?" he asks, placing a kiss on my cheek.

"Sally has taken a lot of calls from journalists about our *relationship*, and Stephen and security have had to deal with problems at the gates—media camping at the main entrance."

"Are you okay, though?" he asks, sounding concerned.

"Yes, I'm fine. I just don't like being the centre of attention. And I don't want anything that's in the papers to affect things here. I think I will have to look at my marketing for the hotel. The hotel has a good reputation, and I won't allow my personal life to interfere with my job here."

"Sorry. I feel bad about this. It's my fault," he says. "If it wasn't for me, you wouldn't be getting all this attention."

"That may be so, but with you staying at the hotel there would still be of media interest, so I'm just going to think of it as extra PR for here."

Alex has a point about it being his fault. And I won't be the focus of attention for long, soon enough they'll move on to someone else. Or Alex will move on. I try to push that thought to the back of my head. I want to enjoy the rest of the time I have with him instead of thinking about what will happen when he goes home. My mind starts to wander again, but I try to focus on the ceremony that's taking place in front of me.

"Hey, you're a million miles away, Libby." His arms tighten round my waist.

I hate to admit it, but I do feel comfortable with him. Maybe that's what he does—makes women want him, then tosses them aside. Part of me keeps wondering about the actress, Katherine Hunter.

"Sorry. I'm fine." I smile at him.

Jack is walking towards us. I wriggle out of Alex's arms.

"Hi, Jack. Jack? Alex. Alex? Jack," I say, introducing them. "Jack is a photographer."

"I would never have guessed, Libby." He smirks. "I thought he was just carrying all those cameras to sell to the tourists."

"Libby, I got a few shots earlier of the hotel and loch that might be good for some promotional material. And I hope you don't mind, but ..." Jack looks a bit lost for words. "I'll show you." He lifts his camera, presses a few buttons, then lets me look at the display on the back. There on the screen in front of me is a picture of me and Alex. Jack obviously took that one a few minutes ago. Jack encourages me to look through the others he has taken, though. He's been a bit snap-happy, as I see quite a few with me alone, just before Alex got here, and several of the two of us looking content. In some he's kissing me. In all of them, we both look incredibly happy. I look up at Alex, who smiles.

I turn back to Jack. "Jack, these are good. But I'm wondering why you took them?"

"Well, you know I always take pictures of you every time I'm here; I have since … well, since your granddad. Until now, though, I've never been really pleased with them. They're all missing something. When I saw the pictures in today's papers, all I could think of was how I wished I had been there to take them, to capture you like that. And now here you are, looking just like that! The light was perfect, the backdrop was perfect, and so were you."

"I have to agree with your friend Jack," Alex says, putting one arm back round my waist. I turn and glare at him. I'm not sure I'm entirely happy with everyone seeing us together. I don't even know what's going on with us.

"Jack, what are you planning to do with these photos?" I ask, out of both curiosity and fear.

"Libby, I'm not doing anything with them—except giving them to you," Jack says.

"Oh."

"I know what you're thinking, Libby," Alex says in a low voice. "These pictures will *not* end up in the papers, right? Jack, please tell Libby. Please put her mind at ease."

"Oh! No! I'm so sorry, Libby, I didn't think. No, *of course* they won't end up in the papers. I will give them to you," Jack assures me, and I know he's telling me the truth. "Libby, I'll e-mail you copies and drop off a disk for you on Monday. Look, I better get back to work."

"Thanks, Jack. And the pictures do look great," I say to him.

"It helps when the setting is completely perfect," Jack says, smiling as he walks back towards the happy couple.

"You know, he's right," Alex says, leaning back down and resting his chin on my shoulder. He brings his other hand back round my waist.

"About what?"

"About you being a beautiful woman."

"He didn't say that."

"He didn't have to."

"Do you think comments like that will get you into my bed?" God, I am really surprising myself.

"Your bed … no. Been there, done that, haven't we? It's about time for a different location." The boyish grin on his face has just gotten wider with excitement and anticipation.

Time for a change of subject before the conversation gets too intense to change it. "I should really get back to doing some work before I have to take off again."

"Yeah, I forgot. Going to see the apartment … and dinner with your parents." *He said that like he's going as well.*

"What?"

"Oh, didn't I mention it? Your dad invited Michael and me for dinner, but Michael bowed out. He's going to have an early night. I think the last few days have caught up with him."

"Well, this should make for an interesting night." *Interesting* is one of those words that can cover a lot of situations. My mum is going to take one look at me and just know what's going on. There is no way I will be able to hide it from her. She seems to have a sixth sense when it comes to my love life.

CHAPTER 13

*D*ad is in my office, on the phone. He doesn't hear me or see me enter. "You're right. They do make a lovely couple," he's saying to whoever is on the other end. "But there really is nothing in it, at the moment. The American actress? I don't know. You'd have to ask Alex about that yourself. Yes, I read the reports, but as I said, you could ask him when you do the interview."

Dad turns around in the chair and smiles when he sees me. *Alex is doing an interview.* I do hope his private life isn't the topic of conversation. I'm not sure I want to hear all about that. Dad finishes off his call.

"How long have you been standing there?"

"Long enough," I say.

"Everything going smoothly with the wedding?" he asks. I know he's trying to change the subject. The question is, will I let him?

"Everything's going great. So … who makes a lovely couple?"

"A journalist who wants to do an interview with Alex thinks you two make a beautiful couple; they are wanting you to attend a photo shoot with him." Dad grins. Well, what can I say to that? After all, I've seen the pictures of us together. And if a picture says a thousand words, what do the pictures say about us?

"Dad …"

"Yes, sweetheart?"

I decide not to say anything to my father. What should I tell him? The truth? God, what is the truth? That I am sleeping with his client; that I jumped straight into bed with him the first night I met him? Or tell him yeah, I think we do look like a great couple, and there's nothing I would like more than for us to *be* a couple. But back to the real world— that's not going to happen. I can just see his face.

"You were about to say something?"

"No, it's fine Dad." I sigh. He looks at me with a puzzled expression on his face. "I have a few things I want to check with Kieran. I'll meet you out front later on."

"Yes sure, just text me when you are ready to leave. Alex is coming with us," Dad says. "Is that all right?"

"Fine." What else can I say?

It turns out that everything is going well in the hotel, and I'm not needed at all, so I head up to my room. I want to phone Kirsty now while I have peace to do that, and then I'll change before heading out with my parents and Alex. *How the hell am I going to be able to sit through tonight?*

I call Kirsty, and whilst it's ringing, I start running a bath. A relaxing bath is just what I need to soothe away all my aches and pains.

"Finally! I thought you were never going to answer," I say to Kirsty.

"Yeah, yeah. I was just getting ready," she says.

"You got a hot date tonight?"

"Mmm."

"Well, do you or don't you?" I say. I really don't know why

she is being so coy about it. I know she's dying to tell me; I can hear it in her tone.

"Yes. I *am* seeing someone tonight," she says. She must be grinning from ear to ear.

"*Well?* Spill! Who are you seeing?"

"Okay, okay. I'm having dinner with Michael." Her reply sounds very smug.

"Michael ... as in Michael Smith?"

"Yes."

"So Michael has blown my dad off for dinner to go out with you? That's magic! You really must've made an impression last night. I do hope it was the impression you made *before* you got so drunk."

"I know." She giggles. "I didn't think I was drunk until we stepped outside, and the fresh air hit me. Was I bad?"

"You've been worse, but there was no way I was going clubbing with you."

"Shit, that bad?"

"So where are you two going?" I ask curiously.

"I'm coming to the hotel, but I know I won't see you since you're going out."

"You've done your homework. You got it all planned." I pause, knowing what Kirsty is like. I'll probably see her at breakfast tomorrow.

There's a knock at my door. "Kirsty, look, I have to go. There's someone at the door, and I have a bath running. Have a nice night ... and don't do anything I wouldn't do."

"You've not left me much, seeing how quickly you and Alex—"

I don't let her finish. "Okay, point made. See you tomorrow."

There's another knock at my door. "Just a sec," I call as I turn the water off in the bath.

I open the door to find a very handsome-looking Alex

leaning against the doorframe. He's holding a suit carrier draped over his shoulder. I suppose he has a suit in it, but I can't imagine why he's carrying it. Is he leaving suddenly? I must have a worried look on my face, because a slow, sexy smile spreads across his beautiful face. *God, he looks hotter every time I lay eyes on him.*

"Well?" I ask. The question hangs in the air for a few moments.

"Well what?"

"What's with the suit carrier?"

"Well, I thought maybe I could leave it here, just in case." He's really not giving much away with his passive expression. Totally unreadable. Well, two can play this game.

"You mean to stay here tonight? Ah, I see. Sorry to be the bearer of bad news, but I'll be staying at my parents' tonight," I say matter-of-factly and trying—really, really trying—to keep a straight face.

The expression on *his* face is priceless. What I wouldn't give to have a camera in my hand at this moment. I giggle and give myself away.

"You had me there," he says, leaning down. His soft lips meet mine in a quick kiss. "Are you going to leave me standing in the doorway?"

"Come in then," I say. I walk towards the seating area. He places the suit carrier over the back of the couch, and before I know it, he has pulled me into a tight embrace. I throw my arms up around his neck in response.

"I've missed you today. You have no idea how much." His voice is low and soft.

I think I do. Although it's been a hectic day here, I've missed him too. Really missed him.

"How could you possibly miss me? You saw me this morning and outside at the wedding." I don't want to admit my feelings just yet. I have to decide what those feelings are first.

He's holding me tightly, flush against me. His gaze is full of lust. Raw lust. Or is it just a reflection of my own eyes I'm seeing? He tugs my hair gently to tilt my head back. He works his other hand down my spine, settling it on my ass. He pulls me in again even tighter. He kisses me—not softly this time but passionately. Lustfully. He wants me just as much as I want him. He pulls away, and I swear his eyes are glowing.

"What took you so long to answer the door? You up to no good?" He's smirking at me.

"If you must know, I was running a bath. And I was on the phone with Kirsty." He has a smug look plastered on that beautiful face. He already knows.

"I'm glad she told you. I don't mind keeping it a secret from your dad, but I didn't want to keep it from you too. Now … running a bath, you say? Is it big enough for two?" he asks with a low, suggestive voice. His smile is wicked.

"Yes," I whisper. "I want you."

His breathing changes. I feel and hear him inhale sharply, trying to get it under control. *My words alone have done that to him. Glad to see I can have the effect on him that he has on me.*

He takes my hand and leads me to the bathroom.

Entering the steam-filled room, I check the water. Just perfect. Well, it is for me, but then I've always loved a hot bath. When I turn to face Alex, he's undressing, and I do the same. By the time I've finished and pinned my hair up in a clip, Alex is already sitting in the bath waiting patiently on me to join him.

I climb in and sit between his lap, leaning my head back against his shoulder. *I could get used to this.* I feel warm and fuzzy, and I can't decide whether it's the bath or Alex making me feel like this. He reaches beyond me for the soap and a cloth, but I take the cloth from him to remove the makeup from my face. When I'm done, I hand it back to him.

"Lean forward." I do as I am told. He soaks the cloth and brushes it over my back several times. Then he slides the soap around my damp skin, lathering my shoulders, slipping down the furrow of my spine, down to the small of my back. He drops the soap and continues caressing me with his strong hands, making delicious circular motions with his palms against my soapy skin. He places a trail of kisses round my bare neck. My breathing quickens.

"Turn around."

I do seeing the new direction we are going. I wrap my arms around his neck, and he slowly guides me into position, teasing me at first with just the tip. Then he pulls me down. I gasp as he enters me fully. I feel my vaginal walls shiver and embrace him, and then I take control. This I will enjoy. I ease up, up, up, and then just as it seems we will separate, I slide all the way back down. Up and down. Up and down. He tries to bring his hands up to my hips to take control, but I pin them in place with mine. This isn't about me; it's all about him. I know I will enjoy this, but right now every move I make I make for his pleasure.

His breathing is erratic. His eyes are closed. I'm watching him as I control the pace. His pleasure is evident in his face. I want to hold on, although my body's own desire is taking control. My head falls back as I focus on the sensation of his skin on mine deep inside me and massage him rhythmically with my pelvic muscles. Taking him higher. Pushing him to the edge. Up and down. Faster and faster. Closer to the edge until he lets go, loudly calling my name. At the same time, I explode around him.

We sit in the same position for a few moments, spent. Finally our breathing returns to normal, and I lean towards him and give him a brief kiss. Then I pull myself up on the bath.

"Where are you going?"

"To get myself ready before my father comes looking for me," I say, laughing. I grab a towel and wrap it round me.

"Shit." That got him moving.

A short time later, we are both ready to meet my father. If I'm honest, I'm dreading tonight. I hope I can manage to stay professional in front of my parents.

"You scrub up well," I say to Alex with a smirk. His hair is still damp from our extended bath, but it still looks great. He's wearing a deep red shirt with black trousers, and he looks hot, but then again, I've not seen him look any other way.

"Why thank you, Miss Stewart. I shall take that as a compliment." He takes my hand and bows slightly. "You, on the other hand, look beautiful—as always."

I've only thrown on a pair of tight jeans, top, and blazer—something I would normally wear when going out with my mum. If I dressed up, she would be suspicious.

Dad texts me that he's ready, and I reply that I'm on my way down. He says he'll call Alex, but I say that I'll swing past his room on the way down and collect him. Alex grins. *It's not funny*, I mouth to him. I hate lying to my dad.

When we get downstairs, Dad is talking with Kieran in reception. Alex gives me a brief smile before looking back in the direction of my father.

"Phil." Alex greets my father with a handshake.

"Alex, Libby. Are you both ready? Your mother will meet us at the restaurant after we've seen this flat of yours."

"I'm still unsure about it, Dad," I tell him.

I give Kieran a nod as the three of us head out of the hotel and towards Dad's car, which is sitting right outside the main doors. He obviously called for someone to get it. I climb into the back, letting Alex sit in the front with my dad so they can talk—and I don't need to.

The drive seems to take much longer than it did last night. The traffic is a nightmare. Alex and my dad don't seem to notice. They are chatting away, mainly about football. I listen as Alex tries to keep up with the comings and goings of Scottish football. They both try to include me in their conversation, and I manage to nod or comment at the right times, but mostly their conversation is just a background buzz to my own distracted thoughts.

When we arrive at the flat, Eric, the estate agent, apologises profusely about Lynn going to the papers. He assures us that he personally dealt with the matter harshly, from which I infer that she has lost her job. Tonight's walk-through is much quicker than the one last night. I still love it, but after seeing it again, I do think it is far too big for just me. I share my concerns with my father, who doesn't seem to think my concerns are justified. When we leave the flat, I tell the Eric I will be in touch by close of play on Monday. He assures me he will put off advertising until then.

We arrive at the restaurant just as my mum is getting out of the cab. Perfect timing. I greet my mum with a hug. God, I've missed her! It seems ages, although it's been less than a week since I've seen her. I pull away from her to let Dad introduce her to Alex, but she's already eyeing me suspiciously.

"Mrs Stewart, it's so good to finally meet you," Alex says, holding his hand out to my mother.

"Please. Mrs Stewart is Phil's mother. Call me Jane." She smiles at Alex.

We all enter the quaint, little Chinese restaurant, where the food is to die for, and the staff are so friendly. It's off the beaten track, so hopefully we won't be seeing photos in tomorrow's papers.

We are shown to our table in a secluded part of the restaurant. Mum takes her seat, and Dad sits opposite her, leaving me to decide which one to side beside. Out of the corner of my eye, I see Alex watching me, and I wonder if he realises how hard this is for me. I decide to sit beside my mum. And no matter which parent I sit next to, I still have to face him. God, I am going to struggle tonight.

We order drinks from the waiter, who is being a bit over attentive to me, much to my father's amusement. Alex looks somber. I smile at him, but it's not returned. I pick up the menu and start to read through it. My father and Alex are talking. Good. The more they talk to each other, the less pressure there is on me. I glance at my mother, who despite having the menu in her hand is glancing between me and Alex. I go back to reading the menu. What else can I do?

The over attentive waiter returns with our drinks. He places everyone's drinks down, leaving mine until last.

"Now last, but by no means least," he says with a smile and a wink.

Seriously? Did he just do that? Alex and my father laugh quietly as the waiter walks away from our table. I kick Alex under the table. He grins at me. He thinks it's funny, although I'm not sure I do.

"I think you have an admirer, Libby," my dad says with a hint of humour in his voice. He returns to speaking with Alex.

"He's not the only one, is he?" my mother whispers to me, smiling.

I turn to face her, but Alex catches my eye. Oh—he heard her too.

"What do you mean?" I ask, although I really don't think I want her reply.

"We'll talk later," she says. "Alex, how are you enjoying

your stay in Scotland? I do hope Libby and the staff at the hotel are taking extra good care of you?"

I splutter into my glass of wine. *Of all the things to say.* Three sets of eyes focus on me.

"Are you all right, Libby?" It's Alex asking the question. I nod. My mother will have a field day with me.

"Well, Jane," he says, "it's a beautiful country from what I've seen so far. And yes, Libby and the staff are taking great care of Michael and me. I hope to see a lot more during my time here once I get the business end of my trip tied up." He has a hint of a smile on his face as he looks to me. Does that mean I get to spend more time with him? Do I want to spend more time with him? Or is me spending more time with him only going to lead to heartache?

The waiter chooses this moment to interrupt to take our order. He is very animated, the type of person I would love in the hotel restaurant, and he's great with the customers. He spends a bit of time explaining various items on the menu before we order.

"If you'll excuse me," I say, rising from my seat as the waiter leaves our table. Again, everyone turns to me.

"Are you all right, Libby?" my mother asks. I hear the concern in her voice. "You look a bit pale. Are you tired?"

"I'm fine. I just need to use the bathroom," I say, turning towards the back.

I hear my mother say, "I think I'll just go and make sure she's all right."

I hold the door to the ladies' open since she's walking right behind me. And there I was wanting a few minutes to compose myself. Instead I'm going to be interrogated by my mother. Oh well, I suppose it's better to get it over with than to have it hanging over my head for the rest of the evening. She looks round the bathroom, and I can only presume it's to make sure that we are alone. No journalists or people with cameras.

"Right, Elizabeth. Do you have anything you'd like to tell me?"

"Like ..."

"Oh, I think you should start with Alex."

"What's to tell? He's one of Dad's clients—one I'm stuck with for the next few weeks." I know that's not what she wants to hear. She shakes her head at me.

"Libby, I'm your mother. I can tell that there's *something* going on. I just don't know what," she says. "I thought at first it was attraction, but you're ignoring him completely now. Is it that you don't get on? Friction between you? Would you like me to ask your father to get someone else to see to him?"

"Stop there, Mum." She's puzzled, and quite frankly, so am I.

"Darling, what is it? I can see he likes you—he's hardly taken his eyes off you since we arrived."

"Oh, Mum ..." God, I am just going to tell her. Get it over and done with. What will she make of this? "How do I say this without you thinking badly of me?"

"Libby, sweetheart, you're starting to worry me. Please, just tell me."

"Okay, here goes. I am kind of *seeing* Alex." Well, at least that sounded better than *I'm sleeping with Alex*, but my mother is not stupid. She now knows exactly what's going on.

"Oh," she says. She sighs. Shit. Maybe I shouldn't have said anything. God, what if she tells my dad? She smiles at me after a few moments. "He is quite handsome. I can see why you would be attracted to him."

"You're not mad at me then?"

"Why on Earth would I be mad at you? I was young once myself, and I still have eyes. I'm not ready for a pine box yet.

You think it all ends when you reach my age?" she says with a smile. I do not want to think about this right now. "The point is, though, it would be great to see you happy and carefree for a change. You've had a lot to deal with these past few months, and you deserve a little happiness." She gives me a hug. "And anyway, I've seen the pictures in today's papers of you two. You look happy together. He might be good for you. All I ask, as your mother, is that you'll be careful."

"Don't, Mum …" I do not want to hear The Talk again.

"Why the sad look?"

"Because I am not naïve. I know there's no chance of any kind of serious relationship between a man like him, especially one who lives in another part of the world, and someone like me."

"Sweetheart, why ever not? You are intelligent, witty, and beautiful … should I go on? I think you put yourself down too much, although god knows why. I get that you have trusting issues, but then who wouldn't after Jeff? But you know, sweetheart, all men are different. You never know what's going to happen in the future. Sometimes you have to take chances. If everyone went into relationships expecting them to fail, there would be no relationships. If I'd had that attitude, neither you nor Ethan would be here today! My relationship with your father was very difficult in the beginning with both of us working, hardly seeing each other, and then me staying home to raise you two. But we managed and thrived. You just never know what's waiting around the corner."

"I guess you're right."

"Come on. We'd better get back out there before they start to worry," Mum says.

"What about Dad?" I ask. "I feel like I'm lying, and I hate it."

"It seems like just yesterday we were both your age. I'll

speak with your father tonight when we get home and gently remind him what it's like," she says, winking. She gives me a quick kiss on the cheek, and we both head back to the table.

"Are you okay? You had us worried," Dad says.

"Everything's fine. Libby's just a little tired." Mum looks directly at Alex as she speaks with a hint of a smile.

"I'm fine, Dad. Mum's right. I'm just a little tired," I say, just as the waiter arrives at our table with starters.

My explanation seems to settle Dad. I have to admit that I am much more settled and relaxed too after my talk with Mum. She always knows the right thing to say. As we eat, we talk and drink. Alex seems relaxed in my parents' company, but then again, why wouldn't he be? He's working with my dad, after all.

The conversation flows easily. Mum asks Alex lots of questions about everything from schooling to business to family. I wonder if he realises that he is being interrogated. I suspect so. He answers all the questions politely. I'm learning a great deal about the man I'm spending time with, and so far I like what I've heard.

She also questions why he didn't go into law like his parents and brother. His reply was it simply didn't interest him enough, but his mother would tell us a different story, of a young, maybe rebellious boy who wanted to take a risk, a gamble. This is a story I'll have to ask more about later.

The waiter clears the starters and brings more drinks to the table. I'm going to have to slow down with the alcohol, or I will end up in the same state as Kirsty last night. God, Kirsty! I wonder how her night with Michael is going. The conversation changes to one of my father's favourite subjects, football.

"Are you looking forward to the game tomorrow, Libby?" my father asks.

"Not really, Dad." I answer curtly.

Mum laughs. "Now I am sure Libby would much rather go shopping, which I know she *hates.* But if there happened to be a certain football player there, she would be more than happy to go. Phil, what was his name? Libby had a huge crush on him when she was what, thirteen?"

"Mum!"

"What? It's true—one minute you didn't like football, then it was all you spoke of." She laughs, knowing this little bit of information is something I would rather she wasn't sharing. "It was quite funny listening to you and Ethan bickering about a sport that up until that point you had showed no interest in, especially when it came to old firm games. He would be cheering on one and you the other. I will say this— never a dull moment." Alex laughs.

"Phil, if Libby doesn't enjoy the football, we don't have to go." Alex holds my gaze. "If Libby has something else she'd rather do…"

"I've already said I'll go. And anyway, it will give me a chance to see Ethan."

"It's settled then. I'll send a driver over for you all in the morning, and you'll pick Ethan up on the way. When you get to Fir Park, you'll be met by Motherwell officials who will take you up to the Millennium Suite. With the game being a lunchtime kick off, they'll serve you a meal after the game. They usually bring rolls and things around before. Your seats for the game are in the director's box. Libby knows the dress code if you have questions." Dad gives us the details for tomorrow.

The rest of the evening flows smoothly, and before I know it, we've finished our meal. I ask the waiter to phone a taxi for Alex and me. Dad did offer to drive us back to the hotel, but it's not even in the same direction, so that doesn't make any sense at all.

When the waiter tells us our taxi has arrived, Dad pays

the bill, and we thank the staff for a great evening. Alex and I say our good-byes to my parents outside. They head to Dad's car, and we go to the taxi. I climb sheepishly into the back, and it doesn't come as a great surprise when Alex gets in beside me. He puts an arm round me and pulls me close; I lean my head against him. I am so tired. I just want to sleep.

"Close your eyes, baby. I'll wake you when we get there." He leans down and places a kiss on my head. My eyes close. All too soon I hear, "Libby, Libby … it's time to wake up. We're back."

"No, I need to sleep," I say, stretching.

"Come on, sleepyhead. You can get straight back to sleep as soon as we get upstairs."

Sleep is what I want, but I'm sure I can be persuaded to stay awake a little while longer. I take his hand as we get out of the taxi. I rummage around in my bag to pay the driver, but Alex has beaten me to it.

The hotel seems quiet, but I know there is a wedding reception in full flow at the other end of the hotel. We stroll through the hotel hand in hand like an ordinary couple and head up to my room. We are anything but ordinary. It doesn't take too long to get to my room.

"Right, Miss Stewart. Let's get you into bed," Alex says, his voice soft and low. *Bed. This could be interesting.* My smile spreads across my face as I look him in the eye.

"No, you don't. I know *exactly* what you are thinking, and as much as that thought appeals to me, you are shattered. I have monopolised too much of your time. Now, pyjamas? What do you usually wear to bed?"

I point to the drawer. He takes out my pj's and brings them over. I take them from him and go to the bathroom to wash and change. When I am finished in the bathroom, I walk slowly back to the bed.

"Come on," Alex says as he pulls the bedcovers down. "In you get."

I do as I am told and climb into bed. I roll straight onto my side. I feel the mattress shift as Alex gets into bed next to me and switches off the light.

"Good night, baby," he says, wrapping his arms around me and giving me a kiss on the back of my head. He's naked. I know I will have sweet dreams tonight.

CHAPTER 14

"*L*ibby? Baby, it's time to get up. Come on." Alex's voice is soft and coaxing. The weight of the bed has shifted. He's sitting beside me. His hand reaches down and moves my hair off my face. His touch is gentle and warm but most of all, familiar. *Familiar*.

"Please … not yet. Surely it can't be time to get up already?" I mutter.

"Yes, it is. Come on. Up you get." He pulls me round with strong arms. I turn and gaze up at him. His eyes are soft and sincere. He leans down with a soft smile and places a soft kiss on my lips. He pulls away too quickly. "Now. Up."

"No. I want you to come back to bed," I whisper. The thought of him joining me back in bed suddenly has me feeling all hot and bothered. My body wants him. "Please? I'll make it worth your while. Why didn't you wake me earlier?"

"No," he says, his voice firm. "I *wanted* to wake you—nothing would have given me greater pleasure—but you looked so peaceful, so beautiful, and so tired. I couldn't be that selfish."

Selfish. I'm sure I would've been if the boot were on the other foot. And pleasure—I'm sure we would both have gotten a great deal of that.

"Come on. Michael is joining us for breakfast."

Shit. I sit up in bed and pull the covers all the way up to my neck. I feel my face redden. He's here? "Is Kirsty here as well?" I ask. No, she can't be, or she would already be in my bedroom. I know her well.

"No," he grins. "I believe she left a short time ago. Now if you don't get moving, you'll be going to a football game dressed like that." He yanks the covers off me and right off the bed.

"Do I have enough time for a quick shower?"

"Yes." He gives me a lingering kiss before turning away and walking out of the bedroom.

Ten minutes later I'm fresh from my shower, wet hair pinned back, and dressed in a black-and-cream dress. I leave the bedroom to join Alex and Michael for breakfast.

"Have you two left me anything to eat?" I ask, entering the sitting room.

They both stop talking and turn to face me. Alex stands as I stroll towards the table. Michael is watching me intently. I can feel his eyes burning through me as Alex pulls me into his arms.

"Good morning again," he whispers into my ear, kissing me. I really wish Michael weren't in the room.

"Good morning, yourself. I've missed you this morning." From the look on his face, he knows exactly what I mean.

"I'll make it up to you, I promise," he says, grinning. The glint in his eyes is full of promise and leaves me with a feeling of anticipation.

"Good morning, Michael," I say, sitting down next to Alex's seat.

"Morning, Libby. I hear you're not much of a football fan these days. I'll sit with you, then. I'm not either." He chuckles. I don't know why, but the expression on his face leaves me feeling puzzled. Uneasy even.

I pour some orange juice and take some fresh-chopped fruit. I can feel Alex's gaze before I turn to look at him. It's then I notice he's wearing a crisp, white shirt, the top button still undone, and his tie draped around his shoulders for later. He's not shaved, but the stubble looks good on him. I'd like to run my hand along his jawline and feel its roughness as I pull him in for a long, sweet, passionate kiss, but that will have to wait until we're alone. I'm not sure when that will be, since we'll be in company all day.

"Is that all you're going to have?" The question comes from Alex.

"For the moment, yes. I don't have time for anything else. I need to finish getting ready," I say. "And we can get something to eat before the game if I get hungry."

Breakfast continues in unbearable silence. I'm wondering what's going on between Alex and Michael. Michael is a bit weird this morning. Or maybe this is what he's always like. Let's face it; I don't know him at all.

"If you'll both excuse me, I'm going to dry my hair," I say, getting up. Michael is still watching me intently, and Alex is looking between Michael and me. I don't know what's going on, and I'm not sure I want to know.

No sooner have I closed the door behind me than I hear raised voices.

"Don't. Seriously, Michael, we're not doing this." Alex sounds angry. Do I want to stand here behind the room door eavesdropping? Yes, I think I do.

"Oh, come on. You're telling me I can't do anything? She's more my type than yours. I'm sure I can have some fun with her. I know you would have fun with Kirsty."

Shit, I really didn't need to hear that. This is all too good to be true. I knew there would be a catch somewhere along the line. I hear a thud, as if someone has slammed a hand down on the table.

"I'm warning you. We. Are. Not. Let me repeat … We. Are. Not. Playing. This. Game," Alex says. "Libby is different."

Different how? What game? At once I want to call off today. I pick up the hairdryer and start drying my unruly hair. Once it's dry I pin most of it up, leaving some down around my face. I put some light makeup on and slip into a pair of black heels. I stand in front of the full-length mirror. I suppose I will do. My face looks haunted. I'm not sure I want to face either of those two. Should I pretend to be sick?

Get your act together, girl. What's changed? Just tell him you overheard them. Demand answers. How bad can it really be? I put on some jewellery, grab a handbag, and practice my best teeth-whitening smile. Fake, but it will have to do.

I leave the safety of my bedroom and find only Alex waiting on me. Should I talk to him just now about what I overheard? I might not get another chance today.

"Libby, what's wrong? You don't look so good." The concern is evident in Alex's voice.

I shake my head as he walks towards me, meeting me in the middle of the room. He places both hands on my shoulders. I shrug them off. He looks like I feel: wounded.

"For Pete's sake, just spit it out. I've obviously done something wrong."

"Okay," I say, my voice raised and slightly shaky. "I heard you and Michael. You seemed to be discussing … swapping."

He turns away from me. His composure completely gone. Stephen was right, here's a lot more to him than meets the eye. I feel tears well up in my eyes. I can't do this. I need to cancel today. They can all go on their own.

"Alex, the car will be downstairs for you shortly. I'll call

Ethan and make my apologies. I'll tell him I'm unwell or something."

"No," Alex snaps. He turns to face me once again. I'm struggling to contain the tears. I want him out of the room before I let them fall.

"No, what? Look, Alex, please just go!" I shout.

"Libby, please. Let me explain. Please?" He reaches over and tenderly cups my face. I freeze. I am so overwhelmed with emotions that a single tear escapes and runs slowly down my face. He wipes it away.

"You have one minute." After that I will surely break down.

"Okay. Michael and I have been friends for years. When we were younger, Michael was seeing this girl, and I bet him that I could make her *my* girlfriend, steal her away from him. He accepted the challenge. It's a game we've both played once in a while over the years whenever one of us was kind of … jealous, I guess … over the other guy's hot girlfriend. None of the girls even realised. I'm sorry."

"You're *sorry*? Do you have any idea how pathetic that sounds? What age are you? You sound like an adolescent schoolboy!" I shout. "You think that's all right to do, play games with people's emotions? And what … did Michael just presume that because I was so quick to jump into bed with you, he had a chance too? I am not some cheap whore. You've had your minute."

"No, you most certainly are not. That's not what I think of you. Please, Libby, if you were listening, you must have heard my reply to Michael." I nod. "Well then, you already know I'm not playing *any* kind of game with you. Michael knows it now too. He won't bother you. And I know it sounds stupid, but it's kind of Michael's way of saying he approves of you … that he really, really likes you too. *Please* come to the football?"

"Why? Because you want me there or because you just don't want to have to try and explain why I'm not there to my dad?" I stand shaking my head at him. I know how my dad will react, especially given that my mum has probably already told him about Alex and me. "Okay. But you have to make sure Michael understands. He made me very uncomfortable during breakfast. You also have to find out what's going on with him and Kirsty, because I will not stand back and let him play games with her."

"Done. I promise," Alex whispers. He leans forwards and kisses my lips softly. "Come on then. Are we ready to go?"

"Yes, I suppose. Do I look okay? Do I need to touch up my makeup?"

"You look beautiful. You always do." He smiles, holding out his hand to me.

"Let me fix your tie before we go? We can't be having you seen like this leaving here. What will people think?" I giggle as I take his tie from his shoulders. I button his top button and lift his collar up. I place the tie round his neck and, holding it at both ends, pull him slowly to me, staring into his eyes. God, I love his eyes. He raises his eyebrows questioningly, then grins. My intention is very clear. Our kiss is passionate. And in that moment, all my anger is washed away.

We walk downstairs hand in hand. I am not so bothered who sees us together. After all, I told my mum we were seeing each other.

Kieran is working at the front desk, but the big question is why. "Is everything okay, Kieran?" I ask curiously.

"Yes, Sally's just running a bit late this morning. She's on her way, though. She called to say." He looks between me and Alex and smiles. "Oh, am I to presume that you two are no longer a deep, dark secret?"

"No secrets," Alex replies. Maybe I should just ask him

outright what kind of a relationship he thinks we have, since I don't really know myself. How can I possibly answer the questions I am bound to be asked?

"Libby, remember that I won't be in until lunchtime tomorrow, so you'll have to make sure everything is ready. But I'll get the room set today."

"I remember. See you tomorrow then. Mind, if there are any major problems, call me."

"Okay. You two have a good day." Kieran is grinning with his trademark full-on, dazzling, white smile.

We head outside to find a very impatient-looking Michael leaning against our car for the day. I am suddenly not sure I can spend the day with him. I tense up just seeing him.

"It's fine. Just breathe, baby," Alex whispers, so low I can barely hear him. I look at him, and I know everything will be okay.

"What kept you two? On second thought, don't answer that. I have a pretty good idea." His look is smug. What I wouldn't give to knock that smug grin off his face. Then it hits me.

"Jealous, Michael?" My statement is bold and straight to the point. I look at Alex as I walk round the back of the car, open the door on the far side, and slide into the seat in the most ladylike way I know. Alex is laughing, and Michael is shocked. Good. That's the reaction I was hoping for.

"You walked straight into that one. I say you got off easy. She overhead you earlier," Alex tells him.

"Oh." Michael at least has enough class to look abashed.

Alex slides in beside me and straightaway wraps his arm round me. I want to crawl onto his lap and wrap my arms round him, but I restrain myself. I'm going to be doing that a lot today—restraining myself.

"Well, Miss Stewart, you told him. So seriously, are we okay?" he asks me with a solemn look on his face.

"What do you mean?"

"Me and you, after earlier," he asks.

"Yes. But I do have a question. What exactly does 'me and you' mean? I need to know what to say when people ask questions about our relationship. Let's face it. Someone's bound to ask today," I say, looking down at my hands.

"Ah, I see." He's very quiet for a few moments as he thinks about my question. "Well, what did you say to your mum last night? I know she worked it out. It was obvious from the expression on her face."

"Well, she first thought that maybe we didn't get on. She was going to speak with my dad and get someone else to look after you," I say.

"Ha! Then what?"

"Then I told her I was kind of *seeing* you," I whisper shyly, looking anywhere but at him.

"Isn't that what we're doing?" He brings his free hand up to my chin and tilts my face so that I'm looking straight into his blazing eyes.

"I don't know what we're doing," I say, mesmerised by those eyes. "I mean, you live in another—" Just then the spell is broken.

"Ready to go?" Michael asks as he gets into the car. Alex shoots him a quizzical look.

I speak to the driver. "Mark, we need to pick up Ethan first."

"Yes, miss."

"Libby." Alex's voice is soft at my ear. "I believe we didn't finish our conversation?"

"No, we didn't. But I think it will have to wait until later," I say with a grin before placing a kiss at the corner of his mouth.

"You two talk away or whatever else you want to do. Just pretend Mark and I aren't here," Michael says, laughing. Alex slaps him almost playfully on the back of his head.

"Hey, what was that for?" Michael shouts, rubbing his head.

"You know what it was for. Can you remember you're in company? Sorry about him. I don't know what's got into him."

"Libby, about earlier sorry," Michael says as he turns and looks at me.

"It's fine." I just shake my head and stare out the window. Michael is speaking to Alex, but I'm not listening. I have just shut the world out for some peace and quiet. A few moments alone with my thoughts. *Shit*. He didn't really give me an answer to the question that I am sure we will get asked today.

"A penny for your thoughts," Alex says, taking my hand. "You're a million miles away."

"I'm fine. Just enjoying the scenery."

The ride to Ethan's isn't long. Michael and Alex continue talking, although Alex doesn't take his eyes off me. I feel them burning through my skin intensely. His fingers gently stroke my neck whilst he is stroking my thumb with his. I want to moan but remember where I am. When I look at him, he's smiling. He knows exactly what effect his touch has on me. And he told me he doesn't play games?

When we pull up at Ethan's, my dad's car is in the driveway. Strange.

"Give me a minute, will you? I'll go get Ethan." Mark opens my door. I walk up the drive, looking at the house next door, which was *my* home only a few days ago. How things have changed in such a short space of time! Before I reach the door, Mum opens it. She has Lucy in her arms. The wee soul is breaking her heart, sobbing uncontrollably. Mum is rubbing her back, trying to console her.

"Here, Mum. Let me," I say, putting my arms out to take my niece.

"Thanks, Libby. She's been so cranky this morning. I think Ethan is looking forward to some time away from her today. She had him up all night."

"There, there, little miss. For someone so small, you sure make a lot of noise." I gently stroke her back as I talk to her in a low voice. "Oh, sweetheart, you are a bit hot. There, there. See? No need for all that crying," I say, cuddling her tightly.

"You do have a knack with her. Looks like she's missed you," Mum says in a reassuring voice. I've missed her.

My dad and Ethan come out of the house. Ethan is on his phone. Deep in his conversation, he waves his hand to me. Dad looks me over, eyeing me suspiciously. Oh, that's right, Mum has told him about Alex. Finally, Dad smiles at me, and then he walks down the drive to speak with Alex. I hadn't noticed Alex getting out of the car, but he's standing there leaning against it, watching me closely.

"Mum? What's going on?" I ask, watching my dad.

"Nothing to worry about. He's just going to have a quick word with Alex. Are you still coming to ours later? Your dad is thinking about cooking a BBQ."

"Yes. Is Dad okay with me and Alex?" I ask. I'm pacing slightly on the driveway, holding Lucy. She is such a joy. I glance down the drive towards my dad and Alex, who is listening intently to my father but hasn't taken his eyes off me. He smiles when he sees me looking. Dad notices and looks between the two of us.

"Yes, honey. Everything is all right. Nothing to worry about." My mum's answer makes me relax.

Ethan's off the phone. He gives me a brotherly hug. "Libby, you need to give me the lowdown on Alex. Do I need to have that brotherly chat with him?" He bends down and gives Lucy a kiss. "You always know how to settle her, Lib. I think she misses you."

"Mum just said the same thing."

"Well, it *must* be true then." We all laugh.

I hand Lucy back to my mother because we really should get going. My dad gives me a reassuring hug and tells me he'll see us all later. I give my mum and Lucy a quick kiss before grabbing Ethan's arm and walking down the drive to a patiently waiting Alex.

"Come on, you two," Alex calls to us. "Michael is getting grumpy."

"Well, he can stay grumpy," I say as we approach Alex. "Alex, this is Ethan, my brother. Ethan, Alex."

"It's good to finally meet you," Alex says with an outstretched hand. "I've heard a lot about you from your father … and a little from Libby."

"It's good to meet you. So, you enjoy the football?" Ethan looks at ease speaking with Alex. With football the hot topic for the day, I have lost them both.

"*Finally*," Michael says, exasperated. Mark is too professional to let his feelings show, but I can tell he finds it amusing.

Alex introduces Ethan to Michael. With all introductions out of the way, we finally head off for our day at the football. I have a feeling this is going to be a long day. I lean back into the seat and sigh. Alex notices. He takes my hand in his and brings it up to his beautiful face and places a small kiss in the middle of it. I melt.

"You okay?" he asks in a low voice. I nod, even though I am a bit apprehensive. I know there will be reporters there. My father has already told me that. They're interested in

Alex—he is big news, after all—but I will be there too. I just hope I can put on a smile that will see me through. "Everything will be fine. I promise." He squeezes my hand a little tighter.

Somehow, his words don't reassure me.

CHAPTER 15

*A*lex

I don't know what I can do or say to reassure her. Right now, I want to kill Michael. What the hell was he thinking this morning? That's the problem I know exactly what he was thinking. I hope he got my message loud and clear that Libby is different. The different part I'm still trying to come to terms with. I'm dealing with my own feelings, something I've never had to do before. No one has ever mattered so much to me.

No games.

A few short days and everything that was in my life before feels so far away. I'm struggling to explain it to myself so I'm not sure how anyone else will understand. My thoughts for the last few months have been stolen by the beautiful woman beside me, and that was before I even met her.

But now, that I have her in my life I don't ever won't to let her go. She completes me. Consumes me. And all this scares the fucking shit out of me. She makes me feel alive and for once gives me a purpose other than work.

Everything about Libby brings me comfort and hope. Holding her as she slept last night brought me peace and an over-whelming surge of emotions. All I want to do is protect her and love…

Is this really what I'm feeling, love? I do believe it is and I never want this feeling to leave me.

The big question is, how does she feel about me?

CHAPTER 16

*T*he closer we get to Fir Park, the more nervous I get. We'll be dropped off right at the front entrance, but it will still be busy. There is always press at the games—usually to speak with players, but Alex is big news here at the moment. I'm feeling daunted. Alex squeezes my hand, bringing me back to reality.

"We're here," he whispers.

As our car approaches the main entrance, I see a sudden rush of activity. Looks like extra security separating reporters, making a clear passageway. I suppose Dad will have already made the necessary arrangements for today. Still, it doesn't make me feel any better.

"You ready for this?" Alex asks. Mark stops the car and gets out, heading straight to my door. I know he won't open it until I nod.

"As ready as I'll ever be," I say, drawing in a deep breath.

"Come on then, Lib. Let's get it over with," Ethan says.

I give Mark the signal, and he opens my door. At the same time, everyone else gets out. Alex is quickly round the car and at my side, taking my hand—which is just as well, as the questions start flying at us.

"Elizabeth? Can you comment on your relationship with Alex Mathews?"

"Alex, how long have you and Libby been an item?"

"Is it true you two are moving in together?"

"Alex, what about Katherine Hunter? Will you be seeing her when she comes to the UK next week for her film premiere?"

"Alex, how did Miss Hunter take the news of your breakup?"

"If the business deal goes ahead, will you and Libby make your base in the UK?"

"Ethan, it's been a rough few months for you. How are you coping?"

"Miss Stewart, what do you hope to gain from Alex? You've ducked the public eye for years. So why now?"

I feel the panic settling in, but I put on my professional face and my best fake smile and pray they see me through this. My mother has taught me well.

I really want to get inside. This is madness. I glance at Ethan, who tries to give me a reassuring smile, but it doesn't work. This must be affecting him as well—especially the mention of the last few months. Alex brings his hand up to the crowd of waiting journalists. Oh shit, he's going to make a statement. I can feel my whole body start to shake.

"Ladies and gentlemen. I'll make this brief." He looks at me with a smile as he squeezes my hand tighter. "Let me clear up one thing first. Katherine Hunter is my friend. There has never been anything else between us. Since she is a good friend, *of course* I plan to see her when Miss Stewart and I attend the premiere of Katherine's movie." He looks back at me with the smile I love. The announcement that we're going to the premiere is news to me, but I try to keep the surprise from my face. The flashing of multiple cameras startles me.

"As for my relationship with Miss Stewart, I am spending time with a lovely woman"—he pauses to look directly at me instead of the journalists—"for whom I have a great deal of feelings." The smile on his face widens, and I know that if we were anywhere else right now, I would kiss him.

"As for my business dealings, when the time is right, I'll be more than happy to update you all. Now if you don't mind, ladies and gentlemen, I came here to watch some football." With that, security ushers us all inside. Alex keeps a tight grip on my hand.

When the door closes behind us, I let out a sigh of relief, releasing the breath I wasn't aware I'd been holding. While the others talk to the officials who have met us, I try to digest what Alex has just told the media. Basically he has just told the world that he has *feelings* for me. I think I have feelings for him. But surely it's far too soon for … *love* … isn't it?

"Miss Stewart! It's good to see you again. You may not remember me. Andrew. I think the last time I seen you, you were maybe fourteen or fifteen," one of the Celtic officials says. "Probably the last time you went to a game with your father." I do vaguely remember the tall man standing in front of me.

"Andrew, of course. It's good to see you again. Has Ethan introduced you?" I ask, looking at Alex and Michael.

"Yes, all introductions have been made. Now if you'd like to follow me, I'll show you upstairs, Miss Stewart."

"Please, Andrew, call me Libby. But I thought it would be someone from Motherwell who would be showing us about," I say.

"Usually it would be, but your dad pulled a few strings." Why does that not surprise me? "If there's anything you need, just let me know."

Andrew continues talking to the guys until we are all seated at our table. When I glance up, there are a lot of eyes on our table and hushed voices around the room. It's a big space—it can hold up to eighty people. That's a lot of hush. *Oh, I hope it's not going to be like this all day.* Andrew introduces us to Ashley, our waitress for the day, who seems more than happy to have our table to contend with. Well, who wouldn't be? I may be slightly biased, but I'm sitting with the three most handsome men in the room. It's no wonder Ashley's smile could light up an entire city.

Andrew leaves us, telling us he's arranged for Alex and the rest of us to meet the players of both teams after the game. From the look on Alex's face, you would think he was a small boy on Christmas morning getting the one present he had hoped for. He's practically giddy.

"So, gentlemen. Can I get you something to eat or drink?" Ashley asks. Ethan coughs.

"Oh, sorry, Miss Stewart. I didn't mean anything by that." Ha. I know she didn't! I just might as well be invisible, eclipsed by my gorgeous companions.

"Well, gentlemen? Don't keep the waitress waiting." If looks could kill, we'd both be flat on the floor. Two can play this game.

Ethan laughs.

"What?" I ask, after Ashley has taken everyone's order.

"Could you be any more obvious?"

"Could she?" I raise my eyebrows at him, and he knows not to push the subject any further. Matter closed.

"Are you okay?" Alex's voice is soft as he questions me.

I nod. He puts his arm round my shoulder and pulls me a little closer, bending down to kiss my forehead. His hand stays firmly in place as he continues his conversation about football with Ethan, although every now and then, he gently strokes the bare skin on my arm, sending shock waves all the way through my core.

I excuse myself from the table. Alex seems reluctant to let me leave. I suppose he's concerned after the welcoming committee that mobbed us on arrival. But jeez oh! I'm only going to the bathroom. I have no desire whatsoever to face those vultures on my own.

I'm nearly back at the table when I hear a very familiar voice—one I would much rather not ever have heard again. "Elizabeth? Is that really you?"

I would know that voice anywhere. I should do, considering how much time I spent with him. I turn around slowly to see Jeff standing in front of me. Of all places to meet my ex! At a football game with the new man in my life … if that's what I can call Alex. The curious thing is, Jeff hates football. I can't believe he's shelled out for hospitality.

"Hello, Jeff. Good to see you," I say, hoping to just push by. No such luck. He pulls me into a tight embrace and gives me a kiss on the cheek.

"Look at you! You look absolutely fantastic." Jeff is grinning from ear to ear. "I thought it was you when you arrived. That was some entrance." He glances meaningfully at our table, seeming to expect introductions.

I face the table. This could be interesting: Alex's expression is grim, not happy at all. Almost as though he recognises Jeff. More likely, he sees how close to me Jeff stands. I step away from Jeff's hand, which has been resting proprietarily on my forearm.

"Hi, Ethan. How you doing? It's been a long time," says Jeff.

"About four months or so. I'm doing okay. And you?" There is a hint of bitterness in his voice. Well, who can blame him? They were, after all, meant to be close friends, but just not close enough.

"Much the same, I guess."

I think Ethan forgets about the connection between twins some of the time, and this is one of those times. I see the look on his face and know exactly what he wants to do to Jeff at this moment. I wanted to do the same four months ago when Jeff was bullying me about spending too much time away from him. I glare at Ethan, and straightaway he gets me.

"This is Michael Smith and Alex Mathews. Guys, this is Jeff Ross," I say mechanically. I don't want to encourage him to stick around.

"Libby's ex," Ethan says. I scowl at him.

Michael says hello politely, but Alex watches Jeff intently, a slightly puzzled look on his face. Ethan plays with his silverware, ignoring Jeff.

"So, Libby, I see you're making a bit of a name for yourself. I never thought you'd be one for the limelight, all things considering. What is it? Business not doing so well, and you need the money?"

What the hell? I feel my blood boiling, the anger building. What a bastard. Ethan is trying so hard not to look at Jeff that he's dropped his silverware. Finally he looks at me for permission to fire back at Jeff, which I won't give. I won't stoop to Jeff's level.

"Jeff, was it?" Alex stands, taking my hand before continuing. "I understand now why you are the *ex*-boyfriend, not current. I'm going to say this as politely as I can, and I'm only going to say it once. Don't make me repeat myself. Now you and I both know that's no way to speak to a lady. Apologise … now." Alex moves his hand from mine and puts it round my waist, pulling me in tighter to him.

"Sorry, Elizabeth. I was out of order," Jeff mutters.

"Thank you. And now that you've apologised, please leave our table without looking back. And if you ever speak to Libby like that again, that will be the last time you speak at all until you see a good dental surgeon. Do you understand?" The whole time he speaks, Alex keeps his voice level and low.

"Yes, I understand," Jeff mutters, looking down at his feet.

"*Leave.*" Alex's voice is forceful.

I sink into my chair as Jeff walks away from our table, moving as quickly as he can without running. Running sounds like something I should be doing. That might ease some of the tension I feel. *No wonder I dumped him. He's a controlling weasel.*

"You okay, Libby?" It's Ethan's voice that brings me back to now.

"Libby." Alex takes my hand, gently stroking the side, sending shock waves through my body. I can't believe he told Jeff that he was my current boyfriend. He's really full of surprises today.

"Oh, sorry, guys. Yeah, I am fine. He just took me by surprise."

"What happened with Jeff?" Michael asks the question that I know Alex wants answered.

"Our relationship just … ran its course."

"Libby, if you won't tell them, I will," Ethan says. He raises his eyebrows at me.

"Oh, for god's sake. Okay. I dumped him four months ago when Ethan's wife, Lindsay, was killed and his daughter, Lucy, was born."

"Because?" Alex asks.

"He asked me to choose between Ethan and Lucy and him." Ethan leans across the table and takes my free hand, urging and supporting me to continue. "Ethan and I have a connection; it will always be there. He had just lost his beautiful wife, my dear friend, who he'd thought would be there to share all the steps of their lives together—the biggest being raising their gorgeous baby girl together. How could I abandon my brother, especially then? My choice was simple.

Ethan and Lucy needed me. Jeff was meant to be his friend too, but he was so cold towards him." I sip my water to give myself a moment. Everyone's looking at me. "And, well, if truth be told, he was also kind of boring."

That breaks the tension; there is no need to go into all the details.

"You're not getting all soppy are you," Ethan says with a wink of his eye and a smile.

"Me? Never. You should know me well enough by now."

"I don't know what to say to all that," Alex says with a hint of sadness in his voice. "I can't believe he put you in that position. If he was any sort of a man, he would have given you space and support. That tells me a lot about him. He's weak."

"I couldn't understand that at the time, but I do now." I sigh.

Ashley approaches our table with hot rolls filled with square sausage and back bacon, strutting over with a wide smile on her face. And let's just say she's not smiling at me. For the love of god, this really is going to be a long day.

I thank Ashley because Alex refuses to look at her, and my brother and Michael seem to have lost the ability to speak. They are both too busy focusing on her cleavage. *Please, boys, close your mouths.* Their eyes follow her away from the table. Her outfit really leaves very little to the imagination, and I could swear she's undone another button of her blouse since her first visit to the table. I admit, though, it's good to see Ethan showing some life. That's a step in any direction, although I won't be pointing it out to him in case he takes it the wrong way. I know he will never truly get over Lindsay, but it would be good to see his life move forward and maybe through time he will find a special someone.

We eat our rolls and drink tea and coffee. I had expected the guys would order beer, but it's still early. We finish eating just as Andrew returns to our table to show us to our seats outside. On our way out, Andrew introduces Alex to a few people, most of whom Ethan seems to know. They all say near enough the same thing to my brother: *Good to see you out and about.*

I am sitting between Ethan and Alex. Good. I don't think I could have been beside Michael. I think I might struggle with Michael for the rest of their visit. As I look about the stadium, I don't see many empty seats, yet I haven't kept up, and I have no idea if this is a big game or not. The seats in front of us have yet to be taken.

"I thought it would be better if you didn't sit next to Michael," Alex whispers into my ear. I shiver. "Are you cold?" he asks, putting his hand round my waist.

"No, not cold," I answer. I smile and hold his gaze.

"Oh, I see. Was it my voice or my touch?" His voice is soft and low. His hand moves ever so slightly on my waist. I slide my hand down on top of his. My eyes plead with him to stop, but his eyes are telling me there's no chance of that happening. *Don't do this to me here!* I suddenly feel nervous. Aware of my surroundings.

"Please," I beg.

"Please what?"

"I thought you were here to watch football, not turn me on."

"I turn you on?" He's smirking at me. "How much?" he asks, moving his hand from my waist down to my ass.

"Alex ..."

"Yes, Libby?"

"Please remember where you are," I say. "There are cameras *everywhere*."

"Okay. But I'm just as frustrated as you are." He leans down and places a soft and quick kiss on my lips. Far too quick for my liking.

"Well, someone shouldn't have let me sleep so long then. And that same someone shouldn't have had an extra guest in my room for breakfast." My voice is low and seductive.

"Ah, excellent points. I'll remember that next time." The smile on his face is infectious.

"Who says there will be a next time?" I reply with a straight face, but I can't keep it like that for long before I laugh.

"Elizabeth don't tease. Especially when I know you want a next time just as much as I do."

"Well, at least we both agree on that." I bring my hand up to his chin. His eyes are ablaze with passion. Our lips meet, and this time the kiss is lingering. I am the first to pull away, remembering where we are. Maybe today won't be so bad after all.

"Maybe you two should get a room," Michael says.

"Seriously?" My voice comes out a little louder than I expect. I can't believe this.

"What? Libby, I am only saying what everyone else is thinking." Michael laughs.

"No, I wasn't meaning you," I answer sharply. I'm looking at the seats in front of us. I've not seen him in months, and now I am stuck with him, within touching distance: Jeff.

"Libby?" Alex looks at me, and then he realises what the problem is. "Shit. Do you want to change seats?"

"No, it's fine. I can handle it." I hope. Jeff turns Around with a big smile on his face. He's sitting with his boss, Simon, who is the manager of my bank. The other two men I don't recognise.

"Libby, it's good to see you! Ethan," Simon says, shaking our hands. "You both look well."

"Simon," Ethan replies.

"Thanks, Simon. You're looking well too," I say. "How is your lovely wife and baby? It was a boy she had?"

"Yes, Libby. Calum. They're both doing great. He's a bit of a handful already. I'm sure Ethan will agree with me," he says, patting Ethan's knee sympathetically. "I don't usually see you at the matches anymore. Where's your father today?"

"Helping out mum with Lucy," I say. "Alex, this is Simon MacRae, our bank manager and friend."

"Yes, we've already met," Simon says.

"We met at your father's office yesterday." *God, that was quick.* "We could very well be doing some business together if everything works out for me, although I've encountered an unexpected problem that will have to be taken care of first." He glares at Jeff. *Ah, the unexpected problem.*

Suddenly the stadium reverberates with excitement. The players are on the pitch. Ethan gives me a nudge; I'm the only one still seated. I stand and applaud. As soon as the play starts, I sit back in my seat and try to concentrate on the game before me—challenging, since I'm so conscious of Alex's arm round my shoulders.

Focus. It's only a few minutes into the game when half the stadium erupts. Motherwell has scored first. Ethan is cursing to my right, and Alex is just enjoying the game on my left. The game continues. Celtic are awarded a penalty—for what I honestly couldn't say—but the Motherwell keeper saves it. Motherwell seems to be having more chances.

"Miss Stewart?" I turn to see Andrew standing at the end of the row.

"Yes?"

"I believe Ashley forgot to take your half time drinks order."

"Three bottles of Peroni." I look at the guys, and they all nod that beer's fine for them. "Can I have a large glass of chardonnay please?"

"Yes. Your drinks will be ready when you come back inside."

"A *large* wine?" Ethan asks.

"Yes, I have a feeling I am going to need it." He just shakes his head at me and mutters as he goes back to watching the game.

The game. I really should be watching it, but there are two people unsettling me in very different ways. Alex is stroking my arm, which is distracting at the best of times. And then there's Jeff, who every now and then glances back at me. It's nearly half time when I hear the crowd erupt again as Motherwell scores what I think is their second, but it turns out it's a third. I really need to pay more attention. Oh well, not a good day for Celtic fans. Then a few minutes later, the stadium erupts again. This time it's a Celtic goal. Half time score: Motherwell 3, Celtic 1.

We head inside on the stroke of half time for our drinks and snacks. I had forgotten that's all you do at football games —eat and drink. There is no way I can sit down to a full meal after the game and then have a BBQ at my parents' house. I mention as much to the others, and Alex suggests that we don't bother with a meal here. We settle for finger sandwiches—honey-roast gammon, roast turkey, and creamy tuna, mayo, and cucumber, and I insist the guys try the scotch pies. The scotch pie is the traditional half time snack at every football stadium in the country. Perfect. I send my dad a quick text to let him know we will be over at theirs earlier than originally planned, which Dad replies is fine.

Ten minutes into the second half, the stadium surges to life again, including my party; the game is back on at 3–2. It looks tight from what I can tell. It is. Ten minutes from time, and Celtic scores again to tie the game at 3–3. But no, Motherwell scores again to make it 4–3. Surely that's it, game over, but the Celtic fans get behind the team one last time, urging them on, and with one last corner kick into the box, they score. Final score: 4–4. For all the neutral supporters, a great result. I'm just relieved it's over. We are that much closer to getting away from the stadium and the gauntlet of media.

We head back inside. Andrew's waiting to take us to meet the players. This I could really do without, but I know the guys are keen to go.

"Guys, why don't I wait here while you all go ahead? My ears are ringing, and I really just want to sit here for a bit." I'm not in the mood for a meet and greet, having to smile at the right times and be polite.

"Libby, is everything okay?"

"Yes, Alex, everything is fine. Relax. Take your time. I'll still be here when you're all finished. I'll order a drink or something."

The guys hesitate, but I assure them I'm fine. Ethan's look is skeptical, but I send them all packing. Ashley comes over to the table looking extremely disappointed that it's only me she'll be serving for now, and she looks downright angry when I tell her that we won't be staying for a meal. I suppose she'll have to find someone else to shamelessly flirt with. I order another large white wine.

There is a steady stream of visitors to my table, so I don't get a moment to myself. That's unfortunate, since peace and quiet is rather what I'm wanting right now. Just when I think I've finally got a few moments alone, the voice I've come to despise today is there again. This time it sounds as though he's had a good bit to drink.

"So, 'lizbeth, he's left you already!" Jeff leans over my shoulder. "I'll just join you then. Looks like you could do with some company."

"I'd really rather you didn't, Jeff." I look him square in the eyes, and there is an old, familiar look in his bloodshot eyes. "You've been drinking."

"I may've had a few," he says. This is the first time in years

I have seen him this drunk. This could be an interesting conversation. "Where's the boyfriend?"

"He and Ethan are off meeting the players, if you're so interested." I answer drily.

I wish he would leave. I feel his arm on the back of my chair, then all too quickly, I feel his fingers on the back of my neck.

"Did I tell you how beautiful you look today?"

"Yes. Thank you." If I keep it short, he might go away. Wishful thinking on my part.

"Well, it's true, shweetie. I've really mished you," he says. I can smell the beer with every slurred syllable. His fingers brush against my face. This feels wrong. So wrong.

"Jeff ..."

"You don't have to say a thing, 'lizbeth. I know you shtill want me. An' I want you just as much as you want me."

"Seriously? Jeff, you are *delusional*." I try to shove my chair a foot away from him, my anger building, but he's holding my shoulder with one hand as he touches my face with the other. The look in his eyes tells me I need to get away, but it's too late. I see his face leaning towards me, and the grip he has on me is getting tighter. I try to pull away from him before his lips meet mine, but I'm too slow. The damage has been done.

I push him off. I am sitting in the middle of a full restaurant, so why is there no one here when I need them?

"Libby, I want you. I need to have you." He moves his hand from my face and runs it down the front of my body, finally resting it on my leg.

"Jeff, I do *not* want *you*," I say, my voice getting louder. "Go away!"

"No, I *really* want you," he growls as he attempts to slide his hand under my dress.

"I SAID, I DON'T WANT YOU! GET YOUR HANDS OFF ME!"

"I think you heard the lady," Alex hisses, pulling Jeff to his feet. Jeff struggles to stay upright, but I'm not sure if that's Alex's hand on Jeff's wrist or the alcohol Jeff's indulged in.

"Yeah, I heard her, but I know her better'n you. All you want is a quick fumble, nothing more. I'll be the one still here after you've dumped her and gone back to the States," snarls Jeff. I think he's trying to sound gallant, but it comes out sounding more like a threat. "I'll be the one left here to pick up the pieces."

I realise that all the people in the room have their attention turned to our table when I hear whispers and gasps. Ethan has me wrapped in his protective arms, and Michael is trying to coax Alex into letting go of Jeff. Alex looks pissed off, whilst Jeff just looks pissed. That I find funny because he was always so against drink.

Suddenly the room is a rush of activity, with security all heading in our direction. They take Jeff from Alex, and I can only presume he will get escorted off the premises. I feel Ethan's protective arms leave me, only to be replaced by Alex's. I lean my head on his chest, close my eyes, take several deep breaths, and finally relax in Alex's arms. I am fighting the urge to cry. How could this day get so bad?

"I am sorry, baby," Alex says.

"Sorry for what?" I lift my head slightly to look at him, and our eyes lock. His eyes grow wide. "I am sorry for leaving you alone and for you having to go through that. Although I am really surprised that he was ever your boyfriend. He doesn't deserve someone like you."

"Okay, point made. And I am not going to let him ruin our day anymore." I smile at him. "Have you finished your meet and greet? Because if you have, can we get out of here and just head to my parents' so I can relax?"

"Of course, baby, whatever you want," he answers, hugging me tightly.

"You're leaving already?" Michael says.

"Yes."

"Well, do you mind if I take off? I am going to go catch up with Kirsty."

"Go ahead," Alex says. I don't even have the inclination to question Michael.

Andrew gets a taxi for Michael, who heads off to pay Kirsty a visit. I hope he behaves with her. As much as Kirsty likes games, I don't want her to be taken advantage of or to get hurt. But I'm sure she's more than capable of looking after herself.

While I'm lost in thought worrying about her, Ethan has organised things so that we don't have to leave through the main entrance. I love my brother. I don't think I could face that again today.

CHAPTER 17

"*H*ey, are you all right?" Alex asks as he tucks a strand of hair behind my ear.

"Yeah, it's just been a challenging day with one thing and another. And we still have to talk," I murmur, thinking about today's turn of events and the conversation from last night with my parents. I am curious to hear about how he built his empire. I'm sitting in the back of the car leaning against Alex, who's had his arms wrapped round me since we left the football. I close my eyes to take a few moments for myself, and I feel myself relax for the first time today. I feel Alex's fingers trace my shoulder. His breath tickles my neck. I'm afraid to open my eyes. What if this is all a dream?

"Libby?"

The sensuality in his voice has my stomach in knots, and my heart skips a beat. My mind is racing. Am I always going to feel like this around him?

"What?" I whisper, looking timidly into those beautiful, brown eyes, eyes that could tell a thousand stories. Maybe one day I will hear all the stories he has to tell.

"We'll talk back at the hotel when we're alone, okay?" he says.

The journey from the stadium to my parents' isn't a long one, but it's a challenging drive with all the winding country roads. Everyone's quiet, even Ethan, and we all seem to be lost in our own thoughts. I'm looking forward to sitting in my parents' having a comfortable, relaxing time with some good food—and no unwanted guests or media.

Both my parents are great cooks. Because of my father's line of work, they entertain often, whether at home or out. Mum did most of the cooking at home when I was growing up, always using fresh ingredients and never any of the processed crap that fills the shop shelves. I used to love watching and helping her.

By the time we pull into the long drive of my parents' house, I definitely feel more at ease. This is home; it always has been, and it probably always will be. It's changed a lot over the years. It was once a small, cosy cottage, or so I have been told, but it's been extended over the years. I don't remember it ever being small.

The car stops in front of the house. Mark tells me to phone him when we're ready to leave, and he will take Alex and me back to the hotel. Ethan plans to stay here tonight. Mum must be in her element, having both Ethan and Lucy to spoil all night.

"This place is great," Alex says as he gets out of the car and looks around. "How much land is there here?" God, so much; Ethan and I used to get lost for hours playing.

"I really don't know. You'd need to ask my dad," I say, smiling at him with what I think is pride. I am glad he likes my family home.

I grab Alex's hand and drag him inside. Ethan is already way ahead of us. He must have been missing Lucy. As we walk through the house, the smell coming from the back is amazing. Dad has already started cooking on the BBQ.

"Hi, Mum," I say as we enter the kitchen. She smiles when she looks between us. I still have a hold of Alex's hand. I look at him. He smiles and shrugs lightly.

"Hi, sweetheart, Alex. Did you have fun at the football?"

"Yes, it was a great game, great atmosphere. It has me wondering what an Old Firm game would be like," Alex says enthusiastically.

"Oh, don't get Phil started on that …"

"Get Phil started on what?" My father enters the kitchen as if right on cue.

"Alex was just wondering about the atmosphere at an Old Firm game, dear," Mum says as she hands him a plate with raw steaks on it.

"Well, Alex, follow me and I can tell you while I cook these." Dad looks happy, and Alex looks interested.

"Where's Ethan?" I ask, looking around and not hearing any noise.

"When he came in, I was pacing the floor with Lucy. She's still a bit hot, so he took her out into the garden. Why don't you go and get them? You seem to have a way with our beautiful girl."

"Are you sure? Do you need a hand with anything in here?"

"On you go. Give your brother a hand." Mum gives me a reassuring smile. "Oh, Libby, I seen the statement Alex made today. You know you can talk to me anytime. No pressure—when you want to talk, I'm here. But I think this relationship is going to work out just fine."

I can only nod in response as I head outside in search of my brother. It doesn't take me too long to find him. He's at the far end of the back lawn singing. I love hearing him sing. He has such a beautiful voice. He is cradling Lucy in his arms. Such a wonderful sight. I can see the love he has for his baby girl. I stand watching them for a few moments.

When he stops singing, I approach. He's looking down anxiously at his daughter. Lucy does seem a bit on the grumpy side.

"What do you think is wrong with her? I don't have a clue. Maybe I'm not cut out for all this."

"Is this coming from the same person who just sang so beautifully to his little girl? She's just going to be like the rest of us, with good days and bad. Besides, even Mum doesn't know what's up with Lucy today, and she's the one with the experience, not us. Anyway, give her to me; I'll go change her and see if that helps." He places my niece in my arms.

She's definitely out of sorts, crying in my arms. I try to comfort her with soothing words to no avail. I leave Ethan with my dad and Alex, who smiles at me with his eyebrows raised. I pass him and head inside. His smile takes my breath away.

"Mum?" I call, entering the kitchen.

"Yes, Libby. Is Lucy all right?"

"Mum, do you think she could be teething?" I ask. Well, I don't know much about babies.

"You know, sweetie. You're absolutely right—that is a possibility. You know, when your time comes, you'll be a great mother."

"Mum … I'm going to change her. Where are all her things?" I've never really thought much about having kids, and until the first time I held Lucy in my arms, I wasn't sure I even wanted them. Once I held this precious girl, I knew I did … but not for a good few years yet.

"In the living room. I'll send your dad for some teething gel for this little one. For now, give her a piece of ice—wrap it in a cloth so she doesn't choke—to chew on. That'll help her some."

I'm sitting on the sofa with Lucy in my arms. She's content for the moment, cooing at me, and it's not long before a very familiar feeling runs through me. I glance up to find Alex watching me intently. How long has he been there?

"Do you need something? Or are you just standing there admiring the view?"

"I like the view, of course, but I wanted to see if *I* could help *you*. But you seem to have the situation in hand." He walks towards me and plops down beside me on the sofa. "She is such a beautiful baby. I see a lot of you and Ethan in her."

"Do you? I only see one person when I look at her: Lindsay. She's her mother's double," I say. I can hear the sadness in my own voice.

"I should confess that I was only being polite about seeing if you needed a hand. Babies and I don't usually go very well together."

Babies and him don't go well together? We'll see about that. I turn slightly towards him. "Nonsense. Are you ready?" Without giving him a chance to refuse, I hand Lucy to him. "Relax. If you don't, she'll sense your tension." He looks terrified. "So how come you're inside when there's all the footie talk outside?" I ask, smiling. He's relaxing a little.

"Ethan and your dad went off to a shop for teething gel. I'm guessing that's for this little one." His smile is infectious. I love seeing him smile. I see that Lucy does, too. She's staring up at him. "You're all such a close family." His face has darkened, saddened.

"Yeah, I suppose we are really close. We have our moments like most families, but the bond between Ethan and me—I really can't put it into words. And as for this little one …" I tickle Lucy under her chin, and I am rewarded with a giggle. "She has insured that the bond stays firmly in place. She means the world to us all. She's so precious."

"Yes, I can see that." Alex looks down at Lucy and then back at me with admiration in his eyes. "It must be hard on Ethan."

"You've no idea," I say, looking at Lucy. She's settling into his arms. Her tiny eyelids are heavy, and she's struggling to keep them open. Only a matter of time.

"Tell me, then." His voice is softer. "Help me understand."

"Ethan couldn't bring himself to look after Lucy at first. Mum and I went to the hospital and brought her home, as he couldn't even manage that. I moved into his house, which was right next door to his anyway, and I did everything in this little one's first few weeks home, from getting up for night-time feeds to bathing her, taking her out for walks, chatting with the health visitors. You name it, and I did it."

I lower my voice. Lucy's asleep.

"Ethan couldn't even do much of anything for himself. He was deeply depressed for weeks. I hated seeing him like that, but I made Lucy my first priority. He wouldn't even hold her. He was completely broken, but then … he'd lost the love of his life. That broke my heart. After a month or so, I spoke with the doctor and health visitor. They both made suggestions on how to help him. I was to start off easy with him—you know, start by leaving the room when Lucy got upset to see if he would go to her. I didn't leave her screaming for long periods of time, of course. At first, I would stand at the room door and watch him. After a few days of this, he still hadn't made any attempts to go to her. I thought it would never work. Then one day I had to deal with a problem at work over the phone, and it took a bit of time to work things out. I could hear Lucy crying—she was so upset!—and it went on for a bit longer than I would've let it. And then there was silence. I was a little scared, actually, and when I ended the call, I ran in and heard him sobbing."

Alex is listening intently, but it doesn't go unnoticed that he smiles tucking Lucy's blanket up around her more tightly. *Don't go well together, indeed.*

"I found Ethan standing in the middle of the room, cradling her, his tears flowing down. He was so upset. He held her as if his life depended on her, and in a way, it did. I knew then that they would be okay, and it made me happy … and a little sad too. And that was the first time he really spoke to me in nearly six weeks. He asked for my help. He wanted me to show him how to care for her."

I look at the beautiful girl now. She's sound asleep in Alex's arms without a care in the world.

"Libby, you truly are an amazing person," Alex says. He leans forwards, trying not to disturb sleeping beauty, and places a slow kiss on my lips.

"Thank you, but he's my brother, and I would do it all again in a second for him if I had to." It's true. I would. "I'm just so relieved that he's doing so well now with her on his own. It's been a long road. I made some tough decisions that affected us both, but in the long run, I know they were the right decisions to make. He knows I'm always here when he needs me, but I knew the longer I stayed doing everything, the harder it would be to walk away from her." The tears run slowly down my face. Alex wipes them away with his free hand. His touch is warm and gentle on my face.

"I think I know how you feel. You'd do anything for those you love." There's a sadness in his voice. Does he speak from experience? Should I ask him? Or wait until he wants to tell me?

"Yes, I would." I hear Dad and Ethan come back into the house. "Come on. I'll go put her down, and we can join the others."

"I'm fine with her. You just lead the way."

Ethan is out in the hall when we leave the living room. He raises his eyebrows when he sees Alex has Lucy.

"Interesting. How long has she been sleeping?"

"Not long. Hopefully she'll stay settled and let us eat. Because I am starving, and it smells delicious," I say as we head through to the kitchen. Lucy's pram is out in the garden. I bring it in so Alex can put her there. She doesn't wake.

"Libby, you're always starving. Where the hell do you put it?" Alex asks.

We eat at the kitchen table. I'm not sure who my parents were expecting; there's enough food to feed a small army— steaks, chicken, burgers, salads. The guys all have a few beers. Mum opens a bottle of wine for me, though she refuses to join me in a glass. I know that's because she wants to fuss over Lucy. The food is great and the company even better.

Alex looks at home with my family. That thought makes me feel sad, as I know he will be going to *his* home in a few weeks.

Late afternoon turns into evening. It's been great spending the day there, and I have loved watching Ethan with Lucy. He's so comfortable with her now. I'm so happy for them both. They do need each other. It's eight o'clock when Mark arrives to pick us up. I'm looking forward to some time alone with Alex when we get back to the hotel. I've already sent Kieran a text to have some chilled wine sent to my room.

We say our good-byes to everyone, saying we'll see them tomorrow.

"Remember what I said, sweetie. I'm always here to talk. But I think everything will be fine." Mum pulls me in tight. "Do you think you could get some time off Tuesday? I want to take you dress shopping."

"Why?" I ask.

"Because you're going to need something special for

Wednesday night's premiere down in London," she says. She smiles. "You can help me find something, too."

"What? Why?" I stammer.

"Your father and I are attending as well."

"Brilliant! Love you, Mum. See you tomorrow." I leave her embrace and take Alex's outstretched hands.

He slips his arm round my shoulder as we walk to the car. "I've had a great day with you. I hope you survived okay?"

Mark stands by the car with the back door open. "Thanks," I say to him as we get in the car. He nods in acknowledgement. "The day wasn't so bad considering what happened with Jeff. I really can't believe I wasted two years of my life on him."

"You know how it goes. We learn from our mistakes."

"He was a big mistake, so I must have learned a lot."

I lean into Alex while Mark drives us back to the hotel. Now would be as good a time as any to talk. I cuddle against Alex's arm round my shoulder, and he smiles at me sweetly. Then he turns and looks out the window. I sense a change. He's deep in thought.

"Alex ... can we talk?" He glances at Mark. "Mark has been a driver with my father for years. I'm sure he's heard a lot worse over the years than anything I want to talk about."

"Okay, go ahead then."

"All right, a couple of things about today. The film premiere? When were you going to ask me? I'm not sure I'm comfortable meeting Katherine Hunter."

"I was going to mention it today, but then we were ambushed by the media circus. Things kind of got out of hand at the stadium, don't you think?"

"Yes. Ambush is a good word for it. That's the kind of public spotlight I've tried to avoid all my life," I say. "Well, since Tony, I should say. Before that I never worried about it."

Alex pulls me in tight and strokes my arm. "I am sorry. It's all my fault." I can hear the anguish in his voice. I grow still in his arms.

"No, this isn't your fault," I say. "But to get back to the matters I wanted to talk about. The premiere—when is it? I will need to organise the hotel."

"Wednesday night. Your dad wants to fly down in the afternoon. The hotel rooms are booked," he says with a no-nonsense attitude.

"We're staying over?" I question.

"Unless you have a better idea?" He sounds snappish. *What's up with him?* Maybe he's regretting some of the things he said today? I shake my head and sigh.

I unstrap my seat belt and slide over. My dress rises slowly as I straddle him. I hope this works. He glances down, his eyes running ever so slowly from my bare thighs up my body. I try to keep composed. It's taking all my willpower. When his eyes finally reach mine, I see the wicked spark slowly emerging in those deep, brown eyes. I have definitely got his attention. All focus is entirely back on me.

"Libby, what are you doing?"

"What does it look like? I'm putting a smile back on your handsome face and hopefully putting you back in a better mood." I grin wickedly. Some parts of his body are definitely feeling happier.

"I was slightly distracted. A few things on my mind. But now you are my distraction … and a mighty fine one at that."

I wrap my arms round his strong shoulders. A few days ago, just the thought of being this forward with a man would have had me feeling embarrassed. And yet here I am, not nervous in the slightest.

"As tempting as you are, Miss Stewart, I would much rather be alone with you." Alex leans in with his mouth so close to mine, I can almost feel the kiss I am eagerly waiting for. My body is eager for his touch. His eyes tell me their own story, what he is desperate for. He wants me just as much as I want him. "Sorry, baby. It will be worth the wait, though." He pulls back with an extremely smug look. Oh, he knows exactly what he's doing. Well, as I keep telling him, or at least thinking at him, two can play this game. I remove myself from his lap, straightening out my dress at the hem, turn face to the window, and cross my arms.

"So. The film premiere," I say, though I don't turn to look at him. "Were you going to ask if I wanted to go? Or were you always just expecting me to do as I'm told?"

"No, Libby. I wanted to ask you if you would accompany me as my plus-one, my date. But as you well know, I was somewhat put on the spot today. I would have asked before we went to the football, but the business with Michael distracted me, I guess. I cleared this up a few moments ago?" I nod. "My sincere apologies. Now was that all you wanted to speak about, or is there something else?"

God, what can I say to that? I have a mountain of things running through my head. What does Katherine Hunter mean to him? What do I mean to him? After his comments to the waiting vultures, I want to know. Then there's his cryptic comment about doing things to protect our loved ones … what did he mean? I know there's a meaning behind it. I could tell from the expression on his face.

"Tell me what Katherine Hunter means to you." My voice is low. He doesn't answer for a moment. Was it so low that he didn't hear me?

"Libby, turn around."

No, he heard me all right. I turn slowly round but can't bring myself to look into those beautiful eyes. I keep my eyes down, looking at my hands. He cups my face with both his hands, tilting it, so I have nowhere else to look but directly into his face. He brushes his thumb slightly over my cheek.

I'm trying to concentrate on my breathing, which is always a difficult task in proximity to Alex. My mind is racing with all the possible things he could say to me. Does he regret what was said today, or does he want me?

"Katherine Hunter is a family friend. I've known her and her family for a number of years. There are no romantic feelings—on my part, at least. I wouldn't presume to speak for her. She's got a mind of her own—like you." He pauses, trying to gauge my reaction. "Yes, there have been a few photos of the two of us out together lately, but your dad's in the business, so you know—that sort of thing is beneficial to people like us. And since she's my friend, I'd like you two to meet. I'm sure you'll love her."

He leans forward, and this time there is no hesitation on his part as our lips meet. The passion is there. When he pulls back from me, all I see is desire.

"What else do you want to know?"

"Well, you did say something about us at football, and I was wondering what you meant?" I mutter nervously. Why does this question make me nervous?

"I see." He's gazing at me intently. "Libby, I meant every word I said. Yes, you are a lovely woman, and I'm loving the time I'm spending with you. But yet again I find myself apologising to you."

"Why?"

"Because I'm too selfish where you are concerned. Your life is going to be scrutinised by the media—not just here but worldwide—and all because of our relationship. I'm not being vain, just honest, when I say that I'm big in the news right now. I'm young, and I get more successful every day, and that makes for good headlines," he says. "I should do the right thing where you are concerned and walk away to give you back your privacy. I should, but I don't want to. I don't think I would even be *able* to do that, to walk away now."

I am totally lost for words. He's completely taken my breath away. He doesn't want to walk away from me. What will that mean when his visit is finished?

"You're deep in thought, baby," he says, stroking my face.

"I'm just thinking that I'm happy," I say, snuggling back into his arm.

"I'm happy too. You've made me feel happy." He sighs. "These feelings are all completely new to me. I never thought I was ready for, wanted, or had time for a relationship just yet, but with you it feels … different."

Happy and content. That's how I feel right now as I sit in the back of the car with Alex's strong arms around me. Taken care of. Is that what I crave? Someone to take care of me? Could Alex be the one to take care of me? I always thought of myself as independent. I can't even begin to explain my feelings. Can I really have such strong feelings for someone I've known only a few days? Is it lust or love? I suppose only time will tell.

CHAPTER 18

*W*hat the hell?

I am standing in the middle of the sitting room surveying the case and suit carriers slung over the back of the couch.

"I see they made the trip." Alex laughs at my confusion.

"These belong to you?" I eye him curiously.

"Yes."

"So why are they here?"

"I just thought …"

"You thought what?"

"Well, if you would let me finish my sentence, you would know," he says, sighing with a mock exasperation. "I thought I would free up a room for you. I've spent every night with you so far, and I want to spend *all* my nights going to bed with you and my mornings waking up with you. Was that too presumptuous?"

Alex approaches me cautiously. He's a wise man. Who am I kidding? I want the same. I have enjoyed my nights and mornings with him, both in bed and out of it.

"I hope you're not angry. If you are, I can move them

back, although I think I'd have to share with Michael, as Kieran has already booked my room out."

"So ... I'm stuck with you?" I grin.

I walk toward the table where Kieran has left a bottle of champagne chilling, along with some rather tasty-looking strawberries. This could be the perfect way to end what has been, on the whole, a good day. I can shrug off the whole Jeff incident. Alex puts his arms round my waist and rests his chin on my shoulder.

"What are we doing for the rest of the evening?" he asks. His voice is low and seductive. I have really got a feel for being in his arms. It feels like the safest place in the world.

"I want to get out of these clothes and shoes and spread out on that couch with your arms wrapped around me, then maybe see what else we can get up to. But most of all just enjoy your company," I say. The grin on my face must tell a story.

"I can certainly help on all accounts." Alex's mouth curls at the edges into a sexy smile. God, I love that smile. There must be a thousand meanings behind it, but the only one that interests me is that he wants me. Me. "But I'll let you go and change by yourself because if I come through there, the only certainty is that we will end up in bed. You go change, and I'll open this." He picks up the champagne bottle and removes the wire cage over the cork.

I quickly change into shorts and a vest top. I wash the makeup off my face and unpin my hair letting it fall softly round my shoulders before returning. Alex has moved the suit carriers from the couch, probably to the entry closet. His suit jacket and tie are now draped round the back of one of the chairs, and his shoes are placed neatly on the floor underneath. The champagne is open and already poured. There is music flowing round the room.

He hands me a bubble-filled glass. I have a feeling this

will go straight to my head after the wine earlier. He takes my hand as he goes towards the couch. I take a drink before placing the glass on the small table that he's moved. He positions himself on the couch, pulling me so that I am between his legs, leaning into his chest. I love the closeness between us.

"So you share my father's love of football?"

"I'll let you in on a secret. I couldn't come all this way without seeing a football game. Your country has such a passion for it. But I could've watched any game."

"What do you mean?" I ask, surprised.

"I mean I do my homework. It wouldn't have mattered what *teams* I watched today. I just wanted to experience the buzz. Let me put it another way. If you come—no, let me rephrase that—*when* you come to America, what sport would you like to go see?"

Seriously? He wants me to go to the States? A visit with him. Would I? Of course I would.

"That's an easy question. Baseball."

"That's how I feel about football. So I did some research. Simple." He takes a drink.

"But all that talk about an Old Firm game and how excited you were today?"

"Libby, I think we can agree on the fact that most people know about the Old Firm—the Celtic and Rangers rivalry. Unlike a lot of people in my country, I really enjoy the sport, but I also wanted your dad and Ethan to feel comfortable with me. I studied up, read up on the Scottish teams. Like I said: I did my homework. I knew the right things to say to your dad and Ethan. I really liked meeting both sets of players. That's not something I get to do every day. How many people can say they've done that? Most of the day was perfect." He strokes my cheek.

"I'm just sorry I couldn't protect you from the media and

Jeff. I can always try to control the paparazzi …" He sees my raised eyebrows asking a silent question. "Baby, there's *always* a way to at least try to manage the media, and for you I would be willing to try anything. But as for Jeff, that's not so easy. I hope our paths don't cross again, because he'll get no second chances with me."

"As far as I'm concerned, you did protect me from Jeff. You're my very own knight in shining armour," I say. "But I can't guarantee you won't run into him again during your visit." I lift my glass of champagne and take a drink. "Your paths are bound to cross again if you do business with his boss. He could be here tomorrow with Simon."

"Well, if so, I hope he behaves better than he did today," Alex says sharply. He kisses my cheek all too quickly. I sigh. "What's wrong?"

"Nothing at all."

"Libby, don't give me that." His eyes lock with mine. The gaze we share is intense. I'm beginning to understand that look. He shakes his head at me. "No. Well, not yet anyway. I'm enjoying sitting here with you just talking."

"Okay. What do you want to talk about?"

"Anything at all."

"I have a question," I say, grinning at him. "When am I going to America? And why?"

"Libby, that's two questions. Okay, I'll answer," he says. "I would love you to come home with me when I am finished with my work here. There are so many places I'd love to take you, but what I really want is for you to meet my family. My mom is looking forward to meeting you. She's been on the phone a few times since the story broke."

God, I wasn't expecting that. He spoke to his mum about me? He wants me to meet her? God, this is moving fast. How will I find the time between running the hotel and the trial in a few weeks. Ethan will need me for that. There's absolutely no way I can leave him to deal with that without me. I take a deep breath.

"I don't think that's possible—at least not right away." Alex looks puzzled and hurt. "I would love to … honestly, I would. But Ethan needs me here. The trial starts in a few weeks." He looks puzzled. "The man who caused the car accident in which Lindsay died—there is a plea hearing this coming week, and if he pleads not guilty, there will be a trial. I don't know much about the legalities of it all, but I do know that no matter what, I want to be here for Ethan."

"Is that the only reason you are saying no?" He can't hide his disappointment.

"Yes. No. There's this place as well, I suppose."

"Libby, I would never ask you to make a choice. Ethan needs you here, and I understand that. But what about *after* the trial? You must have some holidays you can take? I do know how to compromise."

"Of course, I do. I could probably take a few weeks off. I would need to make sure Kieran is fine for cover. And of course, there's my father."

"I'm sure both your parents would be happy. They seem very focused on wanting both you and Ethan to be happy. And at the moment that's all I really care about—making you happy." He traces his thumb along my lips.

Happy. At this moment I am deliriously happy, but for how long? I am falling way over my head, and there's not a thing I can do to stop the smash that is bound to happen sooner or later. *Why am I always waiting on bad things to happen? Why can I not just focus on here and now?* Alex pours some more champagne into both our glasses.

"A toast then," he says, handing me my glass.

"To what?"

"To happiness." Our glasses clink together before we each take a drink. "And to one of the most beautiful, thoughtful, and caring women I've ever had the pleasure of meeting."

I flush. I don't take compliments well. He is full of surprises.

"Anything else you want to talk about? I've told you about my family. We are all pretty close, much like yours. But I presume it's more the business you want to know?"

"Well, I suppose I am interested to learn more about you and your business. I want all the details, so don't leave anything out."

"As I said last night, the law never really appealed to me, and I think my parents felt let down in a way. Not that, that's how they feel now; I know they are proud of me. But I was a bit rebellious, as my mom would put it."

"So why casinos?"

"Because it was a gamble, pure and simple. I thrive on the rush, the adrenaline. The casinos I've kept—that's my business—but the other businesses that I've bought and turned around before selling on, they all gave me the same feelings. There are always risks in what I do. Some have worked out extremely beneficially for me, and someday I might not be so lucky, but I've managed to invest money wisely, so I don't think there will be a time when I am broke. But even if that happens, I think I will still be happy."

"So that explains some things. But how did you first start out? Where did the money first come from?"

"You really want to know? Well, my grandfather left all of his grandchildren money, and let's just say I invested some wisely and some not so wisely, although the unwise investments actually paid off. The casino rewarded me well."

"Are telling me you made your fortune through gambling? Surely not."

"Afraid so. I don't mean I have gambled my money away on the tables, personally. Well, let's just say I have done extremely well out of a business deal that looked like I would lose a lot That's the reason I was so interested in this group when it went into administration."

"What about your hotel," I ask curiously.

"I only acquired that recently. It wasn't doing well and I got it at a good price. I wasn't intending keeping it, but you never know. Now I am sure we're not going to sit all night and talk business, are we?"

No, I don't suppose we will.

"Strawberry?" he asks, holding the red fruit just in front of my lips. I nod and open my mouth, but he pulls it playfully away from me and puts in in his own mouth instead.

So, he's in a playful mood. I put my glass down on the table and turn around. I take his glass from his hand and put it down as well. I position myself so that I am straddling him and pick up the bowl of strawberries. I make a big deal of inspecting them for the perfect one to feed him. He opens his mouth, and I tease it onto his tongue slowly. He starts to close his lips over it, but I pull it back out and pop it in my own mouth.

"Hey, that's not fair!"

"What? You did the very same to me." I laugh as I take another from the bowl. I slide it into his mouth, but I let him eat it this time.

"Mmm, these are good," he says.

I take another strawberry and place it between my teeth, leaning close. He leans down, mouth open. *This has possibilities*. His mouth closes round mine. His lips are soft. He bites and pulls back quickly, eating his half of the strawberry.

I need to kiss him. I've spent the whole day with him, and now I need more. A lot more. I kiss him as if my life depended on it. I close my eyes, lost in the moment. My arms go around his neck. He has one arm on my back and the other hand wrapped in my hair. His tongue invades my mouth, coaxing me, but I really don't need much coaxing. Heat surges through my body.

He pulls my hips down onto him. I grind against him, trying to work myself into a pleasurable position, but the feeling just intensifies. I moan as I hug him tighter. He pulls back. No, I need this. I need this connection between us. And I am sure he needs it too. I open my eyes.

His eyes meet mine. He is so hot. I want him. I move my arms from his neck, at the same time placing small kisses on his face. My hands stop at his shirt, and I slowly start to unbutton it. I pause after each button and place a kiss on his skin.

"Libby … what are you doing?"

"You can't tell?"

"I think I've figured it out."

Soon I have all the buttons undone, and I slide his shirt off, tossing it on the floor. My hands do a bit of roaming from his strong back to his muscular chest and down to the waist of his trousers. This is all about his pleasure, not mine. I slide off his lap and undo his trousers, sliding them and his boxers off and tossing them onto the floor beside his shirt.

"Libby, I feel a little … exposed here in my birthday suit. Why do you still have all your clothes on?"

"Well, if you must know, I am admiring you in all your glory," I say. "It's a very impressive suit, Mr Mathews."

"You are easily impressed, then, Miss Stewart," he whispers. I giggle.

I take a slow sip of champagne, then position myself on my knees on the couch. I touch my lips to him, running my tongue over the smooth tip, feeling the tiny bubbles pop on my tongue. He inhales sharply and closes his eyes. He's hard. He groans. I glance up at him through my eyelashes. His eyes are still closed.

"Fuck," he moans softly.

I take him farther into my mouth, deeper, sucking him in, working my tongue against him. I pull back slowly and run my tongue over and round the tip, teasing him. I'm still watching him. He opens his eyes, which are blazing with fire, and I open my mouth wider to take him in deeper until he's pressing the back of my throat, filling my mouth completely with his hardness. He reaches down and takes a tight hold of my shoulders, and I can tell he's fighting the urge to move his hips.

"Libby, that feels so good. Don't stop. Please." It sounds more like a whimper coming from him.

I slide him out, then thrust down, deep, then pull back again, sucking him, and at the same time, massaging the base of his shaft with my hands. I'm not sure how much longer he'll be able to take it. Christ, I don't know how much longer *I* can take it; I am so turned on by the sounds he's making, by the way he's writhing and trying not to control me. He starts to move, thrusting with me. I push him all the way to the back of my mouth and pull back. Again. Again. It won't be long. Harder and deeper. Again and again, pushing him to the edge.

"Libby" he cries out.

I can feel the warm, salty fluid bursting from him. I swallow quickly as his thrusts slow until he comes to a stop. His rapid breathing starts to slow down.

"Libby, that was amazing. I don't know what to say. You completely took my breath away."

Good. Mission complete. He pulls me back up towards him. The grin on his face is wicked. He pulls me into his arms tightly and kisses me hard, his tongue pushing into my mouth, exploring, tasting. My tongue meets his with the same passion. He slowly pulls back and stares intently into my eyes. His eyes are smouldering. I break the spell by turning and lifting one of the glasses of champagne. I take a sip first before lifting the glass to his mouth. He takes a long, slow drink. The look on his face tells me he is purposely drawing this out. I pull the glass away and put it back down.

His eyes run over my body. He has a mischievous look in those beautiful, brown eyes. He is up to no good.

"Miss Stewart, as I said earlier, you are wearing way too much clothing," he says. "I think we should get rid of that top, don't you?"

"I don't know. I've always really liked this colour on me," I say with a giggle.

"Arms." His voice sounds authoritative. He pulls my vest top over my head. "Now we're nearly even."

As he runs his hands lightly over my breasts, I try to focus on his face rather than the sensation that is sweeping through my entire body. But that doesn't help me. His expression is full of desire, and his eyes are full of fire.

"Now the shorts," he whispers. He quickly removes my shorts and panties in the one go. "Much better."

He's hovering above me, watching me, his deep, brown eyes hypnotizing me. I could stay under his spell forever. He leans down and places a soft kiss on my lips. I wish I could read his mind. His lips move slowly to my throat, kissing me.

"I want to kiss you all over. Every single inch of your body. And when I finish, I'm going to start all over again," he says softly.

I am breathless with his words. He trails small kisses up and down each of my arms. He stops at my breasts, and the kissing gets deeper. Kissing and sucking. He sucks and pulls on my nipples with precise care and attention. My already too-sensitive skin reacts to his touch, shivering and burning at the same time. I'm not sure how long my body will hold up with this continued teasing. It's already showing signs of letting me down.

"Please try and keep still, baby."

"I can't. I need you," I whimper.

"Libby, you have me. I'm right here with you." He's smiling.

"Alex, please …"

He shakes his head and continues his travels down my body. His lips glide over my belly. It won't be long until the fire that's slowly burning within me is out of control.

I close my eyes as I feel him between my legs, pressing them farther apart. Then he's right there, licking and sucking, softly. My body moves.

"Libby, I asked you to keep still."

"I can't," I say. "I don't want to. I just want you. I need you."

"I know you do."

He continues licking and sucking. Again and again. His tongue dances slowly over my clit. I'm so close to losing my self-control. No, I lost that self-control when I first clapped eyes on him. He slides one finger inside me, then another. He moves them round, stretching me, and at the same time, his tongue moves around and around. I can't take much more. I am so close to the edge.

"Alex, please," I whimper.

"Not yet, baby."

Not yet? Is he serious? The licking and sucking. Deeper and deeper. Dizzy. My head is spinning out of control. The mist descends. My body needs the release. I can no longer hang on. I let go, calling his name. It takes a few minutes for everything to come back into focus. The mist has lifted. I am still panting when he crawls slowly up my body.

I open my eyes as his lips descend on mine with a consuming passion. I can still taste him, and as he pushes his tongue into my mouth, I can taste myself.

"Libby, you know we're not done yet."

I can only nod my head. I don't think I have the ability to speak yet. He stares at me, maybe trying to second-guess me.

"Turn over," he commands.

I slowly turn over, so I am lying on my front. He pushes both my legs up the couch so that my ass is in the air. How dignified.

"Arms? Take your weight on your arms. Comfortable?"

Comfortable, no, but anticipating what's about to happen.

Before I can reply, he plunges deep inside me and stills as I cry out.

"Are you okay?"

"Yes," I whisper.

He grabs my hips as he slowly starts to move. My breathing quickens as he goes deeper with each thrust. The pace picks up, and he continues to slide in and out of me. The desire is burning within, building.

"Libby, I hope you're close." He groans.

I can't answer him. I am so close as the tempo builds. His hips meet mine harder with each thrust, and my body responds the only way it knows how. I shatter around him, and he stills, finally letting go with his own release. He collapses on top of me, and I sink deep into the couch. I am panting, struggling to catch my breath, totally spent. I wish I could find my voice. I need him to move off my back. As if he hears my unspoken thoughts, he quickly rolls onto his side, moving me to face him.

"Hello," I say.

"Hello, yourself. You okay? That wasn't too rough, was it?"

"No, I'm fine." I glance down my side. I have a few small, red finger marks on my waist. His eyes follow my gaze. He places a hand on the marks and massages them softly.

"Sorry. I just got carried away. You seem to have that effect on me." He's different, concerned.

I lean towards his face and place a soft, lingering kiss on his lips. He looks surprised.

"Am I forgiven?"

"What's to forgive? We had sex. Intense, amazing sex. I have a couple of red marks, but they're nothing. I can't even feel them," I say, trying to reassure him, but I'm not sure it's working.

"Intense, amazing … are you sure?"

"Did I not just tell you that? What's wrong?"

"It's just … I never want to hurt you," he says.

This conversation has gotten way too serious all of a sudden. I sit up and take his hand gently, tugging it.

"Come on—let's get cleaned up and into bed," I say with a giggle, hoping to lift his mood.

My giggle seems to have done the trick. There's a glimmer of light in his eyes that wasn't there a minute ago. His grin is mischievous. He gets up off the couch in one quick move and pulls me up, and before I know it, he's picked me up and thrown me over his shoulder.

"Put me down!" I shriek, pounding my fists on his back playfully.

My words fall on deaf ears. He's laughing at me as he strolls into the bedroom and then into the bathroom, where he finally sets me down on the cold, tiled floor. As I stand brushing my teeth, Alex tosses in my shorts and vest.

"I thought you might like these back."

"How thoughtful," I say. "Do I really need them?"

He stands staring, shaking his head as I pull my clothes back on. I notice he has pulled on a pair of pyjama bottoms, ones that hang low on his hips, showing off that toned physique. I walk towards him and stand on my tiptoes to place a very brief kiss on his lips before walking into the bedroom. I know his eyes have followed me into the room; I can feel them.

In bed I go through the messages on my phone and reply to a few e-mails. It looks like my day tomorrow will be a long one. Kieran has left a message saying that Karl is short staffed in the kitchen tomorrow; two highly experienced staff have walked out, and Kieran thinks we could also do with an extra pair of hands at the function. The joys. I call him.

"Hi, Libby. You got my message then?"

"Hi, Kieran. A bad night, I take it?"

"Oh, Libby, you've no idea, although Karl says he's seen this coming. He just didn't think they would walk out on a busy weekend. But I think they had planned together to quit at the same time at a time like this when it would hurt us most. So please tell me you have a plan, honey?"

Alex chooses this moment to climb into bed beside me and snuggle up, making me giggle.

"Libby?"

"Kieran, yes, I have a plan. Of course I do." Alex is studying me closely. "I presume you've already tried to get some agency staff?"

"Yes, before I called you."

"Okay, then. If you think we need extra to cover waiting at the function, perhaps you could cover that? It's only for a few hours. I don't anticipate that there would be any major problems on a Sunday afternoon."

"Right, fair enough. But what about the kitchen? There is no way Karl can put out lunches *and* a four-course meal for three-hundred people, all on his own."

"He won't be on his own," I say quickly.

"Well, spit it out."

"I'll be in the kitchen all day." I look at Alex as I speak. He smiles, shaking his head at me.

"Libby, are you sure? You're meant to attend the event tomorrow," Kieran says.

"Of course I'm sure. I've worked in that kitchen often enough over the years—and anyway, there is no way I am letting my staff put in extra effort tomorrow while I sit back and do nothing. You know I wouldn't let that happen. Make sure Karl has the other chefs in early and double-check that all the waiting staff are in, and if anybody has the day off, call them, or I can call them."

"Right. Okay, honey. That sounds like a plan. I'll be in extra early in the morning. Let's meet in the kitchen at six to coordinate with Karl, okay?"

"That sounds perfect. Can you let Karl know tonight for me that I'll be covering so he doesn't panic? Starting from breakfast on. And if I have to work all day and night, I will. I'll let my dad know of the change of plans."

"Yes, I'll let Karl know. I think he was *hoping* you'd help, because the other option was me, and you and I both know that I'm hopeless in the kitchen." Kieran laughs.

"Oh, I know. Now, I'll see you bright and early. Six a.m. Don't be late."

"*I* won't. Now tell lover boy to leave you in peace tonight so you can make it on time. We can't have you falling asleep in the soup tomorrow."

Alex has obviously heard Kieran. He playfully shoves my shoulders and pulls me towards him, laughing.

"Good night, Kieran."

"Good night, honey."

I flop back in the bed. *God, I hope I can pull this off tomorrow.*

"Libby, are you okay?" The concern is there in Alex's voice.

"Yes, I'm fine. But now I really have to get some sleep. Please?"

"Why are you asking me?" says Alex. "Were you planning something more? Haven't you had enough yet?"

"My plans for the rest of the night were just to lie in your arms and talk. I want to learn more about you, Alex. I want to know it all—no stone left unturned."

"We have plenty of time to talk. There's loads more I want to know about you as well." He leans towards me, and our lips meet, not with passion or lust but with what I think is *love*. Maybe I'm just reading too much into this. "Come on then, Miss Stewart. You have a busy day ahead. I'll miss you tomorrow."

CHAPTER 19

"*T*wo full Scottish breakfasts and one smoked salmon!" Kieran shouts as he enters the kitchen. "How're you getting on?"

"We're good. Aren't we, Chef?" I answer.

"Libby Stewart, if you call me that once more, I won't be responsible for my actions," Karl says, laughing.

I laugh too. For eight in the morning, we are all in good spirits. The hotel is full, so breakfast is extremely busy. Kieran is working the restaurant floor with two members of the waiting staff. He made a few last-minute changes to today's rota so we would have enough staff between the function and the restaurant later on. In the kitchen this morning, it's just me, Karl, and an assistant. Karl is leaving me to do the breakfasts so he can make a start on the lunch meals. I'm so glad it's a fixed meal; at least that gives us a fighting chance.

Karl and I are so busy in the kitchen that the morning is flying by. So far, so good. We're not stressed yet, but it's still early. At nine thirty Kieran comes into the kitchen, singing

229

away. He's very cheery considering he's not a morning person, and he's already been at work for over three hours.

"Okay, guys, that's all the breakfast guests. Everyone's been accounted for between the restaurant and room service," Kieran says with a huge smile on his face.

Relief sweeps over me. Round one completed. Just the rest of the day to get through, and then we should be laughing.

"Right, Miss Stewart. Are you ready for next round?" Karl asks.

"Of course. I'm having fun," I say. Well, if I'm honest, I'm really enjoying it. I love cooking, and I love the buzz of a fast-paced kitchen. If I hadn't done management, this is where I would be, deep in the heart of the hotel.

"Libby, I have one guest who wants to complain to the chef. Can you deal with it please?" Kieran is pleading with me, but he looks rather suspicious.

"Libby, I can go if you like," Karl says. Kieran is shaking his head. He doesn't think I've noticed.

"It's fine. I'll go," I say. I follow Kieran out into the restaurant, and he turns and smiles at me. I know exactly which table I have to go to before Kieran gets there. Alex and Michael are sitting by the window. "I understand that there's a problem, gentlemen?"

"No problem with the food. The only problem I had was that when I woke up in your bed, you were already gone." Alex smiles, holding out his hand to me. I take it even though I am working.

"Alex ..."

"Can you two give it a rest for five minutes? Libby, don't take offence, but I'm kind of glad you'll be working all day so I don't have to sit watching all this mushy shit," Michael says, laughing as he gets up from the table. He walks over to talk with Kieran and give us some privacy.

"I like this on you," Alex says, motioning at what I'm wearing. It's just typical chef clothes—black-and-white-checked trousers and black jacket, my hair pulled back in a hairnet. "Can you keep those on later? You look kind of hot right now, and I think I would take great pleasure in helping you out of those."

I feel myself blush. I knew that was what he was thinking. It's written all over his face, from the smug grin to the look of desire in those beautiful eyes.

"I want to kiss you," he whispers, "but I won't. I'll try and be patient today, although where you're concerned, I'm finding that extremely difficult."

"I'd better get back. It's just me and Karl right now. The other guys come in about an hour."

"So, you're really going to work in there all day then? What time do you think you'll finish?"

"Of course I am. I never back down from a challenge," I reply quickly.

"Do you need a hand?"

"Have you ever worked in a kitchen before?" I ask. He needs to say no; he would be too much of a distraction for me.

"Do you want me to be honest?" I nod. "Well then, no, I haven't."

"Sorry, Alex, you would get in the way," I say. "I'll try to see you as soon as we've finished serving the meals, but we'll have other lunches to serve here in the restaurant as well. I'm sure my parents will look after you, and Kirsty is coming as well. I'm *positive* Kirsty will keep everyone at the table entertained."

"Okay. I better let you get to work. If you still have any energy left over later, maybe we could do something tonight … maybe go out to a club or drinks?"

"We'll see how I feel when I finish—whenever that will

be." I give him a brief kiss before walking away from him for the rest of the day.

The rest of the morning flies by. I work with Karl the whole time, which goes well considering that I've never worked alongside him. I have worked in the kitchen before, so I know my way around, and it helps that I can actually cook. When the other chefs arrive, they all set about their tasks. The atmosphere in the kitchen is relaxed, considering we are down two highly experienced chefs. The young guys have proven their worth so far today. I think a bonus could be in order.

My parents pop into the kitchen when they arrive. Dad tells me the hall looks perfect, and he's proud of me for the way I've handled today. I know how much today means to him—the charity event is always well attended, and a lot of money is raised for the kids' hospital. My parents don't linger in the kitchen long, as they have guests to see to. I am a bit nervous. I know that Jeff is at my father's table, along with Alex. I told my mum what happened yesterday. She promised to keep an eye on things with them and Kirsty.

"Right, guys, and Miss Stewart. Gather round," Karl says. He's about to read the menu for today's event.

STARTERS
Seared Scallops with Black Pudding and a Sweet Chili Glaze
or
Wild Mushroom Risotto

INTERMEDIATE COURSE
Pea and Fresh Mint Soup

❧

MAIN COURSE
Fillet of Venison with a Red Wine Jus
or
Caramelized Onion and Goat Cheese Tart
(Both served with new potatoes and seasonal vegetables)

❧

DESSERT
Cranachan Cheesecake
Tea and Coffee

HE FINISHES off by telling us what we are all doing for service. Just as I have been so far today, I will be working with Karl. I am plating up at the serve over.

I can hear the MC informing every one of the running order of today's events as we start plating up. Just on cue the waiting staff, along with Kieran, arrive to start taking the food to the tables. At the same time, the first lunchtime order comes in from the restaurant. Now the fun begins.

Oh. My. God. By three thirty we have served a four-course meal to three-hundred people, and we've served eighty covers in the restaurant. It's time for everyone in the kitchen to have a break. I decide to go and see everyone at my father's table. Seated there are Mum, Dad, Ethan, Alex, Michael, Kirsty, Jeff, Simon and his wife, and an empty seat where I should be.

"Afternoon, I hope you enjoyed your meals?" I ask.

"Sweetheart, everything was perfect! How have you coped

in there today?" Mum's voice is caring and concerned, but I know she has faith in me.

"Mum, it's been great. Such fun! The guys have all pulled their weight today, and I have really enjoyed working alongside Karl." I think I see a flicker of suspicion on Alex's face. Surely, he's not jealous? "Is everything going well out here?"

"Yes, everything is running smoothly. I wish you could be out here with us," Mum says.

"I can't believe you've spent the whole day working … in the kitchen especially!" Kirsty squeals. "You'll need *two* showers before we head out tonight."

"What do you mean 'out'?" I ask, staring at Kirsty.

"We're going clubbing," she announces.

Clubbing. What a thought. I was thinking of a long, hot soak in the tub with Alex. That sounds so much more appealing, as I have a very good idea how that would pan out.

"I said maybe, but I can tell you right now that my feet are killing me," I say.

"Only if you feel up to it," Alex says, studying my face.

"Oh, come on, Libby. We've not done that in ages!" says Kirsty. "You know it'll be fun. And we have to take the guys out at least once." Her voice sounds quite whiny.

"Okay. I guess I'll be alright," I say, watching Alex. He smiles, shaking his head.

Out of the corner of my eye, I catch Jeff gulping down his wine and quickly refilling his glass. God, I hope he at least manages to keep his opinions to himself today. And I hope he doesn't get any ideas about following us to the clubs. Alex follows my gaze and frowns before mouthing, *its fine; don't worry about him.* But after yesterday how can I not worry?

I continue talking to everyone except Jeff. I can't bring myself to even look at him. I've only been at the table for a few minutes, and in that short time, Jeff has finished off two large glasses of red wine and is working on a third. Not a good sign. His body language is sending off some really strong vibes, and they're certainly not good ones. If looks could kill, I wouldn't be standing any longer.

When I make my way back through the function suite into the kitchen, I can feel at least two sets of eyes following me. Alex's isn't the set that worries me; I've gotten used to his gaze the last few days. No, the one giving me cause for concern is Jeff's.

"Libby, come on. Join the rest of us on break, won't you?" Karl shouts from across the kitchen.

"In a few minutes. I want to get all these dry ingredients back in store. I won't be long. Could someone make me a cup of tea, please?"

"Okay. You have five minutes to be in the canteen before I come looking for you," he says with a grin.

"I'll be there. Don't worry about that."

I make a start on getting all the dry ingredients back in the store. It will take a few trips. I gather up some of the jars of spices and carry them across the kitchen. I can't believe I gave into Kirsty so easily about a night out clubbing, although I am looking forward to dancing with Alex. I bet he can move. Just the thought of it sends shock waves all the way through my core.

I open the storeroom door using my elbow since my arms are full. I make sure to put everything away in its correct place, as I know how fussy Karl is. That's not true. He's not fussy. He's professional, exceptionally well organised, and extremely efficient at his job. That's a much better description of him.

I open the door to leave and gasp. Without thinking, I take a step back to steady myself. I wasn't expecting Jeff, of all people, to be standing in front of me.

"Well, Elizabeth," he says, his voice harsh. "You were rather rude at the table, don't you think? Manners are everything. Didn't Daddy Dearest teach you anything?" Jeff takes a step inside the storeroom.

"Well, after the way you spoke to me and treated me yesterday, did you really expect anything else from me?"

"Oh, I expected *lots* from you, Elizabeth, but you always leave me feeling let down, disappointed," he snarls.

"I let *you* down?" My voice is raised with anger. *How bloody dare he?* He feels let down. How does he think I feel with him? "I can't believe you think I've let you down. Didn't you ever give a thought to how I might be feeling?"

"No, why should I? You chose Ethan over me."

"Of course I did. And I can't believe you asked me to choose. Ethan needed his family and his friends' support. I thought you were one of his friends, but you turned your back on him—and on me. How could you do that to him? You never think about anyone but yourself."

"I never turned my back on you. I needed you."

"Lucy and Ethan needed me more. I'm sorry that's how you feel."

"I still need you, and I will have you. You are mine." He moves farther into the storeroom, letting the door close behind him. He's scaring me.

"What do you want, Jeff? I have work to do. So if you don't mind, I need to get on …" I take a step towards him, but he throws up his hands and grips my arms, stopping me.

"What do I want? Oh, Libby, Libby, Libby … I thought that was obvious." His voice is soft, almost tender. He brings his hand to my face and lets his fingers slide across it. There was a time when Jeff's touch had the same effect on me as Alex's does now. Now it makes my skin crawl. It makes me feel dirty. "I want you. Like I said, you're *mine*."

"Jeff, I am not yours."

"Do you think you're his? That bloody Yank?" he hisses through gritted teeth. "You're just his latest plaything. Do you really think he wants you? Look at you. You're a kitchen girl! You're a glorified hostess! He can have anyone he wants. Why would he *possibly* choose you?"

That strikes a nerve because I've been thinking the exact same things. My expression must give it away, because Jeff looks at me differently.

"Elizabeth, I want *you*. That hasn't changed in the last few months. I love you, and I know you still love me," he says, quietly pulling me closer.

"No, Jeff. I don't love you. And if you really loved me, you would have stuck by me when I needed you most. Instead you forced me to choose. Well, I made the right decision four months ago. And I'm sticking to it."

"And you think he loves you?" Jeff shouts. "Do you love him? You're a fool. He's *using* you, just like your dad is. You're just there to make headlines for your dad's clients. When are you going to get that into that thick skull of yours? Have a look about you."

That's done it. Now I'm mad. Maybe that was his plan all along. Why did I waste so much of my time with him? He is still playing mind games, and we're not even together. I bring my hand up swiftly, ready to slap him. He really deserves this.

But I've not been quick enough. He grabs me by the wrist, roughly, stopping my hand from making contact with his face. His grip is tight. I pull against it, but he's strong and more than a little drunk, so he has no compunctions about hurting me. I can't believe I am stuck here with him. Karl will surely come looking for me shortly, won't he? He said he'd give me five minutes. He has to, because at this moment that seems like the only way I am getting out of here.

"You stupid bitch!" Jeff shouts as his other hand makes contact with the side of my face. Ouch. It bloody stings. He pushes me and my back hits off the metal shelving behind me. "You didn't answer my fucking question! Do you think he could ever love you the way I do?"

"No. I *hope* not. That's not love, that's … sickness," I answer, holding back the tears that are bound to flow sooner rather than later.

I stand my ground. I don't pull against him. What's the point? It's only aggravating him more. I hold eye contact with him, and all I see is darkness in his eyes. I don't know the man before me. He's a complete stranger. Deep within, there was once someone I cared a great deal for, but he looks long gone. I am frozen to the spot. I need to try and stay focused.

"So how long have you and him been at it?" he growls.

"Jeff, let go of me. You're hurting me. Please."

"I can tell by how cosy you two look that you've already fucked him."

"That's none of your bloody business!" I shout angrily. "Now let me go!"

"No, Libby. Where would be the fun in that? I think we should have a little fun together for old times' sake. Stop fighting."

I try to look defeated while I consider what to do. All the fighting in the world is not going to help me, but I refuse to give up. He releases his hold on me and runs his fingers down my cheek, brushing them along my lips. Then suddenly his lips are on mine, crushing me. I taste the bile rising from the back of my throat. Dear god, I think I am going to be sick. The smell of alcohol is turning my stomach. His fingers trail down my face and neck, and then they pause at my breast.

Now his intentions are very clear. I can't let him do this. I push and pull against him. I feel his teeth bite down on my bottom lip; I can taste my own blood. He takes a step back and draws back his hand, then slaps my face again.

"You *know* you and I belong together. We could be so happy if you let us," he says.

Happy. I once thought I could be happy with him. I once thought I would spend the rest of my life with him. *Why did I never see this side of him? He's a lunatic! Where the hell is Karl?*

"Jeff, please," I sob.

"Elizabeth? Please what? Make you happy? I can always do that. Make you come? I was good at that too," he snarls, gripping both my wrists tightly.

"You could *never* make me happy. Only miserable. I would rather be alone forever than to be with you." I draw in a deep breath. "And as for making me come, you were never any good at that. Me, on the other hand—I'm very good at faking it. But I guess in all our time together, you never noticed. You were too wrapped up in yourself. You are one selfish bastard. Alex is different. He cares about *me*, and he certainly knows how to make me come." My voice breaks with my sobs. My face is soaked with tears.

He draws his hand back again, but this time he clenches his fist. The punch lands right in my stomach, winding me. The power of the punch knocks me flying into something long and sharp. Something's punctured my back. It feels deep. There's warmth, wetness, and searing pain. I see the floor coming up fast, and then I'm laid out on my side, my cheek pressed to the cold floor.

Eyes blurry with tears and pain, I see Jeff loosening the belt on his trousers. *Maybe I should just stop fighting it.* I close my eyes. He pulls at my jacket. I just want this over with.

"Please, Jeff, it doesn't have to be like this," I plead.

"Elizabeth, there were two ways of doing this—the easy way and the hard way. You chose the hard way. Let's face it: you're not known for making smart decisions, are you?"

Karl, please, where are you? I can't move. I can't fight back now. I feel his weight on top of me.

I hear voices in the distance. I draw in a deep breath and scream.

"Help!"

"Shut up, you stupid bitch," Jeff shouts as he punches me in the face again. I close my eyes. I don't want them to ever open again.

The voices are getting closer, but I have nothing left in me to call out. I can only hope its Karl looking for me.

Suddenly there's a crashing noise.

"Get the fuck off her!" It sounds like Alex. "Go get Ethan!"

It *is* Alex. I open my eyes as I feel the weight moving off me. As my vision slowly comes back in to focus, I see Alex dragging Jeff across the storeroom.

"What the fuck?" Alex lands a punch on Jeff's face. "YOU. THINK. IT'S. OKAY. JUST. TO. TAKE. WHAT. YOU. WANT?" He punctuates every word with another punch. Jeff cries out in pain.

"Alex! It's okay—stop before you kill him. He's not going anywhere now." Michael's voice cuts through the chaos. "Ethan, take care of your sister."

"Libby? Libby, are you okay?" Ethan's voice is comforting as he holds me in his arms. I can hear his sobs, and I can feel his tears. It's not fair. Ethan doesn't deserve any more pain in his life. I need to stay strong. He needs my strength.

I can hear more voices. Please, I don't want anyone else to see me like this.

"No!" someone screams. My mum.

"Has anyone called 999 yet? And can I get a cover? She's shaking. She's cold," Ethan calls out. "Libby? Come on, squeeze my hand. Can you hear me?" He pulls off his suit jacket and tucks it around me.

I squeeze his hand as hard as I can. I love him so much. My eyes flicker open. I see the pain and anguish in his face. I focus on his eyes and smile weakly at him.

"Alex, I said stop now! He's not worth it!" I turn my head towards the shouting. Michael is pulling Alex off Jeff, who is on the floor, not moving. Michael turns Alex to face him. "Alex, pull it together. Libby needs you, man. *This. Is. Not. The. Same.* Go to her."

Alex nods slowly and takes several deep breaths. He's struggling.

"Ethan, can I …" Alex's voice is lower.

"Only if you're calm. She's bleeding, she's probably in shock, and she really doesn't need more of a flap right now." I glance at Ethan's hands, which are covered in blood. My blood.

"I understand. Please, Ethan. Let me closer. You go to your mom; she's upset."

Alex swaps places with Ethan, who was sitting with me on the floor. My eyes are heavy, but I'm scared if I close them again that I won't be able to open them. Ethan hesitates, looking at his hands.

"Ethan, wash your hands before you talk to your mom," Alex whispers. "Libby, baby, everything's going to be okay. It's all right." He gently strokes his fingers along my forehead.

"Alex," I sob, not knowing if my words come out.

"Libby, don't think about anything. Don't talk. It's going to be fine."

His voice is soft, reassuring. My head pounds. The noise. So many voices all speaking at the same time, Mum crying. *Oh, Mum, don't cry.* It hurts, everything hurts. My eyes are so heavy, and it feels so much quieter when they close. Alex whispers that I will be okay, and I focus on his voice.

I feel Alex moving away from me … where is he going? I reach out my hand, needing contact. I try to speak, but nothing comes out.

"Hush, sweetie, it's all right. You're in safe hands. I'm going to take good care of you. I'll just have a look at your back, and then we'll give you something for the pain," she says. Her voice is calm and reassuring. I recognise the patch on her shirt—a white X on a blue circle topped with a red crown—the Scottish Ambulance Service. I try to nod. "That's great, sweetie. You can hear me. Okay, let me see you wiggle your fingers. Hands? Toes. Excellent. It's safe to move you." She slides me onto a backboard. "Let's get you a bit more comfortable and off to the hospital."

She and another paramedic lift the board and manoeuvre me through the kitchens and out the back of the hotel to the waiting ambulance. After what seems like an eternity, they set me down. It's much quieter in the ambulance, but the pounding in my head is still unbearable.

"I want to go with her," Mum says, sobbing, "in the ambulance."

"Of course, you can travel with your daughter."

"Phil …"

"Jane, it's okay. You go with her. We'll follow." I can only imagine that Dad is giving her a kiss and a hug just now. "I'll see you shortly, honey. We'll be right behind you. Mark's already brought the car round, see?"

I hear scuffling outside the ambulance and Michael's voice pleading for Alex to stay back. "Where are you taking him? Surely he's not going in the same ambulance as Libby—not after what he's done to her!" Alex shouts angrily.

"No. He needs treatment as well, but he won't go in the same ambulance. He will be going to the same hospital, but I expect he'll be discharged rather quickly," says the paramedic. "By the way, sir, I would advise you to get your hand looked at when you come in as well. And you might want to do that *before* you speak with the police." She sounds sympathetic towards Alex.

CHAPTER 20

lex

WHAT THE FUCKING hell has happened today?

Libby is a remarkable person she doesn't deserve the punishment that she's been dealt by his hands.

"Alex! Get in the car." I stare after the ambulance that has just driven off, anger consuming me. "Alex?"

Phil's frustrated voice pulls my attention back to now, back to reality. I need to be with her. I need to hold her in my arms. "Yes, erm, sorry," I mutter getting in the back of the car where Ethan is waiting, looking as lost as I feel. Mark is driving and Phil is beside him in the passenger seat. I have no idea where Michael or Kirsty are but I'm sure they will be following us straight to the hospital.

I stare blankly out the window losing myself in my thoughts. That bastard, I should've dealt with him yesterday and this today wouldn't have happened. This is my fault. I grip onto my trousers as the vision of what I saw in that store floods my mind. He was going to rape her. This is a man that she once had feelings for and vice-versa, is that what their relationship was like? I fucking hope not because if it was I might kill him myself.

He's hurt her, really fucking hurt her and I'm struggling.

Struggling with my past and my present. Lines have all blurred together and I can't tell what's now and what should be safely tucked away in the past.

Phil and Ethan are talking and even though they are both in the car, their conversation sounds so far off in the distance. All I can hear is Libby's cries for help and all I can see is blood. I need to get a grip, pull myself together otherwise I'll be no use to anyone. She needs my support and strength, not some man who is out of control.

"We're here," Phil says turning toward me before getting out of the car. I look out the window taking note that Mark has stopped at the main entrance.

I take a deep breath to calm my growing nerves because I don't know how she is. How bad she's been injured; there was a lot of blood. I get out the car trying to stay composed when all I want to do is rush inside and be with her. Ethan places his hand on my shoulder, I can't even bring myself to smile at him. He must be worried sick. I can only hazard a guess as to they relationship they share, the closeness. Their bond. Poor Ethan.

Phil leads the way inside, with Ethan and I following on. He stops at the desk giving Libby's full name. The lady behind the desk searches through the computer for a few minutes before telling Phil that she's not on the system.

"What the fuck!"

"Alex calm down," Phil tells me. "My daughter was brought in only a few minutes before us, I'd say."

"Okay, she might not have been booked onto our system yet, but why don't you all go and wait in that room over there and I'll get someone to go and find out details for you."

"Thank you."

Again, I follow behind Phil, not taking in my surroundings, although from the noise, I sense it's very busy. Phil opens to the door to a small and vey private waiting room with six chairs. I sit down and wait without speaking to anyone. I've not been able to string a sentence together since I watched her being taken into the ambulance with Jane's whimpers and cries for her beloved daughter.

I've only known Libby a short time and I know how I feel, helpless. Phil and Ethan talk but I don't participate in the conversation. I'm boiling mad that bastard has been brought here. Clenching my fist in my hand, I know I should get cleaned up especially before I go to her. I don't know how long we wait before the door opens, but I sigh seeing Michael and Kirsty. I know he won't be offended, he'll know I'm just desperate for news on how she is.

I fucking hate hospitals.

I hate this part.

The waiting for news on a loved one. Because regardless of what I tell myself I do love her, probably have done since before we even met. Crazy, totally crazy.

But that saying springs to mind, 'you can't help who you fall in love with."

And I wouldn't change my feelings.

Love at first sight, is such a cliché, but it's happened to me although if anyone ever tried to tell me this would happen, I would never have believed them.

The door opens, this time a nurse. "Mr Stewart, I'll take you to your daughter."

"How is she?" I ask standing for the first time since we entered the room.

"She's coming around. I'll be in a better position to give

you more news as soon as the doctor is finished with her. Now, I'll take Mr Stewart, then I'll come and get you to have a look at that hand," she says with a sympathetic smile.

"As soon as I know how she is, I'll be back," Phil says patting me on the shoulder. I nod and slowly sit back down and hang my head in my hands.

She's going to be okay. She has to be okay.

CHAPTER 21

*M*y head hurts. I'm frightened to move. My whole body aches. I feel as if I've been run over by a steamroller. I hear voices, low, whispered voices, and I slowly open my eyes, but everything is blurred. Why are my eyes so sore? There are so many figures in this clean, white room. I blink a few times, trying to clear my vision. I need to see them. I turn my head to the side. Mum is sitting by the bed holding my hand.

"Mum." I move my hand in hers.

"Oh, Libby. Thank god." Her voice sounds relieved, and I can see fresh tears in her eyes. "Phil, can you go and get the doctor?" Dad leaves the room.

"Mum, I'm okay." I smile, but even doing that hurts. My face must be in some mess. "Where's Ethan? And Alex?" I ask.

"In the waiting room with Michael and Kirsty. The doctors would only let your dad and me in. Once the doctor has been in, I'll get them for you."

I nod. My dad enters the room with a nurse, followed by an older gentleman wearing a white coat.

"Good evening, Miss Stewart," the old man says with a

smile. "I'm Dr. Young." I giggle. "Well, I'm glad you still have a sense of humour, albeit at my expense." His smile just got wider. "How are you feeling? Be honest."

"Where to start … let's see. My head is pounding, my face hurts, everything's blurry, and as for my stomach and back, I can't even begin to describe the pain," I say. "Other than that, I feel fine."

"Libby!" Mum does not approve.

"Mrs Stewart, it's perfectly all right. I have heard much worse." The doctor speaks directly to my mother, then he turns back to me. "Now, Miss Stewart, you have quite a few injuries but fortunately nothing life threatening. You have severe bruising to your ribs, but the X-rays showed nothing broken. You sustained a deep puncture wound to your back, but it missed all vital organs. We took care of that earlier; it's been cleaned, stitched, and dressed. Twenty-four stitches it took. I'm afraid you'll have a bit of a scar, although it will fade some with time."

"What about my eyes? Why can't I see clearly?" I ask.

"Nothing to worry about. Your face is badly bruised and swollen. The swelling will take a bit of time to go down, and the bruising will—"

"Can I see it, please?" I ask, interrupting the doctor. "And can I get up?"

"We're monitoring your blood pressure, which is always a bit wonky after a trauma, so I don't want you up out of the bed just yet. You've been through an ordeal, and you need rest to help speed the recovery process. If you really want to see your face, I can bring you in a mirror."

"Thank you."

Mum and Dad leave the room to let the staff do their job. The nurse takes my blood pressure, which is still a bit high. She puts up another bag of fluids but says that should be the last bag, as I am awake now and should be able to drink. She takes some blood from me, filling several small tubes.

"Miss Stewart, when was the last time you had something to eat?" the nurse asks.

"Breakfast this morning," I reply.

"Would you like some tea and toast or soup?"

"Yes, please, although I'm not sure I can manage it. Will I be able to see my brother and Alex now?"

"Yes, I'll get them just as soon as I'm finished. I have a mirror here. Do you still want to see?"

"Yes, I may as well get it over with."

She hands me the mirror face down. She looks anxious. I lift the mirror slowly. I take a deep breath before turning it round.

"No," I gasp. That can't possibly be me. I don't recognise myself. There're bruises everywhere. My eyes are quite swollen. I have cuts on my lip and a larger one at the top of my forehead, maybe from when I fell. "I don't think makeup will cover this up, do you?" Tears run freely down my face. The nurse hands me a tissue.

"Libby ... do you mind me calling you that?" the nurse asks. I shake my head. "You've been very lucky. This could've been much worse. I won't lie to you. And no, makeup won't cover it up, it will take a few weeks to heal completely, but it *will* heal. Now I have a few other tests I need to do."

"What tests?" I ask nervously, although I have a feeling I already know.

"Libby, we need to ..."

"Stop!" I shout. "He didn't do it. He never got the chance. Alex pulled him off me before he did." I start to cry.

"Oh, sweetie, you cry all you want. I know this is unpleasant for you, but for peace of mind, I would much rather the tests be done—and I am sure the police would as well." I nod in agreement with her. "I also have a camera here to take the photographic evidence that the police will need. Is that okay with you?"

The tests don't take too long, and before I know it, I have a cup of chicken soup in my hands. It tastes delicious, but my mouth hurts with each mouthful I drink. I only manage half the cup.

"Shall I collect your brother and Alex?"

"Yes, please," I answer, looking at her name badge.

"Okay, you can have a few minutes with them. But then a couple of police officers need to speak with you. I should send them in first, but I expect you'll be a bit more settled after you see your loved ones."

"Thank you, Sam. I really appreciate it," I say to her as she heads out the door.

I am left on my own. It gives me time to think. I can't believe how this day turned out—or that Jeff has done this to me. If only I'd just taken a break with Karl and Kieran. If I had done, then this would never have happened, and I wouldn't be here. Why did Jeff have to do this?

My room door opens. Ethan stops in the doorway and gasps.

"So, Ethan, are you going to just stand there with your mouth open, or are you coming in?" I try and make light of the situation. "Where's Alex?"

Ethan walks towards me. He bends down and gives me a kiss before sitting down on the edge of the bed, taking my hand.

"Alex is with the police, giving them a statement. Jeff wants to press charges against him."

"What?" I screech. "How can they charge Alex? If it wasn't for him, who knows what would have happened!"

"I know, I know. You won't get any arguments from me. He saved you," Ethan says, shaking his head sadly. "But Alex did make some job of Jeff's face. The guy's got a broken nose, two missing teeth, and even more bruises than you have."

"I need to give my statement. Can you go and get someone?"

"Libby, they'll be here shortly."

"But they *can't* charge Alex. He hasn't done anything wrong. Jeff was going to …" I start crying. I can't even say the words.

"Libby, please." Ethan takes me in his arms while I sob uncontrollably. "Libby, everything will be fine. Dad is with Alex. Alex's lawyer is getting the first available flight from America."

"Seriously?" I pull back from him. Ethan nods. "What a way to meet his parents."

Ethan looks confused. I suppose I'd better tell him. "Both of Alex's parents *and* his brother are lawyers. I wonder which one I am going to meet? I'm scared that they'll blame me for this."

"This is not your fault, Libby. How could anyone blame you? And as for Alex's parents, don't worry about them. We'll set them straight. You have enough going on."

"I know. So, have you. Is there still a hearing tomorrow?" I ask.

"Yes, I'm going with my lawyer first thing. After today I would love it to be postponed. I'd rather stay here. I just want to make sure you're all right."

"Ethan, I'll be fine. A few days' rest and I'll be as good as new." He really doesn't need to be worrying about me with everything else going on. He needs to stay focused on himself and Lucy. It's going to be a tough couple of weeks, raking over the past few months. Just when he was finally making some headway in his life.

"Libby, you don't have to be the strong one all the time. Just once could you let me take care of you? You're always there when I need you. Now it's time for me to return the favour. You're my sister, and I love you—and I really don't know where I would be today if it wasn't for your persever- ance and your unconditional love."

God, he's made me cry again. Only a few days ago, I had him in my arms comforting *him.* Now here we are again, with everything backwards. We stay like this for a few moments. The closeness we had before Lindsay's death is definitely back.

"Is it okay if I come in?" Alex asks from the doorway.

"Yes, I was just leaving. I need to go and collect Lucy." Ethan gives me another kiss before whispering something into Alex's ear, then heading out.

I've wanted to see Alex since I woke up, and now that he's here, I'm at a loss for words. Worry and sadness are etched into his beautiful face. As he walks slowly towards me, I dip my head shamefully, and the tears flow freely.

"Hey, Libby, it's all right. It's over. I am so sorry I didn't get there sooner." He puts his strong arms around me. "I should have seen it coming the way he was drinking."

I can't speak. I'm just numb. The reality of what happened is just sinking in. Alex places a kiss on the top of my head.

"Libby, please. I feel totally helpless. I don't know how to help or even if I can help. What do I do?"

I draw in a deep breath and try to wipe the tears away. Alex hands me a hankie. I lift my head and meet those eyes I adore so much. Where I usually see passion and desire, now I see only concern, pain, and tiredness. I look straight into those eyes as I speak.

"Alex, it's a lot to take in … what happened today. For the second time in my life, I felt completely helpless, vulnerable, and scared. Not a lot scares me. I wasn't even that scared when he was hitting me, because I knew I could fight back, push him off me. I would never have given in," I say. I force myself to hold back my tears. "But the pain … I hit the ground, and I couldn't move. I heard him loosen his belt, and I couldn't do a thing about it. I didn't give up; I just wanted it over with. I didn't stop fighting, because I never had the chance to start. It was like all my energy had drained away. I'm so ashamed. When I couldn't fight, I just closed my eyes and kept thinking the sooner it's over with, the better."

"Libby …" Alex pauses as if searching for the right words. But I don't need the words; I can hear the tenderness in his voice. "When I found that bastard on top of you, his pants open, I just wanted to kill him. Then it got me thinking how I first came onto you. I was no better than him. For that I will always be sorry and grateful. Grateful that you gave me a second chance."

I don't know how to reply to that statement. Alex sits on the bed beside me, and I do the one thing that feels so natural to me; I sink into his arms. He wraps them loosely round my waist. I inch myself closer to him, ignoring the pain shooting through me when I move. Bloody hell.

"Thank you," I say.

"For what?"

"For being here with me. For saving me. For falling into my life."

"Shh, shh. It's all right."

We sit cuddled together in silence for a few minutes. Then we are interrupted by a knock at the door. I look up to see a uniformed police officer in the doorway, accompanied by someone I assume to be from CID.

"Sorry, we hate to interrupt, but we do have some questions for you, Miss Stewart. Mr Mathews, if you could please step outside for a moment?"

"No! No, I don't want Alex to go."

"It's all right, baby. I'll be right outside."

"Miss Stewart, your mum could sit with you," says the officer.

"No, I don't want her upset more." It's true. My mum's crying earlier today will haunt me.

"Officer, can't I stay with her if I don't say anything?" Alex asks.

"Oh, all right then. No interrupting. We already have your statement."

"You won't get any interruptions from me," Alex says, shifting his position on the bed. For a moment I think he's going to move away from me, so I grip his arm. "It's okay. I'm not going anywhere."

"Right. Let's get started. Miss Stewart, I'm Detective Inspector Lorna Tate, and this is my colleague, Constable Neil Phillips."

I go through all the details from yesterday at the football, and I describe the events of today. Hearing it all out loud, it sounds like a bad movie. She asks lots of questions about my relationship with Jeff, including the timing and circumstances of our breakup. Alex tries to stay calm and quiet as I go over every detail, but it doesn't work. I feel his chest tighten, and the word "fuck" leaves his mouth all too often. DI Tate glares at him in warning to keep quiet, but she doesn't say anything.

I didn't think it would be this hard to talk about what happened, but I find myself stammering and pausing a lot. DI Tate keeps reassuring me that I am doing extremely well. If it wasn't for her words of encouragement and the warmth of Alex holding me, I'm not sure I would be up to this. I am tired now. It's been such a long day. I don't even know what time it is.

"Officer, are you nearly done with the questioning?" Alex asks. "Libby looks exhausted. I really think she needs some rest."

"Yes, Mr Mathews, I agree we should leave it here. We have enough to press charges against Mr Ross," she says. "He'll be taken into custody tonight. His injuries aren't severe enough to keep him in hospital overnight, so he'll be spending the night in a cell."

"Thank you," says Alex.

"No thanks necessary. We've taken up enough of your time tonight. Miss Stewart, when the doctors discharge you, will you be going to the hotel or your parents' home? I understand that your mother wants you at home."

"I haven't given it any thought."

"That's fine. I have your mobile number, so if we need to speak with you in person, we'll contact you first by phone. Again, thank you for your time. We'll leave you to it. Get some rest." She closes the notebook in which she's been jotting things down and shakes my hand, then Alex's. "Mr Mathews, you'll be at the hotel should we need you again?"

"Once Libby's discharged, I'll be wherever she is. Until then I'll be here."

"I'm sure we'll speak again soon. Hopefully I'll have good news for you by then," DI Tate says. "And Mr Mathews? If it's any consolation, if I'd been in your position, I would have done the same thing."

With that they leave, and I breathe a sigh of relief. I sink back into Alex's arms. God, I've not even asked him what's happening about him. I completely forgot that Ethan said Jeff wanted to press charges.

"Alex?" My voice is barely a whisper.

"Yes?"

"Ethan said Jeff wanted you arrested. Will everything be okay?"

"Nothing for you to worry about. I just want you better."

"But you're worried enough that you called your lawyer."

"Libby, your father's lawyer is dealing with it. I called me parents, knowing that my mother would be frantic if she found out about this online or in a newspaper. As for my father, he told me that they were both taking the first flight they could get. He wants to make sure your father's lawyer is doing a good job—which I don't doubt for one minute he will do. But I am sure my mom is the main reason for the unscheduled trip." The smile on Alex's face is warm and sincere.

"I guess I'll be meeting your parents sooner rather than later?"

"Yes, and please don't worry about it. They're going to love you," he says before kissing my head.

My eyes close voluntarily. I no longer have the energy to fight the sleepiness that is hanging over me. I am not sure how long I sleep, but it seems like days later that I hear voices.

"Are you sure you're all right? I've never seen you that mad." It's Michael speaking. He's out in the hallway.

"Yeah, I am fine now. It just took me back instantly to ten years ago ... although this time I was in a position to do something about it," Alex says. "Look, Michael, I don't want to talk about this. In case Libby wakes up, you know?"

"Okay, understood. So have the doctors said how long they plan to keep her here?" That was a quick change of subject.

"There are no physical injuries that need observation so probably in the morning after she gets some sleep."

"What about you? Are you coming back to the hotel tonight with me and Kirsty?"

"No, I'm staying here."

"Okay, Kirsty wants to come in and see Libby before we go. Is that all right?" Michael asks.

"Yeah, of course. Although you should warn Kirsty that they've given Libby something that knocked her right out.

She didn't even stir when her parents said good night to her. I've to call Phil first thing in the morning to let him know what's happening."

I hear Michael's footsteps as he walks away down the hall. Alex returns to my room. What happened ten years ago? My mind races. How bad could it be? Alex would only have been fourteen or fifteen. I suddenly remember the sadness in his voice during a conversation yesterday about Ethan. I'm now restless and have questions I want to ask him.

I open my eyes slowly and shift my position on the bed slightly. My mouth is dry. I lick my lips. Alex notices and releases his hold of me to pour a glass of water. He puts a straw in it. God, I'm not a baby. I take the straw out of the glass in his hands and take the glass from him as he watches. I put the glass to my mouth.

"Ouch." I forgot how sore my lips and mouth were.

"See? There was a reason I gave you the straw. Here," he says, as I shift uncomfortably in the bed. I take a slow drink through the straw. It quenches my thirst. "So how long have you been awake?"

"Long enough to hear your conversation with Michael."

He takes the glass of water from me and gently places it on the cabinet beside the bed. He has yet to look me in the eyes. I sit waiting for his gaze to meet mine. His body is tense.

"Alex, please ... explain."

"Libby, can we talk about it later? You've been through too much already today without having to listen to stories from *my* past. It's old news. It can wait."

He doesn't get to finish, and I don't get to speak. Kirsty and Michael walk into the room.

"Oh, honey, you're awake. Michael said you'd probably be sleeping. How're you feeling? I suppose that's a really stupid question."

"Kirsty, I'm fine. Or at least I will be when the cuts and bruises heal. But I think I'm going to have to say no to going out clubbing tonight, if you don't mind," I say. When I try to laugh, my lips crack. Even that hurts.

"Elizabeth Stewart," Kirsty hisses. "That is not funny in the *slightest*. I've been worried *sick* about you. If I saw Jeff right now, I'd kill the bastard with my bare hands."

"Sorry," I say. "But if I don't laugh, I might cry. I don't want to waste time feeling sorry for myself."

I glance at Alex and Michael, who seem to be having an unspoken conversation about their earlier conversation—or rather about the fact that I heard it. I gently squeeze Alex's hand. His response is to put his other arm round me with a smile.

"You're always so much better than I am at picking up the pieces," Kirsty says. "Alex thinks you'll be allowed to leave here in the morning. I'll come to the hotel to sit with you when Alex has to leave to go to his meetings."

"Guys, I don't need babysitting. And I thought you needed to be in at the office early tomorrow?" I ask Alex.

"Your dad rescheduled for the afternoon. Your mom was going to take care of you at her house, but she's watching Lucy tomorrow and—"

"God, no, Lucy can't see me like this! I look like a monster!" I say. I find I'm once again having trouble keeping my eyes open. I can't hold back a big yawn.

"Oh, honey. You're tired. We should go and let you rest," Kirsty says, leaning down to give me a kiss. "And it's not babysitting, it's company."

"Okay, you win. I'll see you tomorrow."

Alex gets up from the bed and walks them out of the room. I can hear him speaking with Michael outside. I'll ask again tomorrow. Right now, I'm too exhausted to think about it. My eyes close as sleep overcomes me.

"Libby? Libby, what is it? It's all right; I'm here." Alex's voice brings me some comfort.

"Alex, what's wrong?" I say.

"I think you were having a bad dream, baby. Do you want to talk about it?"

"No, not really," I answer.

"That's all right. I can guess what it was about," he says, running his hand across my brow. "You're a bit hot. You sure you're feeling okay?"

"Yes. What time is it?"

"It's seven thirty."

"In the morning? Why is it so dark then?" I ask.

"Yes, in the morning. The nurse wanted to open the blinds earlier, but I asked her to leave them. You had a bit of a rough night—tossing, turning, and crying through the night. She agreed that you should sleep a bit longer."

"Alex, now that I am awake, can we leave here? I want to go back to the hotel. I want to have a nice, hot shower. I want to be clean."

"I'll see if the doctor can check on you now," he says. He gives me a kiss before leaving the room.

I know it will take more than a shower to feel right again.

CHAPTER 22

*I*t's early evening, and I'm just out of the shower again. I've lost count of how many showers I've taken today. It seems like the only time I get a minute's peace and quiet is when I'm in the shower. The endless phone calls from my mother are starting to get to me. I know she's concerned and worried, but she really needs to give me a break. Alex too. He sent a text right after he left me for his meeting, then another one every hour on the hour.

Kirsty spent the whole day with me at the hotel, after having spent the previous night here with Michael. She spent the entire day fussing over me, but I did enjoy her company—to a certain extent. She says I made the papers again. Sunday's papers ran with a story and a picture from the football game, saying how good Alex and I look together. Today's papers have all run with the same story and added what they know about the incident yesterday. Three days in a row. Surely there must be some other news besides me? Around six o'clock, I told Kirsty just a little white lie, saying that I was exhausted and just planned to go to bed. She reluctantly agreed to leave so I could rest, but I really just wanted another shower before Alex got back.

Kieran was a constant visitor to my room throughout the day as well. He cried the first time he saw me, and I found myself crying with him. He was so upset. I was meant to be working today, so I got Kieran to bring up some of the important paperwork, which Kirsty helped me with. She also offered to come in and work for a few days while I was off, but I told her there was no need that I would be back to work tomorrow. Her response to that was, "We'll see." Kieran was surprised by what I said as well, but I can't sit holed up in this room for days. I'll go mad.

The police officers visited again today. They asked me more questions and answered some of mine about what's happening with Jeff. He appeared in court today and was remanded into custody—no less than what he deserves. We'll just need to wait and see how he pleads. I'm not looking forward to a trial. God, I can see the headlines already for that.

Kieran told me that Alex's parents have checked in to the hotel, which makes me nervous, even though he says they seem like nice people. Of course, they will be nice people—I really don't expect otherwise—and Kirsty, Kieran, and Alex have all told me I have nothing to worry about. But how could I not? Shit, I really wish I wasn't meeting them under these circumstances. It is my fault, after all, that their son is facing assault charges. *Oh god, they might hate me.*

Stephen also paid me a visit. He wasn't shocked by my appearance. He'd been at the table talking to Ethan yesterday when Michael ran out to get help. I can't remember seeing him in the storeroom or anywhere yesterday, but it's still all a bit of a blur. Karl came by at lunchtime to bring a special room service delivery for me and Kirsty. He kept apologising for leaving me on my own, which is absurd since there is no way he could have known that Jeff was going to attack me. I tried to assure Karl that it wasn't his fault, that if anything, it was my own for not joining them for the break, but DI Tate assures me that it was no one's fault but Jeff's. If he hadn't done it then, he would probably have done it some other time, given the state of mind Jeff seems to be in. Karl told me not to worry about the kitchen or the restaurant either, as he and Kieran have brought in a couple of temps for a few days while he holds interviews. He's promised to let me know if there are any suitable candidates for a second interview.

As I'm drying my hair, I suddenly realise that the one person I haven't heard from all day is Ethan. I send him a quick text:

Libby: How did it go 2 day? Do you want to have lunch tomorrow x

Instantly he replies:

Ethan: Lunch would be perfect. Loads to tell you. Today went better than expected. X

Libby: Great x

Ethan: How are you today? X

Libby: Fed up. Sore but ok I guess x

Ethan: Ok see you tomorrow x

I am so relieved to hear that. I had originally planned to go to today's hearing with him to provide some moral support, but instead, here I am staring at my gruesome reflection in my bathroom mirror. I look worse now than I did last night. How the hell is that possible? What's the saying? It will get worse before it gets better.

My phone chirps with another text:

Alex: On my way back. My parents are at the hotel xoxo

Libby: Yes I know Kieran told me earlier x

Alex: You better not be working!

Libby: Been in my room all day and now I am BORED!!!!!!!!!!!!!!!!!!!!!!

Alex: If you are up for some fresh air maybe we could go for a walk later

Libby: Sounds perfect. Thank you x

Alex: See you soon xoxo

I decide to call the estate agents. I hope there's someone still in the office. I *did* tell them I would let them know my decision today.

"Eric, hi. It's Libby Stewart.

"Libby! I didn't expect to hear from you today after everything. You've just caught me." Well, he obviously reads the papers. "How are you?"

"I'm all right, considering. I look worse than I feel."

"As long as you're resting and not working too hard. That's quite an ordeal you went through." He pauses before asking, "So, Libby, what can I do for you?"

"Well, Eric, you can start by telling me you haven't sold the flat."

"No, Libby. I said we wouldn't put it on the market until I heard back from you."

"Well, don't put it on the market. I will instruct my lawyer to make a formal offer tomorrow," I say.

"Oh, Libby, that's wonderful! The current owner will be thrilled. They were looking for a quick sale," he tells me. We spend another few minutes talking before ending the call. I feel as if I've made the right decision. A new start. I make a very quick call to my lawyer giving him instructions for the offer and tell him I want the missives concluded as quickly as humanly possible.

There's a knock on my room door. I consider not answering, but I'm a nosey so-and-so. I get up from the dressing table and leave my bedroom, calling out that I will just be a minute. I open the door to a stunning woman who is maybe in her late forties or early fifties. Sophisticated. The minute I look into her eyes, I know exactly who she is. I would know those beautiful, brown eyes anywhere.

Alex's mother.

"Mrs Mathews," I say, offering her my hand. She steps in the door and embraces me instead.

"Elizabeth! How are you, dear? And please, call me Sarah."

"Come in, please," I say, gesturing towards the couch. I wasn't ready for this. *God, where is Alex? He should be here.*

"Sorry to drop by unannounced. Richard said I shouldn't, that I should wait until Alex was back, but I couldn't wait another moment. I just couldn't sit another minute knowing you were here alone after what you went through. I had to come and see how you were for myself."

"It's fine. Can I get you anything to drink?" I ask her.

"No, I'm fine. I should be asking you if *you* need anything."

"I have had an endless supply of visitors today. If I drink any more water or cups of tea, I think I'll burst."

She laughs genuinely. "I'm sorry, Elizabeth. I should have thought—you're probably wishing for some peace and quiet. I should let you rest," she says, standing up.

"Don't be silly. Stay. Alex will be back shortly. I am sure he wants to see you, and you obviously want to see him," I reply with a smile.

She sits back down. At my mention of her son's name, she smiles. A mother's love and admiration. I can't believe I am sitting here looking so bad. It's not just my face that looks a mess. I'm also just wearing shorts and a vest top.

"As long as you're sure. I don't want to put you out. You must be tired."

"Can I be honest with you, Sarah? I am not that tired just now, but I am fed up with being stuck in this room. I don't know what my father will say, but I have got to go back to working tomorrow," I say.

"What do you mean? Never mind what your father will say. I have something to say on that matter myself," Alex says, closing the door. "Evening, Mom. Did you have a good flight?" He leans down and gives his mother a kiss on her check. Her eyes light up.

He walks over to me, sits down on the arm of the couch, and drapes his arms round me lightly, giving me a kiss on my forehead. His mother watches us closely.

"Yes, Alex, we had a good flight."

"So, Libby … work? Really?" he asks in a flat voice. "It's too soon to go back. You have to give yourself time to recover." Sarah nods in agreement. "And anyway, you'd frighten the guests away." He's grinning, trying to lift my mood, which he obviously senses.

"Hey, you," I say, as I playfully slap his arm. *Shit, maybe I shouldn't have done that with his mother sitting there. First impressions and all that.* She's watching us with a look of amusement.

"Babe, are you hungry? You okay eating here? Or would you like to go out," Alex asks.

"I am a bit peckish. What about you, Sarah?" I turn to his mother, much to Alex's surprise. "You and Richard are more than welcome to join us here. I don't feel up to going anywhere in public just yet. No, let me rephrase that: I don't feel up to getting dressed for dinner."

"Are you sure, Libby?" Sarah asks in a warm voice.

"Yes, of course I'm sure. Why don't you call Richard and ask him?"

Alex gives me another kiss. Sarah calls Richard. While she's on the phone, I head into the bedroom. I won't dress up, but I will get dressed, and I could stand something warmer to wear. As I rummage through the wardrobe, I feel Alex enter the room. I pull out leggings and a jumper. I keep my back to him and remove my shorts before pulling on the leggings.

"I love that ass."

"Alex, watch your mouth," I say, scowling.

"You didn't have to do that. I didn't expect you to entertain my parents this evening. Are you sure you're up to this?" he asks.

"Yes, I'm fine. Although I would prefer it if I looked better."

"Oh, baby, you look beautiful. A few bruises can't change that." He wraps his arms round my waist and turns me round to face him. The look in his eyes is only of concern, but I want the longing and passion back in his eyes. "Libby, don't look at me like that."

"Alex, I want you to kiss me."

"Libby, I want to, I do … but I am scared that I might hurt you," he whispers in my ear. His breath against my neck sets off my desire for him. I stand on my tiptoes. He seems edgy. He must know what I'm going to do, but he's not stopping me. My lips meet his in a long, slow kiss. It takes him a few moments for him to respond, but when he finally does, the pain on my lips is worth it.

He pulls back slowly.

"Are you okay? That wasn't too sore?"

"I'm tougher than I look, you know," I say with a wink. "Now go talk to your parents. Order up some food and wine and some more bottled water for me."

"What do you want to eat?"

"Just something light," I say, chasing him from the room. I need a few minutes before going back to his parents. "By the way, I called the estate agents earlier. I'm putting an offer in on the flat."

"That's great news! I know how much you love it." His smile is warm and encouraging.

"I do love it. I still think it's too big for me alone, so I'm still thinking about taking Kirsty on as a flatmate."

The evening as a whole is going well. His parents are easy to get on with—they remind me of my own—and it's obvious that Alex has the same closeness with his parents as I have with mine. They are extremely proud of his achievements. The evidence is there in front of me.

Sarah takes great delight in telling a few old stories about Alex's childhood, much to his displeasure. I learn he was a bit of a handful compared to her other two children, and looking at him now, why does that not surprise me? Even from a very early age, Alex and Michael were the very best of friends. They shared tears, tantrums, and even girlfriends over the years. The last bit, of course, I am well aware of.

Both boys went all through school together and then on to the same university. Alex worked extremely hard to get a degree in business finance and Michael in economics. Sarah says Michael is like her third son; she loves him just as much as her own children. But like her own, he was always managing to get into bother with her as well.

She tells me about a time when they were both about fifteen and had come home late and so drunk that they could barely string two words together between them. She had wanted to kill them both, but instead Richard pulled a few strings, and both boys found themselves waking up in police cells the next morning. They never, and still haven't, returned to her house drunk. I laugh at that.

I catch Alex from the corner of my eye shaking his head at his mother and mouthing, *No more.*

She goes on to tell me Alex was always very independent and always looking for a challenge, something he could, as she says, "sink his teeth into."

"So, Alex. Will you still be attending Katherine's premiere on Wednesday?" Sarah's tone changes from the warmth that was in her voice speaking about Alex to being flat with the question.

"I really haven't thought about it, what with everything that's happened these past few days." His arm grips me tighter as we sit together on the couch. "We were all planning to go together—Libby, me, Libby's parents, Michael, and, I think, Libby's friend Kirsty."

"Alex! I can't face the media looking like this! It's been bad enough the last few days. You might be used to publicity, but I'm not." Imagine this face amongst all those stunning models and actresses! I also couldn't cope with all the questions.

"Well then, Mom. There's your answer. That should make you happy. We're not going," he says sharply.

"Alex," I say, facing him. "I said *I* wasn't going. That doesn't mean *you* can't go."

"Libby—"

I cut him off. He was going before we started seeing each other, and although I still wonder if there wasn't *something* going on between them, I do know they he considers her a good friend. I can't stand between him and his old friends. "Alex, you've planned to go from the start. She's expecting you. Why should that change?"

"Because you need me here," he says. "I'll call your dad. He's brought forward next week's meetings in London to Thursday, seeing as I was down there anyway. I'll see if he can change it back."

"I am perfectly capable of looking after myself, you know. If your meetings are all set, why change them now? I know my parents are still going. Why don't you take your parents?" Sarah chokes on her wine. "Are you all right?"

"There is no way—no damn way on Earth—that *I* will be going." Sarah sounds angry. I wonder what the history is behind her obvious hostility.

"Sarah, enough," Richard says.

"Sorry, but you both know how I feel about her. I've never hidden the fact."

Alex shakes his head at his mother and mouths, *enough*. So, there *is* a story to Katherine Hunter. Does her story relate to what I heard Alex and Michael talking about?

Alex's mother politely changes the subject. The rest of the evening passes by quickly and without further incident. After another hour or so, I am tired, really tired. I feel myself closing off from the conversations going back and forth. I lean into Alex's shoulder, trying not to yawn, but I can no longer hold it in. I feel myself drifting off. Maybe I will dream of Alex's hands all over my body. Now *that* would be a good dream.

"Libby, I'm sorry. We shouldn't be keeping you up. You need to rest up after what you've been through," Sarah says, her sweet voice waking me from my daze. "You should've said something. Come on, Richard." She pulls her husband by his arm. I go to get up and see them out, but Alex pushes me back into the couch. His mother comes over to me and gives me a kiss on the cheek. "It was lovely meeting you, dear. You are such a beautiful, brave young woman, and I do hope we'll be seeing much more of each other."

"And you. Thank you," I reply.

Richard Mathews says good night, and Alex sees his parents to the door. "Alex, what room are you in? I can get you on the way to breakfast in the morning," says Sarah.

"I'm staying here."

"Oh, right. I didn't think," his mother says, flustered. He's caught her off guard. "Good night, Alex. See you tomorrow." She gives him a kiss before leaving.

The next morning, Tuesday, I awaken to an empty bed. I roll over, and there is a note from Alex on his pillow:

. . .

LIBBY, you looked so peaceful that I didn't have the heart to wake you. I have early meetings. Then your father's lawyer wants to see me and my dad early this evening. I hate to ask, all things considering, but will you look after my mom when my dad's away? Not sure when we'll get back. Probably late. xoxo Alex

I GLANCE AT THE CLOCK. Shit. Its 11.45 already. So much for morning. It's practically midday. Ethan will be here soon. I pick up my phone. I have a few messages:

ETHAN: I will be over at 1. Bringing Lucy x E

Libby: Ok see you soon x

God I hope I don't frighten Lucy looking like this. She might not even recognise me.

Kirsty: How you feeling today?

Libby: Not as sore but tired. I am just up x

Kirsty: Lazy git x

Alex: Hope you slept well. xoxo

Alex: How are you feeling? xoxo

Alex: Are you still in bed?

Alex: ????????

Libby: Just got up. Had a great sleep. Not as sore today but still tired. In answer to; Are you still in bed? answer is yes and I wish you were with me xx

Alex: Don't tease x

I DON'T KNOW where the day has gone. One minute I was just up, and now it feels way past my bedtime. Alex phoned to say he was on his way home at nine o'clock. I told him to go and see his mum before coming to me. I spent the evening with

his mum having dinner and chatting before coming back to my room. I had to make an early night of it, as I am just so bloody tired.

I am so glad I didn't work today. God knows how I would be feeling if I had. The attack on Sunday definitely took its toll on my body—and my mind. I've been trying not to let it show, but I'm a wreck. I hope I can pull myself back together again.

My thoughts drift to Ethan. I can't believe the change in him, and it's all down to fatherhood. Lucy is the apple of her father's eye; of that I am sure. He told me today about how things went at the hearing yesterday. He's yet to tell my parents about it, but I asked if he wanted me there when he did. His reply was a very quick no. He wants to do it on his own.

Yesterday was a plea hearing. The other driver in the accident that killed Lindsay had pleaded guilty. Straightforward enough, but what do I know? Nothing is as it seems. Ethan went to the court with his lawyer, and for the first time, he saw the other guy sitting with his lawyer and his wife. The wife is the reason everything changed.

She's very, very pregnant. She looks as though she could give birth any moment. Ethan told his lawyer that he'd changed his mind and that he no longer wanted the man to face charges. Ethan didn't want another family to go through what he has been through these past four months. He wanted that baby to be born with both parents around. He said they seemed like nice people, both hardworking folks, and that the man had just been a little tired, a little careless. Unfortunate. Wrong place, wrong time.

The lawyers on both sides said it was highly unlikely the charges would be dropped altogether, but they are prepared to see what can be done. The judge promised to give the case special consideration after Ethan made what I have no doubt was a heart- warming plea that left the husband and wife speechless. Both had been expecting the worst, but now they had hope. Ethan told the court that he thought the man had been punished enough, especially since he would always have to live with the memory of what had happened, but that the man's family shouldn't have to be punished as well. He said that there was no just need for another child to grow up with just one parent when the other one is still alive and willing.

Ethan has turned a corner. I don't know what my parents will say. My father's attitude has always been that the punishment should fit the crime. Well, I for one am proud of my brother. That took a lot of guts.

My eyes open in a panic when I feel the bed shift. It's Alex. I never heard him come in.

"Sorry I scared you, baby," he says in a low voice. "You look wiped out."

"Hi. I feel wiped out. It's been such a busy day."

"Tell me you didn't work all day?"

"No, actually, I didn't work at all, you'll be pleased to know," I say. "Ethan and Lucy came for lunch. I'll tell you all about that in a minute. I went for a walk with your mum. We walked a wee distance along the pebble shore of the water's edge, but I did start to get tired, and then we had dinner together. I like her."

"Yeah, I just left her. She really likes you too. She can't wait for you to come to New York. They're going home on Thursday."

"I am still unsure when I can leave the hotel to travel there," I say. "So, your dad doesn't need to be here for anything else then?" I ask.

"No, Jeff isn't pressing charges. I think he realised that it was not in his interest to continue with that."

"Well, I suppose that's something." I'm relieved because I know that Alex didn't do anything wrong. If it wasn't for him, I dread to think how it would have ended. "Have you eaten?"

"Yes, we had our meeting over dinner. Tell me about Ethan."

I tell him the story. He seems as impressed as I am. He asks how the day was with his mum, and I tell him the truth. I enjoyed spending time with her. I feel as if I got to know him a little better. He seems quite concerned by that comment but quickly changes the subject.

"I need to leave here about lunchtime tomorrow. My flight to London is at 2:15."

"That's fine. I have you all to myself in the morning then?" I run my hands over his chest and feel his muscles tighten under my touch. This could work in my favour.

"Don't you be getting any ideas," he says, swatting my hand away. "You're meant to be recovering. And I'll have to say good-bye to my parents since they'll be gone before I get back here on Thursday night."

"You plan on coming back on Thursday? What about your meetings?" I ask, placing my hand on his thigh. He shoots me a questioning glance. *Go on, I dare you to say something.* My hand is not moving. Yet. But I do intend for it to start moving and the only direction of interest to me is up.

"The really important ones have all been scheduled for Thursday," he says. His eyes travel from my hand back to my face several times. "The first one is an eight o'clock breakfast meeting. Your father and I will be in meetings most of the day. I think he's worried about your mum being left on her own. Our flight back is at five o'clock."

"There's no need for anyone to be worried about Mum. She loves London, and she and Kirsty will have a great time gadding about town," I say with a yawn.

"Come on, you. You should be sleeping."

"What if I don't want to sleep? I know what I would

rather be doing." I move my hand slowly up his thigh, stopping exactly where I want. He is straining against his trousers. That's the reaction I was hoping for.

"Miss Stewart, if you don't rest, your injuries won't heal. Then you'll have to go without for a longer period," he says, shaking his head.

"Now, Mr. Mathews, who says I need to do without?" I pull him towards me, but his intentions are very clear. He is fighting me on this. This is one round he is not going to win. I want him—and badly.

CHAPTER 23

"That was perfect. You are perfect, Libby," he whispers as we lie together, trying to get our breathing under control. "I hope you know now how much I want you."

It *was* pretty remarkable. So tender. So gentle. So caring. And dare I say, so loving. Is it possible to love someone after such a short period of time? I am not sure how I feel about Alex; all I know is that the feelings I have for him are something I have never experienced before.

I nod. It's all I can do. He walks towards the bathroom in all his naked glory, and my eyes follow him intently. I could watch him all day. I don't think I could ever lose interest in him. His head turns to me, and our gaze meets. The fire, the passion, the longing … it's all there. It's back. Or never went away.

"Enjoying the view, Miss Stewart?"

"I do prefer a room with a view," I say with a smile as I try to suppress a yawn. I suddenly remember how tired I was—and still am.

"Libby, baby, I won't be long. Do you need anything?"

"Some water and my painkillers."

"Libby …" His voice carries across the room.

"Alex, I am fine. The doctor just told me to take them on schedule until they were gone, and it's almost time. I don't want to get up during the night."

He's back beside me a few minutes later, handing me a glass of water and my medication, which I take. Tiredness overcomes me. I feel Alex climb into bed beside me.

"Sleep, my beautiful girl." He moves until he's touching me. I lift my head so he can put one arm under me. He gently places the other on my waist. I am now in the safest place in the world: safe in Alex's arms.

"I promise I'll wake you in the morning."

"You better, because if you leave tomorrow without saying good-bye, I will not be a happy bunny," I tell him. "Good night, Alex."

"Sweet dreams, baby," he says, leaning and kissing the back of my head.

Alex is deep in my thoughts as I start to drift off to sleep. He already fills a huge part in my life, a part I didn't even know needed filling. But that's just what I am beginning to realise, I need him, and I most certainly want him. How did I not notice there was something missing from my life? Oh, that's right. I've been busy with Ethan, Lucy, and the hotel.

Fear. I am fearful. I am fearful of what will become of our relationship when he goes home. Will it just fizzle out? What do I want to happen? Could a long-distance relationship work? Do they ever? I doubt it. I suppose I should think about learning to accept the idea that when he leaves, that will be an end of us.

As I am finally drifting off, I am suddenly aware of Alex's soft voice. I could be dreaming, but if I am, it's a great dream. His words are softly spoken, but I hear them nonetheless. "Libby, you have no idea how much you mean to me. I had absolutely no idea I could ever feel about anyone the way I feel about you. I'm crazy about you. You're such a strong, beautiful girl, and I want to keep you safe in my arms always. I love you."

I love you?

I awaken to find Alex still in the same position in which I fell asleep, with his arms round me. Did I hear him right last night? I am sure he used the *L* word. Maybe I was just dreaming. Is that how I feel about him? Could I love him? The answer to that is easy. Yes. Although I do feel it's far too early for declarations. I need to go to the bathroom, so I ease myself slowly out of bed, trying not to wake him. I manage it.

I slide back into bed and lie facing him. I need to wake him—he wants to see his parents before he leaves for London—but he does look so peaceful. I can now appreciate the times he left me sleeping, just watching me. I could watch him all day.

I run my hands across his muscular torso and watch as he reacts to my touch, even asleep. His chest rises and falls with every breath he takes. I lean across and place a small kiss on his chest and rest my head there. I continue touching his warm skin, and soon he stirs.

I allow my hands to travel down the line of his belly and settle between his legs.

"Good morning, Libby. I could get used to waking up like this," he says with a smile. "Oh hell, I admit it. I'm *already* used to waking up with you beside me. I'll miss you tomorrow morning."

What do I say to that? I've enjoyed having him in my bed. Do I speak to him now and ask him about us? Us. I don't even know what I want from him. Maybe I need to think this through first. What do I want? A proper relationship with him would mean one of us having to give up a lot. His life and business are based in the States, and mine are in Scotland. Could I give up my life here for him? My family?

God, maybe I am just jumping the gun. He might not even want a relationship. I suppose his trip to London without me will give me time to think about that. But at the moment, I can't imagine Alex not being in my life.

"Good morning. You do need to get up so you can see your parents before leaving."

"I think you've already gotten me up," he says. "And I'm tempted to just stay here in bed all day with you."

"Well, that's not happening. Although …" I move slowly from his chest, and our eyes meet. I know what he's thinking. I've gotten to know that look quite well. And I want to have him thinking of me all day after he's gone today.

I slide my hand over his hard length, stroking and teasing. He lets out a small groan. I keep my eyes on his face as I dip my head and tease him with my tongue.

"Libby …" His voice is strained.

I smile, hearing his voice, knowing it's me who's about to drive him insane. My turn to take care of him … to touch, to pleasure, and to taste. He's not the only one who gets pleasure from this. I gently rub the base of his length with the palm of my hand. I press my lips over the tip and draw him in, teasing him with my tongue.

He was already hard before, but I feel his body responding. His groans are low but not low enough. Pleasure to my ears. I run my tongue along his impressive length. He tightens in response. I draw him in again, teasing with my tongue and pumping with my hand at the base.

His fingers entwine in my hair tightly, firmly holding me in place. He matches my movement thrust for thrust. I feel the tension as he gets closer and closer to the edge. He is losing control, and I am the one controlling his control.

"Libby …" His voice is tight. "Libby, I can't hold on much longer."

I lift my eyes back to his but don't break our contact. I continue with the job in hand, so to speak. My hand. My mouth. His grip in my hair gets tighter as his thrusts get deeper. Deeper in my mouth. I take him as far as I can. It's only a matter of time. I feel the first trembles before tasting his warm, salty fluid slide down my throat.

"Holy fuck," he says, his voice trembling. "That was incredible. You are full of surprises, Miss Stewart. You take my breath away time and time again."

I move slowly back up the bed, and his arms wrap round me as he pulls me in for a kiss. The look in his eyes is one of content- ment. Mission accomplished. I don't allow the kiss to continue, because I know where it will lead, and that is not my intention. Instead, I rise from the bed, much to Alex's surprise, and head straight to the bathroom, where I switch on the shower.

I hear Alex talking to someone in the other room, so I dress quickly, pulling on a pair of jeans and a vest top. I pull my wet hair up into a clip. I can dry it later. I go to the sitting room and find Alex closing the room door. He's dressed in pyjama bottoms that sit on his hips and a white T- shirt. Good enough to eat.

He's ordered room service breakfast, and the table is set for two.

"I thought we could at least eat together before I head off," he says, pulling out a chair for me. Such a gentleman. "My parents are coming here in about half an hour, so we'll have some time together before then. I ordered an omelette for you. Is that okay?"

"Perfect," I say, sitting down.

I take a sip of the orange juice sitting in front of me and relax in the chair. Alex goes into the bedroom, but he comes back in a moment with my painkillers. He pours a glass of water and hands both to me. There is an understanding in the silence between us.

The atmosphere during breakfast is light and relaxed. Actually, today I feel so much better. The pain has eased off a bit, and I am happier today, although the happier part surprises me since Alex is leaving me today.

"What do you plan on doing while I am gone?" he asks.

"Well, I have a few things to take care of around the hotel today, so I'll get those things done. And your mum wants to go out for dinner."

"What, without me?" he laughs.

"Of course. That's the best time to talk about you—when you're not there." I smirk. "I thought I could take them both out tonight."

"Hey, wait a minute. If you're going out, you could've come with me!"

"It's not the going out that bothers me, and you know that. I just don't need the hassle with attending a premiere tonight looking like this. All those cameras, all those questions that are bound to be asked. And with you being in London, I should be able to go out without being the centre of attention."

There is a light knock at the door. That will be his parents. I move my chair to get up, but Alex shakes his head at me as he goes and opens it. Sarah greets him with a kiss and a hug, then walks towards me and does the same.

Alex pours his parents some coffee, and they join us at the table. I move the plates to try and make a bit of room.

"Are you all set for your trip?" Richard asks.

"Just need to grab a shower and dress. Then I'll be ready. My suits are in the carrier, and I have a bag packed for tomorrow. That's all I need," he says. "What about you both? What are your plans for today?"

"Well, I'm going for a pamper session, courtesy of Libby, and your father is going for a round of golf with Stephen, I think." Sarah sounds excited about that. "Then we're going out to dinner this evening."

"Yes, I know Stephen's looking forward to getting outside," I say.

"Promise me you'll take care of Libby this evening for me?" The question is intended for his parents, but his eyes are locked on me. He places his hand on top of mine, and the slight touch sends shivers down my spine.

"Of course we will. You don't even need to ask," Sarah says, watching Alex interact with me. You would think she'd never seen him with a woman before. Maybe she hasn't—not behaving like this anyway. "We'll get going, so you can get ready."

"I'll give you some time alone. I need to go and dry my hair anyway," I say. "I'll see you both this evening. I'll book a table for seven if that's okay for you?"

"Perfect," Sarah replies with a smile.

I get up and leave them to say their good-byes. In the bedroom I sit staring at my reflection. I've finished doing my hair, and it looks half-presentable, if I don't say so myself. I wish I could do something with my face, but it's still a bit sore to touch, so there is no point even thinking about putting makeup on.

"Thank you." I turn to see Alex enter the room. He walks towards me and bends and places a kiss on my head.

"What for?" I ask.

"For what you're doing for my parents." He smiles at my reflection. "My mom is so happy, and as for my dad, you've made his day he loves golf."

He rests his hands on my shoulders and gently rubs, massaging lightly. I close my eyes and enjoy his touch. This I will miss, although he's only going away for just over twenty-four hours. *What am I going to do when he goes home?* I open my eyes and smile at him. The look in his eyes tells a story, and I shake my head. I know that look well. Very well.

"Shh. Get in that shower, or you'll never get away from here today," I say, chasing him towards the bathroom. He goes in reluctantly. Whilst he's in the shower, I have a few calls and texts to take care of. I text Kirsty first:

Libby: Enjoy London. Try and behave x

Straightaway I get a reply:

Kirsty: I will try. Wish you were going as well but at least I have your mum x

Libby: Me too x

I call my mum. She tells me she wishes I were going with them, but she understands my reasons for staying behind. I have to admit I am a bit jealous of them. I'm going to have to keep myself busy around here to keep my mind occupied. Before I end the call, Mum tells me she will bring me something back.

I call Kieran.

"Libby is everything okay?" he asks.

"Yes, I'm coming down to the office when Alex leaves. I presume there's plenty of work for me to catch up with."

"Are you sure? I mean, of course there's work, but it can wait. Shouldn't you be resting?"

"Kieran, if I hear that once more, I might hit the person who says it. I need stuff to do. I'm bored."

Alex walks into the room wearing just a white, fluffy towel round his waist, distracting me from my conversation. His muscles are well defined. He obviously works out a lot, although he's been here a week, and I've not seen him work out once. Perhaps he has some obscenely expensive personal trainer.

"Libby? Libby, are you there?" Kieran shouts, bringing me back to earth.

Alex laughs.

"Yes, Kieran. Still here. I'll be down when the car comes for Alex in about thirty minutes, so make sure you're available."

I hang up and follow Alex with my gaze. I watch him get dressed. He seems to be putting on quite a floor show, which I am more than happy to watch. I lean back on my elbows on the bed and take in the tantalizing sight in front of me.

"See something you like?"

"Of course. As always," I answer.

He walks slowly towards me as he fastens the belt on his jeans. There is a black T-shirt sitting on the bed. I pick it up and throw it at him. He pulls it over his head and ta-da, he's ready except for shoes. He bends down and places his arms at either side of me. It would be so easy to pull him in and let my emotions take over.

"You have no idea how much I am going to miss you. I have gotten so used to being around you. I'm really considering playing hooky and missing the premiere." His voice is soft, and I can feel his breath on my lips.

"I've gotten used to you being here as well," I say quietly, "but I might as well get used to it for when you go back to the States."

I've struck a nerve. Pain is etched all over his face. He can't bear the thought either.

"Libby, I've already told you that I want you to go to the States with me when I return. I haven't changed my mind. Now that the trial might not go ahead, you might be able to get away sooner than you thought. I hope you'll consider it."

His face has been edging ever so closer to mine. We are almost touching. I want nothing more than to run my hands through his still-damp hair and claim him with my mouth. But he acts first. His mouth claims mine with passion and softness. I respond with the same passion, but no softness.

He pulls away slowly, very slowly, seemingly struggling with his emotions. The look on his face tells me I *did* hear him correctly last night. I see love in his eyes, but I also see conflict. That worries me.

"Come on, you. Up you get," he says, holding out a hand to help me up. He pulls me up from the bed and straight into my favourite place, his arms—the safest place in the world for me.

"Thank you," I say.

"What for?" He questions me with raised eyebrows.

"For being here with me through everything this week." I do mean that. It's been comforting.

"Even when you thought I was pushing you away?"

"Yes, even then, because you thought you were doing the right thing. I just needed to know that you still wanted me. I thought you saw me as damaged goods."

"I could never think that about you. Never."

"Come on. Let's get your stuff together and head downstairs. Michael must be waiting on you."

It's strange walking through the hotel. The staff are being overly polite, trying hard not to stare. I greet all the guests who pass by and even stop to help a lady who has dropped the entire contents of her handbag on the floor.

Alex has his bag in one hand and the suit carrier in the other, which annoys him. He did fidget with them, trying to carry them both with one arm so he could hold my hand, but he wouldn't let me carry even his extremely light carry-on bag. I think he was desperate for contact between us.

"Lovely to see you up and about, Miss Stewart," Sally says from behind the desk. "Kieran says you'll be working today for a bit. If I can help in any way, just ask."

"Thanks, Sally. That's appreciated. If you could give me the schedules for room allocations for the weekend and the coming week, that would be helpful," I say, smiling at her.

"No problem. I'll leave them on your desk. What about lunch? Do you want to me organise anything for you?" She is thoughtful.

"No, just tea I think. I only had breakfast a short time ago."

"Mr Mathews, the rest of your travelling party are already outside. I believe Mr. Stewart has just arrived with the car."

"That's your cue to leave, Alex," I say.

"Thank you." Alex flashes a smile at Sally. "Well, Libby, will you walk me out?"

"Only because I know I will see my parents." I grin.

When we get outside, Fraser is helping the driver put Michael's and Kirsty's things in the back of the black Audi whilst they are in a deep conversation. Kieran stands talking with my parents. No doubt my mother is making Kieran promise to keep an eye on me. Of course he'll agree, but the promise is hardly necessary. He'd watch over me without being asked.

"Sweetheart, you look a lot better today," Mum says as we approach. She greets me with her usual kiss and a hug.

Alex heads to the back of the car. Fraser takes his things from him, and they engage in what looks like polite conversation.

"Thanks, Mum," I say. "I feel better today. I don't feel as sore. If only I didn't *look* so bad."

"I've already told you. You could never be anything less than beautiful," Alex says as he strolls to my side.

My mother's eyes dart between me and Alex. He's not noticed yet; he's too busy gazing at me. His eyes are filled with sadness. My mother's eyes are filled with warmth, love, and a happiness that's not been evident for a long while.

"Come on, you lot. We need to get moving, or we'll miss the flight," Dad shouts to everyone.

"I don't want to leave you," Alex whispers as he pulls me into a tight embrace.

"Stop it. You have a friend to see and a business to take care of. I'll make this easy," I say, holding his gaze. I step onto my tiptoes and place a small, soft kiss on his lips, and then I pull back before he can take it further. "Now go. I'll see you tomorrow night."

Alex climbs right into the backseat with Michael, leaving the middle seats free for Kirsty and my parents. I say goodbye to Kirsty, reminding her to behave herself. She assures me she won't. Kirsty wouldn't be Kirsty if she did.

My parents are the last to get in the car.

"Sweetheart, you two are so perfect together. Even after everything that's happened, you still look blissfully happy."

"Mum, I am happy," I say with a sigh.

"Sweetie … I sense a 'but.'"

"He lives over there, and I live over here. I just don't see how a proper relationship can work between us. One of us would have to give up so much, and that one would certainly be me because of his business. I just don't want to get in over my head, although I'm already thinking that's too late."

"Oh, Libby, you do have yourself worked up into a fluster. Well, at least you've got some time to think things over. But while you are thinking about things, remember that all relationships take hard work and compromise. And try not to overcomplicate things. These things often have a way of sorting themselves out, but I think, and please don't take this the wrong way, that you have to get over the insecurities going through that head of yours. You're too busy focusing on problems that don't even exist, so think about the good for a change," she says. "Now don't work too hard. We'll talk later. Okay, sweetheart?" She does have a valid point.

We all say our good-byes. I'm left standing with Kieran

and Fraser, watching as the car drives away. Kieran places his arm round my shoulder, and I lean my head on him.

"Miss Stewart," Fraser says, "are you sure you're okay? You look a bit knackered."

"I'm fine, Fraser, although I suppose as the day goes on, I will get tired. Come on. Let's get back inside. We've got work to do."

We go back inside. Immediately Fraser starts giving out advice on places to go to a young couple. Kieran heads off to attend to a few problems with housekeeping.

I spend the first hour or so going through and replying to e-mails. I didn't think there would be this many. Most are from various suppliers wishing me a speedy recovery, but there's one that really interests me—and it should interest the staff. It's from the hospitality association. It seems the hotel has been nominated for an award. The fact that we have even been short-listed is such an achievement.

There's a knock at the door.

"Come in," I call out. It's Sally.

"Libby, I was wondering if I can get you anything?" she asks. "I'm just going on my break."

"Maybe some tea."

"Nothing to eat?"

"You know what, Sally? Do you mind some company? Are you going to the canteen?"

"Of course. I'd love for you to join me," she says, smiling.

I shut down my computer, and we head to the canteen. It's quiet when we arrive, with only a few members of the housekeeping staff in evidence. We both have a baked potato and salad. Sally decides she'd like some coffee to keep her alert, while I have a sweet tea that might help curb my desire for some chocolate. The conversation goes smoothly between us. Sally is such a likable girl.

Karl joins us for a well-earned break now that the lunch

rush in the kitchen is over. I ask him how the interviews are going. He has four candidates that he thinks are suitable, but he wants to do a practical interview to see how they perform in the kitchen. Sally agrees with me when I say that's a fantastic idea.

Before I know it, Sally says her break is just about over. I decide to head back with her. I lift our plates and take them over to the hatch leading into the kitchen.

"Libby," Sally calls out my name in a panic. I turn around, and she looks worried. So does Karl.

"What's wrong?"

"Libby, I don't want to worry you, but you have fresh blood on the back of your T-shirt," Sally says. "Can I get Stephen or Kieran for you? They're the first-aiders."

"Sally, you don't need to get them. I'll take care of it," Karl's deep voice assures her.

"Karl, I wasn't thinking."

"Right, Libby. My office. We'll have a look." Karl motions me into the kitchen. To say that I'm reluctant is an under-statement. I've not been in the kitchen since Sunday. "Sally, would you mind going and getting Libby a clean top? Libby, do you mind if she uses the pass key?"

"You know, you can be quite bossy," I say, laughing. Karl grins.

"Anything in particular you want?" Sally asks.

"No. Any of the T-shirts in the bottom drawer of the dressing table. Thanks."

Sally leaves, and I go into the kitchen with Karl. He puts one hand on my shoulder, urging and reassuring me to continue walking. He must sense my apprehension. I knew that eventually I would have to get it over and done with, to go back to the scene of the crime, but I didn't think I would feel this anxious.

"It's fine, Libby. You're doing great," Karl says. His voice gives me the confidence to continue with small, slow steps.

When we go into his office, he tells the staff that no one except Sally should be allowed to enter, which is met with sniggers and whispers. One stern look from Karl stops that.

"Right. Libby, if you could lift your shirt?" He's grinning. "You'll need to sit on the desk so I can look at your back." He's as embarrassed as I am, but he's taking it well.

"I bet you say that to all the girls," I say with a laugh.

"Only the good-looking ones." Karl opens the first aid kit. "I'm sorry. You do have to lift your top, please."

I lift my top rather awkwardly. It's uncomfortable. The office door opens, and I hear Sally gasp. "Oh, Libby."

"I presume it looks bad?" I say, struggling to keep my arms up.

"I had no idea it was this bad. It looks really sore."

"Sally, could you hold her top up for me, please? Libby, I'm going to need you to sit still. I'll clean it gently so I can look at it properly. There is quite a lot of fresh blood."

I nod as Karl puts on some gloves before getting to work. The sterile solution he uses to clean my back with is cold, really bloody cold. He's trying to be gentle, but it's not working.

"Sorry," he says, as I shiver. "Libby, the stitches look tight enough, but it's weeping quite a bit and bleeding at one end. I'll put a fresh dressing on, and I can check it later, but you might want to get it checked with a doctor."

"But I'm going out for dinner tonight with Mr and Mrs Mathews."

"What, is my food not good enough for you?" Karl says with a chuckle.

I shake my head. I wonder if it would bother them if we stayed here for dinner. I could relax my rules about the restaurant for tonight. It would mean I wouldn't have to sort or transport, especially if I am tired.

"You know what? I'm being silly to even consider going out when I have an exceptionally talented chef right at my own disposal. I'm going to stay here tonight in the restaurant," I announce.

"Don't be silly! Take your guests out if you'd like. I'm only winding you up."

"No, it makes sense. I won't need to worry about getting back here if I get tired. And let's face it, I've been shattered most of the week. Anyway, I hear we have a few excellent, up-and-coming, young chefs." I smile, and Sally giggles.

"There. A little antibiotic cream, and that's the dressing on. Sally, if you could help her change her top?" Karl says, handing me my T-shirt.

I don't bother asking either of them to leave. I'm sitting with my back to Karl after all. He won't see anything. I let Sally pull my top over my head and pull the nice clean one on.

"Thanks for that, Karl."

"You're welcome. Now let's get you two out of the kitchen so I can get back to work. Two beautiful women—too much of a distraction."

Sally's face turns a lovely shade of red. Poor Sally. She doesn't know how to take Karl. He sometimes reminds me of Kirsty—a big flirt but harmless.

CHAPTER 24

*T*he rest of the afternoon passes by quickly. I get through a good bit of work and have even arranged a meeting with the heads of all departments for five o'clock. I need to break the good news to them about our nomination. I also speak to the beauty therapist and arrange for her to come to my room to see if she can do anything with my face, which she assures me she can.

The guys are all excited with the news of the nomination.

"Oh, Libby, this is great news!" Kieran shrieks with delight. "So is there a big bash that we can all attend? We can all get dressed up in our fancy togs."

"Saturday, 22 November. We'll have to check who all will be available to go. I believe it's in Edinburgh," I tell them.

"I'm not at all surprised by this. I know I've not been here as long as some of you, but this hotel outdoes a lot of those where I've worked in the past. The nomination is very well deserved," Karl tells the room.

I have a hardworking, dedicated team, who all ensure that our guests have the VIP experience. I am proud of them all, and I'm sure my father will be over the moon with the nomination when I tell him tomorrow.

After the meeting I go back to my room, leaving the staff to carry on with all their jobs. Kieran has worked his backside off this week. I don't know what I would do without him, and he does make my job easier. I call Sarah about the change of plans for dinner, and she agrees that it makes sense. She tells me she'll come to my room so we can walk down to the restaurant together. Richard won't be joining us; he's still out with Stephen on the golf course.

I'm secretly pleased by this last news. Maybe if it's just the two of us, Sarah will dish the dirt on Katherine Hunter.

That reminds me of the premiere, so I send Alex a quick text:

Libby: Hope you have a good night x

I don't expect him to reply straightaway, but I am surprised he's not been in touch before now. The beauty therapist does a great job with my makeup. The bruising is still visible, but I don't look like a monster anymore. I put on a skirt and a loose-fitting, button-down top. I don't want anything that will rub against my back, and I don't want to stress the stitches.

I hear a knock at the door, and I open it expecting to see Sarah. I'm surprised to see Karl standing there in his chef uniform. He's holding the first aid case.

"I said I wanted to check it again," he says, walking in.

"It will be fine. You shouldn't have taken time out to check on me."

"Now you're being silly. You can't check it or reach it yourself. Someone has to do it for you. Sit down, and stop being childish."

He opens the case and puts it on the table. I sit down on the couch and lift my top up at the back. He peels off the dressing slowly and delicately. Nothing like the way my mother used to do it when I was wee; she'd just rip the plaster right off. There is a knock on the door.

"Could you answer that? It will be Mrs Mathews," I ask, not wanting to move.

Karl opens the door, and I hear Sarah's loud gasp.

"Oh, good lord," she says, sounding flustered. "Libby, are you all right?"

"Sarah, it's not as bad as it looks," I tell her.

"Don't listen to her. She can't see how bad it looks. Libby, you need to have a doctor look at it. It's still weeping. I think you may be getting an infection," Karl says as he cleans it out.

"Libby, I have to agree with your friend here …" Her voice trails off.

Karl interrupts her. "My apologies for my manners, Mrs Mathews. I should have introduced myself," he says, bowing gallantly. "I am Karl, the head chef."

"Nice to meet you, Karl. Libby, you should see a doctor. It does look bad. I had no idea about this injury. Alex never mentioned it. It's really inflamed. How are you feeling? Do you have a temperature?"

"Sarah, I feel okay, and my temperature is normal. I'll call the doctor in the morning if that will make you both happy."

"Yes, it would. And I'm sure Alex will be happy as well," Sarah says. I smile at the mention of his name. God, I do have it bad.

Sarah holds my top up while Karl continues his delicate work. Before I know it, I'm all cleaned up again with a fresh dressing on my back.

"Right. That's you, good as new," Karl says, putting my top back down. "I'm not in until lunchtime tomorrow, but Stephen is in first thing. I'll send him a message to come check on you in the morning and change the dressing again. He can drive you to the doctor, too. Now if you ladies want dinner, I'd better head back to the kitchen."

"Thanks, Karl," I say as he leaves us. I turn to Sarah, who eyes me cautiously. "Are we ready to go for dinner?"

"Yes, but ... Libby, are there any other injuries?" she asks with concern.

"No, Sarah, the only other thing injured is my pride. Being stupid enough to let this happen."

"You're certainly not stupid, Libby. Strong, brave, defiant —you've not allowed it to affect your everyday life. I've seen lots of people shut themselves away from all their family and loved ones after attacks like this. It can damage so much more than the body," she says, her voice sad.

"Don't get me wrong. I've had my moments these past few days when that's all I've wanted to do, and I've shed a whole load of tears. But I've decided that Jeff Ross isn't worth a single tear of mine."

"Good for you. Okay, no more sad talk. Let's go see what your chef can do," she says with a smile that reminds me of Alex.

The restaurant is really busy for a Wednesday evening. It's great to see, and Sarah seems impressed. The waiter shows us to a quiet table, as I requested, and we order drinks and settle in to read the menu.

"Libby, what would you recommend?"

"Everything, of course," I say with a chuckle. "But is this your first time in Scotland?"

"Yes."

"Well, in that case, there's only one option for you: haggis, neeps, and tatties. And if you don't like it, I'll have Karl make you anything you want. But I'm sure you will love it."

"Okay, why not? What is haggis?"

"I will tell you after you've tasted it." She looks intrigued. Well, there is no point telling her before she even tastes it, because I have the slightest suspicion she won't try it if I do. We get our haggis from a traditional butcher, who makes the haggis in store. It's traditionally made from sheep's heart, liver, and lungs, minced together with onion, suet, oatmeal, and spices. I know it really doesn't sound that appealing, but one taste and I was hooked.

The waiter brings our drinks and takes our order. We don't bother with starters, and we both order the haggis. Conversation flows with ease, considering I barely know this woman. To see and hear us talking and laughing, you'd think we'd known each other forever.

"Sarah, can I ask you something? Don't feel you need to tell me if it's some sort of secret, but I am curious."

"Of course."

"It's about Katherine Hunter," I say.

"I thought it would be. You want to know why I detest her." I nod. "Okay, I'll give you the full story. Alex might not be happy about this, but I think you have a right to know. Katherine's mother and I were close friends. All our kids are quite close together in age. Katherine and my daughter, Sophie, are the same age and were the best of friends, ever since they were little. Now they hardly talk."

I remember Alex telling me he had a younger sister, but not much more.

"Well, I'm sure you remember what it was like to be a teenage girl. Katherine had a crush on Alex and had as far back as I can remember, but Alex was never interested in her like that. Alex was fifteen, two years older, and he still thought of his sister and her friends as little kids, pains in the butt. Alex walked the girls home every day after school, though he hated doing it—he would much rather have been going home with his own friends—but he was always a good kid. He did it out of duty."

"He's still a good kid," I say, smiling thinking of him. She smiles back.

"Anyway, one day Alex and Michael got into some kind of

a scrap at school. They were kept late after school and put in detention—we call it that back home—so the teacher could talk to them. I can't even remember what the fight was about, though it was probably about some girl. Sophie wanted to wait for Alex, but Katherine said it would be okay if just that once, they walked home without him. The girls took the usual way home, but they ran into some older boys on the way home. Now Katherine knew the boys—they were friends of her older sister. The boys had been drinking, and … well, they managed to talk the girls into going into an alley off the main walk. That's when they struck both the girls and pinned them down."

I gasp in horror at the story I am hearing.

"When Alex and Michael finally got out of school, they ran most of the way. They were certain they'd get in trouble for letting the girls walk home on their own, even though it couldn't be helped. When they ran past the alley, they heard screams. Of course they tried to stop it. They managed to get three lads off Sophie, and Michael grabbed her, and the two of them ran off to get help. Alex stayed to help Katherine but ended up taking a bad beating that left him in hospital for over two weeks. But the worst thing for Alex was that he was held down by three or four of the boys and made to watch as they raped Katherine."

"That's horrible! For all of them!" I can feel the tears fill my eyes. "Of course. That explains the way Alex behaved when he found Jeff attacking me."

"Sweetie, what do you mean?" Sarah asks.

"Jeff didn't just beat me. When Alex found me, Jeff had his trousers undone, and he was about to—"

"No, Libby, please don't tell me he—"

"No, Sarah, he didn't, because Alex stopped him in time. But Alex beat Jeff quite soundly before Michael managed to pull him off."

We sit in silence for a few minutes. I suppose we are both trying to digest the other's story. But the silence is broken when the waiter brings our food. As usual, it looks perfect.

"What you've told me tells me a lot about Alex, but it doesn't quite explain your dislike of Katherine."

"No, it doesn't. I'm getting to that," says Sarah, taking a sip of wine. "After the attack Katherine changed. That was to be expected, I suppose. God, Sophie changed a lot too. She shut herself off from us all. But finally Sophie got counselling, and it helped her. Alex started counselling, but he wouldn't go back. Katherine didn't have the same family support that my kids had and still do, we are a close knit family. Well anyway Alex blamed himself for that day's events, and I believe he still does. But Katherine blames Alex."

"Why would she blame him?" I ask out of confusion.

"Because he and Michael managed to get Sophie away to safety and not her. Well, anyway, the distance grew between the girls, but Katherine still kept hovering around Alex. I believe that ever since that day, she's used my son's guilt to manipulate him. She snaps her fingers, and he goes running. She's more than happy to be seen on his arm to further her career, and it's worked—it's a good part of what's helped her get where she is today. She was a second-rate actress, all bit parts and uncredited walk-ons, until he agreed to squire her around Hollywood one season. She doesn't want him; she wants payback. She's extremely jealous of any relationship Alex ever has, and she *always* interferes. Do you know you are the first girl—excuse me, woman—who Alex has ever introduced to us? Oh yes, I see him in the press with different girls, but they never last. I believe Katherine is to blame for that. The pictures of you together must be driving her crazy. She's a manipulative little bitch."

I don't know what to say. I take another mouthful of food,

which I suddenly have no desire to eat. I push my plate away and take a drink of water.

"You should eat more, Libby. This is great by the way. You can tell me what's in it now. I should get you to cook this when you come to New York with Alex."

"Sarah, I'd really like to visit you in America, but I've not decided what I'm doing about Alex's invitation. I have this place to think about. And then there's my brother, Ethan, and my niece, Lucy, to consider." I tell her Ethan's story, which helps her understand my bond with my twin.

"Alex cares about you. That much is obvious to anyone who sees you together," says Sarah. "My wish for Alex, as his mother, is to see him happy and settled. But he has to settle for the right reasons—for love, not guilt. I think that's what frightens me the most, the idea that he might do something silly out of guilt. Sorry. Listen to me rattling on."

"No, it's fine. I care for Alex. Truly I do, but I've known him only a week, so I am not sure what to call what I feel or what to make of our relationship. We lead such completely different lives on separate sides of the Atlantic. I'm so afraid a relationship can't work for us," I say, feeling a bit down at my own summation.

"Oh, Libby, all relationships take work. You just have to decide if it's worth it for you," she says with a smile. "And anyway, it's early on for you both. If it's meant to be, things will work out for you, I'm sure."

"My mother said the same thing to me the other night when we were all out for dinner," I say, laughing.

"Sounds like a woman after my own heart. Who knows—maybe in the not-too-distant future, I'll get to meet her. I'm sure she and I would get along great." I'm sure they would too.

Sarah puts her cutlery down on an empty plate just as Karl comes over to our table.

"Well, Mrs Mathews, I don't need to ask if you enjoyed that, do I?" He flashes a proud smile.

"No, Karl, that was delicious. I've asked Libby if she will make it for the family when she decides to come visit us in the States. They'll love it. Everything was perfect."

"Libby, was there something wrong with yours?" Karl asks.

"Nothing at all. I just haven't really got much of an appetite yet, I guess. I wasn't as hungry as I thought I was."

"Libby, are you okay? You look quite pale," Karl asks.

I wish people would stop asking me that. I know they mean well, but it is driving me insane. Although now that he mentions it, I really don't feel so great. *Oh, give in and tell him.*

"Actually, Karl, no. I don't feel well at all. If you'll both excuse me, I'll be back in a minute. While I am gone, you can tell Sarah what's in haggis," I say, rising quickly from my chair. I race through the kitchen to the staff toilets and make it just in time to bring up everything I've just eaten. I feel dizzy and tired. I clean myself up and return to the restaurant.

As I approach the table, I feel strange—hot and dizzy. I stagger slightly and take hold of a chair. I hear Karl telling Sarah that he's going to call Ethan. I don't even have the strength to argue with him about it. Right now it seems like a good idea.

"Libby!" Sarah shouts.

Everything turns black.

When I come to, Sarah is on the floor beside me with my head resting on her legs. Karl is on the phone.

"No, we need a doctor to come here … yes, yes … no, she is conscious now. No, I think she has an infection in the wound on her back … many, many stitches—I can't remember how many now. Yes, I changed the dressing twice today, and it is weeping quite a bit. Yes, bloody discharge …

yes, certainly. Is it okay to take her back to her room? No, she didn't bang her head when she fainted. Thank you again."

He ends the call to the doctor and immediately makes another call. Sarah is gently stroking my arm in a comforting way, the same way my mother probably would.

"Ethan, it's Karl at the hotel. Listen, I know it might be difficult with the wee one, but Libby isn't feeling well. No, I've called for a doctor to come here. You don't need to rush —I'll stay with her, and Alex's mum is with her as well—but as soon as you can manage. That's fine … of course you have to bring her. I'll see you soon."

"Okay, Libby, we're going to get you upstairs and comfortable before the doctor gets here. Ethan is on his way with Lucy. Do you think you can get up slowly with my help?"

"Yes, Karl. I feel foolish lying here in a busy restaurant. If we could hurry it up?" I say drily.

"Libby, we can't rush. If we do, you'll only wind up back on the floor again," he says. He sounds frustrated.

"Please listen to him," Sarah says kindly.

I nod. Karl shouts for another chef to help, but I tell him no. I don't want to draw any more attention to myself. I feel silly enough. With the help of Karl and Sarah, I manage to get to my feet, albeit a bit on the shaky side. Karl takes us through the kitchen so I don't have to go through all the hotel corridors. He's kept a tight grip of me around the waist. I am certain my feet are flying through the air.

As we enter my room, Karl takes me straight to my bedroom and lowers me gently onto the bed. The last time I was lowered onto this bed, it was by Alex, just before we made love all night. I wish he were here right now.

"Libby, sweetie, where are your pyjamas?" Sarah's soft voice is right beside me again.

"In the drawer." I point the direction of the dressing table.

"Do you mind me dressing you and washing your face?" she asks kindly.

I can only shake my head. I can't find the words. I am so hot, and this bloody room is spinning. My mouth is dry. My eyes are heavy.

I hear Sarah ask Karl to leave the room until she can help me change. He tells her he'll go meet the doctor, and she nods. Sarah's hands feel cold against my skin but soft, soft like Alex's. She takes her time removing my outer layer of clothes. I try to help as best I can, but I feel useless. She is gentle as she cleans my face, removing all traces of the makeup.

Soon I hear voices.

"Sarah, darling, how is she doing?" Richard asks.

"Not great. She's burning up. I'll be glad when the doctor gets here ... and her brother. I don't want to call Alex—I'll leave that up to Ethan. He'll want to be the one to call their parents," she answers. "Bring me another cold washcloth, will you? And some ice?"

I drift off to sleep again.

I hear a baby cry. My eyes spring open. Ethan is sitting beside me, holding my hand. Sarah holds a very tired-looking Lucy on her lap. She's singing her a lullaby.

"What's wrong, Libby? You not getting *enough* attention this week? You thought you needed some more?" He's trying to make me laugh, but he's not fooling me. I can tell he's worried.

"Ethan, you didn't have to come. You should be at home, and that beautiful baby girl should be in bed."

"Look at her. She's fine. She's loving the extra attention, and I'll put her to sleep in the pram soon. It's you I'm worried about." He looks towards Sarah.

"Where's Karl? I though he was here?" I say.

"He's headed down to bring the doctor up," Ethan says. "That will be them now."

I hear more voices coming from the next room. Sarah takes Lucy out of the bedroom, and the doctor comes in. He closes the door. Ethan stays with me.

"So, Miss Stewart. I understand you're having a bit of a rough time of it lately. I'm Dr. Taylor." He inserts a thermometer in my mouth. "I need to check your back now, if that's okay. Can you roll onto your side for me?"

I turn slowly onto my side. Ethan is still holding my hand. The doctor puts on some gloves and removes the dressing. He cleans the wound thoroughly. I wince at the coldness. I feel his gloved hand putting pressure on my back. He rolls me onto my back and reads the thermometer and then takes my blood pressure.

"Right. Miss Stewart, it would appear that you have an infection, which is not uncommon with such a deep puncture. We'll treat it with a stronger antibiotic. Your temperature is a bit on the high side, as is your blood pressure, but I think at the moment I'm happy enough for you to remain here. If anything changes, you'll be admitted to hospital. I'll make arrangements for one of the community nurses to visit first thing in the morning."

"The infection explains how she is just now?" Ethan asks.

"Yes. I can give her something to help her sleep through the night. The fever will most likely get slightly worse before we start to see an improvement."

Worse? I don't think I could feel worse than I do just now. Maybe I should just let the doctor give me something to sleep. Maybe I'll wake up feeling right as rain.

"I need to know that someone will be here the whole night with her," the doctor says.

"Yes, I'll be here," says Ethan. "I'll stay with her."

The doctor tells Ethan when to give me the medication

and what other signs to watch out for. Ethan sees the doctor out and thanks him. I can hear everyone talking in the next room, but I don't know what they are talking about. Although I can guess. Me.

Suddenly I hear Sarah shout. "*That. Damn. Bitch!*"

"Sarah, that's enough! There's a baby here, and Libby is right next door. She doesn't need this just now." Richard seems to be trying to calm her down.

"She makes my blood boil, Richard! You know how I feel about her! And as for Alex, I'll cancel my flight tomorrow and deal with him."

After my conversation with Sarah earlier, I know exactly which bitch she's talking about, but I can't imagine what Alex has done. I'm not sure I want to know—at least right now. Ethan enters the room with his phone stuck at his ear.

"Mum … no, it's not Lucy. If you'll hush and let me speak, I'll tell you. I'm at the hotel. Libby isn't well—Mum, calm down! Karl had to dress the wound in her back twice today, and she took unwell whilst having dinner with Mrs Mathews. Yes, she fainted. The doctor says she has an infection, and he's given us some antibiotic … no, Mum, she's not being admitted into hospital. The doctor says that unless it gets worse, she's fine here. Okay, I'll speak to you again in a few minutes."

I can only imagine how my mother's end of the conversation went. Ethan sits down on the bed beside me. He takes my hand and strokes it gently. Such a simple gesture but one that means the world to me.

"Ethan? Is Mum okay?" I struggle to get the words out, but I want to know what Mum has said.

"She's worried. She wanted to speak to Dad, and then she'll ring back. They were just about to leave and go to some after party," he says. He seems tense, edgy even. He's hiding something from me. Ethan forgets how well I know him.

"Ethan, what's happened?" My voice trembles.

"Libby, are you cold?" I nod. He gets up and grabs another blanket. "Here. You need to stay warm. You should try and sleep."

His phone rings. I try to concentrate on what he's saying.

"Hi, Mum. Yes, I'm with her just now. No, I'm not sure you'll get much sense out of her. Libby? Mum wants to talk to you."

"Libby, sweetheart, don't you worry. Kirsty and I are heading to the airport right now. We're getting a flight back up the road."

"Mum," I croak, but I can't hold the phone. I'm trembling so badly it falls from my hand.

"Mum. I need to go. See you soon," Ethan tells her. He takes me in his arms and cradles me, and I eventually drift off into a troublesome sleep.

CHAPTER 25

I wish I could say I felt rested, but that would be a lie. I don't remember much from throughout the night. There were nightmares. Plenty of them. Tears, I think, too. Plenty of those. There was Ethan, who stayed with me the whole night. Noise. Everything seemed so loud. But now it's just quiet. I open my eyes slowly, blinking a few times to clear my view. The curtains are closed. The room is dark, so I'm unsure what time of day it is. It's too quiet, considering. Something is wrong.

I try to pull myself up in the bed, but it's much harder than I anticipate. My body aches, everywhere. I finally get myself into a sitting position, and I'm able to reach over and put a light on. I hear a noise from next door.

"Ethan?" I call out.

"No, Libby, it's just me," Karl says, walking into the bedroom. "Ethan needed to go home and get a few things for Lucy—I think clothes—and drop them off with your mum. He should be back shortly. He didn't want you to be left alone."

"Oh. Karl, what time is it?" I ask.

"Five o'clock."

"In the evening?" He nods. Christ, I've been out of it for almost a day. "Poor Lucy ... being stuck here all this time."

"No, it was just Ethan with you all night. Your mum took her home after she arrived. She didn't want the wee one to disturb you. But from what Ethan says, a bomb could've went off and you would've slept through it."

"I think I spoke to Mum on the phone. There was a doctor here?"

"Yes, there was. Ethan can fill in any blanks for you. Can I get you anything?"

"Some water, please? I'm so thirsty."

Karl gets some ice water and a straw. He holds the glass for me, and I take a sip. It's cool and refreshing, just what I needed. I could also do with going to the toilet and taking a bath. My hair feels damp as I run my hands through it. So do my clothes.

"You were sweating from your fever," Karl says, answering my unspoken question. "I could run a bath for you, but you're not getting into one until Ethan gets back."

"That would be great, because I must stink," I say with a laugh. "So I presume Sarah and Richard are already away? I didn't even get to say good-bye to them before they left."

"No, they're still here." *Why are they still here?* "As I said, Ethan can fill you in on everything," Karl says, walking towards my bathroom.

I get the feeling that something is going on. Karl is keeping something from me. I wonder if Ethan will tell me exactly what it is. Why are Sarah and Richard still here? On the plus side, it should only be a few hours before I get to see Alex.

I move my legs so they are hanging over the bed. I need to get up. I lower my feet to the floor and slowly lift myself off the bed. I manage to stand, albeit slightly unsteadily. I wander through to the sitting room. Karl must have been sitting watching TV. It's still on. I don't bother with it. It's just good to be up and moving about. Each step I take gets easier.

The room door opens, and Kieran walks in with what looks like a pile of newspapers but stops dead in his tracks. He looks a little shocked and surprised.

"Oh, Libby. You're here."

"Where else would I be? This is my room, after all."

"Yes, of course. I was … eh … just looking for Ethan," he says, stumbling over his words. "I have a few things … no, never mind. Where is he?"

"He will be here shortly. Karl is here, though, babysitting me," I answer with frustration lacing my voice. Something is definitely going on. Even Kieran looks shifty. I've seen Kieran look a lot of ways, but never this bad. I walk towards him. He's still hovering by the door looking to make a quick exit.

"Kieran, what's going on?" He shakes his head and says nothing. "Kieran, please tell me."

"Nothing. Everything is fine." He shifts from one foot to the other, agitated, and tries to hide the papers behind him.

"Kieran, give me those bloody papers!" I shout angrily. I can hear footsteps behind me.

"Libby, what are you doing up?" Karl shouts, looking as suspicious as Kieran. He tries to take my arm to lead me away, but I push his arm away.

"*I am not moving from this spot until someone tells me what the fuck is going on!*"

A voice distracts me, Alex's voice. He's back already? No, wait. It's the TV. Alex is on the TV. He's at what looks like an airport with my dad. Karl moves quickly to get the remote control, but so do I. I get it first.

"*Alex, can you clarify your relationship with Katherine?*"

"What about Miss Stewart?"

"You and Katherine looked very much together last night."

"Have you ended things with Libby?"

"Libby, honey, give me the remote control. You don't need to see or hear this just now," Kieran says, his voice low and soft. He walks to where I stand in the middle of the room, transfixed by Alex's face on the screen.

Kieran puts the papers down on the table and steps in front of me, blocking my view of the TV, but that doesn't matter. I can still hear the questions being fired at both Alex and my dad. Then I remember that I heard Sarah shouting last night about that bitch. At the time I presumed she meant Katherine, and now I know I was right.

"Alex, will you be heading back to the States now that the buyout is complete?"

"Phil, what do you make of the allegations that both you and Alex used your daughter for the publicity?"

"Libby, please," Kieran says, trying again. He puts his arms on my shoulders and tries to steer me back towards the bedroom.

"Kieran, is this what you are all tiptoeing about for?" I push him away from me.

"Libby, leave Kieran alone." My brother's voice echoes in the room. Karl is beside him. God, I never even noticed him leaving. "Guys, would you go and leave us to it?"

Kieran gives me a hug and a kiss and tells me he's sorry before they both leave the room. Kieran has a little-lost-puppy look on his face now.

"Could you eat now?"

"No, Karl ran me a bath. I'm going to go for that and change into fresh, clean clothes. And then I want some answers from you. So you have a short time to think about what you will tell me. And the truth would be a good place to start. Could you also let Sarah know I am awake? If I remember correctly, she was quite worried."

I head towards my bathroom, leaving Ethan with his thoughts. I strip and lower myself into the perfect bath, where I sink into the comforting water and my own less comforting thoughts. Could it really be true? Did Dad use me for publicity? If so, why? As for Alex, well, I don't really know him. It could all have been an act. Maybe it had been planned all along. Both he and Katherine seem to have gotten the exposure they wanted. Good or bad, as far as press coverage goes, it doesn't matter if you're hungry enough for it. Or who gets hurt along the way.

Mum. Shit, I need to speak with her. If this is true, she will be devastated. I finish getting washed, including my hair. I dry and dress in record time, pulling on jeans and a T-shirt. I pull the hairbrush through my hair and put it up in a clip, and then I walk back out to Ethan, who is sitting on the couch with one of the newspapers in his hand. I sit at the other end of the couch. He hands me the paper. The front page has a picture of Alex and Katherine. His arm is around her waist. I feel myself start to shake. She loves him—that much is obvious. It looks as if they are about to kiss. Her hand rests against his jaw. I toss the paper away as my eyes fill with tears. Ethan is at my side with a protective arm around me.

"Shh, it's all right," he whispers. But I need him to tell me the whole story.

"Ethan, I want to hear what you know. All of it, please. Don't leave anything out."

"Are you sure you're ready?" I nod, not really sure that I am. "Okay, then, here goes. Alex is Dad's first high-profile celeb in a while. The PR business has taken a tumble over the past year and a half. This is fact. I know, because before Lindsay's death, I was working with him on some advertising. All his other business interests were and still are going well. You know how well the hotel is going; it's never been in a stronger position, and a lot of that is down to you."

"But I've only been manager a short time."

"That may be so, but think of all the work you did here even before you were appointed. Everything was in preparation. This hotel is your life, and it has been for years. You dreamed of this place being yours since—god, I don't remember when. You were always the one to come here at weekends and help out wherever Granddad would let you. I could never see myself working here. Right. Well, it was Dad's original plan for me to spend time with Alex. I could have coped with some of the publicity without much problem. You know—big-time PR guru's son and American businessman become friends. I show him the sights, get him seen in all the right places. I could go on. Mum and Lindsay knew about this. There was no need to tell you; we all wanted you to concentrate on your studies and the hotel."

"But something happened …"

"Yes. Libby, you know money was not the driving force behind this. If it didn't work, they wouldn't lose anything. But Dad enjoys the lifestyle his PR business brings. He craves the attention. He's missed it. And his plan fell apart when Lindsay … and I became next to useless. If I am honest with you, I never gave any of it a second thought. I had completely forgotten about it until I saw the first pictures of the two of you in the papers."

"I see." I don't see, but I want him to keep talking.

"Dad still needed someone to show Alex about, and you and he were both going to be staying at the same place. And let's face it—you make for much more interesting reading than me. And the pictures, they sold a story of their own. Dad would *never* have gotten as much publicity out of me. Dad made arrangements for a photographer to be at the football and here again on Sunday, just to get a few snaps of you two together. You were only meant to be seen in each other's company a few times. To arouse speculation. You know—will they, won't they? Nothing like the pictures that first made the papers. Dad was just as surprised as the rest of us, with those. You and Alex look so good together in those."

That does it. I can't hold the tears back any longer. The dam has well and truly burst. Everything was a lie, and I was the only one who didn't know? I can't believe they've done this to me. If I had at least known about it, I could have saved my feelings—and my heart.

"Let's get this straight. You all knew about Dad's grand plan? Even when you saw how I felt, you went along with it? Here's foolish Libby, falling for it all, hook, line, and sinker. You know what? I don't know Alex that well, so I can't say I am surprised by him. He took Dad's plan that one stage further. He led me on, making me think … well, what does it matter what I think? It was all one big lie," I say. I pause to wipe the tears from my face. "But all of you … you're my family. You lied to me! I can't even begin to explain how I feel right now."

"Libby, I'm so sorry."

"Sorry!" I shout. "Sorry won't cut it. Right now I don't want to see you. Any of you. After everything I've done for you, this is how you treat me?"

"Libby …"

"Ethan, I don't want to hear it. Just get out!" I shout, pushing him away from me. I can't bear the sight of him just now, and that hurts more than anything else. The hurt in his eyes: it's too little, too late.

"Just go," I growl.

He gets up and leaves, closely the door quietly behind him. I'm left sitting on the couch alone. I pull my legs up close to my chest and start rocking slightly. The tears don't stop. I've been betrayed by the ones I love most. I wonder if even Mum knew.

I am not sure how long I've been sitting here. My phone has been going almost constantly, but I've ignored it. I really don't want to speak with anyone. There is a light knock on my room door.

"Libby, please. It's Sarah. Can I come in?"

I walk over to open the door.

"Oh, Libby, sweetheart." She pulls me into a tight embrace. "It's all right. Everything will be okay."

"I've been such a fool."

"No, sweetie, you haven't. Come on. Let's sit down so we can talk." We move over to the couch. "Have you eaten anything since you got up?"

"No."

"Okay. Let me order you some toast and tea. You need to try and eat."

Sarah orders some room service for us both, tea and toasted sandwiches, before settling down beside me on the couch.

"Ethan came to see me after you threw him out. He said he hadn't yet let you know what the nurse said this morning."

"I didn't give that a thought."

"Not surprising. Okay, your blood pressure is still a bit high, but your temperature was nearly back to normal then, and I think we can say your temperature is probably okay now. She checked your back as well and said it already looked better. We have to change the dressing again tonight. She said that if we had any concerns when you woke, we were supposed to get the doctor back out. So apart from the obvious, how are you feeling?"

"Sarah, I've not given myself a thought, to be honest."

"I had a feeling you might say that. Can you think about it

now? You gave everyone a scare last night. I was really worried about you."

"I feel much, much better than last night. No dizziness. Thank you for staying with me."

"No need to thank me," she says. She takes a deep breath. "Alex would never have forgiven me for not staying with you."

"I think we both know that's not true. Alex couldn't care less about me."

"Oh, sweetie, that's not true. He's been calling nonstop since Ethan first called your mother last night. Both your dad and Alex will be here any time now."

"I don't want to see *either* of them."

"I think you should hear them out. They've both been going out of their minds with worry for you. Ethan has told me the story, so I think I know most of it. People do things for lots of reasons, and we don't always agree with them. But I think you should listen to what they have to say. I'm not happy with Alex—that's one of the reasons I'm still here—and I plan to let him know exactly how I feel. I've seen the pictures of that woman and read the stories, so he has me to face when he gets here. And believe me, if I have any doubts about his answers, well, we'll cross that bridge when we come to it, I suppose."

"Sarah, how can I face either of them? They've both lied to me! And as for Alex, I feel so foolish for letting things go so far between us. He said … he even said he loved me, but he was just using me—for publicity. I don't care about Katherine, but it's obvious from the pictures how much she loves him. So I now I have to ask myself another question: did he use me to make her jealous?"

"Libby, I think you're right that Katherine is in love. But she's in love with the global spotlight that surrounds Alex. Do I think she loves *him* as a person? I have to say no. Do I think he loves her? I know that the answer to that is no. He feels guilty for what happened to her, and as I told you last night, she uses that to her advantage. Do I think Alex has used you for publicity? I'm not sure. He's never needed to use anyone. And as for the pictures of you two, I can honestly say he's never looked happier—and he's not a very good liar. He bursts with pride when he speaks about you. When I think back to Sunday, when you were attacked, he was beside himself with worry about you. I believe he cares about you a great deal. I can believe that he loves you. Could there be more between you? My answer to that question is yes, but that's up to the both of you. Libby, you are a strong, intelligent, and independent woman. If you want to, you'll work things out."

Room service arrives. Sarah pours the tea for us both. This must be hard for her sitting here with me, considering everything that's going on. I do try and eat something, but I'm struggling. I'm just not that hungry. Sarah also gives me some of the medication that the doctor left.

I have a look at my phone. Loads of messages and calls. It looks like Mum has been calling nonstop since Ethan left. Well, I'm going to let her stew. I'll call her tomorrow—if I feel up to it. Lots of missed calls from Alex and a voicemail. Should I listen to it?

"What's wrong, Libby," Sarah asks, checking her own phone.

"There's a voicemail from Alex. I'm not sure I can listen to it."

"As I said, you have a lot to think about, but I'm sure it will all work out just fine in the end. It might just take a bit of time. Right now Alex is in the hotel with your dad. They're on the way up. Would you like me to stay or go?"

"Please stay ... if you don't mind," I reply.

"Of course."

I am nervous now and scared at seeing both of them. But I don't get a chance to think about it too long before the door opens and Alex is standing there, my dad right behind him. Sarah squeezes my hand and gives me a reassuring smile. That's all the encouragement I need. I will make it through the conversations with them both. I may not make the right decision tonight, but I think I'll be okay.

Alex introduces my dad to his mother. She smiles politely. Alex walks towards me and, for the first time in the short time I've known him, he looks unsure of how to approach me. But he does, slowly, with a nod of encouragement from his mother.

"Libby, I've been worried sick since we got the call last night." He bends down and gives me a kiss. "How are you now?" I don't flinch.

"I'm over the fever, and the antibiotics are working on the infection," I say as he sits down in the chair.

My father walks towards me and says much the same as Alex. I can hear the concern in his voice.

"Dad, whatever you want to say can wait. I'm really not ready to hear from you just yet."

"Libby, I'm sorry I—"

I cut him off. "I'm sure you are. Just the same as Mum and Ethan. But at the moment, I don't want to hear the excuses. I love you all—that's not changed—but you've hurt me. You should have kept me in the loop, let me make my own decisions. Now you've seen me, and you know I'm fine. I would much rather you go. Tell Mum I might call her tomorrow."

I do feel bad for speaking to my dad like that. I've never done that before. But then again, he's never pushed me this far. He gives me a kiss and wraps his arms round me. I fight the urge to respond.

"I am so sorry, Libby. I never meant to hurt you," he whispers before turning towards the door.

"Phil, wait there. I'll walk you out," Sarah says, much to my surprise. I stand up to thank her.

"Libby, it's been such a pleasure meeting you, and I do hope our paths cross again. Remember everything we've talked about."

"You're leaving?"

"Yes, sweetie. Our flight back to New York leaves at two in the morning. Take care of yourself. And whatever happens, please stay in touch." She leans in and gives me a kiss on the cheek before leaving with my dad.

And then there were two.

"Libby." Alex's voice is low. He moves from the chair and sits on the couch beside me. He takes my hand.

Such a simple gesture has butterflies in my stomach. I lift my eyes and drink in this man who has turned my life upside down in such a short period of time. He looks as tired as I feel. I want nothing more than to fall asleep in his arms, but I have a feeling that won't be happening again anytime soon, if ever. That thought upsets me—maybe a lot more than I'm prepared to let on.

"So the deal is done and dusted. You are now the proud owner of a chain of casinos in the UK," I say.

"Yes. I thought there would be a longer negotiation process, but everything's now in the hands of the lawyers. I'll need to find someone to manage my UK operations."

"The casinos here … will they become part of your chain, or will you run them separately?" I ask continuing with the small talk.

"Libby, surely you don't want to discuss my business transactions. As much as I would love to discuss this with you, I think we have much more pressing matters."

"Oh, and what would you like to discuss first—the fact that both you and my father lied to me and used me? Or maybe we should discuss your relationship with Katherine

Hunter and how I feel that yet again you used me to make her jealous. Tell me. Which one should we start with?"

"I suppose I deserved that, but I have never lied to you," Alex replies. "Before we discuss that, though, how are you? My mom was really worried about you."

"I don't remember much from last night, but your mum was great. I think she stayed with me most of the night." I smile at the thought.

"She said she took turns with watching over you and Lucy. She fell in love last night; she adores Lucy."

"I do remember hearing her sing a lullaby last night, but as I say, most of the night is hazy. A lot happened, or so I've been told. I still need to get the dressing on my back changed. I will get Karl to do it before he leaves for the night. I think he was here most of the night as well."

"I can do that for you." He strokes my hand and holds eye contact with me. "Libby, I *never* lied to you. I think I've been honest and up front with you from the start."

"How can you sit there and say that?" I wonder. Could he be being truthful? Maybe the problem is my own insecurities. I still find it hard to believe he is interested in me.

"Because it's the truth. Your dad told you about the press for the football and the function here. You can't be too hard on him. He's upset as well at how things have turned out. He thinks the news has somehow come from Jeff. And let's face it, he has motive."

"Dad should have told me long before you arrived that I was supposed to be a prop for your publicity shots. Things might have been different then. Instead, all my family kept it from me. And as for you, what did you think? That you could just take Dad's plans one step further and use me in more ways than one? Do you have any idea how I felt seeing and hearing the reports today of you and your actress *friend*? Humiliated and foolish spring to mind. But you know what?

You and my dad both got what you wanted. You got some great PR out of this." I pull my hand away from him. His touch is putting me off everything I want to say.

"Libby, I can honestly say I haven't used you. You have to believe me." There is sadness in his eyes as he speaks.

I want to believe him, I really do. But how do I know he didn't orchestrate everything from the start? Maybe this was his game all along. Let's face it. He has the right contacts to be in the right place at the right time.

"Libby, no one meant for you to get hurt. And you've been hurt a lot this past week. But you know what? You're not the only one hurting," Alex snaps. I don't know what to say to that. "When I saw the papers today with the picture of me and Katherine, my first thought was of you. I knew how hurt and upset you would be. When we posed for the camera, I didn't think anything of it. Why would I? She's supposed to be my friend. But when I heard the questions the reporters were asking me, and I looked back at those pictures, I suddenly remembered everything my mother has been saying about Katherine over the years. It hit home. She has used me to further her career. But I can honestly say that there has never been, and never will be, any romantic connection between me and Katherine Hunter."

"But she loves you."

"Maybe. But if so, it's the same as Stephen loving you. You don't share his feelings. But you also don't lead him on."

"No, I've not. And especially not the way you've led *me* on," I mutter getting up from the couch. I stagger slightly walking towards the window. I hold onto the window ledge to balance myself and stare out at the dark night sky.

"Is that what you think? That I led you on?"

"I don't know what I think anymore."

He is standing right behind me, so close I can feel his breath against my neck. I close my eyes. I feel his hands slip round my waist. I lean back against him. His lips brush against my bare neck ever so slightly, sending shivers down my spine.

"I have not led you on, Libby. Every touch of your delicate, soft skin I've savoured because I'm selfish. I've wanted you from the first moment I saw you, so yes, I'm selfish. Deep down I knew you were out of bounds, and I should've tried to resist you. But I couldn't. Make no mistake; there's not a single touch or word I've spoken that I regret." He turns me in his arms until I am facing him. His beautiful face is laced with pain, pain that my words have caused. "Libby, believe me when I say you mean a great deal to me."

His lips meet mine with passion and tenderness. Right now there is no hurry for lust or desire. That can wait. I just need his arms around me, making me feel safe. And in this moment, I do believe him, every last word. It's true my insecurities are going to be my own downfall. After all the events of the past few days, I feel exhausted. I just want to fall asleep in his arms.

"Come on, you, let's get you to bed." I raise my eyebrows, questioning his words. "No, baby, *that's* not happening. You need to rest." He scoops me up in his arms with ease. "You've lost weight. If you don't start eating properly, you'll end up in the hospital again. And I have it on good authority that the doctor is coming back to see you tomorrow."

He walks the short distance to the bedroom and lowers me to the bed. He then gets the dressings that have been left for my back, along with the sterile solution. With gentleness he proceeds to clean and dress it. When he's finished, he places small kisses all around it and then helps me change into my pjs.

He moves everything that's lying on the bed out of the way. I lie down on the bed. He lies down beside me and wraps his arms tightly around me. I snuggle in; there is nowhere else I want to be. He's fully clothed. Why do I get the feeling that if I go to sleep, he will be gone when I wake?

I try to fight the sleep, but it's a losing battle. My eyes are heavy, too heavy to keep open, and my body is lax. I finally give in. The last thing I remember is hearing Alex say, "I love you, Libby."

I wake in a blind panic. I reach out, but the bed is empty —just as I knew it would be.

"Alex!" I call out.

"Libby?" Kieran's voice is the only one I hear. I turn to find him sitting in the chair, clutching an envelope as if his life depended on it. Maybe it does.

"Here." He hands it to me. I look at him, but he turns away. I open it slowly.

My dearest Libby,

I couldn't bring myself to tell you that I was leaving tonight with my parents and Michael. And I know the heartache this will cause you, because believe me, I will be feeling it too. There is a problem with a deal I have been working on. I am needed back in the States. I have a lot riding on this deal. I still desperately want you to come for a visit, but I will understand if you want to decline. But don't expect me to stop trying to convince you, because I will call you every night until you finally give in. Which I hope you will. I am going to miss waking up with you in my arms the most. Seeing your beautiful smile is the perfect start to any day. Please promise me you will at least think about it.

I know you have a lot going on with work and family (speaking of which, please make peace with them). I will be in constant contact with your father, so there will be no hiding it from me. I've told you how I feel about you, but I have absolutely no idea if you feel the same. I can only hope. Libby, you can call me anytime. I will always answer and make time for you. You have become such an important part of me in such a short time. I will be back in six weeks, sooner if I can make it, but I hope to see you before then. Please, please think about what you want. I know what I want. You.

Yours always,
Alex

As SOON AS I finish reading, Kieran is at my side, his arms round me—comforting me, wiping the tears that have fallen.

"I need my phone. Where is it?" I ask through the tears that are blinding me with panic. "He needs to know I feel the same."

"It's here. Don't panic. But I'm sure he will have already boarded."

I call him, but it goes straight to voicemail, and I can't seem to find my voice to leave a message.

"Text instead. He'll get it as soon as he lands."

Libby: I know what I want. I just wish you were here so I could tell you. Speak to you soon L xxx

Kieran takes the phone from my hand and stretches out beside me. He comforts me for the rest of the night as my tears flow for the man who has captured my heart.

To be continued

Moving On

Karen Frances lives in Scotland with her husband of twenty-two years and their five children. Her busy days include helping her husband manage their family business while coordinating their children's sports and academic endeavours. She finds escape from the chaos of everyday life in good books, particularly stories of passionate romantic relationships. Her appreciation and passion for romance novels led her to write this her first novel, He's Captured My Heart, a tale of contemporary erotic romance set in Scotland.

ACKNOWLEDGMENTS

It's always hard trying to remember everyone I should thank when it comes to the end of the process, so this time I'm keeping it short and sweet.

To my amazing team that help me bring my stories to life and publication, I'll always be grateful for all you do; Karen, Kari, Krissy, Suzie, Margaret, Pauline and Leah thank you for everything you do.

A huge thank you to all the readers and bloggers who read my stories, taking time to review and recommend my books to others.

I'm extremely fortunate to be surrounded by a supportive family and friends and for that I'll always be thankful.

Printed in Great Britain
by Amazon